Brass Ankle Blues

a novel

Rachel M. Harper

TOUCHSTONE
PUBLISHED BY SIMON & SCHUSTER
NEW YORK   LONDON   TORONTO   SYDNEY

TOUCHSTONE
Rockefeller Center
1230 Avenue of the Americas
New York, NY 10020

TOUCHSTONE and colophon are registered trademarks
of Simon & Schuster, Inc.

This Touchstone edition 2007

For information regarding special discounts for bulk purchases, please contact Simon & Schuster Special Sales at 1-800-456-6798 or business@simonandschuster.com.

Designed by Jan Pisciotta

Manufactured in the United States of America

10   9   8   7   6   5   4   3   2   1

Library of Congress Cataloging-in-Publication Data
Harper, Rachel M., 1972–
    Brass ankle blues : a novel / Rachel M. Harper.
        p. cm.
    1. Teenage girls—Fiction. 2. Racially mixed people—Fiction. I. Title.
PS3608.A7747B73 2006
813'.6—dc22   2005054466

ISBN-13: 978-0-7432-7680-1
ISBN-10:   0-7432-7680-9
ISBN-13: 978-0-7432-9658-8 (Pbk.)
ISBN-10:   0-7432-9658-3 (Pbk.)

for Jaxon

Dorothy went on, "Do you know the term 'brass ankle'? It's not a word you mention in polite society. Just like the word 'nigger'—nobody uses that anymore. I haven't heard that word in fifty years. A brass ankle was a mixed-blood person—Indian, Negro, and white. Three different people. They lived in the country, and had ankles that shined because of the mixture."

—Edward Ball, *Slaves in the Family*

Prologue

When I was seven I told my father that I wanted to grow up to be invisible. He told me to read *Invisible Man*. For him, the answers were always in books.

I did read Ellison's novel, but I seem to have the opposite problem. People see me everywhere I go, remember me places where I haven't even been. They follow me with their eyes, their questions. They ask me things I haven't even asked myself.

"What are you, anyway?"

A bullfrog, a butterfly.

"I mean, where are you from?"

Boston. One fifty-one Tremont Street. My mother's womb.

"Your parents? Grandparents?"

New York. Minnesota. A Brooklyn brownstone. The Blue Ridge Mountains. A sod house in Iowa. A dairy farm.

"But what's your nationality?"

I'm American.

". . . Is that it?"

And German, Irish, and English. Cherokee, Chippewa. African. (Sorry, I don't know from where.)

"You are all those things?"

Yes.

"You don't look black."

Do I look white?

"You look different, like no one I've ever seen."

I look exactly like myself.

Part I
The Road

———

There is no truth but in transit.

—Ralph Waldo Emerson

Chapter 1

———◆◆◆———

We are finally leaving Virginia. The sign that tells me this is small and has a picture of a hand waving. Strange, I think, I left Virginia about six hundred miles ago. I left her standing in the driveway of a two-story house I might never see again. Virginia is my mother, a woman I've never associated with this backward state until now. Thank god we aren't moving here. I wouldn't want to see my mother's name on the back of every car and at the bottom of every letter. Virginia. I don't think I'll ever come back.

West Virginia is not much better, but it's a smaller state, one we can cross in a few hours. At this rate we should make it to Cleveland by dinnertime. Tomorrow we'll drive through all those *I* states—Indiana, Illinois, and Iowa—and finally make it up to Minnesota by Friday. That is the plan. My father always has one, and unlike most people, he follows it. We've been doing this ride every summer for my entire life: Boston to St. Croix, fifteen hundred miles in three days. This summer is the first time we've altered the route, dropping down to Virginia to pick up my cousin. That added an extra five hundred miles on to the trip, but it won't slow us down. He'll make up for it after Cleveland, skimming through the Midwest like a book he's trying to finish. My father likes to drive, likes to sit behind the wheel. Even if my mother were here she wouldn't be driving. She drives too slow and stops at too many rest areas. My father likes to move fast, even when he isn't in a rush. I guess he's not comfortable with where he is; he's always focused on where he's going.

My cousin is not a good traveler. It's been two hours since the last stop and already she's begging to use the bathroom. I don't believe her. She lies the way some people clear their throat. If we were alone my father would tell me to hold it, but he's being nice to her because she doesn't have a father, and has grown up thinking that all vegetables have to be defrosted before you can eat them. Well, she has a father—my mother's brother Renny—but she knows him about as well as she knows us. (Three hours in the car, so far, and my grandfather's funeral when we were five.) Barely more than strangers.

When we get inside the gas station's bathroom she doesn't even go into a stall. Instead, she stands in front of the mirror and watches her reflection pull a cigarette out of her bra. I close my door on her face, a mischievous smile, and smell the smoke before it's even locked.

"Goddamn, that's good," Jess says slowly.

"You act like it's food or something."

"Nah, it's better than food." She pauses. "Except grits. Grits and smothered biscuits. Nothing's better than that."

Jess is from the South, the only one of my cousins, on either side, born below the Mason-Dixon Line. This isn't the only thing that separates us, but maybe it's the most important. So far, I pretty much hate the South. (Except for the food since I love anything fried.) I tried to have an open mind, but by the time we picked Jess up in Roanoke it was locked shut. And I'm not just talking about the rednecks. The black people bother me, too. Everybody stares too much, and they ask more questions than an English teacher. The accent also pisses me off; they talk all slow like you came all the way here just to listen to them. So far my favorite places have been the bathrooms. Cool and quiet like church. Even the old ladies leave you alone in here. Not Jess, though, she acts like the bathroom is her confessional, and she has to share everything that comes into her mind. Sometimes I think she's afraid of silence, maybe because she's an only child. Not me. When you grow up with older brothers you start to love solitude.

When I come out of the stall, she's sitting on the counter between the two sinks. She's so skinny that her ass isn't touching either sink. I haven't done that since I was six. I wash my hands in the cold water, using lots of pink powdered soap. It turns into a paste like one of my mother's facial scrubs, the kind with the grit that will take off a layer of skin. I'm afraid if I rub too hard it will wash away all my color.

"I'm gonna miss Virginia," Jess says. "I've never been gone so long."

"It's been three hours."

"No, I mean the whole summer." She taps her cigarette against the sink. When the ashes touch the water it looks like wet sand. I once read about a black-sand beach in Hawaii. I will swim there one day and remember this moment.

"Virginia summers are the best. They're sunny and real hot, and everyone just hangs out on their porches. The Virginia Players come for the Fourth of July, and then the Virginia music—"

"Will you stop saying that?" I stare at the back of her head in the mirror. The ends are streaked blonde in a way that looks like she dyes it, but I know she doesn't. That would be too much work.

"What?" She looks at me, all innocent.

"How would you like it if I lived in a state called Shelley? If I was born in Shelley, went to school in Shelley, and just loved being from Shelley?"

Jess laughs, exhaling smoke. "My mother would never have a state named after her. She's way too crooked."

"Mine's no citizen of the year either." I dry my hands with a coarse paper towel. Jess puts her cigarette out in the sink and hops down.

"Did yours steal clothes from the Salvation Army Dumpsters? Did she pretend to be crazy to get into some study at the hospital? Did she borrow your neighbor's car to go to Atlantic City and end up gambling it away? Did she get kicked off welfare for pretending she had another kid?"

To my knowledge, my mother has only broken one law.

"No," I say.

"Trust me, the criminals are on my side of the family."

I know she includes herself on that list, probably at the top. Right before we picked her up my father told me she got expelled from her high school for trying to bribe a teacher. I decide not to mention it.

"Aren't you going to pee?" I ask, already knowing the answer.

"Nah, I'll wait till the next stop." She holds the door open for me. "After you," she says. Such Southern hospitality.

As we walk out she smells her T-shirt, checking for smoke. My father has a rule about sixteen-year-olds smoking, even if they're not his own. I stop at the counter to buy a pack of gum. Jess stands next to me, thumbing through the latest issue of *Teen Beat,* the one with Matt Dillon on the cover. When the cashier turns his back she tucks the magazine down the front of her cutoffs. The first of many laws she will break this summer.

I am reading Toni Morrison's *Beloved* from my school's summer reading list. When we cross into Ohio I am with Sethe and we are both running. I look down from the bridge as we drive over the Ohio River. All I can see are the waves of blue sky reflected in the water, thick white clouds breaking in the distance. How many people died in that river, drowning softly in the clouds and sky? I don't think I would have made it as a slave, even with the benefits of being a "house nigger." There are few lives I could imagine living other than my own.

I was five the first time I realized I was black. After watching *Roots* my brothers and I began to fantasize about slavery. Marcus, always defiant, claimed he would have run off just like Kunta Kinte.

"I wouldn't let anybody own me," he said with the unflinching confidence that only a ten-year-old can muster.

"I don't know . . ." Noah spoke slowly. "I don't think I'd want to be one of the black people." He was almost eight.

"You mean you'd pretend to be white?" Marcus looked shocked.

"But I am white." Noah held out his arm. In all fairness, he was a bit lighter than us.

"No." Marcus shook his head. "Mom's white. We're black, like Dad."

"But Dad's brown," Noah said. "Uncle Bobby's black."

"Aren't we both?" I asked.

"Yeah, but all that really means is we're black."

"I don't know if I want to be black." Noah was scratching a scab on his knee.

"You don't have a choice," Marcus said. "None of us do."

We were all quiet for a minute, sitting in a circle on the hardwood floors. I tried to focus on the planks of wood, sanded and stained a golden brown, not much lighter than the color of my skin.

"Reggie Jackson's black," I finally said.

The Yankees had just won the World Series. We'd spent the week marching around the block, celebrating each win like we lived in the Bronx instead of two miles from Fenway Park. We'd even taped the newspaper clippings to our walls, we were so proud.

"I love Reggie," Noah said. "He looks like Dad if he lost some weight."

We all laughed. Even my mother thought they looked alike. She'd called him Reggie all day when he took us to the park to play softball.

"He looks like us," Marcus said, so sure of himself that I had to believe him.

We didn't talk about race again.

"This magazine sucks," Jess says from the backseat. "No good pictures." She tosses the stolen *Teen Beat* into my lap. "You want it?"

"I've got a book," I say, letting the magazine fall to the floor.

"I don't like books."

"Oh really?" My father glances in the rearview mirror. He's an English professor, and he loves books almost more than he loves his children. I smile to myself, wondering how she'll get out of this.

"I don't like made-up stories. They're all a bunch of B.S. Give me something real, with pictures."

"I've got a *New Yorker* you can look at," my father says. "Lots of cartoons." He reaches up to adjust the mirror. I don't know if he included her in his view or cut her out.

"No thanks," Jess says.

I watch her in the side mirror as she puts her window all the way down. The wind pushes her hair back, completely off her face, and she closes her eyes. Suddenly, she looks like a Christiansen. Not like Renny, exactly, but like my grandfather and my aunt. Maybe my mother.

I lift my gaze to stare at the view out my window. The fields of grass and uncut wheat seem endless. I wonder if this is what it looked like a hundred years ago to the people migrating north. Is this what Sethe saw when she stumbled through the woods in bare feet with nothing but a torn dress and her pregnant belly? I wish I could stand at one end of America and look all the way across to the other side. I want to experience something that vast, to lose myself in the miles in between. I want to feel as small and insignificant as I am.

Chapter 2

My great-aunt Frances is a colored woman. That's what she calls herself. She was born in Brooklyn in 1919 and always resented the fact that she was a child during the Harlem Renaissance. She acts like she would have been a painter or a poet if she'd come along sooner, would have danced at the Cotton Club, had an affair with Jean Toomer, or gone back to Africa with Marcus Garvey. That is the main difference between her and her older sister: my grandmother had perfect timing, and never regretted a goddamn thing. (Those were her words.)

This is my fifteenth visit to Cleveland. One for every year of my life. All I've ever seen of the city is the view from highway 271 and my aunt Frances's house. She lives in Shaker Heights, but I don't even know if that's a good thing. The streets are wide and each house has one of those thick lawns like a shag carpet. Her house is too big for a single person, and I get the feeling she doesn't go upstairs a lot. She looks like she might fall asleep on the couch and fix her hair in the hallway mirror in the morning. She probably takes a bath once a week.

When I was younger it was fun to visit Aunt Frances. She taught us how to play High-Low-Jack and told stories about seeing Charlie Parker at Birdland. After her husband died, and then my grandmother within the same year, she started to withdraw from the world. She never leaves her house now, even to go grocery shopping. She calls in her order and neighbors pick it up for her. Her son Paul comes over every Sunday to wash and wax her car but she refuses to drive it anywhere. It's a beautiful car, a 1981

Mercedes-Benz that she promised to give to my brother Marcus when he graduates from college. I think that's the only reason he might stay in school. He's always been her favorite because he has light eyes and her father's complexion. He's everyone's favorite, even mine.

When we arrive the house smells like fried fish and garlic. Burnt garlic. My father grabs my elbow and shakes his head. He is telling me to smile and eat whatever she offers. Jess plugs her nose. She is anything but subtle.

"I'm so sorry, I had the oven on a bit too high." Aunt Frances fans at the air with a dish towel. "At least it's not raw, right, Nellie?"

"Sure," I say, trying to smile.

"Marcus always loved my catfish." She talks through our hug. "And Noah, too, he's been a good eater from the beginning."

"I'm know they're sorry to be missing this." I pull away in time to catch my father cutting his eyes at me.

"Well, maybe next summer," he says, not quite convincingly.

I walk into the dining room to escape the oppressive smell in the kitchen. The table is covered with a clear plastic tablecloth that has a yellow stain on it that I recognize from the last visit. Underneath, the wood looks dark and flawless. During dinner Aunt Frances serves us warm Coke in wineglasses. My father has a beer in a wineglass, too. When she brings out the catfish on a large platter, it looks like a blackened-mushroom dish that Noah made when he was trying to be a vegetarian. It takes almost an entire two-liter bottle of Coke to wash it down. Jess wipes her mouth a lot, so I suspect she's spitting some into her napkin. My father will eat anything.

Aunt Frances doesn't even make herself a plate. Instead, she spends the meal freshening up her gin and tonic. "This Tanqueray is really worth the extra money," she says every time she pours more gin into her glass.

When my father looks at her he squints, as if her face is too bright for him to focus on. I wonder if he's remembering her as a young woman, a thinner version of his own mother, with the same explosive laugh and gap-toothed smile he carries in his own mouth. When did she lose herself, and where? In the empty rooms of this stuffy old house? If this is what it means to grow old, I won't mind dying early like all four of my grandparents. My father doesn't act like it bothers him—he will never stop coming to visit her, as long as she's alive. He's big on obligation, especially when it involves family. He'll come each year to revisit the past, to look at the same old photographs and listen to the same family stories, wondering if his mother is still watching.

After dinner Aunt Frances takes Jess and me to our room, the one I used to share with my brothers. It's Paul's old room, and you can tell she hasn't touched anything since he left. It's like she thinks if she keeps everything the same then time won't pass and he'll always be in here studying for a history final or dreaming about the prom queen. It's a huge room, too big for one person, and for a second I'm thankful that Jess is with me. I'd feel overwhelmed staying in here alone. There is a private bath and a curved window seat, but the best part is the balcony that overlooks the side yard. On hot nights Marcus and I used to sneak up to the roof to lay out. I once fell asleep looking for the Little Dipper.

The first thing Jess does after Aunt Frances leaves is lock the door. Never a good sign.

"Goddamn, that was the nastiest shit I've ever tasted. How'd you eat so much?"

"Give her a break, she's old."

"Give *us* a break, that was the worst fish I've ever eaten." She crinkles up her face. "Shit, it tasted like it *was* part cat."

"Funny," I say, walking away from her.

I open the door to the balcony and step out into the night. The view is exactly as I remember it, like not a minute has passed. The skyline is filled with the same thick buildings, squatting in the distance like pillars of clay. The rosebushes that line her neighbor's yard still brush up against her house, their fragrant petals threatening to grow into the brick. I can hear the faint sound of laughter, and the quiet hiss of a sprinkler system. The smell of freshly cut grass permeates the air. Maybe Aunt Frances can stop time.

When Jess joins me on the balcony the boards dip under her weight as if my father were with her. For a small person she's actually quite heavy. Being with her is like carrying a baby who at first seems so light that you hold on with both hands, worried that she might float away, but by the end of the day becomes an awkward weight that makes muscles you didn't even know you had ache. Still, I bet she weighs fifty pounds less than me.

"Nice view," she says. I can't tell if she's being sarcastic.

She drops her head to light a cigarette, her face falling into shadows. Sometimes she looks older than her sixteen years. In those moments, I feel like a child. She becomes this other person: older, tougher, less feminine, less human, and I can't help but wonder if she ever cries. If I had to guess I'd say either a lot or not since she was a kid. She was crying the first time I saw her, actually, at our grandfather's funeral. I remember thinking that she shouldn't be crying, that she shouldn't be sad even, since I don't think she'd ever met him before. I resented her tears, and the way she sat on my grandmother's lap throughout the service. I wonder if she even remembers that day.

"Do you remember Grandpa Brant's funeral?"

"Of course," she says, taking a drag from her cigarette. "It was raining, and cold, too cold for summertime." She exhales like she's trying to blow out a candle. "That's the first time we met, the first time I saw any of you all."

"That must have been weird."

"Yeah. But everyone was nice. Nice to the poor bastard child, to Renny's little mistake. His first of many—should I be proud of that?" She swallows the last word, her voice barely audible.

"It's funny to think that he was ever the golden child."

"Especially since he's such a fuckup now." She spits onto the lawn below. "I just can't believe he was ever a teacher, you know? That he stood in front of a group of high school students and lectured or whatever." She starts to laugh.

"Yeah, I can't imagine him ever sitting behind a desk. He seems like the type who would die being inside all day."

"Well, I guess that's why he finally quit."

"Quit? Who told you that?" I don't even try to hide my surprise.

"Once when I asked her why he never sent us any money, Shell said he quit his job. She said he couldn't stand having anyone tell him what books to teach."

"I heard he got fired for smoking pot with his students."

She puts her head down and starts to laugh. "And everybody says I'm a screwup. I guess it's no mystery where I got it from." She shakes her head like she's trying to knock something out of it. "God, I hate the fact that I come from him."

I watch her spit over the balcony. "Why are you going to see him then, if you hate him so much?"

Jess shrugs her shoulders. "No reason, really. I guess Shell figures she dealt with me for the first sixteen years, and now he gets a crack."

"So you're going to live with him?"

"Maybe. He wants me to. So I can get to know his other kids and shit, be a family. Fuck that, I just want to see California. See the Pacific." She looks over at me. "Can you see the water from his house? Is he that close?"

"Yeah, he's got a great view. Big bay windows. It's nice up there."

"That's all I want. Then I'll go back home." She looks down at her feet. "People will miss me by then. Can't stay away forever."

I try to imagine her friends. Do they have sleepovers? Do they swap cigarettes and jean jackets, and stories about boys who carry switchblades? Do they hug or shake hands when they see each other? Do they ever touch?

"I'm sure your mother will miss you." I am lying, but I know it's the right thing to say.

"Oh yeah, Shell didn't want me to leave. She hates cooking and grocery shopping. Hates doing all the little things that keep the house going." Jess laughs and puts her cigarette out on the railing. "She'll want me back, all right. Probably wants me back already."

From what my father says Shelley practically kicked her out of the house. If we hadn't agreed to bring her to Minnesota for the summer, who knows where she would have ended up. I wonder if Renny knows he's taking her home with him. I wonder if there is anything she tells the truth about.

"I bet your mom really misses you. I bet you're all spoiled and shit, being the baby and the only girl."

"Yeah, sometimes." I make dents in the wood with my finger-nails. It's soft like warm cheese. I wonder how it can hold all this weight.

"So when's she coming, anyway?"

"She's not. My brothers have summer school and jobs and stuff. Plus she's working on the house." I don't mention that I asked her not to come. That I begged my father to leave her behind.

"You think they'll sell your house?"

"They said they weren't making any decisions until the end of the summer."

"Yeah, but they always sell something during a divorce."

"They're only separated."

"Oh, right." She picks at a scab on her elbow. "Just in case, I guess."

I hear a screen door open and my father's voice from below. Then the sound of laughter. Before I realize it, I am picturing my grandmother, even though I know the laugh belongs to Aunt Frances. The floodlight goes on in the backyard, casting long black shadows onto the ground beneath us. Jess bends over the railing, looking for them.

"You can't see the backyard from here," I say, "and they can't see us."

"Nice," she says, lighting another cigarette.

"Don't you get sick of those?" I whisper, afraid of how the sound will travel.

"Never, I'm hooked." She tries to whisper back but it sounds louder than her speaking voice. "Shit, I can barely remember not smoking. I've been buying since I was ten, but I started stealing from my mom way before that. That's almost half my life."

"It's disgusting," I say.

"You think?" She takes a long drag. "To me it's like a minute in heaven. Closest I'll ever get."

The voices from below get louder as they move into the garden.

"Paul planted carrots because the kids love them, but they just go to waste over here. Why don't you have the girls pick some before you go?"

"I don't think they're ready," my father says. "They look too small."

"Nonsense, they're baby carrots. Here." She must have picked a few and handed them to him.

"Okay, thanks. Nellie loves carrots."

I hate carrots. I don't think I've even eaten a carrot since the last time we were here. Why do parents think they can say anything about their kids, even if it's not true?

"That poor girl. How's she doing with all this?"

I feel my face get hot. I hate to be the subject of conversation.

"She seems okay," my father says. "She's a tough one, more so than her brothers, even though they're older. We don't worry about her in the same way."

"I didn't know your wife worried about anyone but herself."

I hear my father clear his throat. "This is hard on everyone, especially her."

"There you go protecting her again. You're so goddamn faithful it's sickening." She makes a noise that sounds like she's sucking her teeth. "Worry about yourself for once, and those mixed-up kids of yours. The marriage was hard enough on them, but the divorce will be even worse. Now they really won't know who they are."

Silence. I suddenly realize that I've been holding my breath. I exhale slowly, trying not to make a sound, even though I want to scream. When Aunt Frances speaks again her voice is softer.

"Why do you make things so difficult, Malcolm? We always wondered about that, your mother and I. Why move so far away from your family? Why marry such a young woman, and a white girl no less? Why take on so many burdens?"

"It's my life, Aunt Frances. I won't apologize for it."

"Of course not, you're far too stubborn for that. Just like your mother. No apology, no regret."

I want to leap from the balcony and kick my great-aunt in the face. I want to protect him, to explain that nothing is his fault. I want to prove that we aren't mixed-up, that we'll all be fine one day, but I don't have any of the words.

"My mother understood me," my father says, speaking just above a whisper. "She respected my choices." Then I hear footsteps on the gravel again, just one set. I don't know who's walking away.

"Thank God she's not here to see this. To see any of this." Aunt Frances speaks to herself in the empty garden. My father is the one who walked away. Surprising, since usually he's the one who stays.

Soon I hear Aunt Frances's footsteps on the gravel. Then the floodlight goes out and Jess and I are alone again. Even the shadows have gone. Jess is surprisingly quiet and still. She must be dying to speak.

"Did they fight a lot?" she finally asks.

"No, hardly ever."

"But did they talk, spend time together?"

"No. They had really separate lives." Actually, I'm surprised that they stayed together as long as they did. That she didn't leave a long time ago, when she had the chance. But I don't say that to Jess.

"Shell was married once. Not to Renny, to this guy named Dickie. Dickie was a pain in the ass, a real loser, and when they first got together they fought all the time. But they were together, you know, in each other's face. Fighting about bills and cooking dinner and who's the best pitcher for the Orioles. They could fight about anything. It was when they stopped fighting that I knew it was over. She would just look at him and shake her head, walk away while he was still yelling at her. She left him right then, even though we didn't move out for another six months."

"So that makes you an expert?"

"I'm just saying I understand."

"You don't understand anything. You don't even know us." It comes out sounding harsher than I meant it but I can't take it back.

"You're right, I don't even know why I care." Jess flicks her cigarette into the air. "It's not like I'm part of the family."

She goes inside, and I hear the bathroom door close. I know I hurt her feelings but I don't care right now. My feelings are hurt and no one's going to take anything back. There's no reset button on the past.

The mirror in Aunt Frances's bathroom has never been kind. I could blame it on the harsh fluorescent lights or the placement (directly opposite the toilet, catching you at your most vulnerable), or even on the stains, gray smudges that hang over the light fixture like a dusty veil, but maybe there's nothing wrong with the image it projects. Maybe this is the only mirror that tells the truth. I stand in front of it every year and try to see the changes, try to catch the bones growing, the skin stretching. First I look at myself—I'm wearing my usual summer wardrobe: an old Hard Rock Café T-shirt that my father brought me from London, baggy khaki shorts, Adidas flip-flops, tearing at the sides, my hair in a loose ponytail, the curls brushed out—and then I ask the same question: Who am I?

I undress completely before looking into the mirror again. I almost look better naked. More flawed, definitely, but also more innocent, more unique. The soft pale belly, lighter than the rest of my skin; small breasts still not certain how big they want to become; the wide hips, streaked with faint stretch marks from trying to grow too quickly; and my shoulders, wide and strong like a swimmer's. No wonder boys don't ask me to dance.

Ever since I can remember, my whole body has been covered with small brown moles. Some people call them beauty marks, some say freckles—I think of them as the mark of miscegenation. I wonder if this flawed skin is the ultimate sign of weakness, evidence that my blood shouldn't be mixing in my veins. There is a mole on my side so big and black it looks like a tick lodged under the skin. But the little freckles on my arms and chest, the ones on my face, look as harmless as Magic Marker dots. I wonder why these imperfections are the darkest spots I have, blackness coming through as thick raised marks that decorate my body. More come every year and by the time I die I will probably be completely covered. On my deathbed I will finally be a black woman.

I'm still waiting for the day when I stop changing, when I arrive at the real me. I want to look the same every time I stand in front of this mirror. I want to have one definition. Then, when I am finally comfortable, I know I will change again. I'll have gray hair and wrinkles, my nipples will point toward the ground, and my belly will be streaked with stretch marks. I'll be a mother, then a grandmother, then a memory.

Chapter 3

We're thirty miles west of Toledo and it's not quite ten in the morning. The car floats over the familiar turnpike, steady in fifth gear and clicked into overdrive. My father has followed his plan, and we're already making up for lost time. The 6 A.M. wake-up, the quiet breakfast of soggy waffles and sour orange juice, hugging Aunt Frances in her pink velour bathrobe—it is all a distant memory as we move farther west. I focus only on the road, imagine what lies ahead after the next bend, beyond the horizon. I don't let myself turn around, even to glance at Jess or get water from the back of the car. The future is straight ahead.

It's too early for lunch but I am already starving. Jess, I'm sure, wants a cigarette break, but she says nothing. My father, as always, denies his hunger. When the gas gauge drops to a quarter tank he pulls off at a service exit. He drives past the deserted rest area and parks on the self-serve side of the Mobil island.

"Fill it with super," he says automatically as he pulls himself out from behind the oversize steering wheel. I stare through the window at his bare arms, the left one already three shades darker than the right, only then noticing that the sun has done the reverse to me. I withdraw my right arm from the window and admire the color.

"Full serve is on the other side." Jess points to the sign from the backseat. It's not a mistake that he's on the self-serve side, but she doesn't know this, doesn't know him after only two days in the car.

"I'll do it." I open the car door and drop my bare feet onto the oil-stained cement. I do not look at him, but I hear my father snap the credit card onto the roof of the car and walk away. His sandals scrape against the cracked pavement as he heads toward the Hardees.

I lean against our station wagon while pumping the gas. The back end hangs low, filled to the top with our clothes and my father's books. I think about going to use the bathroom, but it's not worth the search for my shoes. Looking down at my bare feet, I notice that they are already as thick and brown as the moccasins lost in the car, but they still aren't ready for the cornfields of the Minnesota summer that lies ahead. I glance at Jess's small white feet sticking out the window and guess that they aren't tough enough to take blacktop, let alone an entire summer in the country.

"Should I go with him?" Jess doesn't move, but points after him. I used to think she loved movement and that's why she pointed a lot, but she's just lazy. She points so she doesn't have to move.

"He knows what we want." I stare at the numbers jerking by and start to think that gas in Ohio is pretty cheap until I realize I'm reading the gallons.

"But yesterday he forgot my Diet Coke."

"He didn't forget. He promised my mom we'd drink water and go to supermarkets instead of eating fast food the whole trip."

"But y'all haven't even driven by a supermarket." Confusion seems to bring out her Southern drawl.

"That's why he's sticking to the water thing." I don't believe anything I'm saying but I have already figured out that lying is the easiest way to deal with my cousin.

By this time she's frustrated and lights a cigarette she took from her tampon box—one of the few things my father didn't go through when he was collecting her stash. The handle pops out of my grip at $13.77, but I tap until $14.00 and watch the gas run down the side of the car. I breathe and smell Ohio in the gasoline and cigarette smoke. I tighten the cap and watch Jess take long drags on her Camel Light. She stands on the island, rolling on her tender feet from heel to toe. Her mouth is open, and I stare at the gap between her two front teeth. She was supposed to get braces, but didn't want to lose her whistle or the ability to shoot water over two parked cars; a trick she picked up in Roanoke but has been perfecting at rest stops along the way.

We are both surprised to see my father cutting through the wood chips that line the Hardees entrance with a bag under each arm and a triangle of drinks. Jess drops the half-smoked cigarette without looking away from him, but my eyes dart to the puddle of gas that has collected near the back tire before swimming toward my barefoot. I take one step to the right and stand on the burning embers as my father hands us each a sweating cup.

"Diet Coke and root beer, don't say I never spoiled you." He gives in to a smile and continues to the driver's side, pleased that his drink surprise has worked. Jess takes the lid off her gift and gulps down the soda. I, too, want to take off my lid, but I dream of dunking my entire foot into the root beer and crushed ice. I don't move.

"Did you pay?" He looks back at me and I twist my whole body toward him, hoping any movement will relieve the burning sensation that's rising through my leg. He doesn't wait for my answer but picks the card off the roof and heads toward the office.

"Shit, your feet must be leather, you didn't even wince." Jess almost looks proud as she swallows her last ounce of soda. She walks to the other side of the car and gets into the backseat while I balance on the rear bumper to assess the damage. The squashed butt falls to the ground as I lift my foot and notice a slightly pink bubble growing just below my middle toe. Even leather needs to be oiled, I think, as I open my first root beer in three days and pour it over my dirty, throbbing foot.

We are a few miles from the rest stop when I notice the smoke coming from the dashboard. I don't say anything for a couple of seconds, just watch it curl toward the mirror. I reach out with my left hand and feel the cool stream flow through my slightly parted fingers.

"What the hell is that?" My father begins pressing all of the buttons on the dashboard. "What did you hit?"

I know I haven't touched anything, but I help him roll the windows up and down, turn on the rear defrost, and flash the hazard lights in an attempt to find a button that will stop the strange emission. We pull to a stop in the newly paved breakdown lane and continue to play with the dashboard. Jess sits up and sticks her head between the two front seats.

"Is that smoke?" she asks, taking a bite of her bacon double cheeseburger.

My father turns off the engine and pops the hood before getting out of the car. I squint and watch his silhouette lift the brilliant sheet of metal, erasing the July sun from my view. The whole car jiggles, so I imagine he's doing something.

"Has it stopped?" he yells between shakes.

"No, it's the same." I put my finger over the spot, hoping it's a leak I can cover with pressure. The thick vapor splits around my finger and becomes two streams.

"Do you guys have the water?" he asks, peeking around the hood.

I turn and look at Jess, knowing that she forgot to refill the thermos at Aunt Frances's house.

"I hate drinking water," she whispers. "Besides, I thought your daddy was kiddin' about getting it from that garden hose."

"Do you at least have some more ice?" I grab for the cup she has tucked into the pocket behind my seat.

"I ate it all. What about yours?"

I decide it's better to ignore her from now on.

"I don't see anything wrong with it," my father yells as he closes the hood. I turn around and notice that the stream of smoke has been replaced by a perfect, tiny flame between the rear defrost and hazard buttons.

"There's a flame, Dad." I put my hand up, half expecting it to be as cool as the mystery smoke. It has burned my pinkie by the time my father arrives.

"Shit." He reaches through the window and takes the keys from the ignition. "Jess, hand me the water bottle from the back."

"We drank it all," Jess lies.

"We've got that sparkling cider from Mom." I remember as I'm getting out of the car. I hate saying "Mom" around him, but there is nothing else to call her; she is still my mother.

The tar is hot and soft as I walk in front of the car to look behind the driver's seat. Jess has left her swimsuit and three pairs of shoes beneath the seat, but I finally find the smooth, warm bottle tucked underneath the floor mat. It's shaped like a champagne bottle and from the other lanes it must look like we're having a party as my father pops the cork and leans in through the window. The bubbly liquid washes down the dashboard and knocks the flame over, but it pops back up with more strength each time. When the bottle is empty, the flames are almost three inches high and have consumed most of the dash. The smell is kind of nice, like burnt apples or fireworks.

"Jesus Christ." Jess finally gets out of the backseat.

"Start unpacking the car," my father orders as he heads for the back end. He opens the door and pulls out the boxes that hold the last thirty years of his life, carefully restacking them on the gravel next to the road. Except for the cabin, everything he owns could burn in this fire. Without talking, we form an assembly line: my father pulls things out of the car, I drag them to the edge of the gravel, and Jess rolls them down the grassy hill and into the overgrown ditch. It seems like hours, but we empty the back end in a couple of minutes. With my hands on my knees, I bend to look through the wagon, checking the progress of the fire. A square of smoke escapes from the edges of the hood while flames break through the front windshield.

My father closes the back door and steps onto the bumper to untie the stationary bicycle from the roof. He pulls it off by himself and carries it into the ditch, making sure to stand it up and straighten the seat before walking away. Only when I see the empty back end do I remember the secret compartment, which my mother packed with things she couldn't wrap: a family picture from my eighth-grade graduation, a spear my father brought back from South Africa, a crocheted blanket my grandmother made, pewter candlesticks, even a few jars of peach jam that my mother grew and canned herself—they are all waiting to burn. I pull on the door, hoping to save the jam, but my father has locked it, and I can't justify pulling him away from his flaming typewriter to save some fruit.

I stumble over Jess as she pulls a mound of clothes out of the backseat and walks blindly into the ditch. Through the smoke I see her swimsuit and shoes still wedged behind the driver's seat. I lean in to grab them, noticing that the leather on the front seats has already caught on fire. The flames continue to spread as I watch, as if my gaze encourages them to grow. Smoke vapors drift through the headrests until I can no longer make out the dashboard or the windshield, where my backpack and cassettes must now be melting. I think about reaching for the tape deck, which still holds the DeBarge mix Marcus made me for the trip, but I know that my arm is too short; I do not know if it's flammable. I try to remember what song was playing when the smoke came but all I can hear is the heat.

The smell of burning leather and electrical wires is becoming unbearable, but the attempts to hold my breath are futile. I surrender with a stifled cough, sucking in the toxic fumes through a clenched jaw as if my teeth could filter the air.

"Nellie, get out of the car," my father says, pulling me out by the ankles. My skin burns as I slide across the backseat, and I don't know which is hotter, my legs or the car's leather. I look back at the worn bench, half expecting to see a sheet of my own skin rolled into the stitched grooves. "At least you saved your swimsuit," he offers, marking my shoulder with a fresh carbon print, blacker than the original hand.

I tuck Jess's suit into the front pocket of my cutoffs and nod.

Jess climbs out of the ditch and wipes the sweat off her face with the front of her T-shirt. It leaves a smear of soot across her forehead, but I say nothing; she is now as black as we are. The three of us are standing five feet from the burning car but can no longer feel the heat; even the smell is disappearing.

"Will you guys flag down some help?" My father cleans his glasses with a shirttail and waits for us to move. We walk around the car and onto the right lane of the freeway. The passing cars have all moved into the far lane, and they slow down to stare at the fire as they crawl by. Jess waves her arms and yells for someone to help but no one pulls over. One woman rolls down the passenger window of a maroon Pontiac and leans out with her Polaroid camera, trying to capture the scene on film. I give her the finger and smile for the first time since leaving Boston.

"Fuck you, lady," Jess yells and lunges toward the car.

The Polaroid lady's husband tries to speed up, but he's forced to slam on the brakes since there is nowhere to go in the backed-up traffic. The lady, rushing to roll up her window, accidentally drops the camera. It falls to the ground near Jess's feet, spitting the developing photo onto the tar. Jess smiles like she won the lottery.

"Thank you kindly, ma'am," Jess says as she grabs the picture and tucks it into her back pocket. Then she picks up the camera, looks around to locate me, and hands it back to the lady while I watch. I wonder what she would have done if I hadn't been here. The lady never utters a word, and finally her husband leans over and rolls up her window.

A siren pulls my attention away from the traffic and back to our roadside attraction. Through the smoke I see my father talking to a policeman, hesitating before he gets into the passenger side of the squad car. He glances at me and I wonder if he's thinking that he's the first black man to sit in that police car without handcuffs. He takes what looks like a napkin from the officer and wipes it across his forehead, then down over his eyes. If the travelers look now they will think my father is crying.

My feet stick slightly as I begin to walk, and I realize that there's a four-foot radius of melting tar around the car. A thin layer has already covered the soles of my feet, and I can feel only the slightest tingle of the earlier cigarette burn. Behind me, sunken footprints scatter in all directions like those of a child flying a kite on the beach. Even though my shoes are two sizes larger than my cousin's, our footprints look the same in the softened tar; I can't tell which path is mine. Jess tries to clean her feet on the guardrail at the side of the road, scraping off the tar like it is sand.

Passing by the front end, I'm surprised to see that the first foot of our '78 Volvo is still perfectly intact. The lights full of squashed mosquitoes, the Massachusetts plate, even the sparkling blue paint remains untouched by the flames that are blackening every other inch. I take a quarter from my pocket and bend in front of the inferno, holding onto the bumper as my feet sink into the doughy tar. A couple of turns on each side and "606 AEH" pops off easily. I slide into the ditch and tuck the license plate into a box of books. Jess follows me and places the AAA sticker she must have peeled from the bumper onto the outside flap of the same box.

My father and the cop wave us away from the police car, so we hop the barbed-wire fence and walk into the cornfield that borders the turnpike. My movements are nonchalant, but it has just occurred to me that the car might blow. Avoiding the foot-high stalks, we cut across the dirt rows faster than any tractor, not stopping until we reach the taller plants, whose ripe husks are in full bloom, their kinky golden hairs a perfect hybrid of my curls and my cousin's flax. The ears of sweet corn seem to float in midair as the pale silk brushes across my face and mixes with my own hair, streaking my dark locks with blond strands, the color burnt off from the tip to the follicle. I breathe in the calm before looking back at the road.

The cars passing by have returned to their traveling speeds but still follow one another in single file, staying in the fast lane. Our luggage grows out of the ditch in uneven stacks, its silhouette like the skyline of an old shantytown. Behind a skyscraper of books, my father nods his head in the cramped patrol car. I don't have to look at my cousin to know that she's watching, too, taking it all in slowly, like a long drag from a cigarette she doesn't want to finish but can't afford to waste. I hear more sirens in the distance and guess that the fire trucks are still a few minutes from us.

There is nothing to do but watch our car burn.

Chapter 4

"D'you mind if I smoke?" the flatbed driver yells into my ear as we exit the turnpike and drive south to a town called Asterville. We're jammed into the cab so tight that Jess is practically on my lap, and I have to lean around her to look at my father. I want him to object, to ask the driver if he's lost his mind, but he says nothing, his bent arm holding his head out the window. I turn back, and the cigarette is lit.

"I seen a lot of weird shit in my day, but I ain't never seen no car light up like that. 'Specially them foreign jobs." He chuckles. "You sure you all didn't start that fire yourselves, hoping to get some insurance money or something?"

I can feel him looking down at me but I keep my eyes straight ahead, focusing on a church steeple in the distance. We pass a chicken farm, but I only recognize it from the large white coops; I smell nothing but smoke.

"I'll tell you one thing, I'm getting me a picture of that carcass. Gonna hang it right next to the Corvette that split in half off Thompson's bridge." He taps the cigarette on the windowpane. "That guy was a tourist, just like you all, only he never left the county. Cedar Creek was his final destination, his resting place, so to speak." He finishes the cigarette and snubs it out on the truck door before flicking it out the window.

Without slowing down, he pulls the truck into a parking lot shared by the Nite-Lite Motel and Tink's Auto Repair. Tink leaves the truck idling and hops out. My father follows and starts helping Tink unpack the flatbed. Some of the boxes are seared, but it looks like most of his books were saved. I don't know if that's a good thing, since I will probably spend the rest of the summer helping him clean them by hand. Jess pulls the pile of clothing out from the back of the cab. Most of it's hers since I left my suitcase in the ditch. I have grown out of my old clothes anyway, and the cabin is full of hand-me-downs I will never outgrow.

"Just repack it all, and we'll see what we can salvage at the lake." My father tosses me a burnt duffel bag. "If we have to, we can replace things there."

The stationary bike he saved from the fire sits in the middle of the parking lot. Tonight my father will ride it outside our motel, and when cars pass by he'll feel like he's going somewhere. I look up at the flatbed. It's now empty except for the shell of the car, the first foot still untouched. My father traces his fingers across the headlights, stopping to scratch a few dead bugs from the smooth plastic.

"He said it was a good thing that we'd just filled up or it might have blown. Something about no air in the gas tank."

I nod, not knowing what to say.

"It was my first new car." He clears his throat. "I drove it right off the lot."

He cleans the mosquito from his fingernail and flicks it onto the overgrown grass. With that one motion, and the way his eyes can't look at me, I know that he's sorry for losing the car they bought when he got tenure, in the name of family expansion and my mother's gardening tools, when now just the two of us and his niece and library and fifty years of life aren't enough to fill it up, or to keep our car intact.

When Tink drives the flatbed into the garage, filled with the charred remains of the only car I've ever known my parents to drive, my father closes his eyes. It's only for a split second, but I know it's long enough to see the look on my mother's face as she got into the new car for the first time, marveling at the clean leather interior and the power windows, as she blessed the little girl in her lap, the freshly scrubbed boys in their seat belts, and the man who gave it all to her, fearing that one day it would not be enough.

"I'll call Triple A and see if I can rent a car. If we leave soon, we can at least get through most of Indiana tonight. I don't want us to get off schedule just because of this." My father walks to the pay phone outside the Nite-Lite Motel and lays a handful of coins on top of the booth. He will never have to ask for change.

"When I'm done you can call your mother. She'll want to know you're okay." He's looking at the phone as he speaks, so I wonder if he's talking to me or Jess. We both stand still.

Tink jumps down from the cab and walks toward us, the lone ignition key dangling from his right index finger.

"You think he'll wanna keep this?" He nods in the direction of my father.

"Yeah, he doesn't throw anything away," Jess answers before I can. I take the key from his outstretched finger, hooking the key ring through one of my belt loops. Tink's eyes cut a triangle among me, Jess, and my father, trying to connect the dots.

"Y'know, it sure is strange." Tink pauses to roll a cigarette. "How the three of you—"

"What?" Jess cuts him off. "How the three of us can have this much crap?"

Tink gives Jess a look somewhere between surprise and disappointment. He sprinkles dried tobacco into the creased rolling paper, balancing it gently between his thick fingers.

"Yeah." He licks the edge of the paper from left to right without taking his eyes off my cousin.

"Like I said, my uncle doesn't throw anything away."

Tink nods, pinching the ends of his homemade cigarette before delicately placing it between his slightly parted lips. He tucks the pouch of tobacco into his chest pocket.

"Don't 'spose you got a light?"

Jess glances back at my father before digging into her pocket for a lighter. She shakes it, and then hands it to him.

"Keep it, it's almost out."

He smiles in appreciation and lights his cigarette before slowly walking back to the garage. Jess looks at me like she's waiting for me to speak. I have nothing to say; I'm not used to us being on the same side.

"The Triple A guy will be here any second," my father says, walking over to us. "I left you some change by the phone. Make sure Jess calls her mother." Then he walks to the edge of the parking lot and waits.

I smell my father's cologne on the telephone handle and it makes me smile. I put in the coins and wait for the phone to ring. Once, twice, three times. I want to hang up. Who am I calling to talk to? What will I say? Four rings, five. If one of my brothers answers I will tell him about the fire. That is a good reason to call. On the sixth ring my mother picks up. She is laughing.

"Hello?" She tries to catch her breath. "Hello?"

What is making her laugh? Who?

I hang up. The coins tumble down through the phone, sounding like more change than I could ever carry. I take them out, one coin at a time, and tuck them into my pocket.

"Nobody home?" Jess asks. She is sunbathing on the grass behind me.

"You're up," I say, nodding toward the phone.

She doesn't use any coins—a collect call, I guess. She said she'd call her mother but she's laughing and swearing a lot so I wonder if she really called a friend. After a few minutes she hangs up suddenly, without saying good-bye. She looks around, scanning the parking lot for my father.

"They picked him up a few minutes ago."

"Oh," she says. "You seen a cigarette machine anywhere?"

I give her a harsh look. "I'm going to find a bathroom," I finally say, starting toward the motel's office door. Jess hesitates, then follows me into the motel.

There is no one behind the desk but we find a door marked

LADIES in the deserted hallway. When we meet at the sinks I can still hear the toilets running. I look at Jess's reflection first, before I glance to the right and see myself. I look darker than I remember. Jess scrubs her face with the tiny bar of soap, revealing tanned cheeks and a forehead full of freckles. We still do not look alike, but in our cut-offs and dingy T-shirts there is a vague resemblance, like a costume designer outfitted us for roles in the same play, and we're both auditioning to see if we belong. By now, I don't know if our performance is to convince the audience or ourselves. I wash my hands, then cup them together and drink the cold tap water until my teeth hurt. I dry my hands by running them through my hair, twisting the remaining threads of blonde further into my snarls. Jess dries hers on the butt of her shorts. We leave the paper towels untouched.

"I'm going to check out the pool," I say, opening the door and sneaking into the hallway. I glance back at the front desk but it's still empty.

The pool awaits at the end of the hallway, glittering through the glass door like pieces of tinfoil are floating on the surface. Nobody is swimming, but two men are lying out on deck chairs. I prop open the door and step onto the sidewalk. There are patches of wet cement where dripping swimmers must have stood. We walk in the puddles to the side of the pool, then sit on the tiled edge.

"Shit, this water's cold." Jess winces as she tests the water with her toe.

I drop both feet into the cool water, knowing that in a few minutes it will seem as warm as the air.

"Should we get our suits?"

"I lost mine," I say, as I reach into my pocket and pull out her swimsuit. It looks surprisingly clean but smells like the turnpike. "Here." I fling it onto the diving board. She glances at it and then looks away.

"Thanks."

The room across from the pool looks like a large greenhouse, but there are chairs and tables, so I guess that it's the dining room.

I see movement inside and think that it's the desk clerk coming to kick us out, but then I realize it's just a cleaning lady. She looks up at us for a few seconds, then goes back to her vacuuming.

I lean forward, dipping my arms into the pool. I scratch at the cinder bits that have freckled my forearms, but they won't wash away. Maybe they were always there.

"God, I want a cigarette."

"I guess a whole car burning up isn't enough smoke for you."

"Jesus Christ, it ain't the same thing." When she smiles I see my mother's dimple cut a line down her left cheek. "I was telling my friend Bic about the fire. He thought I was making the shit up. How it burned so quick and everything."

"Bic?"

"Yeah. *B-I-C*, like the lighter. He loves fire. He would've loved to see that shit burn."

"Did you tell your mom?"

"Nah, Shell wasn't home."

"I thought you said she never left the apartment."

"Yeah, well. She must have." Jess stares at the water. It occurs to me that Shelley might not have accepted the charges. She looks at me.

"What about yours?"

"Yeah, she wasn't home either."

Why are we both lying?

Jess sits up suddenly. "What's the best thing about your mother, the best thing she ever did?"

"Sometimes I can't remember her doing anything right."

"What? Are you trying to tell me that Miss Virginia Kincaid wasn't good to you? My aunt Ginny, everyone's favorite aunt?"

"No, she was all right. When I was a little kid. Now she acts like it's all about her." I keep my feet perfectly still in the water, and soon I can't feel them at all, like I'm paralyzed. I wiggle my toes.

"Now that sounds familiar. Only Shell was always that way. Always a lady first, then my mama." She leans back, resting against the diving board. "When I was little she used to come into my room at night. That was my favorite thing. She'd sit on the edge of my bed and rub my hair. I loved that feeling, her combing it with her fingers. She'd sing to me sometimes, not that she sounded all that good, but I still loved it. I'd just look at her, not saying a word. Before she left she'd whisper real softly. She'd say, 'Don't grow up and get ugly like everyone else, baby. Stay small and sweet and smooth just like this. Stay my little sunshine girl.' " She looks away. "She doesn't think I remember, but I do. How does a kid not remember something like that?" She kicks at the water, soaking the end of the diving board. "I remember every fucking word she's ever said."

The wind blows, and I can smell the hot, clean air of the motel's dryer. It's so nice to smell something other than the fire.

"It must have been hard, to be the only kid."

"Yeah, I wanted brothers and sisters. All the time. I wanted someone else to be there, to see everything I saw so people wouldn't think I was making shit up."

"Who thinks that?"

"I don't know. Teachers, guidance counselors. Nobody gets it till they see it up close. And we don't let them up close, that's one of the rules."

I don't say anything, hoping that if I'm quiet enough she won't realize she's opening up to me.

"I used to think it would've been different if Renny had been around. When I was a kid, you know, not anymore." She runs her fingers through the water. "Maybe he would've fixed something. Isn't that what daddys do?" She withdraws her hand, shakes off the water like dirt. "Your daddy's a fixer. I hope you appreciate that."

I guess she's talking about the fire and getting the rental car but all I can think of is how he hasn't been able to fix our family as easily as getting us back on the road. Running away doesn't seem like much of a fix to me.

"So what's he like, anyway?"

It takes me a second to catch up with her. "Your dad?" I ask.

She hesitates. "Renny."

"I don't know, it's not like I've spent a lot of time with him. He's like all our uncles—he drinks a lot of beer and goes fishing all day long."

"So he's drunk all the time?"

"You can't always tell with him. But he's always got a beer in his hand."

"That doesn't surprise me." She smiles to herself. "But is he . . ." Her voice trails off, looking for words to a question she doesn't know how to ask. She wants to know if she'll like her father.

"He has a dog named Wolf," I say, trying to find something redeemable.

She finally laughs. "He's got a dog named Wolf. That's classic."

"Come on." I stand up and walk out onto the diving board. "Let's get in before we have to get back on the road." The board bends under my weight.

Jess pushes off the edge and glides into the water fully clothed. She swims into the middle of the pool and does somersaults under the water until she runs out of air. The water ripples in her wake, and I notice a gray object floating down toward the drain. I see Jess at the shallow end of the pool, but it is the gray square that I look for as I dive into the water. Freeing the slick paper from the debris in the drain, I swim with it to the surface. It's the Polaroid, developed but slightly blurred. The smoke looks like a tornado surrounding the car and the spongy tar seems to be sinking into the turnpike. My father rises like a giant from behind the police car, and Jess and I look like sisters who can fight fire with bare feet, holding hands.

The car my father rented is a two-door Chevette, brick red, with a coat hanger sticking up where the antenna should be. I think it is older than I am.

"This was all they had," he says, slamming the door. "Try to pack it up while I take care of the Volvo." He walks into Tink's garage, holding out a credit card.

I can't imagine that all of our luggage will fit into it, let alone our bodies. Jess starts laughing behind me.

"Come on, Nellie, this has got to be a joke. The three of us won't fit in this box." She slaps the top of the car, which sounds like it's made of cardboard.

"We don't have a choice." I just want to close my eyes and wake up at the lake. I just want this trip to end.

The trunk ends up being a decent size, and most of the boxes fit inside. I put the breakables and the typewriter up front, at my feet, and shove the extra boxes behind the driver's seat. The duffel bags fill up the backseat, but I leave a little nook for Jess to sit in. We stuff the remains wherever they will fit.

"Where are my legs supposed to go?"

"On top of the clothes."

"Jesus Christ."

I wheel the stationary bike next to the car. "Help me lift it up."

There is no rack on the roof of the car so we put the bike on top of an old wool blanket. We tie it in place with twine, wrapping it around the bike several times and running it through the inside of the car. This same piece of twine held our Christmas tree to the roof of the Volvo last year; my mother had made us keep it, saying we'd use it again. The fisherman's knot she tied is still intact.

"Look, you can use this as a handle to get in and out," I say to Jess, grabbing the knotted twine.

"Or to hang myself."

She gets in, cramming into the tiny space between the bags and the window, her cheek resting against the glass as if she is a defeated dog. My father returns and inspects our work. He nods and gets into the car, his knees barely fitting underneath the steering wheel. He doesn't complain.

"Are we ready?" he asks.

I look around, scanning the empty parking lot for any forgotten pieces of our lives. There is nothing left. Everything we saved from the fire, valuable or not, is packed into the small rental car. Everything we have in the world.

Chapter 5

We stop for the night outside Hammond, Indiana. My father tells us that we are close to the Illinois border, and will still make it to Iowa City by tomorrow night. I know this makes him feel good, to continue to follow the plan. The Best Western is full so we get a room at the Notel Motel. I wonder how long it took the owners to think up that name.

It's late but it doesn't feel like bedtime. My father showers, then watches the eleven o'clock news in a T-shirt and shorts. I can't tell if they are different from what he was wearing before, since nothing looks clean. He eats miniature oatmeal cookies from the vending machine outside our door, chewing slowly like a child savoring an after-school snack, and then drinks a small carton of chocolate milk in one swallow. He makes everything around him seem small and inefficient.

When the lights go out I can't sleep. The air conditioner blows cool air but I am still breathing smoke. My feet search for a cool spot on the sheets, but instead run into Jess's hot legs. She has spread herself across the bed diagonally, taking up twice the space she needs. I listen to my father snoring, the rhythm as familiar as the darkness of a motel room, but there is no comfort in the recognition. When I close my eyes I see the tall flames growing out of the top of our car. I can feel the melted tar turn into sandals on my bare feet, as the cornfield becomes a maze I cannot escape.

The sheet feels as heavy as a wet wool blanket. I kick it off, lay in the dark in a T-shirt and underwear. I lift the shirt over my face, exposing my stomach and chest to the cool breeze of the AC. I close my eyes again and breathe clean air through the cotton, imagine the feeling of wet grass as I begin to dream. The cornstalks have become cotton plants, small yet resilient. I stroke the soft, white buds, enjoy the contrast against my dark fingers. I will walk for miles and never get lost in these rows. I can even hold the thorns and not bleed.

My father is gone when we wake up. My mother would have left a note. He returns with coffee and the local paper, nothing for us. He complains about not finding the *Globe,* but he reads the six-page *Gazette* from cover to cover; it's still news. Jess and I are slow to get ready. I contemplate a shower, but decide against it since I have no clean clothes. When I ask about a Laundromat he says we don't have time to stop. Then he picks up the phone and calls his friend Oliver in Iowa City. They met in graduate school, and have been friends for more than twenty years. I hear him say, "A few hundred miles," which means we'll get there for dinner.

When he finishes the paper, my father goes to the car, giving us five minutes to get ready. Jess can't find her shorts. She checks the dresser and under both beds.

"I know I brought them in from the car."

"How can you lose something in one room?"

She checks the bathroom for the third time. I decide to look in her duffel bag, just in case. I don't find the shorts, but I do find two towels from the motel tucked under some jeans. She walks back into the room.

"You find 'em?"

"No, but I found these." I hold up the towels.

She shrugs. "So what?"

"You're stealing towels now?"

"They're here for us to take. Just like the shampoo and the shower caps."

"There's a difference between toiletries and linen. Are you gonna take the sheets, too? The pillows?"

"Jesus Christ, it's not that big of a deal." She puts the towels back in her bag and zips it up.

"And what about the magazine, and the lighters?"

"Matches are free, why should lighters be any different? Nobody misses that shit, it's not like I'm taking somebody's kid."

"You're taking stuff that isn't yours. You're stealing." I grab my bag and head toward the door.

"So, you gonna rat on me?"

I stop at the door. I can see her shorts peeking out from under the blankets by my father's bed. I pick them up and toss them to her.

"No, I don't care that much."

I leave her in the empty room, no longer willing to be a witness.

Standing next to each other, my father and Oliver Scott look like they would never be friends. They look like opposites, really: my father is tall, thick, and honey-colored, while Oliver is short, skinny, and very black. My father has a full head of black hair and is clean-shaven. Oliver is completely bald and has a neatly trimmed white beard. The only trait they share is that they're both handsome. Oliver in a more deliberate way, one that proves that he's aware of it, that he actually works for it, while my father's good looks are almost accidental, and somewhat surprising.

Chloë is his second or third wife; I'm not sure which. She's not even forty, and has no children of her own. I guess the vacations with Oliver's four daughters are enough for her. She's one of those perfect women who can (and does) do anything, and with ease. She takes care of you without making you feel like you asked for it. She is the type of woman you'd need with four daughters and a few ex-wives, maybe the only kind that would make you consider marriage again.

Oliver's most recent novel was nominated for the National Book Award, but an accomplished man doesn't impress me as much; I have that in my father. Chloë is more than that: she speaks Japanese (she's Haitian and grew up in Baltimore), is a gourmet chef, studies kendo, and illustrates children's books. She is also a doctor. One of her books, about a boy who dreams his mother is a redwood tree, was a favorite of mine when I had just learned how to read. I would bring it to bed with me and read it two or three times in a row, the muted browns of her watercolors transferring effortlessly from the page and into my dreams. When my father embarrassed me by telling her the story, she gave me one of the original prints, autographed and framed. That's what I mean by perfect.

Their dinner table, a beautiful round mahogany, is the only table I've ever seen that looks like it was built for five people. (Growing up in a family of five, you notice that things would always be easier if you were four or six.) There are two wineglasses at every place setting; one is big enough to hold an apple, the other is tall and much thinner. At our house it's always one or the other, never both. And the kids only get water glasses.

Oliver grills the steaks in the backyard, on a wide deck overlooking Iowa City. It's more of a town, really, but the Scotts seem like a couple who would only live in a city, and they make the atmosphere swell in their presence. The food is endless, from tortilla chips with spinach dip to fresh bruschetta on toasted French bread to a three-pepper salad with Gorgonzola and cherry tomatoes to the main course of steak, scalloped potatoes, and sweet corn. By the end of the meal Oliver and my father are arguing about the publishing world. They have this discussion every year, and it always begins and ends at the same place. I bet they've been having this fight since they were in college.

"I'm telling you, Malcolm, it's all about publicity. You have to be willing to go on tour, even to the shitty towns where they ask you to sign their fucking library copies because they won't buy the book till it's on sale."

"Poetry isn't like fiction, Oliver. You guys get all the posters and book reviews. They won't even put a poet on *60 Minutes*."

"What about Dixon?"

"That bastard's just lucky." My father takes a bite of his steak.

"And it helps to win the Pulitzer." They all laugh. Jess looks at me like she wants me to translate. I shrug and sip my wine; I've chosen red since I like the big glass. Jess is drinking the white like it's apple juice.

"You know what your problem is?" Oliver says, sitting back in his chair.

My father turns to Chloë and smiles. "Oh, I can't wait to hear this."

"You just don't want to kiss anyone's ass."

"You're damn right. I've been publishing for twenty years. Why would I start now?" My father gestures with his knife.

"Because you want a career in the nineties, when TV and film and those goddamn computers are going to make us obsolete."

"I have a career: it's called teaching. You should recognize that word, it's what pays your mortgage."

"Of course we teach, and I like it most of the time. The kids out here are so excited and energetic, it's enough to make you sick." Oliver finishes his wine. "But that doesn't put you in the history books. Isn't that what we used to dream about in school?"

"I dreamt about having a family, and being able to take care of them. That's what I'm doing." My father wipes his mouth with a linen napkin.

"Speaking of . . ." Chloë interjects, "I'm sure the girls aren't as fascinated with you two as you are with yourselves. Maybe you could finish that chat in the library while we get the dessert and coffee." Chloë shoos them into the other room. "Come on, girls, you can help me torch the crème brûlèe."

I feel a little tipsy when I stand up, having had two glasses of red wine, and I lean against Jess as we follow Chloë into the kitchen.

"What'd she say?" Jess whispers to me. I can smell the alcohol on her breath from a foot away. I don't know if anyone noticed, but she and Chloë drank the whole bottle of Chardonnay alone.

"It's like a custard. It's good."

"Damn, I thought people like this were only on shows like *Dynasty*."

"Come on, they're not that bad."

"No, I meant it as a good thing."

We put the dessert dishes on a platter while Chloë loads the dishwasher. Then she asks us to bring everything into the living room. I'm afraid to carry the tray alone, but Jess's help might make it worse. We each grab a side, almost tipping it over, but thankfully Chloë doesn't notice. Jess is laughing into her shirt as we shuffle across the room. We make it to the coffee table without spilling, but I trip on the way to my seat and land on Jess's lap. We start cracking up, and I understand why people in the movies always laugh a lot when they're drunk.

When Chloë asks about the drive and the fire, I let my father do all the talking. I don't even like coffee, but I swallow two cups, hoping it will make things sound clearer. Jess eats her dessert like it's an exam she's struggling to pass. We are both thrilled when Chloë suggests that Jess and I walk down to the park to check out a free concert. I kiss my father good-bye on the top of his head and stumble out the door after Jess.

Walking is not the problem, but walking in a straight line is. Especially on the downhill slopes. Jess keeps veering to the left, stepping on my toes with her sandals. I suddenly realize that I forgot to put on shoes. The sidewalks are still warm from the day's sunshine, but the cement is rough on my bare feet. I walk the last few blocks on people's lawns, dodging sprinklers and the occasional pile of dog shit. When we get to the park it's still pretty empty. A guy setting up the stage tells us the first band goes on in twenty minutes. We find a nice patch of grass away from the stage, down by the river. When I lie down the world starts spinning.

"Damn, I haven't been this buzzed since my going-away party." Jess lights a cigarette. "We got all fucked up on screwdrivers and peppermint schnapps. It was nice until I puked. The sweet shit is gross coming back up."

She lies back on the grass right next to me, so close I can feel her hair against my face. I watch the end of her cigarette light up every time she brings it to her lips.

"This isn't your first time, is it?"

"What?"

"Getting drunk."

"No, of course not." I think she knows I'm lying.

"So why don't you ever talk about it? About drinking and boys and stuff?"

"No reason—why don't you?"

"I figured you didn't get into it, that it was below you or something." She blows the smoke straight up into the sky. "Have you ever had a boyfriend?"

"Of course." I keep my eyes focused on the stars. "In seventh grade I had two."

"At the same time?"

"No, not really. I broke up with the first one after I'd kissed the second one during a school trip."

"Oooh, you're a cheater," Jess teases.

"I didn't cheat on him. It's not like we were married."

"I bet it still caused a scandal."

"Please, he got together with another girl that afternoon."

"I guess it wasn't true love then," she says.

I don't know if there is such a thing at fifteen. Even at forty.

"Have you ever been in love?" I ask.

"Hell no." Jess sucks on her cigarette. "I haven't even had a boyfriend. I've messed around with a lot of boys, but never anybody special." She tries to blow smoke rings but they don't form right. They float in the air like jellyfish clouds. "I even had sex once, if you could call it that. We were under the bleachers during a football game. Everybody was yelling and cheering, they didn't even know we were down there. When our team scored the crowd started stomping on the bleachers—goddamn, it sounded like they were gonna bust right through and end up on top of us. But they didn't. They sat back down and it was over. I thought I'd feel something after, that maybe it'd make me like him better, but it sort of did the opposite. God, I still can't stand even looking at that kid."

"Why did you do it then?"

"Something to do, I guess. Something different."

"But why him? Why not someone you really liked?"

"I don't know. He was just there." Jess turns onto her side. "Jesus Christ, I sound just like Shell. You know how many times she's given me that bullshit line when she brings home some loser? God, her blood's a fucking curse."

I don't believe in the idea of a family curse; I am not going to be like my mother. I will love one man and marry for life. If I can't be loyal to my family, I won't have one.

"And I don't have it from just one side. Renny's not much better. Christ, maybe he's even worse. He knocks up my mom and runs away—how fucking predictable is that? Then goes off and finds another girl and wrecks her life, too." Jess sits up suddenly, then steadies herself with a bent elbow. "How long was he married to her anyway?"

"They broke up a few years ago, when Becca was a baby." I don't tell her that his second wife told my mom that she should have left Renny earlier, when she was pregnant with Teddy, and that her kids would be better off if they never saw him again.

"See, I got failure all around me. And they wonder why I can't stay out of trouble."

I roll onto my side, facing her. "Don't you want to do better than them? To prove them wrong?"

"Why bother? Who's there to notice if you're doing okay? They only pay attention to the fuckups."

There is some truth to that in our family. The academic failings of Marcus and Noah are the constant dinner table discussion, while my 3.7 GPA barely gets mentioned.

"Don't worry, though, I'm not going to totally follow in her footsteps. I'm not having a baby when I'm seventeen, that's for sure. Christ, I may never have one at all."

"Don't you want to get married?" I pull at the grass near my feet.

"Why do I want some guy hanging around, picking fights and making me do shit for him? I can get a dog if I want something to take care of." She puts her cigarette out on the ground. "You know how some girls dream about their wedding day, and having babies and shit? I don't think about that stuff. I don't dream like that."

"Then what's there to look forward to?"

She shrugs. "Today. Tomorrow. Just surviving day to day."

"And then what?"

"I don't know." She wraps her arms around her knees and pulls them to her. "You know how when you hug another girl your boobs touch? That's like the closest I've ever felt to another person. That's the feeling I'd want if I got married, to be so close you don't know where you end and the other person begins." She looks at the river, the water so black it barely looks like it's moving. "But when I think about it now it feels like drowning."

When I was younger I used to hug people like I was jumping into water; now I stand at the edge and dip my toes in first.

"It's not worth it," Jess finally says, "dreaming about the future. I don't even remember my dreams anymore, at least not the ones with guys in them. Sometimes I dream about girls, though. We're not having sex or anything, we're just talking and laughing. Once I was sitting on some chick's lap. Another time she was brushing my hair." She's quiet for a minute. "Sometimes, when I jerk off—" She stops short and turns to me. "Are you one of those prissy girls who pretends not to masturbate?"

I shake my head. "They're my only sexual experiences." I feel like I might be blushing.

"Good." Jess smiles. "I hate it when girls are all prudes. Anyway, that's what I think about sometimes, how it feels when they're holding me."

I've thought about girls when I touch myself, but it's more because my mind wanders and some girl from school pops into my head. But I try to block her out and go back to Sugar Ray Leonard.

"We had this counselor come into school last year," I tell her. "She said it was normal to fantasize like that. She said it doesn't mean you're gay."

"I know that, I'm not queer or anything," Jess says. "I've never even kissed another girl. I just have better thoughts about girls than guys." She bites on a blade of grass. "You know what my best sexual experience was? You promise not to tell anybody?" She has a huge smile on her face.

"Okay."

"Oh my god, I can't believe I'm gonna tell somebody this."

Now I'm scared.

"I fooled around with this neighbor girl when we were, like, ten. She had a really high bed, and I stood at the end while she laid down on the mattress and took off her shorts. Then we switched positions and she went down on me. I remember her bedspread was pink and had all these tiny blue flowers on it."

"When you were ten?"

"Swear to God," Jess says. "She came and everything. Is that crazy or what? We never even talked about it after."

I don't know whether to believe her since she lies all the time. Still, her voice sounds different, and she had no trouble looking me in the eye. The sound of music interrupts us as the band begins to tune their instruments. People must have filtered in quietly because all of a sudden the park is covered with bodies. The effects of the wine are almost gone, but now I'm dying for a drink of water. My mouth is dry and stale, and my lips feel tight like I've been eating salted peanuts. I look at the river and contemplate jumping in with my mouth wide open.

The crowd claps as the lead singer welcomes them to the show. I lie down on my stomach and prop my head up with my hands, close my eyes, and listen to the music. I can feel each blade of grass as it cuts into my legs and elbows, the earth's only line of defense. In a few minutes my ribs will get sore, but right now the grass is a mattress I could fall asleep on. My toes dig a hole in the cold dirt, looking for comfort, or a place to hide.

*   *   *

I wake up early, with a headache and a sour stomach. I don't know how my uncles can drink so much every day. No wonder they can't hold down real jobs. In the basement I find an industrial-size washing machine, so I clean all our clothes in one wash. The dryer gives off so much heat it feels like I'm standing in front of a woodstove. I watch my clothes through the window in the dryer, twisting and dancing with the other things: the shirt and socks my father was wearing during the fire, Jess's cutoff jeans. They are closer than they would ever get while being worn. Two mix-matched socks travel together, bound by static cling and a centrifugal force they can't comprehend. When the cycle ends they will get separated and may never touch again.

When the clothes are ready I fold them all and pack them together in a canvas bag that Chloë left out for me. I take it to the car and tuck it into the backseat, fearing that a few hours in the rental car will make them dirty again. I accidentally dislodge a box behind the driver's seat, knocking a pile of books onto the floor. One catches my eye immediately, the fire-singed copy of *Tempered Blues,* my father's first book. I pick it up and finger the burnt edges, then turn it over and stare at the photograph on the back. He looks so young without glasses, and small. Smaller than I ever remember him being. I flip through it, reading a few of my favorite poems. The inscription is the hardest part to read. *For Virginia, what is sacred is sublime.* Whenever I read his poetry I almost can't believe that it came from my father, from the same person that I know. But I guess I don't know the person who wrote those words, just like I no longer know the woman they were written for. I don't think I ever knew them.

Sometimes I wish I could remember my childhood better. Those first few years—were they as happy as the pictures show? As perfectly simple as the lines of my father's poetry? Were they worthy of metaphor and simile, of being canonized in literary journals? I am sometimes embarrassed by my father's talent. It makes me feel like he's on a higher plane than the rest of us, or worse, that we're all on that plane with him, because of him, and must one day prove we are worthy of staying. At fifteen, do you really have talent? Do you know it if you do? I'm good at soccer and swimming; I've studied Spanish and Latin, and am a good overall student; I can paint a decent watercolor and knit a pair of wool mittens. So what? I will probably end up working for the Department of Health.

I repack the box, tucking that book into the bottom. Then I jam the box in behind the driver's seat, making sure it won't fall open again.

When I get back inside everyone is awake and breakfast is served. Over fruit smoothies and eggs Benedict my father tells us that we're staying in Iowa City another night.

"Oliver asked me to read with him tonight. His agent's in town and we thought this would be a great opportunity. He's been trying to get me to meet her for years."

"I thought you had an agent."

He looks at me over the top of the newspaper, his eyes saying everything he won't.

"What's an agent?" Jess asks.

"Someone who makes you money."

Her eyes light up. "I need an agent."

"Lonnie's even coming down from Minneapolis, to back me up on sax. You remember Lonnie, right? He always carried those lavender candies you loved."

"But what about the Fourth of July?"

"They celebrate down here, too," he says, with a hint of a smile. "You can go to the fireworks in town if you want. Chloë said they shoot them right over the river, at the park you went to last night." He blows on his coffee before taking a sip.

"What's the difference? Fireworks are fireworks." Jess pours herself a cup of coffee. My father notices, but doesn't say anything.

"But I've never missed the ones at Blackfoot Lake. Ever."

My father looks up. "I didn't know it was such a big deal to you, Nellie." He returns to reading the paper. "I'm sorry."

Jess finally breaks the silence. "Can't we go up alone? I mean isn't there a bus or something?"

We stare at each other, then at my father. He looks up.

"Uh, I'm sure there is. . . ." He hesitates. "Would you want to do that?"

In all the ways I've conceived of this trip I never thought a bus would be involved. On the other hand, I never thought I'd miss the fireworks. I shrug and then turn it into a nod. He pauses, as if weighing the pros and cons in his head.

"Okay." He points to the phone book on the counter. "Find out when the next bus leaves."

The man on the phone tells me there is only one bus a day to St. Croix, and it leaves in forty-five minutes. Chloë and Oliver return from their run just in time to give us directions to the bus station. My father buys two one-way tickets and gives me five dollars for lunch. Aside from the coins in my front pocket, it's all the money we have. I forget to bring my wallet, and Jess doesn't even have one. We're both wearing shorts, T-shirts, and sandals. I'm carrying *Beloved* in my back pocket, the Polaroid from the fire as my bookmark; Jess has her cigarettes rolled up in the *Teen Beat*. Neither one of us bring a bag, or even a long-sleeve shirt. This is the lightest I've ever traveled.

Chapter 6

I've always liked trains more than buses. I like the wide seats, and the rhythm of riding on steel tracks. I like going through open fields instead of driving on the crowded freeway, to see the natural world instead of the man-made one. This bus is pretty comfortable, though, and it's cool being above the other cars and away from the road. The view is better, too. Cornfields line the horizon, a wave of bright green that floats all the way to Minnesota. If I knew what to look for I'm sure I could see the border.

We each take two seats, across the aisle from each other. It's nice not having her over my shoulder like in the car. I kind of wish I had come alone, but I guess my father didn't want to be alone with her either. Maybe I can pretend I'm traveling by myself and not talk to her the entire trip. It's only ten hours, I know I could do it. Jess, on the other hand, wouldn't even last an hour. (Within the first five minutes she asks me what time it is, if I have any gum, and how old our great-grandmother is.)

The bus leaves Iowa City on 380 North but changes to 20 West before Waterloo. I imagine we'll stay on 20 till 35 North, which will take us right into southern Minnesota. This is the same route we would have taken with my father. I picture the map, feeling better as I watch the trip unfold in my mind. The road changes suddenly, as all the lanes merge into one, and the interstate becomes a two-lane country road.

The bus stops for gas outside a town called Dike, after being on the road for about two hours. The driver tells us to be back in ten minutes. Jess lights a cigarette as she gets off; a trail of smoke lingers behind her like a bad smell.

"I'm hungry. Let's get some doughnuts or something." She nods toward the 7-Eleven next to the gas station.

"The money's for lunch," I say. "I'm not wasting it on junk food."

"Since when are you all healthy?"

"Since it's all we've got."

"Let's just look." She grabs the bottom of my shirt and pulls me with her. The other people from the bus have beaten us inside and there's already a long line.

"Okay, bathroom first," Jess says. This is the first time I don't have to pee and Jess does. I follow her inside anyway.

"Oh, damn it," Jess says from the stall. "I got my period. Do you have any tampons?"

"No, but they have a machine on the wall. Hang on."

I pull a few dimes from my pocket. The machine only has pads, but I get her one anyway and slide it under the door.

"What's this?"

"That's all they have."

"Jesus, it's a fucking diaper."

"At least it's not that old-fashioned kind, with those straps that you pin to your underwear. My mother used to use those."

Jess comes out looking more annoyed than usual. She pulls at her underwear. "I can't wear this."

"What else are you going to do?"

Jess makes a face and washes her hands. Inside the store, the line's gotten even longer. I don't remember that many people being on the bus. We walk around, looking for a snack. Jess holds up two cupcakes covered in pink coconut flakes; I shake my head. She grabs a package of hot dogs; I shake my head. When she picks up a can of boiled eggs, I mimic vomiting. She laughs.

"Let's just run across the street to that Hardees," she says. "It'll only take a few minutes."

"No way, we'll miss the bus."

"Look at that line, the driver won't leave all these people. Plus, he's not going anywhere soon."

When I look outside I see the bus driver flirting with a woman driving a convertible. When she moves to get out of the car, he starts pumping the gas for her.

"Come on, the bacon double cheeseburger's ninety-nine cents."

I finally give in. "All right."

We run across the street and place our order. The restaurant is completely empty so the food comes up quick. We run back to the gas station carrying the food in a hot, greasy bag. The entire thing must have taken less than five minutes. Still, the bus is gone.

"No way," Jess says. "No fucking way."

"We're dead," I say slowly. "We are so dead."

"I can't believe he left us. That he left the other people." She gestures toward the 7-Eleven. We both look over to see it, but the line is gone.

"This is like the fucking twilight zone. This is crazy."

"No, I'm crazy to have listened to you." I look down the road but I don't even see the taillights. It's like the bus was never here. I start walking in a circle.

"Come on, there's got to be other buses."

"First of all, we don't have any money." I begin counting on my fingers. "Second of all, that was the only bus. And third of all, we don't have any money." I shove three fingers into her face. She shrugs.

"Well, can't your daddy just send us some?"

"What? We're only, like, a hundred miles from him, he might as well come pick us up."

She takes a sip of her soda. "Do you think he'll mind?"

"Are you kidding me? Do you know how pissed he'll be? He won't speak to me for at least a week, maybe more. He'll treat me like I'm five again." I sit down on the self-serve island, trying to calm down.

"Okay, we'll get a ride then, we'll hitchhike. It's only a hundred miles, I've gone farther than that before."

"If we go back to Iowa City he'll find out we missed the bus. Plus he'll know we hitchhiked and I'll be in twice the trouble. No way I'm showing up back there." I take my feet out of my sandals and rub them on the ground. The bottoms are still black from the melted turnpike. The tar, like color, won't wash off.

"Fine, we'll hitchhike to Minnesota then. It's only, what, a few hundred miles?"

"Yeah, like four hundred. That could take us days."

"No way, all we have to do is find some trucker going north. He'll take us the whole way, probably." She kicks at the curb. "We might even beat the bus."

"And when we get there, what do we say to everyone at the lake?"

"We'll call them from the bus station just like we planned. They'll never even know." She sounds convincing. On the other hand, listening to her got us here in the first place.

"Come on, what choice do we have?" She holds out her arms, palms up to the sky. She looks like someone checking for rain, or a grandmother waiting for a hug. For the first time I notice that I'm still holding on to the Hardees bag, my knuckles curled tightly around the top. The burgers are still warm. They're the only luggage we have to carry.

"All right, let's go." I stand up and head toward the road.

We don't speak while we're walking. I eat my burger slowly, knowing it could be my last meal for a while. Jess eats like she always does: quickly, and in large bites. I wonder if she savors anything. When she's finished she tosses her wrapper into the ditch. One summer during the drive out here Noah made the mistake of littering. My mother pulled over and made him walk back to the ditch and pick up his trash, plus all the other crap that was sitting around. We had to be there for at least twenty minutes. I bet that was the last time my father let her drive. When I finish my lunch, I stuff the wrapper into my front pocket.

We pass a sign for Route 20 West; beneath it a smaller one reads MN STATE LINE: 292 MILES. I'm glad it's a two-lane road; hopefully that will make it easier to get picked up. We both start walking backward, with our thumbs sticking out. I feel foolish, and after a few minutes I drop my hand. Jess sticks with it; she looks more natural anyway. The first few cars pass us by, not even slowing down. I think of being on the Ohio Turnpike and trying to flag down help during the car fire. It's funny how people are interested enough to look, but not to actually pull over and help. I wonder what I would do if I drove by a pair like us. I might keep going, too.

A black Dodge drives by slowly, the driver bent over and staring at us. Jess drops her thumb and turns her back to the road.

"Gotta watch out for the weirdos." She tucks her hands into her pockets. When he speeds up and drives away, she turns back to the road and starts up again.

The sun is warm on my face. I look up to find it high in the sky so I figure it must be around noon. I start to sweat on my forehead and under my bra. It's not too hot, but a few more hours and Jess will start to burn. I don't mind the extra exposure, especially on my legs. I'm hoping to end up quite dark by the end of the day.

A beat-up pickup truck passes by. After a few seconds we hear a horn honking. When we turn around we see that it has pulled over onto the shoulder farther up the road. We run to catch up. All I can see is that the inside of the cab is packed with people. An old Mexican woman sticks her head out the passenger window.

"¿Adonde vas?" she says to me.

"Norte," I say, "to Minnesota." Thank god for Spanish class.

"We go west, to Fort Dodge," she says.

She turns to the driver and they start speaking in Spanish. Fort Dodge is farther than we need to go, but I guess they could drop us anywhere along the way. She turns back to me.

"We take you to the next big town, where the highway goes north." She smiles. "Okay?"

"Thanks," I say. *"Gracias."*

She nods and slaps the side of her door. *"Vamos, chicas."*

Jess laughs as we climb into the back. "They think you're Spanish?"

I shrug. It happens to me all the time. Especially in New York City, where all the Puerto Ricans think I'm one of them. When I was a kid this guy in a museum thought I was his niece and wanted to take me home. My mother had to get a security guard involved.

The back of the truck is filled with tools and paint cans, but we find a fifty-pound bag of dog food to sit on. It's windy once we start moving, and in minutes all the sweat on my body has dried. It feels strange to sit backward, to see the world only as you pass it by, instead of watching it come upon you. I lean my head back, against the small window that separates us from the Mexican family. I glance inside the truck and find a young girl staring at me. She can't be more than three. It looks like she's chewing on a piece of beef jerky. After a few seconds she takes it out of her mouth and offers it to me, painting on the window with her saliva. I shake my head. She puts it back in her mouth and smiles. She waves at me; I smile and wave back.

We get to the interstate in less than two hours. They drop us in the parking lot of a Shell gas station, right next to the freeway entrance. When I go to the window to say thanks, the old woman presses a napkin into my hand. She says good luck and they drive away. Two pieces of corn bread are wrapped inside the napkin. I offer a piece to Jess.

"Damn," she says, biting into it, "that old lady acted like you're her grandkid or something."

The corn bread is warm, and as I chew it becomes a sweet paste that I wish I could suck on forever. When Jess finishes eating she takes out a cigarette.

"I'll be right back," she says, walking toward the Shell station.

I figure she's getting matches so I decide to wait outside. The afternoon sun is getting lower but it's still hot, and after a few minutes I go inside to cool down. Jess is in the back looking at magazines.

"Can't you do that later?"

"Nah, this guy's eyeing me. I gotta look relaxed."

"What?" I'm confused.

"Shhh," she says, showing me a box of tampons under her shirt.

"What the hell are you doing?"

"Cover for me, go distract him."

"No way, I'm staying out of this."

"Come on, I don't want him to see me."

"And what about me? It's not like I blend in."

"Fine, then. But don't get in the way." Jess walks around the magazine rack trying to look nonchalant.

"Can I help you girls with something?" the cashier says from behind the counter.

"No thanks," Jess says. "We're just looking."

I squat in the candy aisle, searching for a pack of gum. When I stand up the cashier is next to me.

"What are you looking for?"

"Gum."

"Any particular type?"

"Sugarless."

"Flavor?" he asks.

"I don't need any help," I say. "I can read." Why is he all over me when Jess is the one with the tampons down her shorts?

"I'm just trying to be helpful," he says. "Customer satisfaction is very important to us."

"Meet you outside," Jess says as she exits. I watch her light a cigarette through the window, a huge smile on her shameless face.

"So, which gum were you interested in?"

"You know what, I just lost my appetite." I feel his eyes on me as I walk away from him. I walk to the door slowly, making sure not to touch anything. There is a large circular mirror hanging on the wall above the exit. I glance up and see that his eyes are still following me, watching each step until I'm outside his range.

"Thanks," Jess says. "Nice work."

"I didn't do it for you." I keep walking toward the freeway entrance.

"Whatever, it still helped me out." She follows me.

"No, the fact that that guy was a racist bastard helped you out."

"What are you talking about?"

"The way he came over to me, how he was watching me."

"He asked you if you needed any help."

"Yeah, looking for gum. What am I, five? He didn't trust me in the store, it happens to black people all the time."

"So?"

"So, it's fucked up."

"Yeah, but you can't seriously think that guy was being prejudiced to you. I mean, it's not like he thought you were black or anything."

"Why not?" I stop and face her.

"Come on, Nellie, you don't exactly look black." She takes a drag off her cigarette. "You're not like a 'real' black person."

"What does that mean?"

"Look at yourself, you've got soft, curly hair and the lightest brown eyes I've ever seen. Plus, your face looks more like Grandma Floss's than anyone, if she'd had a really great tan."

"So just because my mother's white that means I am?"

"None of y'all are really black. Look at your aunt Frances, she's barely darker than me. And your daddy's hair is all soft and he speaks all proper and shit. I mean, you drive a fucking Volvo. Nobody in Virginia drives a Volvo, white or black."

"So that means we're not black, the fact that we have a nice car?"

"You know what I'm saying. I grew up with black people, with black skin and kinky black hair. Those folks are from plantations, with grandparents who were all slaves. Those are real black people. Your family's something else. You're all these different mixed-up things—"

"So what does that make us?"

"I don't know. There's no one word."

"Exactly." I start walking again. "And until we come up with one, we're black."

I hear the crunch of the gravel as I pound along the side of the road. I want to walk faster and farther than my legs can take me. I wish I could walk right out of my body and into the atmosphere, dissolve into the air like smoke.

Chapter 7

————◆◆◆————

Interstate 35 seems crazy after the relative calm of Route 20. There's noise coming from all around, and when the cars speed by it feels like they're going to suck us onto the road with them. The speed limit is fifty-five but it looks like every car, truck, and trailer is going well over eighty. When they pass I have to duck my head so gravel doesn't fly into my eyes.

"No one's going to pick us up on this road," I yell to Jess.

"Give it some time," she yells back. "We'll find someone."

We walk like this for more than a mile, our heads down and thumbs out. I didn't know how tiring it was to walk backward. I feel like I'm using leg muscles I never knew I had. After a while we give up and turn around. We pass a sign for a weigh station up ahead. The small sign that hangs beneath it reads CLOSED.

"Why are weigh stations always closed? I mean, what's the point of having them if they're never going to be open?"

"I don't know," I say.

"And why do they need to weigh them anyway, to make sure the truckers aren't stealing stuff?"

I shrug and keep walking. When we get to the weigh station it's actually open, and there are three 18-wheelers waiting in line to get weighed.

"This must be our lucky day," Jess says, running ahead.

"What are you going to do?" I run to catch up with her.

"I'm getting us a ride."

The last truck in line is the first we approach. The driver's wearing big sunglasses and has a patchy beard. He smiles down at us.

"How're you girls doing?"

"Fine," Jess says, looking up at the cab. She grabs my arm and we keep walking.

"Hey, you need a ride?" he calls after us.

"No thanks," Jess yells over her shoulder.

"Wait, what happened?"

"That guy's a total perv. Didn't you see the porno shots taped to his mirror and the Playboy-bunny sticker? You gotta notice everything."

I guess she really is good at this. The next truck driver seems a lot better. He's older and has a really big potbelly, the type to put on a beard and dress up like Santa Claus for his grandchildren.

"Where you going, mister?" Jess calls up to him.

"Minneapolis, Minnesota." He says it like it's a foreign language.

"How about helping us out with a ride?"

"Wish I could." He points inside the cab. I lean forward and see three guys squeezed onto the bench with him. "These guys just beat you."

"We're going to see Prince," one of the guys yells out.

"Paisley Park, baby." Another guy throws his arms into the air.

"Sorry," the driver says, looking like he really means it.

The last truck's empty, but we see the driver inside talking to the weigh station worker. He's small, barely bigger than me, and wears a Yankees baseball hat. I take that as a good sign. He signs some papers and they shake hands.

"Don't worry, this last one's going to be ours," Jess says.

We stand on the passenger side, the truck idling loudly behind us. When the driver comes out I realize it's a woman. I was wondering why she looked so clean-cut and normal. When we were younger my cousin Caitlin and I wanted to be truckers. We wanted to leave our families at home and hit the open road by ourselves. I guess we thought we'd be the first women doing it.

"Let me guess," she says, "you ladies need a ride?"

We nod in unison. The name Leora is sewn onto her shirt in cursive letters.

"Where you heading?"

"To Minnesota," I say. "St. Croix, it's near Edison."

"Well, I can take you across the state line, but then I'm heading west on I-Ninety to South Dakota. Come look at the map. I'll take you as far as I can."

We climb into the cab, and I'm instantly surprised by how roomy it is. The interior is a maroon leather, and it's covered with stickers from all over the country. And it smells better than I would have imagined, sweet like raspberry pie. I wonder if it's her perfume or an air freshener. This is much better than that tiny Chevette my father rented, or the Trailways bus that left us behind.

"What kind of tunes do you like?" Leora pulls a box of cassette tapes out from under the seat and hands it to Jess.

Jess picks a Bruce Springsteen tape while I scan the map. Leora releases the brake with her left hand and we slide out of the weigh station like a cruise ship pulling out of the harbor. The ride is so smooth it doesn't feel like we're moving; instead, it looks like the trees are gliding by us. I roll down the window and enjoy the breeze, surveying the landscape like I'm going out to sea.

Jackson, Minnesota, is a town I've always liked. Mostly because of Reggie Jackson, but also because they have an A&W that we could always convince my father to stop at. They have huge root beer floats and a car-hop service like on *Happy Days*. It makes me feel like I've gone back in time and I'm in high school with my parents. It's sad to think that we wouldn't have been friends.

We're right outside Jackson, where I-90 and 71 meet, when our time with Leora comes to an end. She brings us to the A&W to drop us off, but ends up buying us dinner. Turns out she ran away from home in high school and hitchhiked around the country. It made her want to be a trucker, and help other people out on the road. She doesn't believe our story; she thinks we're runaways.

"Don't worry, I'd never call the cops or anything," she says as we're saying good-bye.

"We're going to Minnesota to visit our family. Really, we have a place to stay."

"Whatever," she says. She starts writing in a matchbook. "Here's my truck number and the phone number for my company. You can call anytime to find out where I am."

I don't know if we should take it but Jess pockets it before I can say anything. We shake hands and she climbs into the cab. Then she rolls down her window and tosses out a U.S. map of the Midwest.

"Don't leave home without it," she says, shaking her finger like a mother.

"That's one nice lady," Jess says, watching the semi drive off.

I unfold the map and find Minnesota. Jackson's not on it, but I do see Highway 71 and Edison, the only town near the lake that's big enough to have a movie theater.

"Now we're pretty close, it's just a straight shot north to Edison. Then a few miles on Highway 15 and we're in St. Croix. From there we could walk to the lake if we had to."

Jess shakes her head. "Just give me the bottom line: How long?"

"I don't know," I say, "it's more than a hundred miles. If we find another ride soon we can be there by dark."

Jess already has her thumb out as we walk out of the A&W parking lot. Seventy-one is a flat and perfectly straight two-lane road that cuts a field of corn in half, like a perfect middle part. The sun drops lower in the sky as we walk, and soon it's only warming my left side. An old dusty car passes by us going in the other direction. I hear the change jingle in my pocket, knowing I don't even have enough money to call St. Croix, let alone pay for a ride there. I can only rely on fate, and the help of strangers. I want to remember this feeling of absolute vulnerability, to memorize it's vast landscape, so I will never end up here again.

"I didn't expect it to be so flat out here," Jess says out of the blue. "In Virginia you can never see too far."

"I bet you never thought you'd miss a mountain range, huh?"

Jess shrugs. "I never thought about it until now. How it lets you hope there's something better out there, just around the bend. Out here there are no surprises."

We walk in silence for at least ten minutes before Jess starts whistling. It reminds me of my father, who whistles when he doesn't want to talk, but has to make noise.

"Need a lift?" I hear someone shout from behind us. I turn around to see a huge red tractor coming down the middle of the road. The driver, a middle-aged guy wearing overalls and a white cowboy hat, slows down next to us.

"I'll take you into town if you don't mind standing on the back," he yells over the engine.

Jess looks at me; I shrug.

"Okay, thanks," she yells back.

"Just watch your feet when you're getting on. See those little platforms, stand on those. Then hold on to the bars behind my seat."

He reaches back and helps each one of us onto the tractor. As soon as we're holding on he takes off. We can't be going faster than ten miles per hour, but looking down at the road still makes me dizzy, and I almost lose my balance. I decide to keep my head up and my eyes focused on the cornfields in front of me.

I must have been around four the last time I was on a tractor. We were visiting my great-grandmother's farm and I was riding on Grandpa Brant's lap. I remember being scared as we went down each row, crushing the dead stalks in front of us while turning over the soft earth behind us. I could feel the vibrations of the engine through his legs, all the way into my bones and way up into my chest. I felt my heart beating in the loud, broken rhythm of a tractor engine.

Before I realize it we're pulling into a town called Windom. The farmer slows down and we hop off the back end of the tractor. When we yell our thanks he lifts his cowboy hat, showing the deep groove in his matted hair that comes from a lifetime of wearing hats. Even if he never wore a hat again, he still wouldn't be able to flatten that groove. Some marks stay with you for life.

Highway 71 cuts right through the center of Windom. In the middle of town it becomes a strip with nothing but fast food restaurants and gas stations, but after that it turns into a quiet neighborhood full of cute two-story homes, with long front yards lined with sunflowers instead of fences. We decide to walk through town, hoping it will be easier to get picked up on the other side.

We pass a fruit and vegetable stand in a gravel parking lot. An older couple sit in lawn chairs under a crab apple tree. The ground around them is littered with the small, bitter fruit. A sign on the table says tomatoes for a dime.

"Just leave the money in that can," the old man calls out.

I drop the coins into the can and choose two large beefsteak tomatoes, the kind that make perfect round slices for hamburgers. I hand one to Jess before biting into mine like an apple.

She looks at me sideways. "Couldn't we have asked them to slice it?"

"Come on, they're better this way," I say, taking another bite. The taste of this perfectly ripe tomato, more than crossing the state line, is what finally convinces me that I'm back in Minnesota. I lean forward, letting the juice drip down my chin and onto the gravel, happy to be outdoors in the summertime in a world with no napkins.

Jess reluctantly bites into hers, sending a stream of tomato seeds onto her shirt.

"Oh, Christ," she says, dropping the half-eaten tomato into the dirt. She tries to wipe off the stain but makes it worse. "There goes my only shirt."

She sucks the seeds off one by one, and spits them onto the ground like they're poisonous. Then she cleans her hands on the butt of her cutoffs and pulls the crumpled *Teen Beat* out of her back pocket. She flips through it as we walk, silent for a long time.

"Damn, Ricky's hot," she finally says, holding up the centerfold picture of four guys from some rock band. "He's my favorite. Which one do you like?"

I quickly understand that I'm not allowed to like the same one. I tilt my head to read the name of the angry one with the scar over his eyebrow.

"John," I say.

"That's cool. My friend Jenny used to like him, but I don't think she does anymore. I'll give you all the pictures I was saving for her."

"Thanks," I say, wondering if I've just agreed to plaster my walls with the pages of *Teen Beat*.

"Okay, now let's say you had to marry one. Who would you pick?"

"None of them."

"Come on, you have to pick one."

"Weren't we just talking about *not* getting married?"

"It's just a game," she says. "Come on."

"None of them," I say again. "I wouldn't marry a white guy."

"Why not?" She looks shocked.

"Because then my kids would be white, or mostly white. Why would I want that?"

"But you just said all that stuff about being black."

"Well, that's because my father's black. It's different if you have at least one parent; then the kids are in the middle, a blend of both sides. My kids would only have me."

"And what if they looked just like you?"

I picture my future child, light brown with soft, dark curls, his face a passport into any nation but his own. I shake my head. "That's not enough." I look down at my hands, the color not even enough for me.

"All right, so forget about marriage, what about dating?" Jess closes the magazine.

"I don't know," I say. "Maybe."

"So wait, you've never even kissed a white boy?"

"No, I have. The first boy I ever kissed was white. With blond hair even."

"Damn, you went real white. Where'd you find him?"

"We were in South Carolina, near Myrtle Beach. It rained so we spent the whole vacation in the indoor pool. He even taught me how to kiss underwater."

"Wow, a real Cassanova." Jess puts the magazine back in her pocket.

"What about you?" I ask.

"What, my first kiss?"

"Would you date a black guy?"

"No way, my mama would kill me. Everybody in the town would kill me. It's not worth it." She lights a cigarette.

"What if he was the man of your dreams?"

"I'd never know that. I wouldn't give him the chance to show me."

"Well, it's your loss." I look away. "Black men are hot."

"Like who?" She inhales the smoke.

"Sugar Ray Leonard."

"Who's that?"

"The boxer." I can't believe her. "All right, every member of De-Barge."

"They're too pretty, just like Michael Jackson. They don't count."

"Okay, Gregory Hines."

"Who?"

"*The Cotton Club? White Nights?*"

She shrugs.

"What about Billy Dee Williams?" I offer.

She stares at me blankly.

"From *Star Wars,* Lando Calrissian, the only black guy in the movie."

"Come on, he's old," she says.

"Look, it's not my fault you don't know any of the younger ones. They're still hot."

"Not the ones that get together with white chicks."

"What does that mean?"

"You know, it's always the average ones who cross over."

"What, like my father?" I stop walking and glare at her.

"No, I didn't mean—"

"My father's ten times better-looking than your dad, and at least he's not a drunk who abandoned me," I yell in her face.

"Look, I don't give a damn about my daddy," she yells back. "I don't need him or his family, and I don't need you or yours."

"Sure, you're so tough, you don't need anybody."

"Not here I don't. I don't even know why I agreed to come to this stupid lake."

"Yeah, right, where else are you going to go? Back to Roanoke, where your mother can't handle you?" I lean into her face.

"You don't know a damn thing about my mama and what she can handle." She pushes me backward with two clenched fists. I stumble, but stay on my feet. "Besides, she's not my only option, I got plenty of places to go. Anywhere I want."

"With what money?" I straighten my shirt, rubbing off her touch.

"I don't need money. I've never had more than two bucks in my pocket and I've made it this far."

"Fine then, go discover America. Enjoy the open road on your own." I wave her away like a cloud of smoke in my face.

"I will," she says. "It'll be a lot nicer by myself anyway." Something about the way she walks away, without any hesitation, makes me even more angry.

"In case you're wondering," I call after her, "you are like your father. Just like him."

She lifts her arm in the air and gives me the middle finger without turning around. She's walking so quickly that the magazine begins to inch out of her back pocket. I'm sure when it falls she won't stop to pick it up.

There's a part of me that knows I should go after her, tell her to come back, maybe even apologize, but I can't bring myself to do it. I don't want anything bad to happen to her, but I don't want her here with me. She is no longer better than being alone. When she makes it to the next intersection she turns right, and my eyes inadvertently follow her down the street as they might follow an interesting stranger. At the next corner she blends into a crowd of people coming out of a movie theater and after a few seconds I don't even recognize her.

Chapter 8

I'm not lost. I'm not sure where I am, but I know I'm not lost. You're not lost until you don't know where you're going.

On my third birthday I disappeared for an hour on my tricycle. While everyone else was in the backyard trying to pin the tail on the donkey, I got on my tricycle and pedaled away. Even then I wasn't lost—I was looking for something I couldn't find. Apparently, I made it down several side streets and to the corner store, where the lady recognized me (of course) and called my mother. I don't remember waiting for her to arrive, or what she said when she got there, but I do remember her being out of breath and how her heart was galloping against my chest as she hugged me. I remember her hand on the back of my head during the whole walk home, the gentle rock of her apologetic stride.

I remember never feeling lost.

There are never phones when you need to make a phone call, just like there are never trash cans when you have garbage. Finally, in the parking lot of an abandoned store that used to sell mattresses, I find a pay phone. I step into the dirty glass box, tight like a coffin, and am thankful that the door is long gone. My first thought is to call my father, to tell him everything, but I quickly change my mind and decide to call Aunt Maisie instead. When the operator comes on the line my mind blanks and I end up giving her my home phone number in Boston. When she asks for my name I hesitate, then say, "Nellie," like it was a word I've never said before.

Noah answers the phone and accepts the charges.

"Hey, Nells, how's the trip?"

"Well . . ." I don't know where to begin.

"How's the lake, have you been in the water yet?"

"Actually we stopped off in Iowa City and Dad got tied up with Oliver. You know that scene." I clear my throat. "So how are things there?"

"Fine, the same. School sucks but at least I'm passing this time. And they've got me on the bar at night so I'm finally making some real money. That's it, really, nothing too exciting." He sounds like he's drinking something, Tab probably. "Mom's fine. She's having a yard sale this weekend and is going crazy giving away all our old things. Hey, do you want your old skis?"

"No, I guess not—"

"Good, 'cause they're already out in the yard."

I wonder if my bed is out there, too.

"Hang on, Marcus just walked in." He hands the phone to Marcus, who sounds out of breath.

"Hey, girl, how's it going out there? How's the Big Man?"

"He's fine, I guess. Things are fine."

"You miss home yet?"

"I don't know. Where's home?"

"Come on, Nellie, we don't know what's going to happen."

"What about this yard sale?"

"It's just to get rid of old junk. It doesn't mean anything."

"Fine, whatever."

He pauses, and I can picture him in the doorway, his hands hanging from the moldings as if he were about to tear the wall down. "Look, you're right, okay, things are messed up, but no matter what happens with them, things for us were going to change anyway. Noah and I are both out of the house come the fall—"

"And what about me? I'm still in high school."

"Yeah, but you only have a few more years. We're all growing up,

Nellie, we don't need them in the same way. Don't rely on them to always be there for you, okay?"

"They're my parents—who else am I supposed to rely on?"

"I don't know." His voice suddenly drops. "Yourself, I guess."

I scratch at the graffiti painted on the walls. "Are you trying to make me feel better or worse?"

"Listen, try not to be upset, okay? Everything's going to be fine."

I inhale slowly, wishing I believed him.

"Mom's not here, in case you wanted to talk to her. She's out buying tags for the sale."

"No, that's all right."

"You can't avoid her forever, you know. She's still your mother."

"Yeah, well, maybe the summer will be long enough." And as the words come out I know that they're not true. A few months is not long enough and fifteen hundred miles is not far enough. These are things that can't be measured in distance or time.

The man at the park is probably the most handsome man I've ever seen. He's tall and thin, with straight black hair that falls gracefully into his eyes. He's wearing dark jeans and a sweatshirt, but doesn't appear to be too hot. He looks like the kind of guy who rides really fast on a motorcycle. He has long white teeth, perfectly straight, and is exactly my color.

I am standing at the water fountain, watching him between drinks. There is a little girl with him, no more than four years old, and he pushes her on a metal swing. She throws her head back and laughs, occasionally yelling, "Higher, higher."

I look around the park but there is no one else there. I'm sure the girl is his daughter—she looks just like him—but as he stands there behind her, repeatedly pushing her into the air, he looks like someone who has never held a child before. Plus, he doesn't look much older than eighteen. After a while he walks in front of the swing set and sits down on the grass. When the girl flies in front of his face he falls backward in an exaggerated motion, as if she had kicked him over. She laughs with her feet pointed toward the sky. They continue this game until she slows down and hops off the swing. Then she runs over to the merry-go-round and jumps onto the steel platform. When she falls over, she catches herself with two outstretched hands.

"Be careful," he calls out, standing up.

"Come push me."

He grabs the outer rails and starts to push the merry-go-round. At first it spins slowly, but when it speeds up he has to move quickly to keep up with it. He runs in a circle around her. Her hair is blown away from her face and she wears a look of terror. Still, she holds on tight, with both arms wrapped around the bars, and doesn't tell him to stop. Instead, she closes her eyes. Eventually he breaks away and collapses onto the ground next to the ride. She spins around and around, her eyes still closed, as if she's afraid to watch the world as it passes by. She waits until it comes to a complete stop before opening her eyes. Only now does she smile, jumping first onto the ground, and then onto the man. He picks her up and runs with her balanced on his shoulder like a log.

When I finally get my fill of the water, I cut through the park, wishing I had my soccer ball to kick around. The grass is almost too long for soccer, but it's a perfect cushion for my sore feet. I want to lay down in it, maybe even take a nap, but there isn't time. I need to make it as far as I can before the sun sets.

"Would you mind taking our picture?" The man walks up to me holding out a camera. He is even better-looking up close.

"Sure." I take the camera from him. "Do I have to do anything?"

"No, it's all set. Just point and shoot."

The girl is waiting for us, standing still in front of an oak tree. He squats behind her and puts his hands on her shoulders, his dark fingers in contrast to her pale yellow dress. She smiles and holds one of her braids, wrapping the end around her small finger. The other one has come partly undone and the wisps fly around her face. When I snap the picture he is brushing the hair from her eyes. I try to take another one, but the girl steps out of the frame too quickly. He is alone in the second shot, falling back against the tree.

"Thanks," he says, standing up.

"You're welcome." I turn to leave.

"Can I have the camera back?"

"Oh, sorry." I hand it back to him and walk away quickly, trying to disappear.

"Hey," he calls after me. "Are you Sioux?"

"Sue?" I turn around.

"Yeah." He smiles.

"No, my name's Nellie."

He walks up to me, laughing. "I meant the tribe. Sioux Indian."

"No, sorry." I feel my cheeks getting hot.

"You look Indian, especially now that you're blushing."

"I'm mixed, black and white. But my great-grandfather was half Chippewa."

"Well, that's enough," he says. "My mother's a half-breed. You sort of look like her."

"I look like your mother?"

"Don't worry, it's a compliment. She's old but she's still pretty."

"Thanks, I guess." I look at his mouth instead of his eyes.

"By the way, I'm Dallas." He puts his hand out. It's cool when I shake it, and the skin is rough like my uncle Flint's. I wonder if he's a farmer, too. When his sleeve rides up I see the edge of a tattoo wrapping around his wrist. He catches me looking at it.

"It's a python," he says, pulling up the sleeve so I can see all of it. "What do you think?"

"It's big."

"Yeah, that's what a lot of girls say." He starts to blush, becoming a deep red-brown I'd love to be. "I mean, it had to be so you could get all the detail. I sat there for eight hours."

"Didn't it hurt?"

"Yeah, but I wasn't exactly sober, if you know what I mean."

"Dallas, come push me." The girl is back on the swings. He looks over at her, then back at me.

"I gotta go," he says.

I nod, wishing I could get on the swings and have him push me instead. I imagine the feeling of his hands on my back.

"So maybe I'll see you around some time?" He walks away backward, still facing me.

I shake my head. "I don't live around here." I can't stand the fact that I will never see him again.

"Neither do I." He smiles that cute-boy smile that means they think they have all the answers. He puts his hand up, not quite waving, and then turns and walks toward the swing set. As I leave the park my heart is beating as if I were running and I feel more awake than I've ever felt. I can't stop smiling, even when I remember that it will be dark in a few hours and I am still more than a hundred miles from the lake.

The neighborhood on the other side of the park must be the rich one. The houses are much bigger, a few are three stories tall, and one even has a swimming pool with a plastic slide. Next door, their neighbors have an aboveground pool with a black tarp covering it. I watch the family pile into their minivan as I pass in front of their house. Walking by I realize that the large black object in their backyard can't be a pool—it looks more like a flying saucer. I peer through the bushes to get a closer look. It's a huge trampoline, the kind that divers and gymnasts practice on. I haven't seen one since gym class in the fifth grade.

I look down the street, making sure the minivan is gone. Then I slip between the bushes and sneak over to the trampoline. I take off my sandals and grab the side of the trampoline above my head. It's not as easy as when I was ten, but I manage to pull myself up and onto the rubber edge. It gives under my weight, making it hard to stand still. I begin by bouncing softly, to test the springs, and the strength of my own legs. After a few seconds I have lost all fear. I thrust my legs into the woven vinyl sheet, flying higher and higher with each bounce.

I try to focus on objects in the distance: a milk truck, a telephone pole, the top of a nearby house. I want to fly over them all. It feels incredible to float through the air, to feel as light as a paper airplane or falling snow. The air accepts me each time I jump, holds me up without wings, helps me defy gravity with sheer desire.

Chapter 9

I can't walk anymore. There are no mile markers on this road but I've been out here for hours. The sun just set and the sky is an indigo blue, my favorite shade. If there was a pay phone out here I might give in and call my aunt Maisie or uncle Flint. I thought about calling from the last town, but how do I explain being alone in the middle of Cottonwood County? I know they'd come get me if I asked, but I don't want to give up yet. I need to make it there by myself.

I try not to think about Jess, but I can't help but wonder where she is. She probably doesn't even know. She has no sense of direction and would be too stubborn to ask. There's a part of me that's surprised that I haven't run into her yet, since this is the only main road out here. Every time I turn the corner I think I'll see her walking up ahead of me, the smoke from her cigarette like a signal fire. Maybe she called Leora, and is halfway to South Dakota by now. Maybe I'll never even see her again.

I stop to rest at a Texaco station by the side of the road. It's weird being in a bathroom without her. I buy a handful of hot balls with my last nickel, hoping the sugar will give me the strength to continue. The candy is too hot for my mouth, and I stand over the water fountain letting the cold water numb my tongue. My saliva is red as it flows down the drain, like I'm spitting out blood.

Outside I sit on the curb, watching the cars pull in and out. I try to guess which ones will go self-serve, and which will go full. A guy in a gold El Dorado pulls up to full-serve. I lost that one. After he talks to the attendant, he gets out of the car and walks toward me. He looks about thirty, and has the large, soft body of an ex-football player. He stands over me, smelling like fried food and liquor.

"Got anything for me, sweetheart?"

I don't look at him.

"Come on, whatever you're sucking on, can't you give me a piece?" He rubs his hands together and blows into them like they're cold. They look strangely long, like feet.

I jerk my head toward the door. "They've got them inside. A penny each."

He makes a noise that falls between a laugh and a snort, and walks into the gas station shaking his head. I put another hot ball into my mouth; this time the heat barely registers.

A few minutes later the guy comes back out, a frozen pizza under one arm and a six-pack of Schlitz hanging from his finger-tips. He opens one up and drinks it down in a long gulp, then crushes the can in his hand and pitches it into the grass.

He lets out a loud burp. "You think you can do that?"

I look away. "I don't like beer."

He squats down next to me, leaning in close. I can feel the stubble on his cheek even though he's not touching me.

"What do you like?"

I don't move, but my heart starts to beat faster.

"That'll be ten dollars, sir." The attendant walks over to us. The guy stands up and hands him a crumbled bill from his shirt pocket. A can of chewing tobacco comes out with it, falling to the ground. When he bends over to get it, I see a bump in the back pocket of his jeans that looks like the outline of a switchblade. I stand up quickly, almost knocking over the attendant as he heads into the station. I keep moving.

"Hey, where you going so quick?"

I walk a little faster, thinking I should probably go back inside but not wanting to pass by him to get there. I head toward the road, knowing I can always drop into the ditch and outrun him in a field. He cuts me off right by the entrance, pulling up next to me in the El Dorado. He leans out the driver's side.

"Come on, don't you want to come party with me? I got a lot of nice stuff, things you've probably never tried." He grabs my arm with his thick, hot hands.

"Let me go, asshole." I try to pull away but his grip is too strong.

"Come on, don't be like that." He puts the car in park and tries to get out without letting go of me. "Calm down, all right, people are going to get the wrong idea."

"Then let go of my arm." I'm surprised by how calm I sound.

"Get into the car first." His voice is getting sharper.

I look around the empty lot, wishing there was someone outside to see this, to hear me if I screamed. He tries to get out again, but I kick the door shut and scratch at his arm with my free hand.

"Oh, you wanna fight me? You wanna make it hard?" His voice flares as his eyes fill with fury. He grabs for something inside the car. I pray that it's not a knife; I am more afraid of getting stabbed than getting shot. I reach in and try to honk the horn, hoping to get someone's attention. I tell myself to scream, but no sound comes out. Suddenly, I feel a strange sensation in my arm, cold at first, then quickly becoming hotter. Is this how it feels to be stabbed? I look down and see him holding the car's cigarette lighter against the inside of my arm. It feels like he could push it through to the other side.

I lean into the car as far as I can, punching the center of the steering wheel. The horn is deep and loud, and I don't stop honking it until he pushes me away from the car. I stumble backward, falling onto the gravel.

"Your loss, you stupid wetback," he says, hating me with the wrong slur.

The attendant finally comes outside, but when he doesn't see anyone near the full-serve island he goes back inside.

The El Dorado pulls away quickly, almost crashing into an old car that's turning into the parking lot. I stand up slowly, wounded roadkill intent on surviving. I don't bother to wipe the dust off my clothes. The old car stops suddenly, and the driver comes running over to me. It takes a few seconds for me to register that it's Dallas.

"Who was that?" He gestures toward the El Dorado as it disappears down the road.

"I don't know, some creep." I hold my arm up to the light.

"Are you okay?" He reaches for my arm.

"Yeah, it's just a burn."

"Jesus Christ, Nellie, it's bleeding."

I pull my arm away. "I just need a bandage."

"Hang on, I've got some in the glove box."

Dallas comes back with two bandages. He puts them on gently, but the pressure sends a shock of pain through my arm. When I wince he blows softly onto my covered skin.

"What happened?"

"Some guy just started messing with me."

"Where, in the parking lot?"

"Yeah, I was just sitting on the curb and he started bothering me. It's not a big deal, I'm fine." I hold the bandaged arm away from my body. The pain moves in prickly waves from my elbow to my fingertips.

"Come on, let me take you home."

I shake my head. "It's too far."

"Where do you live, the Cities?"

"Boston."

"Okay . . . that might take a while." He runs his fingers through his hair. After a few seconds it falls right back into his eyes.

"Actually, I'm just going to Silver Lake. It's north of here, just outside St. Croix."

"Off Highway Fifteen, right? That's not far."

"It's more than a hundred miles."

"It's a lot closer than Boston."

"Don't worry, I can make it there by myself." I pop a hot ball into my mouth. The firey sweetness is a temporary distraction.

"What, are you going to hitchhike?"

"I've done it before."

He crosses his arms. "So you'll take a ride with a stranger, but not with me?"

I shrug.

"Come on, Nellie, you can't be that stubborn." He leans closer and looks me straight in the eyes. It almost kills me. "You know, I probably shouldn't admit this, but I was looking for you right now."

"At the Texaco?"

"Not exactly. I was headed for the Dairy Queen; no one comes through town without stopping there." He puts his hand on my shoulders. "Come on, let me at least buy you some ice cream." He walks toward the driver's door. "You can use it to cool down that burn."

I lean over to look into the car, as if seeing the inside will tell me what to do. It is large and surprisingly clean, like a rental car. No fast food wrappers, no blankets, no coloring books spread across the backseat—no signs of a child.

"Where's the girl?"

"I just dropped her off, with her grandparents."

"Your parents?"

"No. Her mother's."

"Where do they live?"

"Just outside Windom."

"Where do you live?"

He hesitates. "I move around a lot."

"Is she yours?"

"Yes." He leans on the car door. "Any other questions?"

I gesture toward the car. "Is this a Mustang?"

"No, it's a Galaxy. Nineteen seventy-two." He taps the roof. "I just got it running again."

"Seventy-two, that's the year I was born."

"Damn, you're still a baby." He smiles across the shimmering green roof.

"How old are you?" I ask.

He gets into the car without answering, then reaches across the front seat to open my door. "Nineteen," he finally says. "But it's been a long nineteen, I feel at least thirty."

I slide in next to him. Inside it smells like a new leather jacket.

"Here, the seat belt's a little screwy." He leans over and grabs my lap belt, clipping it into the shoulder strap before belting me in. His hair falls against my cheek, giving me the chills. He pulls back. "Sorry, I'm still not used to it being so short." He tries to tuck the loose hair behind his ears but it falls out.

"You call that short?"

He nods. "I used to have a braid down to the middle of my back, just like in the movies." He gestures with his hand, approximating the length. "It hadn't been cut since I was born."

"So what made you finally do it?"

He hesitates before he answers, starts the car and lets it idle for a while. "I got sent to a reform school when I was sixteen. They shaved my head."

"What did you do?"

"Stole old ladies' purses, broke into grocery stores, borrowed cars."

"No, I mean when they shaved your head."

He shrugs. "I acted like it didn't even bother me. I told them to go even shorter, to take the guard off and go right down to the scalp." He clears his throat, but his voice sounds rougher when he speaks again. "I regretted it, though, 'cause I couldn't go outside for the next week. It felt so delicate, you know, like a baby's head. It felt like even the wind could break it."

"They shouldn't be allowed to do that, to change any part of your body."

He exhales. "But that's exactly what they want to do—that's their goal, that's how they break you." He looks over at me. "The worst part is, I remember looking in the mirror and thinking that my face was ruined, like I'd lost all my teeth or had my nose cut off. It was like it wasn't even me." He glances at his reflection in the rearview mirror.

I smile. "And now, is this you?"

"Not yet." He runs his fingers through his hair. "It's still growing."

He puts the car in drive and pulls out of the gas station slowly, as if he doesn't know if he's ready to move on.

There's a long line at the Dairy Queen when we first pull up. These country ones are always busy, since people out here don't have anywhere else to go. We stand in line together and Dallas pays for both of us. I like the fact that everyone knows we're together. They also think we're the same. I can see it in their eyes, the way they stare and then look down at their feet. I'm passing as an Indian.

"Kind of feels like we're in a museum, huh?" Dallas whispers into my ear. "Like we're on exhibit."

"Yeah, but we talk back," I say, a bit too loud.

"That's what they're afraid of." He catches an old man staring at us; Dallas stares right back until he looks away. Then he smiles at me like he just won something.

The only table we can find outside is next to the trash can and has no umbrella.

"Come on," he says, leading me back to the table. "It's the colored section."

I sit down with my back to the other tables. Dallas straddles the bench, facing me.

"So I don't get it," he says, working his way through a banana split. "If you live in Boston, what are you doing way out here?"

"I've got family here. My mother grew up on a farm in St. James."

"I didn't know they had black farmers in Minnesota."

"They don't. She's the white one. My father's from New York City."

"Wow, that's a different world." He takes a spoonful of my ice cream. "Which one do you like better?"

I pause. "My father."

He laughs. "No, I meant which part of the country, the East Coast or out here?"

"I like them both, for different reasons. I like the sky out here, and how it's quiet at night. But I like all the different people in the city, how you hear all these crazy languages on the subway, how every street has a different smell."

"You're lucky," he says. "I've never been further east than Chicago, and that was only because I had to drive my mother to a powwow in Elgin. She's got a glass eye so she can't drive at night."

"You talk about your mother a lot. You must be close."

He nods. "She's been good to me. I owe her." He sucks the chocolate off his spoon. "I guess you're not close with your mother."

"Not now."

"Yeah, that's how it is with me and my father. We can sit in the same room for hours and never speak. Even when we were both drinking we didn't get along. And now that I'm sober it's like he hates me even more, like I remind him what a fucking cliché he is."

My ice cream has melted and I put the cup down on the bench between us. He gestures to it and I nod, and then he picks it up and drinks it down like soda. He seems to have an endless appetite.

"What made you quit?"

"I don't know, I guess what makes everyone quit. I finally hit the bottom." He scrapes the bowl clean, then lays the spoon in the empty dish. "That's kind of pathetic, huh? Having to start over at nineteen."

I shake my head. "I think it's brave."

When he's finally done I carry both our empty dishes to the trash. On the way back I step on a magazine lying in the dirt. It's all beat up, but I can see that it's a copy of *Teen Beat*. I pick it up and dust it off. It's bent in half lengthwise so it could fit into a pocket. Jess was here.

I look around, half expecting her to be standing in the parking lot, a cigarette in one hand and an ice cream cone in the other. But she's not there, not in any direction that I can see.

"Did you see someone drop this?" I ask him.

"No," he says, "but it looks like it's been there awhile. Take it if you want."

"No, I don't want it . . ."

"You don't have to be embarrassed, Nellie. They're fully dressed, right? That's better than some of the magazines I've been caught with."

"That's not it." I don't want to explain, so I tuck it into my back pocket, imitating Jess.

As we walk back to the car we pass a pay phone. There's a matchbook lying in the gravel, but it takes me a few seconds to recognize it. When I pick it up, I'm not surprised to see Leora's neat handwriting inside the flap. I guess I was right about Jess calling her. She really is gone.

"Are you going to pick up all the litter in this parking lot?"

"No, I just . . ." I glance at the road before looking at him. "This is my cousin's stuff. We got separated earlier."

"You were traveling together? Today?"

"Yeah. I guess she was here." I walk back toward the car, still looking around.

"So, wait, where is she now?"

I shrug.

"Is she alone?" He has a worried look on his face, as if he were talking about his own daughter.

"She's sixteen. She can take care of herself."

"Just like you, right?" He gets in the car and starts the engine. "Come on, let's go find her."

"Dallas, she's fine. She doesn't want me to find her." I slam the door behind me.

"And that's why she left you this trail?" He looks at me.

"That's just her laziness." This time I fasten my own seat belt.

"There must be a whole lot more to this story that you're not telling me."

"There is no story. We were together and then we weren't."

"Why were you hitchhiking in the first place?"

"We missed the bus, okay? We didn't want to get in trouble so we decided to get there on our own."

"So why not stay together?"

"We fought, okay? She's a pain in the ass."

He shakes his head and puts the car in drive. "Then there's even more reason to find her."

We pull out of the parking lot and get back on 71 North, driving way below the speed limit. Dallas has his window down, and the breeze blows his long bangs away from his face.

"I'm sure she got picked up already. She's probably home by now." I'm trying to convince myself.

When cars pass by from the other direction their lights shine on Dallas's face like spotlights; he squints, but never diverts his eyes from the road. I scan both sides of the highway, looking for Jess's familiar frame in the dark and delicate shadows of the night.

We've driven more than twenty miles and still no sign of Jess. There's no way she could have, or would have, walked this far. And if she did get a ride, she could be anywhere.

"Are you cold?" Dallas asks me. "You're not even wearing long pants."

"I'm fine."

"The fan belt's broken, so it takes a while for it to heat up. Here, take my sweatshirt." He unzips his sweatshirt and hands me his arm so I can pull the sleeve off over his wrist. He balances the steering wheel with his knees while he frees the other arm. My mother used to drive with her knees so she could pull her hair back into a ponytail. She also drove a stick shift holding a cup of hot coffee. She used to seem so tough.

He drapes the sweatshirt over my legs, his fingers giving me the chills.

"Thanks."

Now he's wearing just a white tank top. The ribbed cotton is stretched tight over his hairless chest. He's not that built, but he looks wiry and strong. He places his right arm on my headrest, his hand resting inches from the back of my head. I can smell his deodorant, spicy and sweet like nutmeg.

"How's the burn feeling?"

"Okay." It's become a dull throb that I can ignore most of the time.

"Don't forget to put aloe vera on it. That will help the scarring." He looks over at me, then drops his right arm onto my lap again. "This is what happens when you don't use aloe."

His entire arm is covered with small round marks, from below his wrist to the top of his shoulder. They are slightly lighter than his skin, and range in size from dimes to half-dollars. It looks like someone splattered wax on his arm, except the burns are sunken in, not raised. It's horrible-looking, but something makes me want to feel it. I gently run my fingertips across the skin.

"Does it hurt?"

"No, it happened years ago, when I was just a kid. If it wasn't so ugly I'd forget I even have it."

"What happened?" I can't keep myself from asking.

"I was boiling water to make macaroni and cheese. My dad came home and started yelling at me because we didn't have any meat for dinner. He got pissed when I wouldn't fight with him." He flexes his arm; it feels like steel in my hands.

"Before I knew it the water was running down my arm. It felt really cold, like it was almost frozen—I guess I was in shock or something. The noodles were all over the kitchen floor. When I left for the hospital my mother was still on the floor picking them up." He brings his arm up to his face, examining the burns. "I'm gonna get a tattoo to cover it one day, maybe another python. Then you won't even be able to see it."

"Is that why you got the first one?"

"No, that one's covering up a shitty tattoo I made in high school with a ballpoint pen. God, that thing was ugly."

"What was it?"

"It said, 'Grace,' but it was so sloppy you could hardly read it. That's my daughter's mother, my first girlfriend." He looks over at me. "I wanted to do something special, you know, give her something that would last forever." He looks away, his voice softening. "It didn't, though. Her name stayed with me longer than she did."

We are both quiet for a while, scanning the edges of the empty road as we pass through each town.

"I think you're right," he finally says. "About your cousin. We should have found her by now." He lays his arm on the seat behind my neck and taps out an unfamiliar beat. I look straight ahead, staring at the night sky. The stars are low and bright, and in the reflection of the windshield, they look like they're sitting on my lap.

"See that sign right there?" Dallas points to a small brown sign tucked in the trees. "The Lower Sioux Indian Reservation? That's where I grew up."

There is a gravel road hidden in the tall grass below the sign. It looks like it would lead to a fishing hole or to nowhere at all. I look back as we pass by. I don't see any houses, but I can see a bunch of lights through the trees. It looks like someone hung lanterns in the forest.

"My mother still lives there, and my aunts and uncles, my grandparents on both sides. Almost everyone I know. I think it's good for Serena, to be raised around all that family." He looks at me. "That's my daughter. She moved in with my mother last year, after Grace died."

I nod. "Serena, that's a pretty name."

"Grace chose it. I wasn't there for the birth." He runs his fingers through his hair. "She gave her my last name, though, that made my mother happy."

I wait a few seconds. "Do I have to guess?"

"Sorry." He laughs. "Firecloud. Serena Marie Firecloud."

"That's pretty, Serena Marie."

"You don't like Firecloud?"

"No, I do. It's . . ." I stop myself, searching for the right word. "Intense. It fits you, though. It sounds real and imagined at the same time."

"And what about you, Miss Nellie . . . ?"

"Kincaid. Eleanor Davis Kincaid, after my grandmother."

"Eleanor, that's kind of an old lady name. I like Nellie better. Nellie Kincaid, that's got a nice ring to it. It sounds like you're a singer or something." He tugs on a piece of my hair. "You're going to be famous with a name like that."

I'm glad that the car is dark so he can't see the blood as it rushes into my cheeks. I lay my head back and close my eyes, wishing that this night could go on forever, that the cabin was a thousand miles away, and that I never had to get out of his car.

"There's a lever next to your door if you want to put the seat back and take a nap. We've still got almost an hour."

"No, I'm fine." I sit up and blink my eyes, trying to look alert.

"Seriously, you can sleep. I won't kidnap you."

I smile and tell him that I have to stay awake to keep an eye out for Jess, that I don't generally sleep in cars, and that I don't want him to miss the driveway. What I don't say is that I have to really trust someone in order to fall asleep next to him, and that I can't remember the last time I let that happen.

Chapter 10

I've given up looking for Jess by the time we get to Edison, a town only twenty miles from the lake. I don't know how I'm going to show up without her, what I'm going to say to her father, what I'm going to say to mine. Dallas convinces me that I need to face them with a full stomach, so we slow down on the main drag, looking for a drive-thru we can both agree on. I'm holding out for a Hardees, the site of our last meal together, and when I finally see one at the end of the strip I tell Dallas to go there.

We're stuck at a red light when I think I see her, walking through the Hardees parking lot. She's partly in the shadows, and her head is down, but something about her movement is unmistakable: the tense shoulders, the purposeful walk, the way she looks at her feet and not the road ahead of her. It's Jess. I'm guessing her choice of the Hardees was no mistake either. For someone who wanted to get lost, she sure left a lot of clues.

I watch a couple of teenage guys try to talk to her, but she blows them off, waves them away with her cigarette likes she's too busy to speak. When they leave she pulls their wrappers out of the garbage can and finishes their burger scraps and fries without looking up. She takes out a soda, but can't bring herself to drink it, so she chucks it back into the can and goes inside.

By the time we walk in there's no sign of her in the main dining area. I leave Dallas in line and head to the bathroom, a cramped room with wet toilet paper all over the floor. The door to the only stall is closed, and even though she's trying not to make a sound, I can tell that she's crying. I stand against the wall, waiting for her to come out. Then I hear a thud as the toilet paper dispenser crashes to the ground. Half of an empty spool rolls past me.

"Fuck."

"Are you all right?"

"The thing just fell. I didn't break it." She sounds defensive.

"Jess, it's me, Nellie."

Silence.

"Jess, I know you're in there." Before I realize it I'm on my tip-toes looking over the top of the door. Jess is sitting on the toilet, fully dressed, staring back at me.

"You always stick your head into other people's bathroom stalls?" She's wiping her face on her T-shirt.

"I had to make sure it was you." I step back from the door.

"And if it wasn't?" She comes out and stands next to me at the sink. Her eyes are puffy and she has red blotches all over her skin from crying.

"What are you doing here?"

"I had to pee, and then I was blowing my nose," she says. "Any other dumb questions?"

"I mean, how'd you get here?"

"I hitchhiked. You didn't think I walked, did you?" She notices the bandage on my arm. "What happened to you?"

"I got burned, it's not a big deal."

She grabs my wrist, bringing my arm into the light.

"It's bleeding through the bandage," she says. "Who did this?"

"Some jerk was messing with me. I wouldn't get into his car so he burned me with the lighter."

"Jesus Christ, he tried to kidnap you?"

"I just want to forget about it, okay? It'll heal." I pull my arm out of her grip.

"Wow, I never thought anything bad could happen out here, since we're in the country and everything."

"Assholes are everywhere." I grab a roll of toilet paper off the countertop and carry it into the stall with me. "I got us a ride, Jess. He'll take us right to the lake."

"Us?"

"Yeah, if you want to come."

She's quiet for a while. "And what do you want?" She turns on the water.

"I just want to make it there. I'm tired and cold and I don't want to get in any more fights." I flush the toilet and meet her back at the sinks.

Jess is washing her face with cold water. She holds a palm against each eye, pushing deep into the sockets.

"I haven't cried like that since I was a kid," she says. "Since Grandpa Brant's funeral, I bet." She uncovers her eyes and looks into the mirror, watching me. "I cried for hours that day, cried for this old guy I'd never even met." She lets out a quiet laugh. "You know why? Because I felt sorry for myself. Because I'd lost a grandpa before I ever even knew him."

Jess wipes her nose with the back of her hand. I try to stay completely still. When she speaks her voice is barely audible.

"I guess I'm lucky I ran into you." She doesn't make eye contact.

"It's not an accident. We were looking for you." I don't say that it was Dallas's idea, that I had given up on her.

"Here, I think this is yours." I hand her the folded copy of *Teen Beat*. "I found it at the Dairy Queen."

"Yeah," she says, "I thought you might go there."

"And I found that matchbook, from Leora. Did you actually call her?"

"I thought about it." She sniffs and spits into the sink. "But I don't really like South Dakota all that much."

I smile, knowing that she's never even been there. "Come on, Dallas is waiting for us."

"Dallas? As in Texas?" Her face turns sour. "That's another state I don't really like."

I try to hide my smile.

"How do you know we can trust this guy? I mean, you did pick him without me."

"Actually, he picked me."

"Christ, that's even worse." Jess shakes her head.

"No, you'll love him. He's got this tattoo of a snake wrapped around his wrist." I grab my arm to demonstrate. Her eyes get wide and she gives into a smile.

"Cool," she says.

I knew that would do it. She respects anyone with the guts to carry a permanent mark, anything that can connect you to the scene of the crime.

There is no sight as familiar to me as the bend near mile marker 37 on Highway 15 in Redwood County, Minnesota. It's as clear and unchanging as a photograph: the gravel pits with their sandy mountains on the north side of the road; the train tracks running parallel to the breakdown lane, hidden by overgrown grass; the sign for the Lazy Bee campground, two miles ahead; the twin oak trees that guard our driveway like sentry. Even in the dark I recognize it all.

"Slow down. See the two oaks and the mailboxes, the driveway's right there."

Three silver mailboxes, fastened onto a two-by-four and nailed into a dead tree stump, glisten in the moonlight: one Christiansen, one Matthews, one Kincaid. The names are stenciled neatly onto the sides in black paint, looking as fresh as the day they dried, sometime before I was even breathing. Some things don't change.

"We're here," I say loudly to the backseat. Jess sits up slowly, her face a cross between terror and excitement.

When we were kids, arriving was always the best part, and we were sick with anticipation every year. First the familiar sights along the road; then the smell of the freshly cut grass and the lake; then Aunt Maisie's dogs, Sunset and Maggie, running through the fields to meet us, like they, too, had missed our presence all year long. My cousins would join the dogs and run the half-mile drive-way alongside the car, holding on to the windows and our out-stretched hands. Everyone seemed to be talking, but nothing was heard or remembered. And then we finally stopped, piling out of the car and into the arms of our relatives, swapping hugs and laughter, comments on how much we'd changed or how little, how quickly time flies and yet how terribly long it had been since we'd seen one another. "Welcome home," Aunt Maisie used to say, and it was always the last thing I remembered hearing.

But tonight we will sneak in alone, hoping the dogs won't bark and my cousins will all be asleep. I tell Dallas to pull over at the be-ginning of the driveway, that we will walk the half mile to the cabin.

"Come on, let me drive you to the door."

"Do you want us to get caught?" I ask.

"What are you going to say, that you walked from the bus sta-tion?"

"We'll tell them we got a cab," Jess says. "They do have cabs around here, right?"

"Yeah, we'll say we took a cab."

"But wouldn't a cab drop you off at the door?" Dallas asks.

"This thing doesn't look like a cab, Dallas, even in Minnesota." I get out of the car and pull my seat forward to let Jess out from the back.

"Damn, those things are tall," she says, looking up at the oak trees. "And here I thought our great-grandmother was old."

Dallas gets out of the car but leaves the engine running. "You guys take care of yourselves, okay? Don't take any more rides from strange men."

"Thanks a lot," I say, "for everything."

"I'm just glad I could help."

"Hey, can I bum another cigarette off you?" Jess asks him. "Who knows when I'll get back into town, you know?"

Dallas reaches into the car. "Here, take the pack." He tosses it to her.

"You have no idea how much you're saving me right now." Jess takes one out and holds it between her lips, patting her pockets for a light. Dallas reaches into his front pocket and takes out a lighter. He hands it to her.

"Keep it, I need to quit anyway."

"Thanks." Jess lights her cigarette and starts walking down the driveway.

Dallas searches his pockets. "I feel like I should give you something, too."

"No, don't worry about it." I start backing away. "The ride was enough."

"Here, take my sweatshirt." He leans into the car and grabs it off the seat. "It's cold out and you're not even wearing real shoes."

"It's a five-minute walk, I'll be fine."

"No, I insist." Dallas wraps his sweatshirt around me, the cotton soft and smelling like it was just washed.

"Thanks," I say, "but you could have just given me your phone number." I can't believe that just came out of my mouth.

"I wish I had one to give you. I'm kind of between places. . . ." He starts to stutter. "How about if you give me yours. I promise I'll hang up if your parents answer."

I smile and shake my head. "We don't have one either. We're just here in the summers and my parents thought it wasn't worth it. Plus they always said it's more relaxing, never waiting for the phone to ring."

"I understand, kind of like going back in time."

I nod, wanting time to stop. "Well, what are you doing tomorrow, for the Fourth? Our neighbors have a big pig roast every year. You're welcome to stop by."

"My people don't really celebrate that holiday, if you know what I mean. . . ."

"Right, sorry."

He starts laughing. "No, I'm just kidding. I'll try to make it."

Then he grabs the zippered edges of his sweatshirt and pulls me into a hug. It's over before I can register the feeling of being in his arms.

"You're a sweet kid, Nellie, don't let that change." He leans in and gives me a quick kiss on the cheek. His lips are surprisingly warm. I can still feel them as he gets back into his car and drives away.

It takes me no time to catch up with Jess, her lit cigarette a miniature flashlight in her outstretched hand. She walks slowly, hesitates after each step like a cat walking across a comforter, as if she's afraid the road will give out under her weight. We pass under the shadow of a cottonwood tree and I wonder if there's anyplace on earth that's darker than this road. Around the bend lies Aunt Maisie's simple orange house, sitting quietly in an open field like a forgotten pumpkin. After that we'll pass the vegetable garden and the sloping fields of corn, the overgrown raspberry thicket, and finally the barn, with its arched doorway turned down in a frown. At the bottom of the hill we'll see Uncle Flint's house, finished with a natural wood that Grandma Floss demanded, and right next door we'll find our cabin, a small green house that blends in so well it seems to grow right out of the trees. And if you look beyond that, rippling in the distance like a bowl of liquid mercury, there waits our very own Silver Lake. I can see it all right now, even though nothing is in front of me.

Jess flicks her cigarette onto the ground, her torch extinguished.

"So this is it," she says, looking around as if she could see in the dark. "This is our inheritance."

I wonder if she knows that her father doesn't technically own any of the land. That he is the only one of the four siblings who doesn't have a house on this lake, and isn't going to leave any part of this legacy to his children.

"I can't believe we made it," I say out loud, but what I'm thinking is, I can't believe we made it together.

I look up at the trees surrounding us, their outlines so familiar against the dark sky. It still shocks me that the stars are so much brighter out in the country. The sky must be thinner here, or we are just closer to the Milky Way. I find the Big and Little Dippers with ease, and keep looking for Orion as we walk on, knowing I'll make it all the way to my front door without ever looking down, trusting that I can walk home on a path lit up only by the stars.

Part II
The Lake

———◆──✦──◆———

Geography is fate.

—Ralph Ellison

Chapter 11

I hear a woman screaming. Is it my mother? No, my mother doesn't scream. I open my eyes to a dark room. What time is it? I look at the window, notice how the sun paints a thin border of light around the shade: it's still afternoon. I glance across the room, the other bunk bed empty since my brothers claim they're too old for naps, and wonder which cousin, which aunt, has interrupted my afternoon nap?

The screen door bangs against the cabin, then someone runs through the living room, yelling my father's name. It sounds like Aunt Maisie. I sit up in bed, then climb down from the top bunk slowly, holding on to the polished wood with two small hands. My heart is beating fast. I don't want the ladder to end or my feet to ever touch the floor.

"Malcolm?" Aunt Maisie calls out again, her voice almost a whisper now. I hear the door to my father's study open, then his heavy footsteps. They stop right outside my bedroom door.

"What happened?" My father's voice is calm.

"Flint just called. Dad had another heart attack, right in the field." Aunt Maisie's voice cracks. "He's gone."

I freeze on the bottom rung of the ladder, one foot dangling in the air. There's a long silence, then a muffled thump. I imagine them hugging, Aunt Maisie collapsing in his arms.

"Where's Ginny?" my father asks.

"She took the boys agating, down by the campground, I think."

"Okay, I'll go find her."

"Do you want me to go with you?"

"No, I want to tell her. Stay here with Nellie, okay? Take her swimming when she wakes up."

"Okay, I'll wait down by the lake." Aunt Maisie clears her throat. "Should I say anything to her?"

"No, wait for Ginny and me to get back. We'll tell her together."

When I hear them walk into the living room, I sneak over to the door, trying not to make a sound. I have to stand on my toes to see through the keyhole. They're standing together near the front door, Aunt Maisie with her hand on the screen. She looks back at my father, her eyes all puffy like she was stung by a pack of wasps.

"At least he went in the field, doing something he loved," Aunt Maisie says. "That's the best way, don't you think?"

"Yes, that's what he would've wanted." My father puts his hand on her shoulder. She just turned twenty-seven, but she looks like a child.

"They didn't give him enough time, Malcolm. He wasn't even sixty, for godssake. That's not enough time." Aunt Maisie walks out, the screen door banging in her wake.

My father stands alone in the door frame. He takes off his glasses and cleans them with the bottom of his shirt. He wipes his forehead with the back of his wrist, then takes a deep breath, like he's going underwater.

My grandfather is dead.

I back away from the door, stepping on a wet bathing suit in the middle of the room. It's probably not even my own. By now my eyes are adjusted to the darkness, to the angles of a room cluttered with toys and clothing, memories packed and unpacked each year. Two sets of bunk beds line the walls, bolted together in an L shape, so my brothers and I can share the small bedroom. I don't ever want to leave the warmth of this room. I try to imagine living the rest of my life in these four walls.

My grandfather is dead.

I am five years old and I just learned how to dive. My grandfather has a dimple in his chin, and the whiskers that grow out of it scratch my fingertips like thistles. He smells like burnt leaves and peppermint candy, and he lets us eat hot dogs for breakfast. These are the things I will remember. I will forget his voice and his small teeth and the way he closes his eyes when he laughs. I will forget that his hands were always warm.

My mother will tell me that he taught me how to shuffle a deck of cards, but I won't remember on my own. My father will write poems about him, how it took him six months to shake my father's hand, but how when Marcus was born, his first grandchild, he cried in the nursery and said he looked like a warrior, but I will know him only in those lines. My brothers will tell me how he was the only one who could take me into the water before I could swim. They will show me photographs of him vacationing with us in Florida, but I will only remember running on the beach without a shirt on. I won't remember how the water seemed warmer when he swam with us. I will forget all the little things that make him my grandfather; I will even forget that he loved me.

I hear a woman laughing. Is it my mother? No, my mother doesn't laugh. I open my eyes to a dark room. What time is it? I look at the window, notice how the sun paints a bright border of light around the shade: it's morning already. I glance across the room, find Jess in the other bunk bed, still asleep. The laughter is coming from outside, from someone swimming in the lake. I slide out of my bed, careful not to wake Jess, needing to greet the cabin by myself.

There is no silence like an empty house. It's strange to be here without my family, to unpack the cabin and open it alone. I miss the sounds I never even consciously listened to: my brothers' footsteps from the attic as they made the forgotten space their own; the erratic song of my father's whistle; the quiet hum of my mother's sewing machine. Even the monotonous taps of my father's typewriter would be a welcome sound right now. It seems wrong to be here like this, as if I've broken into a stranger's house.

The living room carpet is worn and feels like fur on my bare feet, as if I'm walking on the back of a huge dog. I glance around the room, taking it all in: the wedding photograph of my grandparents next to the door; the gold clock shaped like a star, looking like it belongs at the top of a Christmas tree; the winterberry wreaths my mother made, hanging delicately between the windows; the floral-print love seat with arms that flatten out into a bed; the huge orange couch that actually holds all five of us; even the woodstove squatting unused in the corner. All exactly the same.

I walk into the kitchen, noticing all the things I didn't see last night, since we were afraid to turn on the lights. There's a vase filled with orange poppies on the kitchen table, next to a bowl of ripe peaches and a loaf of chocolate zucchini bread. Already the cabin smells like summertime. A note on the table says, *Welcome home, girls!* in Aunt Maisie's curly handwriting.

I hear the front steps creak and look up to see my cousin Derry standing on the porch with a huge smile on her face. She opens the screen door and slips quickly inside. I count to three and then her brother Tyler stumbles in. He knocks into the sewing machine, something he does almost every time he enters the cabin, even though it's always in the same, exact spot.

"Shhh." Derry elbows him. "Dad'll hear you."

"He can't hear us all the way over here." Tyler tries to stabilize the sewing machine.

"What do you mean?" Derry says. "I could spit on our front porch from here."

"Whatever, we're not going to get caught."

As they walk into the kitchen I surround them both with a bear hug. Our three-way hug is the closest they ever get to being affectionate, and the only time they touch unless they're punching each other. They're exactly a year apart (Derry six months older than me, Tyler six months younger) but have always been the same size, so we all pretty much treat them like twins.

"So how have you been, how's the lake?"

"Fine, always the same." Derry shrugs and leans back into the wall.

"I'm just glad you're here," Tyler says. "Now we know summer's really started."

"Come on, Ty, that's not true. Summer really starts in May, when your dad has you out weeding the garden."

Derry holds up her hands. "Look at my fingernails." The cuticles are raw and dirt-stained. "How can I go on a date with these hands?"

"How can you go on a date with that face?" Tyler teases her.

I pinch him on the cheek. "You know you look just like her," I say with a smile.

"Thanks a lot." He crosses his arms and pretends to be mad. "So how much is the old man paying now? Two bucks, two-fifty?"

"No, he's up to three dollars an hour now, but we still don't get paid for lunch."

"Quit complaining, Tyler, we play cards half the day."

"Well, that's true." Tyler smiles. "Gotta beat the old man somehow."

"Does he know you're over here?"

"Hell, no, we don't get any morning breaks."

"Yeah, we should sneak back soon," Derry says.

We all look up as Jess walks into the room.

"You guys remember Jess, right?"

"Not really—" Tyler stops short when Derry's elbow lands in his ribs.

"Yeah, sure we do," Derry says.

"Hi." Tyler raises his hand like he's pledging allegiance to the flag.

"You look just like the pictures," Derry offers, "same hair and everything."

"Pictures?" Jess turns around. "Who sent you pictures?"

Derry looks at me. "I don't know, they were Grandma Floss's, I think. We found them when we moved into her house."

"I bet they're from Grandpa Brant's funeral," I say.

"Oh." Jess sits down. "Whatever."

"So where's your dad?" Tyler looks into the living room. "Where's the Big Man?"

"Yeah, why did you guys get in so late?"

"Uh, that's kind of a long story." I turn away. "He's still in Iowa City."

"We took the bus up," Jess says with her head down.

"We heard your car blew up back in Ohio or something. That must have been cool." Tyler's eyes are wide. "Well, not that you lost the car, but . . ."

"Yeah, it looked just like on *Chips.*"

"We've got a picture," Jess says. "Wanna see it?"

Jess reaches for the copy of *Beloved* that I left on the kitchen table.

"You're on page one forty-nine," she says, taking out the Polaroid. She hands it to Tyler, whose face lights up as he looks at it. Derry eyes it over his shoulder.

The screen door suddenly flies open like a gust of wind has blown through the cabin. Uncle Flint enters so quickly I don't remember seeing him in the doorway. He grabs Derry by her hair and Tyler by his upper arm. The Polaroid falls onto the floor.

"Let's go, peckerwoods. You're still on the clock." He drags them out of the kitchen.

"Dad, you're pulling out my hair." Derry leans into him, grabbing her scalp.

"Let go of me." Tyler manages to pull away. "I can walk by myself, asshole."

"What'd you say?" Uncle Flint kicks him from behind with his steel-toed work boots. Tyler takes off down the stone walkway, running over the twigs and acorns in his bare feet. Uncle Flint follows him, chasing him into the fields. I stand in the doorway and watch Derry walk home alone.

"Meet Uncle Flint," I say after a long silence.

"Jesus Christ, he seems like a pain in the ass," Jess says, leaning back in her chair.

"That was nothing," I say, walking back into the kitchen. "Last summer they were over here playing cards and he kept calling for them to come home. It must've been around ten-thirty. A few minutes later he just busts right in the back door, almost pulling the screen off its hinges." I get a knife and start cutting into the bread.

"Derry and Tyler took off out this door, each one running in a different direction. Derry came around the back of the cabin as fast as she could. We didn't have any lights on, so it was pitch black back there, and she tripped over one of my mother's cast-iron flowerpots. She flew about twenty feet into the air, and landed right out there on the sidewalk." I grab a plate and serve up the bread.

"She tore a three-inch gash in her left shin, needed twenty-eight stitches. She asked me to come to the hospital with her to make sure she didn't faint when she saw the needle. Uncle Flint waited in the car while I stood next to her and watched the ER doctor sew her back together. When he asked how it happened she told him she was playing football with her brother."

"And he believed that, it being eleven o'clock at night and all?"

"He had no choice. She had no choice." I step over the Polaroid as I walk out of the room.

At times the lake water does look silver. When the sun is high at lunchtime or on a windy day when the water is so choppy it looks like knives are floating on the surface, it becomes clear why they named it Silver Lake. Of all the lakes I've ever swam in, and there must be close to three hundred in Minnesota alone, I've never seen that color in any other body of water. Grandpa Brant used to say it was all the nickels he threw in every time one of his kids pissed him off. He said if we raked the bottom of the lake we'd find a layer of coins holding down the muck.

It's not particularly hot in the morning, but everyone is swimming. Everyone who can swim. Marley and Jake, Uncle Flint's youngest kids, are playing with flippers in the shallow water. They just turned five and six, and look like miniature blond versions of

Derry and Tyler. We are supposed to be watching them, and we do glance at the beach occasionally, between dives and belly flops off the raft. Tyler swims back to the beach every once in a while and gets into splashing fights with them, not quitting until they run screaming from the water. Then, to make up for the torture, he plays with them for a few minutes, building sand castles with deep moats.

The adults have already come and gone. Uncle Flint's back in the fields, and his wife, Dawn, who went back to college last fall, is probably in her room translating a German novel. Aunt Maisie is either baking or weeding her garden, and her husband, Cal, is where you will find him any day from May through September: fishing in the middle of the lake in their run-down dory. And then there's Renny, who, rumor has it, disappeared early this morning before any of us were awake. Aunt Maisie said he's traveling alone this year because his ex-wife caught him drinking and driving with the kids in the car and won't let him take them out of the state. Jess actually seemed upset when she found out, like after all these years she didn't want to wait another month to meet them.

Like many things we have at the lake, our raft is homemade, a project Cal worked on while he was recovering from an accident that ended his carpentry career and almost ended his life. The design is simple: a ten-by-ten-foot plywood square, bolted to four tin barrels that keep it afloat. It's covered by a bright green plastic carpet, almost like Astroturf, that keeps us from skidding off, and there's an orange ladder on one side to help the little kids and older folks get on. It's close to sacrilege for a teenager to use it, since struggling like a seal to pull yourself out of the water is half the fun. I think it's supposed to hold about a dozen people, but during a family reunion we once fit twenty-eight people on top of it and even then it didn't sink—we just ran out of room. Some of the fancier homes on the lake have fancy rafts to match, with diving boards, safety rails, and canopies, but ours is simple and functional, and we like it that way.

Right now the girls have control of the raft. When my brothers are here, they usually spread out across it and take up almost the entire surface, leaving us to fight for corner seats. Now all four of us can lie out, Caitlin and Derry on one side of me, Jess on the other. Sometimes Caitlin's younger brother, Cody, tries to squirm in between us, but mostly he belly-flops off the side, trying to get us wet. Caitlin and Cody, Aunt Maisie's only kids, are both adopted, but they look so much alike you'd never know it.

"Cody, knock it off," Caitlin says, shaking off the water. "I'm freezing." Like most sixteen-year-old girls, Caitlin is in her swimsuit to get a tan, not to get wet.

"I'm trying to help." Cody bobs in the water with a huge grin. "The water's warmer than the air, you know."

"Yeah, well, they're both cold."

Cody gives in and swims to the beach, watching the younger kids build their sand castles like he's going to be judging them later. At eleven, Cody's caught in the unfortunate position of being too young to hang out with the teenagers and too old to get thrown in with the little kids. Most of the time he fluctuates between the two groups, linking us together in games whenever he can. You could hand that kid a can of beans and a shovel and he'd come up with a game to play.

Caitlin sits up and squeezes more lemon juice into her light brown hair. It squeaks loudly as she pulls it through the ends.

"Why not just bleach your hair like a normal person?" Derry asks.

" 'Cause then it'll look fake. The lemon juice streaks it blonde in a natural way, just like Jess's."

"I don't use lemon juice," Jess says with her hand over her eyes, blocking out the sun.

"What do you do?"

"Nothing."

"Nothing?"

"Well, I wash it, of course, but that's pretty much it. Sometimes I use conditioner."

"Well, aren't you lucky." Caitlin tosses the used lemon into the middle of the raft. It lands next to our pile of supplies: sunblock, tanning oil, shaving cream, razors; all that's needed for a long day at the beach.

"I guess you get your color from your dad then." Derry looks at Jess.

"What, he's a blond?" Jess asks. It's like she's talking about someone she's never met. I guess that's kind of true.

"He was as a kid," Derry says. "Both him and my dad were."

"Well, my mama's got blond hair. I think I get it from her."

"Speaking of natural blondes . . ." Caitlin motions toward the middle of the lake. "Look who's coming to visit."

We all lift our heads to see a light blue speedboat heading straight toward us. A cute blond in red trunks waves from behind the steering wheel.

"Visit? He better be coming over to give us a ride," Derry says, waving.

"Who's that?" Jess asks.

"Luke Jasperson, he lives on the other side of the lake. His family is the one having the pig roast this afternoon."

"His dad and my dad are best friends," Caitlin says. "They used to work together before my dad's accident."

"And they used to double-date back in high school." Derry looks at me. "Didn't they take Aunt Maisie and Aunt Ginny to their senior prom?"

"I don't know, ask my mother." I'm lying, of course. There's a picture of the four of them all dressed up and standing in front of Grandpa Brant's Buick before the dance. It's still hanging above the piano at Aunt Maisie's house.

"Damn, so you're almost related," Jess says to me.

"Not quite."

"Good afternoon, ladies. Happy Fourth of July." Luke cuts the engine and lets the boat coast toward the raft. A smile breaks across his face. "Nellie, you're back."

When his boat is close to the raft he drops anchor. Then he climbs onto the bow and does a back dive into the water.

"Show-off," Caitlin says as he surfaces.

"Don't act so jealous, Cate, I'm willing to teach you. But you would have to get your hair wet." He pulls himself onto the raft.

"Very funny," Caitlin says, lying back down.

Luke shakes the water from his hair like a dog. When he runs his fingers through it, it falls perfectly into place as if he were using a fine-toothed comb. He has the kind of hair that women spend hours in a salon trying to mimic.

"Something's different," he says, staring intensely at me. I smile, waiting for him to guess. "You grew out your hair," he finally says.

"Good guess."

"I like it. It makes you look older."

I tuck a loose curl behind my ear. "Thanks."

"So, when did you get in?" he asks, sitting next to me.

"Last night." I sit up to give him more room. "This is our cousin Jess, by the way, Renny's daughter."

"Just when I think I've met them all, another one pops up." When he leans over to shake Jess's hand he drips water on me. It's surprisingly warm. "So where are you from?" he asks her.

"Virginia."

"Wow, you Christiansens are all over the map. Not only does every one of my relatives live in Minnesota, they all live right here in Redwood County."

"Well, we have to spread out, otherwise there would be too much beauty in one place," Caitlin says. "We wouldn't want everyone else to feel inadequate."

"You're so thoughtful, Cate."

"I try."

Luke taps me lightly with his big toe. "Did you guys bring her out?" He squints in the sunlight, his pale blue eyes losing against the sun's bright rays.

"Yeah, my dad and I picked her up a few days ago." I look at Jess, who's lying back down with her eyes closed. "Damn, doesn't it seem like weeks?"

"Years," Jess says without moving.

Luke leans back onto the raft, resting his elbows on the worn carpet. He looks a lot older this year, and seems more comfortable in his body. I can't believe he is the same boy who used to take forty-five minutes to get into the water and then swim with inner tubes tied to his skinny arms. Just like one of my cousins, he's grown up right in front of me.

"What's wrong?" He catches me staring at him.

"You look taller," I say quickly.

"Finally someone notices." He stands up straight like a little boy. "I grew almost three inches this year. But I'm still one of the shortest guys in my class."

"That's because these Minnesota country boys are giants."

"And what, you like those delicate East Coast city boys?" He smiles at me.

"Please, I tower over those shrimps."

"I don't know, Nellie, you don't seem that tall anymore." Luke puts his hand out. "Come on, stand up." He pulls me up and we stand back to back.

"Well?"

"Luke's taller," Derry says. "Maybe two inches."

"Yes!" Luke puts both hands in the air.

"Well, it's about time," Caitlin says. "You are seventeen, after all."

"Not till September," I say, sitting back down. I always remember birthdays.

"Whatever, he's older than the rest of us."

"Not that much." Luke scans the beach. "So where's the rest of your family?"

Out of the corner of my eye, I see Caitlin kick Luke in the ankle and shake her head. He looks confused as he tries to keep his balance.

"My dad's still in Iowa, he'll get in later tonight." I look out at the calm water. "My mom and my brothers are staying out east this summer. My parents just separated."

"Oh." Luke looks embarrassed. "Sorry."

Caitlin looks at her watch. "Don't you have some work to do? You are throwing the biggest pig roast of the summer in less than an hour."

"You know my mom, she won't let us touch anything but the pig. I just came over here to see if anyone wanted a ride over in the boat."

Derry stands up suddenly. "I thought you'd never ask."

"Wait, we've still got some time. Who wants to play Shark?"

"I do," Tyler yells from the beach.

"Me, too." Cody starts swimming toward the middle of the lake.

"Not It," Derry says, diving off the raft.

"Last one in is the Shark."

We all dive off the raft in different directions. When I look back from the beach Jess is sitting on the raft by herself.

"What the hell is 'Shark'?" she asks.

"It's like Tag but in the water. You're the Shark, so you try to tag us."

"You can go anywhere in the lake but land is out of bounds."

She points at Luke. "So if he swims all the way home I have to go after him?"

We all nod from the water.

"Hell, no," she says, crossing her arms.

"What, are you chicken?" A voice from the shore makes us all turn our heads. Renny is leaning against the swing set with a beer in one hand and a doughnut in the other. He's wearing jeans and boots but has taken off his shirt, which hangs from his back pocket like a tail.

"I don't see you in the water." Jess stares at him from the raft.

"I've got to digest first." He walks slowly toward the beach. "You don't want me to drown, do you?" He laughs a little too loud; Jess doesn't say anything.

"Hey, Nellie, where's your old man?" Renny looks over at me.

"He's still in Iowa City. He should be back late tonight."

"Tell him I'm looking for him, okay?" He takes a sip of his beer. "We've got a lot to talk about."

This is not a message I want to deliver, since Renny has never been one of my father's favorites. Even when they were both teachers they didn't seem to have a lot in common, and once he got fired the gap between them widened so much that it's hard to believe they were ever in the same place. And no matter how many books Uncle Flint reads, he's always going to be too provincial for my father's tastes. They are from different worlds, and knowing each other for more than twenty years doesn't seem to have bridged that divide. I used to think it was about race or geography or profession, but I actually think it's much simpler than that: they are different types of men. I've never spent any real time with Renny, but I have with Uncle Flint, and there's something I like about him. He's interesting to talk to, even though he has a crazy temper and seems a little off, like a really old person or someone from another country.

"Anyone seen that crazy brother of mine?"

"What time is it?" Tyler asks him.

Renny looks at his watch. "Eleven-fifteen." He wears it on a two-inch leather band that snaps onto his wrist like a cuff.

"He'll be back by eleven-thirty. You know he never misses his soaps."

"I'll never understand how he watches that goddamn shit box so much. You kids should really talk to him."

"Too late," Derry says, smiling. "He's already got us addicted."

"We're going to watch the wedding," Marley says, jumping up and down. "Roman and Marlena are getting married."

"Oh, Christ." Renny shakes his head.

"What's the big deal?" Jess calls out from the raft. "It's all made-up stories."

He glances at her sideways. "Do you watch that shit, too?"

"Sure," Jess says, "I like all that fake family stuff. It's really inspiring."

Renny lifts his beer in the air. "To the future." He finishes it in one gulp. "It's yours to destroy." Then he walks away from the beach with the empty bottle dangling from his pinkie finger.

Luke swims over to me. "I can't believe Renny's her father," he whispers.

"You'd never guess, huh?"

"Well, he wasn't exactly warm."

"They've only met a few times. He and her mom split up right after she was born."

"Yeah, but that's his daughter."

"Maybe he doesn't see it that way."

Jess dives into the water and swims to the beach in one breath. She gets out and walks to the cabin without stopping to grab her towel.

"Okay, I'll be the Shark," Luke says, lunging at me.

I swim away backward, holding my right arm out of the water so he doesn't tear off the bandage, and force him to follow me into the lily pads. Even with one arm I am a good enough swimmer to evade him all day, but I can't help but wonder what his touch would feel like underwater. I think of Dallas's strong hands, imagine them to feel as soft as the lily pads against my thighs. I kick away from Luke until he finally gives up, going after an easier target.

Chapter 12

When I think of my mother and Palmer Jasperson they are always touching. Maybe that's the mark of first love, the need to hold on to someone and lose yourself in his form. In the few photographs I've seen they are always in the same position: Palmer standing behind her, his chin resting on her shoulder while his arms encircle her waist. His hands are clasped below her belly in a loose knot as if he were a sweater she carried in case it got cold; her hands are at her sides. He is smiling, looking straight at the camera, while her eyes are slightly off-center, as if something behind the photographer had caught her eye at the last second.

I imagine them holding hands in his truck, Palmer shifting with his left hand so they wouldn't have to let go as he changed gears. I know that my mother wore his letterman's jacket, she's wearing it in almost every photograph taken during her senior year. She even has it on in some of her college pictures, with my father standing right next to her, his elbow touching the worn leather sleeve. I'm sure it was only a jacket by then, a piece of comfortable clothing that she grabbed without hesitation, but I look at it now as a sign: she couldn't or wouldn't give up the past.

My parents never touched during my childhood. I never thought of it as strange because nobody's parents touched each other, at least not in front of us. But separately they were both affectionate people. Maybe I just don't remember, or it was all done behind closed doors. Still, I wish there were some photographs of them intertwined, leaning against each other like they wanted to become part of the same space, or even just holding hands. Instead, they were holding on to us.

I do remember them dancing, though. My father is surprisingly graceful for a large man, and he would hold my mother softly, spinning her around like a silk ribbon he was afraid to wrinkle. She always looked so young in his arms, her eyes closed as he spun her around, a slight laugh escaping her lips as she surrendered to gravity, trusting his arms and the open space they had created. Other couples would stare at them, trying to copy or find flaws in their step, but there was no discernible pattern. Their dance, like their relationship, fell outside the lines of a traditional routine, and that originality was what made it beautiful. Like a jazz musician riffing through a solo, they had to believe in the improvisation.

The heat from the open fire is almost too much to take. Occasionally a breeze comes off the lake, cooling my damp backside, but nothing can temper the flames that heat my face and chest. The front half of my swimsuit is already dry, but droplets of water still race down the backs of my thighs, collecting in a puddle at my feet.

I stare at the tall flames, watching them tickle the pig as it circles on the spit. Palmer buys one every year and roasts it all day over the open flames. When it's done, the skin on the outside is crispy, but the meat is tender underneath and can be pulled off in long, juicy strips. The pig has been dead for hours, but the eyes are still open; it's watching me watch it cook. I could look away or turn around to dry my backside, but I won't. Uncle Flint always says never turn your back on an animal, dead or alive.

Caitlin and Derry, disgusted by my enthusiasm for the stuck pig, huddle around a bowl of potato chips at a safe distance.

"That is so gross," Caitlin says with a scowl. She was already thinking of becoming a vegetarian, and I bet that this meal alone will put her over the edge.

"Why do they have to keep the head on?" Derry asks. "That makes it so much more . . . personal."

"Come on, girls, eating meat is supposed to be personal." Palmer walks up to us, waving a long metal fork. "Hunting, fishing, anything where you're taking life from one animal in order to sustain another is pretty damn personal. And there's nothing wrong with that. Hell, your uncle Cal and I used to name every buck we shot, till he got so damn good we had a whole barnful and couldn't remember who was who. That's what makes us different from other carnivores; we can appreciate that they're giving us their lives."

"They're not exactly giving their lives," Caitlin says. "You're taking them with a shot right between the eyes."

"Cal, help me out, your daughter's trying to start something," he calls over to Cal, who's sitting on a deck chair in the shade.

"Shit, I quit trying to fight that mouth when she was in diapers. Give up now." Cal gets up slowly and stumbles over to the picnic table. He holds on to a keg of beer to steady himself. I can't tell if he's drunk already or just stiff from sitting in a deck chair all day. Palmer looks over at me with his eyebrows raised.

"How about you, Nellie?" It always sounds weird when he says my name, like it's a nickname that only he uses. Like he named me.

"Sorry, I'm not a big hunting buff."

"Well, that's because you've never been." Luke walks up to me with his arms folded across his chest. "Come out with us this fall, you'll change your mind."

"I'll be long gone by hunting season."

"How about fishing then?" Palmer says. "We're out there every morning by sunrise."

"You've got to be kidding," Caitlin says. "We're teenagers, we need our sleep."

"I remember what it was like to be a teenager. I'm betting you need to recover from the night before." Palmer laughs and takes a sip of his beer. He swishes it around in his mouth before swallowing it.

"Okay, Dad, don't you have some guests to entertain, some meat to serve, some beers to open?" Luke puts his arm around Palmer and escorts him away. He looks back at me and rolls his eyes.

Jess forgot her swimsuit and sits on the dock with her feet dangling in the water, watching the rest of our family swim. Other
guests have been in the water, some have even swum out to the raft
and done belly flops off the diving board, but nobody has lasted as
long as my relatives. Each of my cousins has been in the water
since he or she got here, only getting out to grab a quick bite of
food, or to run to the bathroom. I wonder if it's because we're
really that comfortable in the water, or just uncomfortable on land.

After lunch Luke's older brother, Troy, brings out the speedboat
for waterskiing. When it's my turn, Luke jumps off the boat and
swims over to me in the water. He helps me into the life jacket,
tightening the canvas straps like it is a parachute he's afraid I'll slip
out of. Then he readjusts the rubber boots and helps me slide my
feet inside, asking if it's too tight or too loose, if I'm comfortable,
and if I have enough room to move. He swims out to get the rope
and fixes the wooden handle so I can place my hands next to each
other. I float there in ready position, the top two feet of my skies
peeking out of the water perfectly parallel, my fists turning white as
I hold on to the handle with all of my strength. Troy revs up the engine and raises his hand into the air to signal that the boat's all set.

"You ready?" Luke asks.

I've been waterskiing since I was a little kid, but I still get but-
terflies every time I do it. I try to calm myself, running through the
movements in my head. Finally, I nod.

"Keep your feet together and just pull yourself up, okay?" Luke
is treading water beside me, his hands holding the rope between
my legs. He lifts his arm out of the water, motioning to Troy. I
watch the boat as it drives away, straightening out the slack in the
rope, but a few seconds pass before I feel it pulling me. It's slow at
first, like a towline just dragging me along, but soon it's going
faster, pulling me through the choppy water in a forward squat.

"Pull up, Nellie," I hear Luke say as I lift myself out of the water,
feeling the power of the boat and the power in my own arms. Water
runs down my body as I stand up; I feel almost weightless, skim-

ming along the surface of the water like a skipped rock. I think I
hear them cheering for me on the beach, but soon I hear nothing
but the sound of the whirling motor.

I ski back and forth behind the boat, crossing my own waves as I
lean back to get the full sensation of each bump. This is the part that's
similar to downhill skiing, the rippled water as stiff as a snowbank, and
I bounce off the waves like they're moguls. After a loop around the
long lake we finally head back to the beach. I see Luke's head bobbing
in the water way out beyond their dock. He waves, but I don't dare let
go of the handle to wave back. Troy swings into the shore and then
cuts sharply out, hoping to throw me close to the beach but not into
the lily pads. I wait until the last minute to let go, flying across the
water with my hands out in front of me. This is the magical moment,
when I'm moving without the help of the engine, when I can walk on
water. I spray two perfect fans of water on either side of my body, a
flanking fit for a queen. For some reason I stay above the surface for a
long time, skiing past their raft and into the neighbor's beach. Finally,
I feel myself slow down as I begin to sink into the water. My skis pop
off behind me as I fall into the waves, surrendering to the lake.

When I come up from underwater Luke is swimming straight
at me, a huge smile on his face. "That was beautiful," he says. "You
really nailed the landing."

"Isn't that what they say in gymnastics?"

"I don't watch gymnastics," he says, tucking the skis under his
arms as if they were flotation devices. "Can't you just take a compliment for once?"

"Sorry." I lean back in my life jacket, trying to catch my breath.

Troy brings the boat back around, killing the engine about
twenty yards from us. "Who's next?" he calls to Luke.

"Me," Luke yells back. "I'm starting on one ski so pull out fast."

"I hope my brother doesn't get killed trying to impress you,"
Troy says to me, turning the boat around.

"I've done this a thousand times with the ski team," Luke as-
sures me, slipping into the ski. Then he gives Troy the ready signal.

"Good luck," I call out as Troy slams on the gas and pulls Luke out of the water. He gets up without a problem and is soon holding on with only one hand. I watch the speedboat disappear from my view, my body still rocking in the waves it left behind.

And then I see Dallas. He shows up in a birch-bark canoe, paddling out of the speedboat's wake and right toward me. He looks like his ancestors must have looked two hundred years ago, his long brown arms effortlessly pulling the oars through the water. I am falling in love with history.

As he gets closer, he takes the paddle out of the water and lays it across his lap, gliding toward me. He starts clapping and says, "Bravo, bravo," but it sounds more like "Hello, hello." I drop my face into the water and smile. The taste of cold fish and pennies floods my mouth, but I don't care.

"You never told me you could walk on water," he calls out.

I grab the side of the canoe, slowing him down. "Where'd you come from?"

"I followed you from the outlet. It was hard to keep up, though, you're pretty fast on skis."

"The boat does most of the work."

"I think I spotted your cabin on the other side, the one with the tree house, right?"

"How'd you know?" I swim backward, pulling the canoe closer to the beach.

"You look like the type of girl who'd hang out in trees."

I shrug. "It's got a great view."

"It looks sturdy," he says. "You must be some kind of carpenter."

I reach the dock and tie his canoe to one of the stakes. "Not really. My uncle helped a lot. He worked construction before he got injured." I climb onto the dock and take off my life jacket. "He broke his neck diving off this dock a few years ago. The water's really shallow this side of the lake."

"Wow, and he's not paralyzed?"

"He's got a limp and his hands shake sometimes like he's got

Parkinson's. The doctors say he was lucky, though. They don't know why he can even walk."

Dallas steps onto the dock. "If that ever happened to me I think I'd drink myself to death."

I glance at Cal, who's napping under a tree, empty beer cans littered around his chair. "I think that's pretty much his plan, too."

"You think I could talk to him, just to find out who he used to work for? I'm pretty good with my hands and . . ." He nods toward the canoe. "I made that by myself."

"See that guy?" I point to Palmer, who's cutting pieces of meat off the pig. "That's Palmer Jasperson, he's the one throwing this party. His company does most of the new building around here."

"Jasperson Construction, right? When I was asking about work in St. Croix, that name kept popping up. I heard he even lived on this lake."

Suddenly, I'm suspicious. "So is that why you came by, to meet Palmer Jasperson?"

"Is that what you think?" He follows me down the dock. "Come on, Nellie, I'm not here to see him. It's just funny that he's your neighbor, and that the party's here, since I was already coming to see you."

He looks so sweet and honest, but I know better than to trust what people say. I want to believe him, but I don't quite let myself.

"Whatever." I jump off the dock, landing in the wet sand. "Just forget about it."

"Nellie, wait." He follows me onto the beach, oblivious to the fact that his boots are getting wet. "I don't want to forget about it."

"You're standing in the lake," I say, motioning to his feet.

"So?"

"So, you look ridiculous."

"I look ridiculous? *I* look ridiculous?" He leans over and picks up a handful of sand. He throws it at me, hitting me in the stomach. "Now *you* look ridiculous."

I immediately start splashing him, first using my hands and

then my feet. His clothes are quickly soaked, but instead of running away, he runs right at me. He tackles me into the water and we both go under. I'm laughing so hard that I swallow some water as I go down. I come up coughing, the lake water burning my throat like chlorine, but I'm still laughing. Dallas comes up laughing, too, his wet hair a slick black mask covering the top half of his face. His arms are still wrapped around me. I hope someone, somewhere, is capturing this on film.

Dallas skips the water-volleyball game, complaining of a sore wrist. I'm pretending to play, but really I'm watching him dry off in front of the fire. My heart sinks into my stomach as I watch Luke's cousin Melanie walk up to him with a plate of food. She's from the Cities and has to be at least twenty-five. Staring at them makes me miss a ball right in front of me.

"Wake up, Nellie, the game's over here." Luke splashes me from behind.

"Sorry." I turn back to the game in time to see Derry slam the ball over the net. While my team celebrates winning the serve I sneak another look. They've moved away from the fire and when I find them again they are talking with Palmer and Uncle Flint by the dessert table. Dallas puts the corncob in his mouth so they can shake hands; it makes Palmer laugh and he pats him on the shoulder with his other hand. Dallas nods and smiles while he listens to Palmer; he runs his fingers through his hair only once.

"Are you all right?" Luke swims over to me.

"Yeah, what do you mean?"

"You seem distracted. Usually you're more into the game than anyone."

"I'm fine." I clap my hands together and raise my voice. "Come on, let's win this one."

When Luke swims away I watch Palmer hand Dallas a business card, which he slips into his shirt pocket. They shake hands again and Dallas appears to be thanking him. When Palmer walks away

Dallas turns to Melanie and smiles at her, holding her arm when he should be holding mine.

When the game ends, I swim out to the raft instead of getting dessert with everyone else. Luke follows me out there, swimming with two slices of watermelon held above his head. He hands me the melon before pulling himself onto the raft. We sit next to each other with our feet dangling in the water.

"So what's the deal with the Indian guy?" Luke says, trying to sound nonchalant.

I shrug. "He's just a friend. What's the deal with your cousin Melanie?"

"Don't ask me, I'm not her bodyguard." He spits the seeds into the water between his feet.

"Can't she find men her own age?"

He shrugs. "She likes anything that's new, anyone different that'll piss off my Uncle Rich."

The raft's carpet is rough against the backs of my legs and I imagine the imprint it will leave, like sitting naked in the grass. "Isn't that what they say about you?"

"What do you mean?" He looks over at me.

"Well, look at us. All these cute little blonde girls and you're out here talking to me."

"First of all, you're not new, I've known you my whole life. And second of all, you don't piss off my parents. They think you're the smartest one out of all the Christiansen grandkids. Hell, your dad's all famous and our parents go all the way back to high school." He gestures with the watermelon rind. "Come on, Nellie, they love you."

"And what about the other part, me being different from everyone else?" I toss my rind into the lily pads, where it floats like a lost buoy.

"That's what makes you better than everyone around here. You've been places and seen things these girls can't even imagine." He sits up straight. "Whenever we study other places in school, states all around the country, I think to myself, Wow, Nellie's been there, she's met those people, she's had her picture taken in front of those buildings. That's so amazing, that you have all those experiences floating around in your head all the time, and yet you still come back here, you still hang around and talk to me." He looks back at the party, at the swarm of people on his lawn. "There must be a hundred people here," he says, "but the only one I want to talk to is you."

I look into the water, feeling guilty that the person I want to talk to most at this party isn't Luke.

"You need a ride to the fireworks tonight?"

"No, Caitlin's driving us." I scan the yard, looking for Dallas. When I find him he's bringing Melanie a piece of cake. Maybe Luke would be a better choice.

"We'll be at the tracks around eight. You can meet us there if you want."

"Okay," he says, smiling. "I'll be there."

"Race you back to the beach," I say suddenly, slipping off the edge of the raft. I don't hear his response, if there is one, or the sound of him jumping into the water behind me. I swim freestyle at first, but when I feel the water swirling around my feet as he gains on me, I switch to the butterfly, a stroke that I know he can't beat. I pull my body through the water as fast as I can, kicking with both feet together, and leave him behind.

When I get to the beach I notice that Jess is still sitting on the dock. I bet she's only left it to sneak into the woods to smoke. She calls out to me as I swim by.

"So when did your man show up?"

"My man?" I try to look innocent. "What man?"

"I only see one man over there, if you take out the old ones and the ones we're related to." I know she's staring at Dallas but I refuse to look. "You'd better get to work if you don't want that blonde going home with him."

"What am I supposed to do? Elbow her out of the way?"

"That's what I'd do."

I turn around to see Dallas putting suntan lotion on Melanie's back. I let out a loud groan. "Give me a break. I can't compete with that."

"How will you know if you don't try?" she asks. "That could've been you."

I shake my head. "That'll never be me."

Eventually he catches me staring at them. "Hey, Nellie," Dallas calls to me. "Where'd you disappear to?" He waddles over to the dock, standing above me.

"Still haven't dried?" I look up at him.

"Not quite," he says, wringing out some water from the cuff of his jeans. "Here, let me help you up." I take his hand and he pulls me onto the dock. He's standing in his socks, which have left a trail of wet footprints behind him.

"So I finally met Palmer. He told me to come by on Monday and he'll see what he can do for me. Melanie introduced us, but I told him I knew you. I hope that's okay."

"Sure, whatever."

He leans forward like he's going to tell me a secret.

"So, are you going into town later, to see the fireworks?"

"Yeah, of course."

"Well, good, maybe I'll see you there."

"You're going?"

"Melanie found out I don't drink so she asked me to be the designated driver." He shrugs. "I don't mind. I figured I couldn't say no since she just helped me out with her uncle."

I nod, knowing I'm out of my league. I can't even vote, let alone walk into a bar.

"Well, have fun."

"Yeah, you, too." Dallas starts backing away. "I'll keep an eye out for you."

"There are thousands of people there. You won't be able to find me."

Dallas smiles at me. "I found you last time, didn't I?" And then he gets into his canoe and paddles away.

The disappointment is still sinking in as Marley and Jake come running down the dock, their small feet slapping the wooden planks with each step.

"Nellie, Nellie, watch me!" Marley shouts and jumps off the dock with her eyes closed. She lands in water that's only six inches deep, but reacts to the splash as if it were up to her chest.

"Wow, very impressive," I say, clapping with enthusiasm.

"My turn, my turn," Jake yells, jumping off after her.

"Damn, those kids have a lot of energy," Jess says, watching them. "I don't think I was ever like that."

"Come on, even when you were little?"

"Nope, I've never liked to run around and jump off things. I've always been perfectly happy to just sit back and watch."

She surveys the scene, her gaze barely stopping on anything long enough to focus. But when she sees Renny, sitting on the ground with an arm around his dog, her eyes lock on him and she doesn't turn away.

"You talk to him yet?"

"Nope."

"Why not?"

"Why do I have to do all the work? I came halfway across the country, the least he could do is walk across the grass." She keeps staring right at him, hard, like she's trying to make him disappear. Eventually she gives up and looks away.

Later, while she's digging in the cooler for a soda, I see Renny notice her. He doesn't move, but something about his body changes when he sees her. He doesn't say anything, but he watches her carefully, like how you'd watch a bird that lands surprisingly close to you. How your body freezes when you first see it, how you hesitate, not wanting to scare it off with any sudden movement or sound, not wanting it to feel the weight of your gaze or even something as delicate as your breath. How you wait with dread for the moment it recognizes you and flies away.

Chapter 13

We line the train tracks the way the second string of a football team lines the bench. At first the steel is cold through my jeans, almost like sitting on ice, but soon it feels no different than the rest of me, and I wonder if I'm warming it up or if it's cooling me down. When the tracks start to rumble I feel the vibrations in my legs first, then they travel up through my rib cage and into my teeth. I imagine this is what an earthquake feels like. Everyone hops up quickly, scrambling away from the track like it's suddenly on fire, but I know that the train is still a minute away. I am always the last one to stand up, those final seconds when I feel the most alive. The power of the engine rumbles through my chest and my heart beats as fast as if I were running alongside the train. I hold my breath until the train passes, then take in large mouthfuls of the windswept air, thankful to be fifteen and to be alive.

We stand together on the pebbled slope, waiting for the wind to die down and the stillness to return. Caitlin touches the tracks with her bare foot, checking for heat, before she and Derry sit back down. Jess searches the ground for a penny she left on the track.

"You shouldn't do that, you know," Caitlin says. "It could make the train derail."

"Whatever, I've done it hundreds of times in Virginia and they've never had a problem."

"And if they crashed and a whole bunch of people died, you wouldn't feel bad?"

"Come on, these aren't passenger trains, they're full of grains and shit." Jess picks up the penny and admires its flat shape. "Look how thin it is, like a guitar pick or something." She hands it to me.

"Do you play the guitar?" Derry asks.

"No," Jess says, "but now I could."

I rub the penny between my fingers, surprised by how smooth it is. Lincoln's face is stretched out wide and I can no longer make out the date. I hand it back to Jess and she tucks it into her pack of cigarettes. I wouldn't be surprised if she kept all her valuables in that tiny cardboard box.

Luke shows up at sunset with a picnic basket full of leftovers from the barbecue. His friends Johnny Stark and P. J. Lipperson are with him, and they're carrying a large cooler between them. They pull out two six-packs of Grain Belt and offer us each a beer. Everyone takes one except Derry, who hasn't had a drink since our camping trip last summer when she drank a four-pack of Bartles & Jaymes and puked for two days straight. I don't even like beer so I sip mine slowly, like it's hot tea. Luke looks skeptical but he takes a drink.

"God, Johnny, what is this stuff?" Luke spits it out on the track.

"It's two ninety-nine for a twelver, quit complaining."

"Are you sure it's not skunked?"

"Come on, it's not that bad."

"It'll do the job," Caitlin says, closing her eyes as she drinks from the gold can. She must smell her childhood in that can, recognizing her father in the smell of warm beer the way some kids recognize cologne or a leather coat.

"You gotta love this town," P.J. says, sitting down next to Derry. "Where else can you get a beer for a quarter?"

"There's a place near my house where you can get a six-pack for ninety-nine cents." Jess opens her beer with a loud crack and gulps it down like juice. "And it tastes a lot better than this stuff."

"No way, where the hell do you live?" P.J. sits up.

"Roanoke, Virginia."

"Oh," he says, sitting back. "Well, aren't you lucky."

"You sure are a long way from home," Johnny says.

"Yep." Jess takes another sip from her beer. "I sure am."

We stop talking when the fireworks start, silenced by their beauty, like when you walk into an art museum. The fireworks are brilliant against the black night sky, each one flying higher and exploding brighter than the previous one. When the colors fade there are still trails of smoke in the air, lingering like the exhaust trail of an airplane. Some of the sparks hit the trees in front of us, and they fall through the branches like October leaves falling to the ground.

I sneak a glance at Luke's illuminated face, his eyes wide and his expression a mixture of surprise and wonder. He takes in a small breath as the fireworks explode like thunder, as if he has to brace himself for the beauty that is about to unfold. He squeezes my knee without looking at me and leaves his hand there, his fingers drawing a sketch onto the fabric. I look to see if my cousins are watching, but they're not paying any attention. Caitlin and Derry are lost in their own worlds, paired off with Johnny and P.J. as if we had played spin the bottle. Jess is lying back on the tracks, a pile of empty beer cans around her feet. She is whistling softly, a tune that I've heard before but can't quite place. Is it a song that my father played for us in the car, one that he whistled when he didn't want to speak?

"What's that song?" I ask her.

"Ask your daddy, he's the one always singing it."

"It's jazz, you don't sing it."

"I don't know, the way he whistles . . . it kinda sounds like he's singing. I mean, doesn't it sound like I'm singing?"

Luke leans into me. "She's wasted," he whispers.

"What'd you say?" Jess sits up quickly. "Wooohh, that wasn't a good idea." She lies back down, quiet for a few seconds. Then she speaks with the enthusiasm of a child.

"These fireworks are awesome."

"Jess, the fireworks ended about five minutes ago."

"Yeah, I know. I'm just replaying them in my mind. The colors are, like, burned into my eyeballs and whenever I shut them they just explode again. I wish you could see it."

"Come on, let's go swimming." Caitlin stands up and pulls Johnny after her. Derry and P.J. get up, too, still wrapped together in a blanket.

"Don't you think it's cold?" Derry asks.

"I'll keep you warm," P.J. says, wrapping both arms around her.

"But we're not even near the beach," Luke says.

"Who cares about the beach, we'll swim out to the Tower." Johnny finishes his beer. "Come on, Jasperson, I want to see if your diving has gotten any better since last season."

"I'm always going to be better than you, Stark."

"We'll see about that," Johnny says over his shoulder as he and Caitlin disappear down the slope. Derry and P.J. collect the empty beer cans before following them down to the lake.

"Come on, Jess, we're going," I say, slapping her knee.

"Why? Are we out of beer?"

"You've had enough beer."

"But I'm just starting to feel good." She sits up slowly. "I'm just starting to forget who I am."

Luke pulls her up and we walk down the hill together, Jess stumbling like a sleepy child between us. When we get to the edge of the lake we find nothing but the cooler and a pile of clothes. Jess searches the cooler for an unopened beer, tossing the empty cans onto the grass. She finally finds one, and sits down on the cooler to drink it.

When I first look out at the lake I can't see any movement, but after a few seconds I see four heads bobbing in the water as they make their way out to the two-story raft we call the Tower. The waves surrounding them look silvery white and I glance up to find the moon half full, floating behind a patch of gray clouds.

"It'll be full next weekend," Luke says. "Sunday, I think. We should go out on the boat."

"Sure," I say, unzipping my sweatshirt. I hesitate, but then offer it to Jess. "Here, you look cold." She drapes it over her legs like a blanket. I wonder if she realizes that it's the one from Dallas.

I look at Luke. "So, are we really going to do this?"

"Why not? It'll be fun."

"You guys are fucking crazy." Jess takes a sip of her beer. "This is a huge lake, I bet the water's not even warm in the middle of the day."

"Come on, it can't be that cold if those four wimps are out there."

"Good point," I say, taking off my pants. When I'm standing in nothing but my underwear and the tank top I'm wearing instead of a bra I turn to Jess. "You'll be here when we get back?"

"Sure, unless I decide to walk home."

I stare at her, trying to give her a look my father would give me.

"Calm down, Mom, I'm not going to leave the shore."

Luke strips down to his boxer shorts, which are aquamarine with big pink flowers on them. He looks down at them, suddenly self-conscious.

"My mother," he says with a shrug.

"Yeah." I pull at my tank top, sprinkled with roses and a satin bow. "My mother."

Since there is no beach we have to step into the muck at the edge of the water. The first few seconds are the worst, the cold water like a pair of pliers squeezing my entire body. There's an old dory tied to a wooden post farther down the shore. I almost mention it to Luke but decide not to show any weakness. When the water is up to my waist I dive in and start swimming. I start with a quick crawl, but when I'm warmed up I change to the butterfly, showing off. Luke keeps up with me and soon we are halfway to the Tower. By now, the water feels almost warm.

The Tower looms in the distance, a giant skyscraper in the middle of the black lake. There are no lights on it, since it's illegal to use after sunset, but we know the structure well enough to climb its metal ladders and walk its uneven platforms in the complete dark. I used to be afraid to swim in the dark, even at our own lake, but now the mystery is what draws me in. I think about the turtles asleep at the bottom of the lake, or the fish swimming right below our legs, and I silently thank them for letting us trespass.

It's cold on the Tower, especially standing out on the diving board, and no one stays up there for long. The goal of all jumps is to create the most splash, preferably in the face of someone swimming below. The most popular one is the watermelon, a cannonball-style jump with one leg tucked in and the other locked at the knee and cutting straight through the water. Caitlin and Johnny are by far the best, and their final jump is a double melon, their synchronized bodies entering the lake at the same time and drowning the rest of us in a huge wave.

Luke is the first one to start diving, his jackknife so pretty it reminds me of a bird-of-paradise in full bloom. Johnny isn't content to have Luke best him, and soon they're caught in a diving competition, the four of us judging from the warmth of the water below. They are both talented, their technique flawless even on the stiff, metal platform, but Johnny is more rigid, as if he's always thinking about what to do next. Luke looks like he's not thinking at all, as if the graceful twist of a forward half-pike is pure instinct.

After Johnny concedes we all climb onto the Tower for one last jump. Derry and P.J. skip off the diving board with their arms linked but manage to land yards apart and facing in opposite directions. Caitlin does a forward somersault, entering the water feet-first with her arms spread out like a bird. Johnny goes off "convict style," headfirst with his hands held behind his back as if they were tied in handcuffs. I'm still thinking about what to do when Luke joins me on the diving board.

"Do a back dive," he says.

"Are you nuts? I won't even do one off the raft at home."

"Come on, I'll hold you." He steps toward me. "Just lean back and let gravity take over."

"I'm not really interested in breaking my neck."

"Trust me, Nellie, I won't let anything happen to you." He puts his arm around my waist and guides me to the edge of the diving board. "Now lean back into me. That's good, see, I've got you."

The moon and the cloudy sky flash before my eyes. I want to close them, to trust my instincts, but I can't; I have to be able to see where I am going. I stare at the upside-down water and watch the trees as they fall into the sky from the shore. I feel dizzy in his arms.

"I don't know about this, Luke."

"It's okay, it's much easier than it looks. I'm just going to lean you out a little, okay?" He steps forward and the board jiggles under his weight. The world is bouncing upside down.

"Oh god." I grab his shoulders.

"I've got you, Nellie. I've got you." He leans closer to me. "Are you ready?"

I try to stay perfectly still. *I can do this,* I say to myself, *I will do it. People do brave things all the time, things that frighten them, things much harder than this. I will be one of those people.* I lean back and let the world drop away.

"No, wait." The words slip out of my mouth. "I can't do it."

"Okay, okay." He pulls me back up. "You're not ready." He still has his arms around me. "I'm sorry, Nellie, I didn't mean to push." I don't want him to ever let go.

"No, it's okay, I'm all right." My heart is beating so fast he must be able to feel it. "I just need more time, some practice, maybe."

"Practice?" he says softly, his face inches from mine. "But you can't practice without doing it."

He hasn't moved, but suddenly he seems closer to me. I am afraid to move. One slight shift, either closer to him or farther away, will change things between us forever. Suddenly I find myself moving forward, pressing against his body as if the wind has blown me into him. I feel his lips on mine, warm and tasting like the lake during a rainstorm. I picture the droplets falling onto my skin and think of the first time I swam on my own, my father having tossed me off the dock and into the lily pads, reminding me not to walk on the backs of the snapping turtles but to swim, swim, swim.

I am swimming.

I hear a strange sound coming from the water. It sounds like a loon's cry or maybe geese talking to each other from across the lake. We pull apart and look toward the shore. Everything looks the same, still and dark, nothing out of place. Derry, Caitlin, Johnny, and P.J. are halfway to the beach, heading for the waterslide and oblivious to any sound but their own laughter. I hear the noise again, but this time it sounds softer and more human, like someone calling my name. I look back to the shore where we left Jess, expecting to see her standing on the cooler in some intoxicated pose, but instead she is on the water, standing in the dory I myself had thought of borrowing. She calls my name again, her arms waving hello with one of the paddles. Then she holds it above her head like a warrior. The dory rocks back and forth a few times and then it tips, the water rushing in as it flips over, sending Jess sideways into the lake.

I dive in without hesitation and swim toward her as fast as I can. When I get there she's floating next to the canoe, still holding on to the paddle. I pull her head out of the water. Her eyes are closed and she doesn't answer when I call her name. A cut from her scalp begins to bleed down her forehead. I grab her rag-doll body around the chest and swim her to shore. Her hair is wet, and it tickles my neck under the water like seaweed. They say that this part of the hair is dead, the part we brush and braid and pull back into ponytails, but how can anything so soft be dead?

I keep saying her name, telling her that everything is going to be okay, but I am really talking to myself. Luke is swimming next to us, silent except for the sound of his breathing. He helps me pull her out of the water and up to the grass, where we lay her out on the pile of clothes. I prop her head up on somebody's jeans and find a weak pulse in her neck. She is alive, and finally knowing that makes my eyes well up with tears. Luke starts CPR, his hands locked together and pressing into her chest in timed intervals. He tells me to hold her nose and breathe into her mouth on every third compression. After four rounds of this she finally starts coughing. We roll her onto her side and she continues to cough, eventually vomiting up lake water and pints of cheap beer.

When she's done she sits up and wipes her mouth on the bottom of her shirt. I hand her a sock, which she uses to wipe up the blood on her forehead. She could probably use a few stitches. Luke is beside her, still on his knees, and his hands are crossed on his lap as if he's doing some sort of meditation. I realize that I'm sitting on a bed of hydrangeas, aware of my body for the first time in what seems like hours. I pick one of the huge, white flowers, as bright and round as a snowball, and hold it gently in my hands. We don't speak; we don't even look each other in the eye.

When the others return we don't tell them what happened. I don't know why, we never discussed keeping it a secret, but when they show up, full of laughter and their own stories, we let them speak without interruption. We act like we have been doing nothing but waiting for them to return.

"So you finally puked?" Caitlin motions toward the pool of vomit beside the cooler. Jess nods. She is wearing my sweatshirt now, the hood covering her damp hair and the swollen cut. She looks at me, but after a few seconds I look away. We both know we will never talk about this night again.

When we get back to the cabin the Chevette is sitting in the driveway. My father is home. It looks out of place under the crab apple tree, still stuffed with all of our fire-tinged possessions. I'm sure that he's waiting for me to unpack it, hoping I can make sense of all that remains. It's well past midnight and on any other night he would be long asleep, but I know that he's waiting up for me, expecting a full report. Still, Jess and I sneak in quietly and head straight for our room. I hear his footsteps slowly approaching the door.

"Nellie," he says. Then he knocks twice, softly.

I go to the door and open it just a crack, as if I don't know who's on the other side. As soon as I see him I realize how much I've missed him. It's been less than two days but it feels like months. It feels like years since I've seen my mother.

"Hi." I fall into his arms like a child.

He leans down and kisses my forehead. "You're cold."

"The windows were down in the car."

"Where's Jess?"

I open the door wider, letting him look in. Jess waves from the bottom bunk, where she's under the covers fully clothed.

"It's pretty late, huh?" He tries to make it sound like an observation, not an accusation.

"Yeah, well, the fireworks and everything . . ."

He squeezes my chin between his thumb and index finger, something he's been doing since I was a child. "I know. We'll talk in the morning then." He looks me up and down, as if to make sure I'm still whole. His eyes stop on the bandage on my arm.

"What happened here?"

"Oh, it's nothing. I got burned trying to make an omelet this morning."

"Here, let me see." He tries to peek under it without taking it off. "It looks bad, Nellie."

"It barely hurts anymore. I've been putting aloe on the blister."

"I've always hated that damned electric stove. I tried to tell your mother."

"I'm fine, Dad."

He reluctantly drops my arm. "Maybe I should make the eggs from now on." He tries to smile, but has a guilty look on his face, as if he's blaming himself for my injury. Now I'm certain I did the right thing by lying to him.

"So was it worth it?" He leans against the door.

"What?" I'm playing it cool.

"Coming up here on the bus, going to the pig roast and the fireworks. Was it what you wanted?"

"I don't know . . . some of it, I guess." I am thinking of Dallas and Luke and the fireworks exploding over Blackfoot Lake.

"Well, sometimes that's all you can hope for."

He walks into his bedroom and closes the door. For the first time I think about how strange it must be for him to be in this cabin without her, and to sleep in their bed alone. If I was younger I could go in there and ask to sleep with him, for his sake and for my own. I could admit that I wanted to be surrounded by something familiar, like the smell of his hair oil or the sound of his snoring. Instead, I lie in the top bunk of my own bed, feeling completely alone. My family is scattered across the country like a photograph torn into five pieces and thrown into the wind, never to exist in the same way again.

But I am not alone. Jess is here, tossing and turning below me as she fights sleep and her own dreams. She still coughs occasionally, the air escaping her mouth in a soft whimper. She may try, but her body will not let her forget.

Chapter 14

Every picture I drew in the fifth grade was of a tree house. Pencil sketches, Magic Marker drawings, watercolor paintings—regardless of the medium, I would use the same image, replicate the same dream. I was obsessed with the idea of blending the inside and outside worlds, hoping to find nature and civilization in the same wooden box perched in the wide-open arms of a maple tree.

Our final project in art class that year was to paint a picture on a three-by-three-foot piece of glass, creating the scene on one side in order to view it from the other. I divided the pane of glass into three horizontal sections: the sky, the horizon, and the grass. The only thing connecting them was a huge brown Y, a child's simplified version of a leafless tree. I remember layering the coats so thick that my teacher was afraid I was trying to build a three-dimensional model out of water-soluble paint. I told her I was trying to re-create the texture of bark and the exact shade of the sky seconds after the sun has fallen. She didn't ask any more questions after that.

I took twice as long as my classmates, even working during recess, but when I finished I thought it was a representation as perfect as a photograph. I hung it up on my bedroom wall and pretended I was staring out the window at a real scene, a world I had created in my own mind and built with my own hands. It was my first exercise in the architecture of desire.

When he wakes in the morning, the first thing my father does is go for a swim. He walks to the end of the dock and dips his big toe into the water, drawing it back quickly from the cold. He drops his towel and leaves his sandals near the edge, neatly lined up next to each other. Then he takes off his glasses and lays them on top of his sandals. He dives in and swims half the length of the outlet before coming up for a breath. There is hardly a splash from his dive, the water looking no more disturbed than if a shoe had fallen off the dock, and I wonder how such a large man can make almost no ripples. He has perfected the art of fitting in, of blending into any situation without losing himself, something I am still trying to master.

But in this moment I do blend, my perch in the tree house a perfect hiding place. It's a refuge that has served me well, ever since I nailed in the first board last summer, going from paper to bark as I transferred my childhood sketches onto the outstretched arms of the tallest oak tree in our front yard. The main structure is a single-story box, suspended on long two-by-fours with a small window that opens onto the lake. The roof is made from sheets of tin I found in the county dump and paid my cousins to drag all the way home. I thought that by making it waterproof the tree house would become a perfect fort during a rainstorm. Unfortunately, the sound of raindrops hitting the tin roof is so maddening that we don't last very long, and have spent most rainy days inside the cabin. The lookout tower, a wooden platform above the main room that's partially covered by a low-hanging branch and has a 360-degree view, is my favorite part of the tree house. It's perfect for sunbathing, and for spying on swimmers and fishing boats, since it's mostly hidden from the lakeside. This is where I'm standing as I watch my father take his annual "first swim."

I search the metal lockbox for the binoculars, a gift from Noah after he gave up bird-watching for music videos. They are just as I left them, the cracked leather strap wrapped around the rusted center joint. I clean the scratched lenses on my shirt and bring them to my eyes, surprised by how clear the image is, and how close.

I watch him cross the outlet in a matter of minutes, his freestyle as perfect as it must have been during his years as a lifeguard. He comes back with a breaststroke, his arms extending in front of him as if he is trying to touch the beach with each stroke. When he gets closer I can see his whole body underwater, the snap of his kick so strong it looks like he could break someone's neck between his legs. Even in the water, and from a hundred yards away, he looks like a powerful man. No wonder everyone is afraid of him: his students, the other faculty, the man at the athletic center who dared to ask him for an ID; everyone is intimidated. But he's not a scary man, not a mean one—he is simply an honest one. He is who he is at every moment, to every person he meets, regardless of his title or position. And that's what makes people uncomfortable. I think most people in his life walk the line between fear and love, holding on to both feelings at the same time, never quite certain which one will lead, never certain which one they're feeling at any given moment. I've decided that I feel them both at all times, twisted together so tight that I can't imagine one of them existing without the other. At this point, I wouldn't even want them to.

When he reaches the beach he doesn't stand up. Instead, he floats on his back with his eyes closed against the morning sun, the soft current moving him slowly along the shore.

"Hey there," Renny calls out as he steps onto the dock and walks out to greet my father. "I hear you had a tough time getting up here." Renny tucks his hands under his armpits, looking lost without a beer to hold.

"Not the easiest drive I've ever had. We handled it, though, the girls and I."

Their voices float along the water and I can hear every word perfectly.

"When Maisie first told me, I thought for sure Jess had something to do with it, maybe dropping a lit cigarette or something."

"It was mechanical. There's no one to blame."

I scan between their faces like a surveillance camera. When I focus in on my father he is shooting water through the gap in his teeth just like Jess. I wonder if Renny notices and if he recognizes it as something that his daughter does.

"So how is she? How does she seem to you?" Renny lights a cigarette, carefully blowing the smoke away from my father's face.

"She seems like a normal teenager going through a rebellious phase."

"No, I meant Shelley. How's she doing down there?"

My father skims his hands over the top of the water. "She's fine. She looks the same as always, maybe a little tougher."

"Is her hair still long? I always liked her hair best when it was long, the way it used to flip up at the ends and bounce when she walked. God, I loved that bounce."

"She had it back, in a ponytail," my father says slowly. He starts speaking slowly when he's angry.

"Oh, too bad."

My father climbs the ladder onto the dock. Now he is almost a foot taller than my uncle. Renny takes a few steps back.

"So how are things with Jess?" my father asks.

Renny shrugs. "You know how kids are, most of the time you can't tell what the hell they're thinking and if you can, you end up wishing you couldn't."

"Have you sat down alone with her?"

"Not yet. I'm thinking I'll take her out to Regal some night. I don't know what to think; she gets defensive when I give her attention and gets resentful if I don't. Plus she acts like she's embarrassed by me." He shakes his head. "Don't tell me I have this to look forward to with the other two."

"Every kid's different. You just have to take it one day at a time, it'll all work out." My father dries himself with a towel.

"And what if she doesn't forgive me?"

"Give her time to get to know you, to trust you."

"I don't know if I've got that kind of time."

My father looks worried. "What does that mean?"

"I've got a chance to make some real money and put some aside for my kids—"

"When you say 'real' do you mean 'honest'?"

"Money is money, Malcolm, I can't afford to be picky." He looks across the lake, staring at the forest on the other side.

"Don't tell me you're working with Flint now? Jesus Christ, Renny, you used to be a teacher. Why'd you even bother going to college?"

"I went to college to get away from the old man."

My father looks toward Uncle Flint's house, shaking his head. "He's putting the whole family at risk, and for what? Just so he doesn't have to get a job like the rest of us."

"He's trying to give us a future. Farming's not enough anymore, it was barely enough for my folks. We need something to fall back on."

"You're shaming your parents' name. You know that, don't you?"

"They're gone, Malcolm. It doesn't matter anymore."

"Your kids aren't gone." My father gestures toward the swing set. "And what about Flint's kids, they have to grow up here. All our kids are growing up here."

Renny lowers his voice. "All I want is for them to have something when I'm gone. I want them to be able to say that I gave them something."

"And it doesn't matter what that thing is? What it takes to get it?"

"I've got a plan, Malcolm; for the first time, maybe, I've got a solid plan. But it's not going to work if I've got a kid hanging around giving me attitude all the time."

"I didn't know you had a choice."

"Well, I don't, really. Shelley's obviously had it, she as much as told me that on the phone. I know it's my turn, I know I can't put this on anyone else, but what good am I going to do my kid if I can't even do for myself?"

They are both quiet for a few seconds, my father keeping his eyes on the dock as he slips into his sandals. Renny looks out to the water.

"I don't know, I guess it'll be okay." He spits into the water. "Pretty soon she'll be eighteen and then she can do whatever she wants, right?"

"She's sixteen, Renny. That's two years from now."

"Yeah, I know. But that's not so bad, right? Two years, that'll fly by." Renny looks at my father for approval. My father puts his glasses back on, like a colonel putting on his hat.

"You're talking about life, Renny. It shouldn't just fly by," he says, dropping his towel onto the dock. "How many years do you think you're going to get?" He walks off the dock without looking back.

Renny stands there motionless for what feels like several minutes. Then he picks up the discarded towel and lays it out on the dock to dry.

My father goes to town every day to do three things: buy the newspaper, mail letters, and prove to the locals that black people exist outside of the ghetto and movie screens. When he goes to the grocery store each week he always pays with a hundred-dollar bill and smiles at the cashiers when they examine it. He knows they blush because they've never held one before, and have never seen a man with such beautiful skin and without hair on his knuckles. The bag boys fight over who gets to carry his crate of peaches to the car, knowing that the tip is always a bill, not the nickels and dimes the old ladies search for in the bottom of their purses. Then, when he drives away with the windows down and the radio up, saxophone screaming in a language they don't understand, they compare notes.

He's from the Cities, right? Or was it New York?

I don't know, somewhere they drive Volvos.

He used to play baseball, right? Or was it football?

He had a good arm, and, boy, could he hit.

Isn't he the one who marched with Martin Luther King, the one who preaches and writes books?

Yeah, he went to jail, right?

He took a bullet, right?
He was a soldier, right?
He was a hero, right?
He was a teacher, right?
He married a white girl, right?
He is a Negro, right?

For the rest of the week we eat mostly out of the freezer, defrosting dinners that Aunt Maisie cooked for us. When the freezer is empty, my father makes broccoli and baked chicken for dinner—the only meal he can cook by himself. But one night I smell something else in the oven, something sweet like apple pie or banana bread. I open the oven door to find my mother's cast-iron pan full of corn bread, the yellow batter already turning a crispy golden brown. When the heat feels like it's burning my face, I close the oven door.

"Wow, Dad, you went all out."

"Don't give me all the credit. Jess made the corn bread."

"She did?" I look at Jess, who's already sitting at the table.

She shrugs. "I found the cornmeal in the cupboard and just borrowed the other stuff from Dawn. I hope it's all right, I didn't really use a recipe."

"None of the real cooks do," my father says, putting his hand on her shoulder. She flinches, then tries to smile.

"I did most of the cooking at home," she says. "Shell didn't really have the patience."

"Feel free to keep that up here," my father says, dishing up the food. "Nellie doesn't really like to cook."

"I can cook. Mom didn't like to share the kitchen."

My father cuts into his overcooked chicken and chews with the thoroughness of a man with false teeth. "We'll all be sharing the kitchen this summer," he finally says, with a tone that ends the conversation.

Halfway through the meal Uncle Flint shows up at the front door. He drops a bucket full of vegetables on the porch and talks through the screen door as if he were the mailman. He will do this all summer long, bringing us the best picks from his garden.

"These red potatoes are pretty nice, just dug them up today. And there's a cantaloupe at the bottom, real sweet already, but I'd eat it tonight before it turns. I'll just leave them here for you."

"Thanks, Flint," my father says.

Uncle Flint nods and shuffles his boots on the porch.

"Do you want to come in?" my father asks.

"No, I wouldn't want to interrupt."

"Come on, at least bring the food inside before the dogs get it."

"Okay, sure." Uncle Flint walks in slowly. He digs out the melon and holds it up. "See, it's kind of soft already, you should really eat it tonight. Here, let me cut it up for you." He finds a knife in the sink and slices the melon into long strips, which he lays out on the cutting board. "There, that'll be good." He steps back from the table, his hands tucked into his back pockets. He always seems nervous around my father, like a kid afraid of being yelled at. It's like watching Derry or Tyler standing next to him.

"Have some." My father motions to the fruit. He's always polite, but I know he doesn't really like Uncle Flint. And even though I'm not sure what he and Renny were talking about on the dock, I now know that there's a reason why.

"Oh, no, I brought that one for you. I have more than a dozen at the house."

"Come on, we can't eat a whole melon in one night."

"You sure?"

"Go ahead." My father points at the melon with his knife.

Uncle Flint grabs a long piece, sucking it up like it's the first fruit of the season. It's strange to see a grown man so excited about food, like he still can't believe that seeds turn into edible flesh and that he has the right to eat it.

I'm startled by a knock at the door, a sound we don't hear too often, but then I relax when I see Aunt Maisie let herself in. She is wearing an apron over a pale green dress, and both the apron and her hands are stained with cocoa powder. She tries to smile, but her face is drawn in, and suddenly my stomach sinks.

"Mr. Pearson called, they found Hettie passed out in the back-yard, laying next to the pump. He took her to the county hospital."

"What happened?" My father tries to sound calm.

"They don't know. They think this is it, though. She's barely holding on."

Jess mouths, "Who's Hettie?" but I don't answer.

"Come on, they've been saying that since Dad was alive," Uncle Flint says. "Grandma has the heart of an ox, it was probably just the heat and her trying to do too much. She'll be fine."

Aunt Maisie looks at my father. "They're thinking it was a stroke this time, but they won't be sure till they do the tests. Apparently she can't feel her left side. The first thing she said when she woke up was that she couldn't feel her wedding ring." Aunt Maisie tries to smile, fingering her own ring.

"What do you think, should we drive down in the morning?"

"Maybe I should go tonight, just in case. I don't want her to be alone, to see the doctors and nurses and Mr. Pearson, and none of her own family."

My father pushes himself away from the table. "I can be ready in ten minutes."

"No." Uncle Flint puts his hand on my father's chair. "I'll take her. I should be there." He tugs on Aunt Maisie's apron strings as he passes her and leaves without saying good-bye. "I'll pick you up in fifteen minutes," he yells from outside. Aunt Maisie places her hand on my father's shoulder.

"He's not ready for this," she says. "He's not ready to be the oldest, to be the head of the family. It's all coming too fast."

"No one's ever ready," my father says, covering her small hand with his own. When Aunt Frances dies he will become the patri-arch in our family, a role he was born for but will probably never be comfortable with.

"She's had a long run," Aunt Maisie says, "outlived her husband

and all her kids. So I guess we can't complain, can we? Not like with Mom and Dad." She picks a hair from my father's shirt and lets it drop to the floor. "And this time we even get to say good-bye." She leans down and kisses my father on the cheek, then comes around the table to give Jess and me each a kiss on the tops of our heads. Jess touches her hair to make sure the cut on her head is still covered, her fall into Blackfoot Lake a secret she has managed to keep all week. Aunt Maisie lingers behind me, combing my hair with her fingertips and rubbing the smells of her kitchen into my scalp.

"Your mom was her favorite. She spent a whole summer with Hettie after high school, helping her fix up the farm after Grandpa died. She even helped her paint the house. She always said that was her favorite summer, eating ice cream cones for breakfast and going to matinee movies, playing gin rummy late into the night." Aunt Maisie tucks a strand of loose hair behind my ears. "Did you know that?"

I shake my head. She walks toward the door.

"We should call her, Malcolm," she says, "she needs to hear it from one of us."

"I know. I'll call her tonight."

When Aunt Maisie leaves we finish our meal in silence. I've lost my appetite but I still pick at the food on my plate, needing to do something with my hands. The chicken is dry in my mouth and I wash it down with small sips of milk, the sound of my swallow almost deafening. I take a bite of cold broccoli; it crunches loud in my head like wood splitting under the weight of an ax.

These are the sounds of my great-grandmother dying.

Chapter 15

When my grandparents bought this property in the early 1960s, most of the lake was still uninhabited. You could walk for miles around the perimeter and not run into any homes. Now most of the lake-front lots have been split up and sold for ten times what my parents paid, but across the lake from us there is still a large chunk that remains untouched. My grandparents bought it right before Grandpa Brant died, hoping to cut it into enough lots for each one of the grandchildren to have an inheritance. Instead, our parents inherited it, and Uncle Flint ended up buying everyone else's share so he could have a nice plot of farmland close to home. Unfortunately the land was too wet for most crops, so it just sat there, the pine trees growing taller and thicker each year, until it ultimately became a forest and the perfect hiding place.

Sometimes we would pitch tents and camp out for the night, pretending to be lost in the woods somewhere in Canada, but mostly this spot has been reserved for quiet walks on those afternoons when you don't want to run into anyone, even yourself.

Today, when I have walked so long that I am no longer certain which side of the lake I'm on, I stop under a pine tree to eat a late lunch. The needles that have collected at the base of the tree, rust-colored in a quiet death, make a perfect bed, and I lie back and look up at the treetops, catching a few slices of blue sky through the intertwined branches. The sound of a twig snapping startles me and I sit up quickly, scanning the area for other signs of life. Nothing is moving; even the treetops are still. I hear the howl of a dog in the distance, then silence. I lay my head back down and close my eyes. A cool breeze covers me, making me wish I'd brought a blanket. That's something my mother would have thought of: a blanket and a bottle of water. She remembers the details, those little things no one else would think of.

My mother is coming. Tomorrow she will be at Hettie's funeral.

The snapping starts again, repeated in the rhythm of footsteps. This time when I lift my head I see a bright red shirt in the distance, seeming to float through the woods. I try to make out the rest of the body, but everything is a blur behind the trees and bushes. The red shirt stops suddenly and looks around. It's dark in the woods and I know he can't see me, but I still don't move. He turns around and stands still with his back to me. I hear a strange sound, like he's pouring out a soda, then I realize he's peeing against the tree. When he finishes, he walks back in the direction he came from. I decide to follow him, staying a good distance back and ducking behind trees when necessary. After a while, he leads me to an open field that I've never seen before, and for a second I wonder if he cleared and planted it himself. There is a tent set up in the field next to the remains of a bonfire. He's obviously been here awhile.

A truck drives through the clearing, coming up from the woods, and I soon recognize it as Uncle Flint's truck. Looking around, I see a familiar car parked on the side of a narrow dirt road, blending into the trees: Dallas's '72 Galaxy. Uncle Flint honks twice and Dallas comes out of the tent wearing that red shirt and a smile. I can't believe I didn't recognize his walk. He runs up to the truck and they talk for a few minutes, then Uncle Flint drives away, disappearing back into the woods. I step out into the field and stand there with my hands on my hips. I'm not really angry but I want him to think I am. He doesn't even flinch when he sees me, as if he knew I was there the entire time.

He saunters over to me chewing on a long piece of grass. I hate how he loves to draw attention to his mouth.

"I was wondering how long it'd take you to find me."

"You could have helped me out by telling me you were staying here."

"I was going to, but your uncle told me to stay quiet about it. I guess he didn't want any extra attention."

"And that's what I am?"

"Just look around, Nellie, this place is hidden for a reason."

I nod, still wondering what his point is. "So what are you doing here?"

"I'm not helping him, if that's what you think. I'm just making sure nobody trespasses. In exchange, he's letting me stay here. I'm not really working for him; my real job is with Palmer."

He sounds defensive, but more than that, a little bit scared. I walk over to the rows of thick green plants, already as tall as my waist. They are too pretty to be basil and too dark to be mint. I break off a leaf and rub it between my fingers. I smell my fingertips—a sweet, earthy smell. No way. I look down the row, see the distinctive leaves and soft buds duplicated in each plant. This row, this entire field, is filled with marijuana plants.

My uncle is a marijuana farmer. He's a criminal.

"This isn't your first time, is it?"

"What?"

"Seeing it up close, seeing the plants themselves, and not just the dried-up shit."

"No, of course not." I brush my hand across the top of the plant. "We grew up in these fields." I don't know why I'm lying to him, except that I don't like him knowing something about my family before I do.

He laughs. "That's kind of fucked up."

"We didn't know, we thought it was just tea. We thought he was a farmer."

"Shit, he is a farmer. That stuff's hard work, it needs a lot more attention than corn and potatoes."

"Yeah, but we thought he was like my grandpa, keeping the family business going." There is a disappointment in my voice that I can't hide.

"He's got a business, all right. In one year he'll make as much as your grandpa did his entire life."

"So that makes it okay?"

He shrugs. "It makes it profitable."

"So why don't you do it then? Why aren't you helping out?"

"Are you kidding me? If I got caught growing weed I'd go right back to that reform school. No, I'm too old now, I'd probably go right to jail. Serena would be dating by the time I got out."

"Then why stay here? Isn't it dangerous just being here?"

He shakes his head. "Your uncle's been here for years without any trouble. The Feds aren't looking around here, right next to lakefront summer homes. Not when they've got Indians they can bust right down the road just for smoking it."

Years. The word keeps echoing in my mind. It's been happening for years, right here, right across from our beach, right in these woods that were our wilderness, and we never knew. Well, the adults knew, but it's not surprising that they didn't tell us. We all know how well they can keep secrets. I wonder if Hettie knew, and if she died thinking that my uncle was ruining the Christiansen name. Did she look at him, fighting tears at her bedside, and feel shame—or worse, pity—wondering how this boy who ate raw corncobs on her lap had become a man, and if he could handle the responsibility she was about to leave to him? Did she gaze at his callused hands as they held her own, thick with veins and muscles from a lifetime of pulling weeds, and was she happy that she couldn't feel them?

Dallas starts to relight the bonfire. When the flames are high he hangs a kettle full of water over the fire.

"Want some tea?" he asks.

I cut my eyes at him, not appreciating the joke. "It's chamomile, I promise." He puts his hands up like I'm pointing a gun at him. "Want to see the box?"

I shake my head. "I trust you."

I warm my hands over the fire, suddenly feeling quite cool. The sun has fallen behind the trees and shade now covers the entire clearing. It feels like nighttime even though it's only four o'clock. By the time I get home it will be dinnertime and after that bedtime and then morning and time to go to the funeral. Then I'll see my mother. I hope she doesn't look like she's been crying, her nose chapped and her neck all covered with those sad red blotches. Seeing her crying always used to make me cry. But maybe this time will be different.

"You all right?" Dallas asks. "You seem heavy, as my mother likes to say."

I shrug. "My great-grandmother died yesterday."

"I'm sorry." He hands me a mug filled with tea. "Were you close?"

"Not really, we all kind of blended together in these last years and usually she thought I was my mother. But she's always been there, you know? Sitting on the porch shucking sweet corn when we came to visit. She was always waiting for visitors to come, needing any excuse to cook and play cards all night." I take a sip of my tea, the flavor surprisingly strong. "She was the oldest person in the family, outlived all her sisters, her husband, and her kids. I just can't believe she's gone."

Dallas blows into his mug, his lips puckered up like he's whistling.

"Is that what you believe," he says, "that dead people are just gone?"

"I don't know. I guess they're still here in spirit or whatever, in our memories."

"In spirit or whatever? Is that the best you can do?" He looks at me over the top of his mug.

"You know what I mean."

He finally takes a sip. "When Grace died I just couldn't believe that was it, that I'd never see her again, that Serena would never get the chance to really know her. That's when I started believing in reincarnation."

"You mean when people come back as other people?"

"People or animals or trees or whatever. Anything that lives, that has a spirit, can be reborn in another form, but the spirit stays the same. They say that the ones that keep coming back have something to learn and that's why they get another chance." He blows on his tea, looking at me. "Haven't you ever met someone who you think you know? Maybe they remind you of someone else or you just feel comfortable with them, like you've already spent some time together. It's their spirit that's familiar."

"That sounds kind of far-fetched."

"Maybe," he says. "Or maybe it hasn't happened to you yet." He smiles into his mug and I decide to let that one go. I will continue to pretend he is just a man standing next to me, and not the flames of a bonfire hot enough to brew tea or warm the air in a dark field, melt the flesh of a girl still forming.

There's not a cloud in the sky the day of the funeral. The sun is hot on my back, soaking into my shoulders, and I wish that I had thought to put on sunblock. I feel a slight sting, then a burning below my right shoulder blade. I tug on the strap of my sundress, wondering if I forgot to remove a stickpin. When I reach the spot something crunches between my fingers. I examine the dead body of a wasp and curse the fact that I had to wear a dress.

I lean over and show the bite to Derry, who searches her pocketbook until she finds some Vaseline to cover it with. The Vaseline helps a little, but the throbbing is still there, a constant ache that distracts me from the service. Maybe it's good to have an ailment during a funeral, the physical pain a nice relief from the emotional.

We're standing in a U-shaped line surrounding the plot where they will lay Hettie to rest. No, that sounds too nice: we're standing around the hole where they will bury her. The earth at the bottom is black and almost looks damp, but the soil that's been dug out, the pile of dirt and rocks behind the coffin, is a light brown powder that looks like it will blow away in the lightest wind. I wonder if it's rich enough to feed the flowers we will plant there.

Right now Hettie's casket is propped up in the middle of our family section: my great-grandfather Homer on one side with their older boys, Percy and Roy, and then my grandfather, Brant, on the other side, the baby and the first to die. Grandma Floss is on the outside, next to Grandpa Brant. They all have matching gravestones, a grayish white that looks too bright for a cemetery, but does look quite pretty from the top of the hill, perfectly aligned like white flags frozen in a photograph. Grandma Floss's gravestone is the only one with a quote, *This is not good-bye*, something she used to whisper to us at the end of each summer. It wasn't until her death that we realized she said it to everyone, the grandchildren and her own children, each time she left us. She even said it to my grandfather, right before they closed the casket and lowered him into the ground. I can hear her voice now, can feel her curly hair tickling my neck, and it makes my eyes well up. It's hard to believe that she's been gone almost five years, that I was only eleven when I stood here last, on a cold gray day in February, and placed a handful of Valentine carnations on her casket, saying good-bye to another grandparent who left without a proper farewell.

Derry has also begun to cry, and I hand her some of my tissues. I wonder who she's crying for, probably our grandparents or maybe her aunt who died from breast cancer last year. Funerals aren't just about the person who died; I use them as a chance to remember everyone who has passed away. I sometimes cry for people who aren't even dead yet, but whom I just miss, or I'll think about my parents dying and try to prepare myself for a life without them. I wonder how it's been for my aunts and uncles, who have lived much of their adult lives without parents. Is there another word, or can adults be orphans?

I look over at my uncles and aunt, the three grandchildren, standing in a line behind the coffin. They always stand in the same order, descending in age from left to right, a slight gap between Renny and Aunt Maisie where my mother should be standing. This is how they were always positioned in childhood photographs, from Sears portraits to shots in front of the Christmas tree. It's weird to think that Uncle Flint and Aunt Maisie have never stood next to each other, him being the oldest and her being the baby. I wonder if they'll always do it, subconsciously following Grandma Floss's theory of order as if she were still in the room lining them up.

A taxi pulls up about halfway through the service and my mother gets out wearing a navy blue dress and sunglasses. The wind blows her hair away from her face, making the hair look fuller than it really is. It also looks lighter. Maybe she got a perm and dyed it, trying to transform herself from the outside in. She also looks like she's lost some weight, but maybe that's just the dress, since color often seems to change the shape of something. She slips into the crowd near her brothers and sister, hugging them quickly, then moves on toward the front. She stops at the foot of the coffin, directly opposite where I'm standing. I drop my gaze so we don't make eye contact but I don't think she knows where I am.

When the minister finishes, my father goes up to the makeshift podium. He is the only man wearing a suit, a dark gray wool that must feel suffocating. He reads Robert Hayden's "The Night-Blooming Cereus" and I hold my breath through the entire poem. I watch my mother mouth the last line with him—*We spoke in whispers when we spoke at all* . . .—her head down and her eyes closed behind the sunglasses. He closes the book and begins to pick all the white roses out of the bouquet behind the coffin. Then he hands them to the immediate family members, including my mother, and one by one they place the roses on the coffin, kiss the polished wood, and whisper their final good-byes. The carnations are left for the children, and I make a wish when I drop mine, pretending that it's like flicking a penny into a water fountain. Usually I wish for good grades or a boyfriend, but today I wish for courage.

At the end of the service I walk around and read all the gravestones, try to memorize all the dates. When my mother walks up to me all I can think is that we're standing on top of my grandparents. She puts her purse down and gives me a long, hard hug, the kind you'd give your kid after he runs into the street and almost gets run over by a school bus. When she pulls away she's smiling. She runs her fingers through my hair and down my cheek.

"You look older," she says.

I pull back slightly. "It's only been a few weeks."

"I know. But that's a long time to be away from your child."
Her voice cracks a little and she clears her throat. "Your brothers
miss you. They were sorry they couldn't come; you know how
part-time jobs and summer school can be . . . unforgiving." She
drops her hand to my shoulder, touching the dress. "This is pretty,
is it new?"

I nod. "I lost most of my clothes in the fire."

"That whole thing sounds awful," she says, cleaning her sunglasses with a tissue. "I'm sorry you had to go through all that."

I shrug. "We're all right."

"How's Jess holding up?"

"She's fine." I look at her across the way; she is watching Renny
with envy as he smokes a cigarette. "Why does everyone always
want to know how she's doing?"

She looks me in the eyes. "How are you then?"

"Fine." Just saying that makes my wasp sting start to throb. I
reach back and rub it.

"What happened?" She looks at the mark. "Wow, you need
some ice on that."

"It's fine," I say, but she's already digging through her pocketbook. She hands me an unopened soda can. "Here, hold this
against it."

Within seconds it starts to feel better but I don't let her know
that. I don't even thank her. Uncle Flint walks by carrying Marley
and Jake in each arm. Jake's asleep, his long bangs matted to his
forehead with sweat.

"They're so big," my mother says. "Every year it surprises me."

"Things change, people grow up."

"They sure do," she says. "Just look at Tyler. My god, he looks
just like my father in his wedding photos." My mother leans back
against her mother's gravestone like it's an old dresser in the corner
of her bedroom. "Don't you wish we could stop time occasionally,
just freeze one moment?"

"If I did I wouldn't choose this one."

"No, I wouldn't choose this one either." She laughs. I used to love making her laugh. It felt like a huge success since it happened so rarely. "You're always so blunt, Nellie, so unequivocal. I've missed that." She puts her sunglasses back on and I'm happy that I can no longer see her eyes.

I don't tell her everything I've missed.

I'm not sure why, but I end up riding back from the funeral with Uncle Flint. Dawn took the kids in their Crown Victoria, so we're in Hettie's old car, a 1955 Plymouth with whitewall tires and the original mermaid-green paint job. The car smells like burnt caramels, as if a bowl of them were roasting under the hood.

"Are you hot? You can roll down the window if you're hot," he says, pointing to the window as if I couldn't find it on my own. Uncle Flint seems nervous behind the wheel and he drives the car like it's a dollhouse with tires.

"No, I'm fine." I don't want the wind to tangle my hair.

"These old cars don't have AC or anything." He tries to turn on the radio but nothing happens. "I guess it doesn't have a radio either. I'll be able to fix that, though; I'm sure it just needs a part or two. Older things are easier to fix than the things they're making now. Things were just simpler then."

We ride in silence for the next few minutes. I haven't ridden in a car with Uncle Flint since last summer when he drove Derry and me to the emergency room to get her shin stitched up. He had sped that night, rolling through stop signs and red lights like they were optional; today he's driving like the old lady this car belonged to, never going more than five miles over the speed limit.

"That was a nice poem your old man read. I didn't get it all, but it sounded nice the way he read it." He unbuttons his cuff and scratches at a scab on his forearm. "It must be nice to be able to say what other folks are feeling, you know? To capture all that emotion in just a few words. That's talent right there, real talent."

I nod without saying anything. I notice the stark contrast between my hand and the white leather seat it's resting on. I have never looked so dark.

"You ever try writing, just to see if you got anything from the old man?"

"Just assignments for English class. Nothing special."

"Well, maybe it hasn't come yet. Sometimes that stuff takes a while." He combs his fingers through his hair but is unable to flatten the cowlick near his forehead. "Growing up I didn't think I had a thing in common with my old man. I hated everything he ever valued and I bet he would've said the same about me. Shit, I never even liked farming: getting up before the sun, being dirty all the time, wearing work boots and wide-brimmed hats. Hell, no, I wasn't interested. But look at me now, working the fields just like him." He smiles. "Damn, he must be laughing right now. Just sitting in that grave laughing."

I can't imagine he'd laugh if he knew what Uncle Flint was farming. But maybe he wouldn't care about the law. From the stories I've heard he seems like the type of guy who didn't like rules of any kind and always wanted to be his own boss. That's probably why he stayed in farming as long as he did.

"What was he like, Grandpa Brant?"

"Well, he didn't laugh a lot, I'll tell you that much." He tugs at the knot of his tie, then straightens it. "No, I guess that's not fair. He laughed sometimes, hard and loud, but that was it—either laughing or shouting—not a step in between. There wasn't a gentle bone in his body, nothing that told him to whisper or tiptoe or touch a thing without trying to break it. Everything was booming in the old man: his voice, his footsteps, his hands. It was all loud." Uncle Flint lifts his hands from the steering wheel and examines them, the fingers stretched out like five-pointed stars.

"And Grandma Floss was okay with that? I remember her being so quiet, so soft."

"Yeah, they were different, all right. Fought a lot. But he never yelled at her, not like he did at us. And he never touched her, never even raised his finger." Uncle Flint's hands are back on the steering wheel, the knuckles turning white from the strength of his grasp.

"I guess she just tried to balance him out, tried to be everything he wasn't. And it worked, too, she made it work. I don't know, maybe they both did. Either way, I only remember her raising her voice once. In my entire life, just one time. She stood right in front of me and screamed at the top of her lungs, this loud cry that never formed into any words. It was right after I told her he died."

My grandfather's death is a story I've heard before, but never from Uncle Flint, the only one who was actually there. He looks at me and seems to read my mind. "Let me guess, you want me to tell you the story?"

I nod, trying not to seem too eager. Uncle Flint loosens his tie a little more. Then he clears his throat as if he's about to sing.

"We were in the fields, me and the old man, tying up all the bales of hay we'd cut that day. I was on foot and he was on the tractor, following behind me about fifty yards. We weren't talking because the tractor was so loud, but every once in a while he'd cut the engine and yell out to me, complain about the way I was bundling the hay or something, tell me to speed it up. It had been a while since we'd talked and then I noticed how loud it was getting, and I looked up and saw how close the tractor was, right up on me. So I yelled for him to watch out, that he was getting too close, and that's when I realized that he wasn't even on it, that it was driving itself. Well, thank god tractors don't go too fast and I could hop on and kill the engine. Then I stood up there and looked around, expecting to see him headed back to the house all pissed off or something. But there he was in the middle of the field, laying out on his stomach like a scarecrow blown over by a gust of wind. By the time I got to him he was almost gone. He was trying to talk, I guess, his lips were moving, but I couldn't make out what he was saying. I leaned over him and put my ear right up to his mouth, felt the air escape, but I still couldn't hear anything. And then his heart gave out and he just stopped trying." Uncle Flint clears his throat again.

"I just sat there for the longest time, watching the life as it left his body. I've never seen anything like that. It was so simple, so quick, not like a pheasant or a deer that tries to hang on, struggling for air and pleading with you. The old man just left. His eyes were still open and they looked real pale, like they were cut out of the ice in January, the color just frozen. And then the strangest thing happened. I looked up and there was a tear in the clouds, and a long streak of lavender sunshine broke through. I'd never seen that shade of purple in the sky before and I've never seen it again. Just on that day, in that moment, a few seconds, really, and then it was gone."

I look over at Uncle Flint, whose eyes are focused on the road. He pulls off his tie and unbuttons the top three buttons of his shirt. He looks like a boy struggling to find comfort in his Sunday best. I've seen him as a father, a husband, a brother, an uncle, but I've never thought of him as a son. Now I realize that he's never stopped thinking of himself that way; he will be their son until he dies, not until they die.

When my mother was a baby and she cried in the middle of the night, Uncle Flint would warm bottles of milk in his armpits and bring her to bed with him so my grandmother could sleep through the night. He also threw Renny off the top of the barn just to prove that people couldn't fly. But when Renny broke his arm in two places, Flint biked him to town on the front of his handlebars. This is the same man who makes my cousins cry with the steel-toed end of his dirty work boots. He also reads to them every night, the little ones falling asleep in the crook of his muscled arm. He is a farmer with illegal crops, but he also grows fresh fruits and vegetables, giving away half his yield so everyone can have a taste. I have seen him be devastatingly cruel and incredibly kind, and I struggle with which one is the truth, which one is the real Flint Christiansen. Maybe he is both things at once, and they exist simultaneously, at odds on the inside, but inside still, mixing but never blending into each other. Maybe love and hate can occupy the same space without either one disappearing, if each force is strong enough to stay.

Chapter 16

When I get back from the funeral I go for a swim alone. The water is almost too warm today, like bathwater, but it still feels nice to float around in it, to be held by something. I swim to the middle of the outlet, staring at the pine trees that line the other side of the lake, wondering what Dallas is doing. I think about stopping by but decide against walking through the woods in my bare feet wearing nothing but a swimsuit. I'm also not looking for any more surprises. I swim back to the raft and lie on the carpeted deck. The sun is softer than it was at the funeral, but I continue to tan, my shoulders going from a deep brown to almost red. Now I could really pass as Indian.

I look over at the cabin and wonder where my mother is. She could be inside reading a gardening book or at the sewing machine fixing a hem, or maybe unpacking her things in the attic, having chosen to sleep in the bed my brothers used to share instead of next to her husband. More likely she's up at Aunt Maisie's, nibbling on sweet pickles and reminiscing with her sister about their childhood. For a moment, in my isolation on the raft, I can pretend that nothing has changed, that we are all here, together, like any other summer. My father is in his study writing while my mother bonds with her sister. My brothers are out for a jog or fishing off the canoe down by Miller's Point. Maybe my grandmother is still alive, and she's standing in her kitchen making oatmeal cookies, measuring flour only with her eyes. But then I remember the funeral this morning, the real reason my mother came out to the lake. How sad that death is what has finally brought us together.

BRASS ANKLE BLUES   161

When I walk into the cabin I hear music coming from my father's study. I don't recognize the song, only the blare of a saxophone that fills the air and covers up the sadness, saying all the things we can't say to each other. I run into my mother in the living room, dusting the curtains and the framed photographs on the walls.

"How's the water?" she asks without looking at me.

"Nice. A little too warm." I dry my hair off with a towel.

"Nothing's too warm after the Atlantic." She looks up. "Maybe I'll take a dip before dinner." She picks up a group shot from the family reunion a few years back, her fingers lingering on the glass too long. I take a step to leave but she speaks again.

"I hear you're spending a lot of time with Luke Jasperson."

"So?" I wrap the towel around my waist.

"So, I think it's sweet, that's all."

"Sweet? What am I, ten?"

"No, you're fifteen and it's still sweet. If you're lucky it stays sweet until your twenties, maybe longer. After that I can't promise anything."

"What a surprise," I say under my breath.

"Why do you say that?" She puts down the picture.

"Never mind."

"No, really, I want to hear. Why is that a surprise?"

"It's not a surprise. I was being facetious."

"Oh, how clever. You're saying that I break promises, that I break vows."

"Whatever. It doesn't matter to me. I don't want your promises."

"Oh yeah, I can see how much it doesn't matter." She walks over to me, drying her hands with the dirty rag. "Well, what do you want then? My apologies? My pride? My head on a fucking plate?" Her voice cracks on the last line.

"Nothing. I don't want anything from you." I back into the wall.

She lowers her voice, trying to regain her composure. "Why do you have to be like this, Nellie? To get so angry all the time, to be so unforgiving?"

"I don't ever have to be this way." It's the truth, but I don't exactly know what I mean by it.

"Then why do it? Why hold on to all the bad things, all the hurt?"

"I don't know. You made me this way."

"No, Nellie, don't give me all that power. I only made you once. Your father and I brought you into the world, but what you've done since then, what you think, who you are—you control all that. You decide if you're going to be destroyed by something. You decide if you're going to survive."

"You're a liar, Mom. I don't believe a word you say."

"Oh, Christ, you sound just like me when I was your age. So full of conviction. So certain that my understanding of the world was right."

"I'm nothing like you."

"Fine, you're nothing like me. You're exactly like your father, your hero, and you didn't get an ounce from me." She tries to walk away but I follow her into the kitchen.

"No, I got something from you." I start counting on my fingers. "I got fear. Disappointment. Anger. And the ability to trust no one, to believe that everyone has a trick up their sleeve. You gave me a lot."

"I didn't mean to give you those things. I really didn't. And I'm sorry if it happened that way. I wish I could change that for you, for all of us."

"So that's it? That's all you're going to say?"

"What should I say? What should I do?"

I point toward the study. "Why don't you ask him that?"

"Don't you think I have? We've tried all this, Nellie. That's what the last year was about, all the counseling and the therapy sessions. We didn't just quit."

"But you're not even out here trying. You're fifteen hundred miles away packing up our house. You're moving on."

"We're only separated, not divorced."

"And that's your way of trying?"

"For now it is. We're not making any promises. I tried that before and I realized they were too hard to keep."

"Oh, so I'm supposed to feel sorry for you because you got married so young?"

"It's not an excuse. It's just an explanation."

"Well, I don't want it. I'm not the one you walked out on. I'm not the one whose heart you broke." A single tear falls from my left eye, always the weaker one.

"Oh, Nellie." She wipes the tear from my cheek. "If only that were true."

I walk out of the kitchen and into my bedroom, closing the door quietly behind me. I lean against it, waiting for my eyes to adjust to the dark room. It takes me a few seconds, and then I realize that I'm not alone. Jess is lying on her bed with a Walkman on, her hands tucked under her head as if she were sunbathing. She doesn't move, even when I whisper her name. She has the decency to pretend she's asleep.

The moon is finally full. Only now, when it's complete, do I remember how beautiful the shape is, and realize how much I miss it during the rest of the month.

"Come on, let's go out to the middle of the lake," Luke says, dragging me down the dock. "Then we can see the whole sky."

"No, this is fine. It's too cold out there."

"Here, get under." Luke unfolds a blanket and offers it to me. I sit next to him at the end of the dock. He tucks the blanket around my shoulder and drops his hand to my waist. I can feel his fingertips as if they were directly on my skin.

"You want to know a secret?" I lean into him, smiling.

He looks nervous. "Sure," he says.

"You can't tell anyone I told you."

"I won't."

I pause to increase the dramatic effect.

"I hate your beach. My entire family hates your beach." I try to hide my smile. "When we were kids we used to dread coming over here to swim. We used to pretend to be sick or say that we wanted to nap instead." I break into laughter and then cover my mouth. "I'm sorry."

Luke smiles. "That's okay, we hated it, too. It's not our fault your grandpa got the best beach on the lake."

"Yeah, but come on, this one doesn't even make sense." I nod toward the shallow water. "It reminds me of the ocean, the way it's all rocky at the shore and then smooth and shallow as you walk out, almost like a sandbar."

"I've never been to the ocean."

"Well, you're not missing much. The saltwater burns your eyes worse than chlorine. You'd like the waves, though. I bet you'd really like surfing."

"I don't know," he says. "I think I'd be scared of sharks and jellyfish or whatever."

"You? Afraid of something in the water? Come on, I thought you were Aquaman."

"Are you kidding, I used to be terrified of the water. After Cal's accident I wouldn't swim over here. I wouldn't even walk on the dock, let alone dive off. I used to imagine falling in and hitting the sand like it was concrete, breaking my neck, my legs, whatever hit first. It took me years to be able to jump off again. And I still won't dive." He holds the corner of the blanket between his thumb and index finger. He rolls it up and down as if he were rolling a cigarette, trying to make it tighter, more perfect each time. "You know my dad still blames himself. He says he should've dug out the beach and made it deeper, or had a sign up saying that it's shallow."

"It's not his fault. Cal grew up swimming over here, he should have known."

"I know, but that's just how my dad is. He takes responsibility for other people, their safety, happiness, whatever."

He kicks at the water with his feet. They look dark brown under the surface, like they belong to my body. I bring my feet next to his to compare the color. Mine aren't much darker, but there is a saturation in my pigment that he doesn't have. They seem to shine, as if my skin were made of copper or brass. As if I weren't quite human.

"I heard about your great-grandmother," Luke says softly. "I'm sorry."

"She was in her nineties. That's a long life, right?"

"Still, it's always a shock when it finally happens, when you actually have to say good-bye."

I wrap the blanket closer around me. "I didn't go to the hospital. I knew she was going to die but I still didn't go. I didn't say good-bye to any of my grandparents either."

"I think it's probably better that way. Then they keep on living in your mind and you only picture them up and walking around, smiling at you and pinching your cheeks." He reaches out as if he's going to pinch my cheek, but ends up running two fingers down the length of my face. They linger on my chin, which he tilts up toward the sky. He stares at me, not saying a word.

"What?" I don't move.

"Your lips, they're perfect," he says. "The shape and how they match the color of your skin."

"Come on, everybody's lips match their skin," I say, hoping he can't see me blush.

"Why do you think other girls wear lipstick? They're painting on the color you were born with."

"They say I have my grandmother's mouth, my father's mother."

"She must have been beautiful."

"I have a few pictures—"

Luke cuts me off with a kiss. As it gets more intense his hand drops from my face and falls into my lap. I hold it with both my hands, my fingers reading the soft skin on the inside of his wrist. I close my eyes and try to picture nothing. There is a splash in the middle of the lake as a fish jumps out of the water. I smell smoke in the distance, and imagine that it comes from a bonfire. I can't help but picture the blaze, the red glow of flames that can light up even the darkest face. Dallas.

"Luke!" someone calls out from behind us. "Luke, you out here?"

Luke pulls away from me. "Yeah?" he says to the dark.

There are footsteps on the dock and then Palmer appears behind the beam of a flashlight. "Sorry to bother you guys." He looks at Luke. "Your grandmother's on the phone. She says it's about your birthday."

"Come on, Dad, couldn't you say I was busy?"

"All she wants is to hear your voice." Palmer takes a sip from his beer.

"I just talked to her a few days ago."

"Luke, she's eighty-five, I don't think it's too much to ask—"

"Okay, okay, stop with the guilt." Luke stands up. "I'll be right back."

"Don't worry, I'll entertain Nellie." Palmer pats Luke on the back.

"That's exactly what I'm worried about," Luke says, walking into the dark.

"I promise not to tell her any of your secrets," Palmer calls over his shoulder. Then he balances the flashlight on one of the dock posts. It shines straight up into the sky, making everything look like it's covered with a light layer of fog. It even softens the brilliance of the moon. We are both silent, staring up at the sky.

"Imagine how bright it is close up," Palmer says, "you'd have to wear moon-glasses."

I smile and give into a little laugh. He looks grateful.

"I know, I know, it's an old joke."

"Really? I've never heard it before."

"Well, it must be before your time then." He leans back against the side of the speedboat, his arms crossed. The boat rocks under his weight.

"I remember those days, when I was your age and everything was before my time. Man, it used to piss me off. Now I wish there were more things like that, more things I was too young to know about."

"You wouldn't be saying that if you were my age."

"You're right. But I'm not, and that's the difference." Leaning against the boat in his jeans and baseball cap, he barely looks older than Luke. This is how he must have looked in high school when my mother fell in love with him, convinced that he was going to take her somewhere. He clears his throat like he's about to make a speech.

"Time moves so fast, Nellie, it really does. I know everyone says that; my parents used to say it to me and I never really listened, but it's true. One day you wake up and your life's half over, and you're still trying to figure out what you're going to do with it. You just can't appreciate time when you've got it, and you never really cherish anything until it's gone."

I wonder if he's just talking about life in general, his lost youth, or if he misses something specific. When I look up at him he's staring at me. No, it's more like he's staring through me. He exhales and shakes his head.

"What?" I ask him.

"Nothing, it's just—" He pauses, probably deciding if he should tell me the truth. "It's just that you look so much like your mother it almost takes my breath away. I know everybody must say that to you, but it really is true. God, when I first saw you this summer, coming out of that water just like she used to, with your hair slicked back and your cheeks a little flushed, that big smile—it was enough to make me think I was seventeen again."

"No one ever says that, no one thinks I look anything like her."

"Well, everybody's blind then. It's not just the physical things, the nose and the body type, it's the spirit. You two have the same energy, the same restlessness, it's just trapped in a different shell. She sees it, too, I can tell by the way she looks at you."

"You haven't even seen us together since last summer."

"So? This isn't some new thing I've just discovered. She's been looking at you the same way since you were born, and it's not going to stop just because you're growing up. You can't run from that type of bond."

"Great, now you sound just like my father."

"Oh yeah, well, you sound a lot like my son. He doesn't like it either, when I tell him he reminds me of myself. When I say that you and he are a lot like your mother and I were at the same age." He hesitates, as if he's picturing an actual scene from the past. "I just hope you two don't make some of the same mistakes."

"What's that supposed to mean?"

He opens his mouth but no words come out. He takes his hat off and scratches the back of his head, then puts the hat back on, pulling it down tight.

"Come on, Palmer, you can't just say something like that and walk away."

"Look, you're so young right now, you're still kids in every way that matters. Keep it that way. Just don't be in a rush to grow up, okay?"

I can't help but laugh. "Sure, leave it to a grown-up to tell the rest of us not to grow up."

"I know, I know, I sound like a hypocrite. Just trust me, okay."

I lean back on the dock. "Famous last words."

"Okay, forget about me, forget about everything I've said tonight." He crosses his arms, hugging himself. "Just trust yourself. At least then you've got no one else to blame."

"Come on, that's such a cop-out. We come into the world having to trust people. You can trust yourself all you want, but you're not the only person in the room."

"But you're the most important. I learned that lesson the hard way, listening to everyone else, following their hearts, and not my own. And I've had to live my whole life paying for that."

The air has shifted and the mood is strangely somber, as if we were suddenly talking about death.

"I'm sorry, I didn't mean to sound all sad and bitter. I'm just an old man talking about old times." He tugs on the brim of his hat. "Now I see why Luke likes spending time with you, Nellie. You have an easy way about you. I hope that rubs off on my son."

"Luke's just fine like he is. He doesn't need to change."

"Yeah, well, he's changed already. This is different for Luke, you know, he's not usually so protective of a girl. He's ready to bite my head off if I ask one question." He smiles at me. "It's okay, though, I was expecting it. It's exactly what your mother did to me, right here on the same dock, in the same lake, almost twenty-five years ago. Maybe he'll be smart enough not to let you get away."

I know he's talking about Luke and me, and he's trying to be nice, but all I can think about is him and my mother. I've never asked him anything about their relationship, but now I figure I've got nothing to lose.

"Is that what happened? You let my mother get away?"

He lets out a long breath. "Well, I didn't go anywhere, did I?" His voice is surprisingly soft. "I'm still right here, standing in the same spot." He looks down, as if checking to make sure.

"What are you saying?"

"Nothing, Nellie. I'm not saying anything." He starts to back away from me.

"And what about her? Would she say 'nothing'?"

"Ask her. Ask her why she left. Ask her if leaving really helped her get away."

He turns around and walks down the dock, his outline becoming smaller with each step, until he's completely covered in shadows.

My mother spends the next week going back and forth between the lake and Hettie's farm, filling up the rental car with each trip. Even with everyone's help, it will take weeks to pack up the entire house, to filter through Hettie's memories, trying to decide which photograph, sundress, LP, bottle of perfume, fountain pen, high-heeled shoe, pair of overalls, candlestick, lamp, frying pan, secret recipe, *Life* magazine, set of earrings, and paperback book is the most important to keep. It's hard to imagine a lifetime being tucked into the confines of a cardboard box. Today, Jess and I are helping my mother pack up the kitchen and parlor; most of the boxes are so heavy it takes two of us to carry each one to the car. I try to figure out why she wants to fill her new house with all these old things. Jess quits before the parlor is empty, sneaking behind the barn for a cigarette break, so I carry the final boxes to the car alone. They are much lighter and I imagine them to be filled with hats, the small ones with feathers that women wore in the 1920s, even though I know that Hettie was never that glamorous.

Resting beside the car, I decide to look through one of the open boxes, a large one labeled *Personal Correspondence*. It's filled with small, brown shoe boxes, each overflowing with letters. When I pull out the first bunch I recognize Grandma Floss's handwriting instantly, the penmanship perfected on a twelve-inch blackboard she held in her lap during her years in a one-room schoolhouse. The letters are tied together in bundles with a long piece of satin ribbon, emerald green and probably taken off a store-wrapped Christmas present. Hettie wasn't one to let any extravagance go to waste, even after the intended purpose had been fulfilled. They look so fragile that at first I don't want to open them, but then a postcard tucked within the group of letters catches my eye. The postcard is a black-and-white photograph of an empty beach at sunset. It says, MIAMI BEACH, in the bottom right corner, large white letters on a black wave; the postage date is March 18, 1955. It's addressed to "The Christiansen Family," but then each person is listed by name, and the list takes up the first half of the card. It reads: *Dear Flint, Renny, Ginny, Maisie, and Mom & Dad, Don't you wish you were here? Missing you all, Brant & Floss.* I guess my grandparents had gone on vacation and left the kids with Hettie and Homer. I bring the card to my nose, imagine the smell of suntan oil and coconuts. My grandmother held this card more than thirty years ago, sitting on a beach in Florida, and now I'm covering her fingerprints with my own.

I skim over the other letters in the stack, and they all appear to be from Grandma Floss. The earliest thing I find is Uncle Flint's birth announcement from the fall of 1940; the most recent, a Mother's Day card from 1979, a glossy picture of a yellow tulip on the cover. Inside Grandma Floss wrote that she thought of Hettie as her own mother. She had even signed Grandpa Brant's name, even though he had died two years earlier. Most of the letters are the same size, having come from the same box of butter-colored stationery, but one letter stands out from the rest. The envelope is slightly smaller, a pale mint green, and worn at the edges like it was carried in a pocket for weeks and read over and over again. The postage-stamp date on the envelope is July 1964, the year my mother graduated from high school and, according to Aunt Maisie, spent the summer living with Hettie. I open it slowly, careful not to tear the thin sheets of paper as I unfold them. The handwriting is different this time, not as neat and deliberate, as if it had been written quickly or under duress.

July 7, 1964

Dearest Hettie,

I want you to know that this is a difficult letter to write. The fact is, I'm not ready to write it yet, but time and nature have a way of forcing you to get ready. What began as a splendid and proud summer (shipping Flint off to basic training, Renny's graduation from the university, and Virginia's graduation from high school) has taken a turn for the worse, as I've recently learned of events that surprise and disappoint me. As a mother, I've always tried to prepare myself for these moments, knowing my children are capable of anything and everything, as all children, all people, are. But I have to admit that my guard was down, particularly concerning Virginia, who has always been so deliberate with her actions. Well, I suppose I should just cut to the bone, as Brant would say.

Virginia has gotten herself into some trouble with the Jasperson's oldest boy, Palmer. He seems the responsible type, and is willing to marry her by the end of the summer, but she promises to be long gone by then. She is certainly in some form of denial, and claims that her plans to move out to California to stay with my sister Clara and start nursing school will not be put on hold. (If only she had thought

about those plans earlier, she might not have gotten into this mess.)
Anyway, we thought some time on the farm might do her good.
Maybe she'll see that she can make a good life for herself here, and
that being a wife and mother doesn't have to mean the end of her life
(which is certainly her greatest fear). She doesn't want to hear it
from me, her own mother and the example that may frighten her the
most, but perhaps from you the words will sound different. She's
always had so much respect for you and your life on the farm, how
you made it work with even the smallest harvest, and how after
Poppa died you ran after the boys, the chickens, and the crows with
the same strong hand.

She needs you now more than ever, in the way that a girl needs a
grandmother, an older woman who is not her mother, but who loves
her in almost the same way, with the same intensity, but perhaps
without the same burden. Please think about it, and respond when
you are ready.

With love,
Floss

Now everything is clear. Clear like the ice over a pond in No-
vember or your sinuses after a long swim. Clear like a well-
rehearsed lie. My mother and Palmer had a baby. She left because
she didn't want to live the same life her mother and all the women
before her had lived. She wanted her freedom and independence,
just like now, and once again, she chose herself.

The word "confront" is so similar to "comfort." This is what runs
through my head when I go in search of my mother. I don't know
if I made it up or if it's a line I read somewhere. Could it be from
one of my father's poems? I find her in Hettie's attic, sitting on the
dirty wooden floor in between a bright red rocking horse and a
mahogany cradle. How appropriate. She notices the letter in my
hand.

"You got the mail," she says. "Who's it from?"

"I found it in one of the boxes. It's from Grandma Floss." I hand it to her.

She stands up and wipes her hands on the front of her pants, leaving a dusty smear. Then she opens the letter. She reads quickly, skimming over it the same way she reads the newspaper. From the way she bites on the corner of her bottom lip, I can tell she's never read it before.

"Well," she says, looking up, "I'm sorry I didn't tell you before. The time never seemed right."

"And it's 'right' now? Today is all of a sudden a good time?"

"None of this was deliberate, Nellie. I just ran out of time. I know that sounds silly now." She touches the cradle, which rocks slightly from the pressure.

"Silly? No, that's not the word I'm thinking of."

"Look, I was very young and scared and I did what I thought was right for me. That's it, end of story."

"End of story? What do you mean, end of story? Where's the baby?" I picture my half brother or sister, a blond, perhaps, with big green eyes like my mother's, adopted by an older couple from the Cities who had a big backyard and a teeter-totter cemented into the ground, anticipating hours of fun. Or maybe it went to a younger couple like Aunt Maisie and Cal, country people who wanted laughter and toys scattered across their open fields. Either way, I can only picture a baby, not a real person who reads novels and tells elaborate jokes, not someone with a favorite food or flower, not someone who has fallen in love. The baby couldn't be grown already, couldn't have really existed this entire time without us.

My mother leans back into the sloped ceiling, her hair blending into the fake wood paneling. She takes in a deep breath and slowly exhales through her teeth. My stomach drops in anticipation.

"There is no baby, Nellie. I had an abortion."

For some reason that never occurred to me. I can't believe that my mother would do something so violent, so deliberate, and so final. My mother today, maybe, but not back then, not the seventeen-year-old girl who had never left the state or raised her voice to her parents.

"How? Wasn't it illegal?"

"Yes. I found an underground clinic in San Francisco."

"You went all the way to California to kill your baby?" I don't mean to sound so heartless but all I can picture is this blond baby I've created, wrapped in a sheet soaked with blood, not breathing. I think of *Beloved,* picture Sethe in the shack with a knife at her baby's throat. I'm trying to remember how murder can be love.

"I'm sorry, Nellie, but I don't owe you an explanation. I don't owe anyone. It was my body." She picks up a wool blanket and begins to fold it into a small square.

"And was it your baby, yours alone?"

"That's exactly what Palmer asked me. All I can say is that it felt like it was. It felt like my decision, my responsibility, my burden."

"You sound like you're talking about a debt, not a baby."

"Well, that's how it felt to me, that's why I chose not to have it. I was seventeen, for chrissake, barely older than you; I was a child myself." She keeps folding the blanket, trying to make it smaller. "I made the right decision for me and I've never regretted it."

"Well, aren't you lucky, never having to suffer through regret."

"No, I'm not lucky. I said I never regretted it, not that I didn't suffer. I mourned that loss for years. I still do. You don't just get over losing a part of yourself like that." She picks up another blanket, this one smaller and handmade, a bunch of crocheted flowers along the border.

"Does Dad know?"

"Yes, of course he knows. He helped me pick up the pieces."

"And you two thought it was okay not to tell us, to keep this huge secret about your past—"

"It was never a secret, Nellie. It was just private."

"So what's the difference? Please clear it up for me, I don't want to get this wrong again. An abortion is private but an affair is a secret, is that right? Are those the rules?"

"We're done talking about this." She walks away from me, still folding the crocheted blanket.

"Why, because you say so? Because it makes you uncomfortable to talk about your mistakes?"

She stops at the edge of the stairs and turns to face me.

"No, because it makes me uncomfortable to see you like this. You can hate me if you want to, if you need to, but I can't stand to watch it from this close. I can't suffer like that anymore, not on purpose. There's no glory in being a martyr at my age." She walks down the stairs holding the blanket against her chest, her chin tucked into the folds as if it were a scarf and she were walking through a blizzard. The wool must be rough against her lips.

For the first time I notice how hot the attic is. I smell the dust and mothballs from two generations of stored clothing and toys and instantly I feel dirty. I wish I was back at the lake, swimming in the cool, familiar water. Sometimes it seems like the only water that will clean me, a baptism to replace the one I never got at birth.

Chapter 17

When I wake up the cabin is empty. No rental car, no parents, no Jess. A butternut squash waits on the kitchen table like a note, a present from Uncle Flint that I decide to open. I've never cooked one by myself, but I want the cabin to be warm, and filled with an earthy smell.

I take the largest knife I can find and cut the squash in half, then scrape out the seeds and pulp from the center, which is no bigger than a tangerine. The flesh that remains is a pale, faded orange, and it squeaks when I rub it, like the bathtub when it's really clean. The pulp is darker, a deeper burnt orange, and it doesn't want to wash off, even with soap. My fingers are stained a dull copper shade and smell sweet like the earth. I hold the gutted halves in both hands, admire their simple curves. The hollowed-out center is beginning to look less vulnerable, and by the time I rub the inside walls with olive oil I can barely tell that something once grew there. I no longer know that something's missing.

I wrap each piece in tinfoil and bake it at 375 degrees for over an hour. When the timer goes off I take the pieces from the oven and unwrap them slowly like a package I'm afraid to open. The heat escapes in a cloud of steam that burns the tips of my fingers. I scrape the cooked meat into a large glass mixing bowl. The flesh is creamy now, and a deeper shade of orange, vibrant like a sweet potato or maple leaves in October, the first ones to turn and cover the ground with their somber glow. It's not as stringy as spaghetti squash, but I remove a few strands of noodlelike skin. When I lay one on my tongue it reminds me of the bitter threads on an unripe banana. I add a chunk of butter, some cream, and a dash of nutmeg and mash the squash until I make ribbons in the mixture. Then I sit down with a soup spoon and eat directly from the mixing bowl.

My mother had an abortion. She ended a life in order to complete her own. What does that mean? What does it look like? I see her wearing a heavy coat, something that covers her knees, even though it was summertime. Her shoes are dark and she isn't wearing socks. Her hair was just washed. She lays on a cold, hard table with her legs in stirrups and tries to think of her favorite things, simple moments from her childhood that made her smile, like opening her Christmas stocking in front of the woodstove, or ice skating after the first freeze, her strong legs taking her as fast as a snowmobile.

She thinks of folding sun-dried towels warm from the clothesline, biting into cold watermelon, and running barefoot in tall grass. She remembers feeling free and innocent. A man she's never even looked in the eye is scraping out her uterus while she recalls how her mother always tucked the blankets in just right, her breath smelling of gingersnaps as she put them to bed with stories from Hollywood, the new Bette Davis picture she had just seen at the drive-in, describing the plot, the actors, the clothing with such accuracy that my mother felt like she'd seen it with them, standing up in the backseat of the car to peer over my grandfather's head.

When they tell her that it's over, that she can sit up now, she pictures herself doing a jackknife off the Tower at Blackfoot Lake, coming out of the water with her hair slicked back and smiling when she hears the applause from the beach, feeling powerful. She remembers when her body was strong. She asks to see it, what they took from her, but the man says it's better if she doesn't look. Still, she glances over while he washes his hands, knowing that her imagination is always worse than the truth and that she'll never forgive herself if she doesn't have the courage to say good-bye. It's not that scary after all, just a small mass of blood and tissue in a shallow tin pan, looking like anything but the beginning of life. It is so thick and dark, the blood almost purple, that she wonders for a second if they took out her liver by mistake. She looks away and feels something drop inside her, her sadness a stone thrown into the lake; it falls to the bottom and settles in the cold mud, hidden from view. She knows she will never sleep through the night again.

Then, as a woman she was never introduced to wraps a thin pink blanket around her shivering body and walks her out the back door, my mother pictures her own mother coming home from the hospital with Aunt Maisie wrapped in a blanket the same shade of pink. She remembers seeing the exhaustion behind her mother's smile, her wince barely visible as she catches one vigorous hug after another, each child more desperate to hold her than the first. Who is desperate to hold me? my mother wonders. Who am I strong enough to catch?

As she walks out of the clinic and disappears into the hills of San Francisco, she swears she can hear a loon cry in the midst of the evening traffic. She can smell the bacon frying in the cast-iron pan on her mother's electric stove.

The St. Croix library is not much more than a poorly lit storage room housed in the basement of a church. The fiction section has nothing from the last two decades, and there's not even a poetry section, but it's got air-conditioning, large reading chairs, and hardly any patrons. I bring my summer reading list, knowing they won't have any of the books I've chosen to read, just to watch the librarian get frustrated and complain about lack of funding.

At five, when the library closes, I sit on the steps outside the church and wait for Aunt Maisie to finish her grocery shopping. She shows up late, as usual, but makes up for it by buying me a Popsicle from the ice cream truck parked down by the town beach at Blackfoot Lake.

"Come on, let's walk over to the playground." She grabs my hand and pulls me through the parking lot like an excited child.

"But what about dinner? I thought Cal had to eat right at six."

"Oh, piffle." She waves me off. "I've been cooking on time our whole married life, he can stand to wait for one night." Then she nods toward the pizza parlor behind me. "I'll tell you what, why don't you just run on over there and order us a pizza. That way dinner will be ready when I walk in the door."

I order the pizza and meet her back at the playground. When I get there her sandals are off, and she's walking barefoot through the dry sand. I watch her pick up a can that someone else dropped and walk it over to the garbage. When she spots the tall metal slide she covers her mouth.

"I don't think I've been down that slide since the kids were little."

She climbs the ladder slowly, looking out at the lake, and over to the small town that surrounds it, but never down. Her skirt is long, but she bunches it up around her thighs and holds it in a big knot between her legs as she slides down, as if it were her steering wheel. She screams with delight as she gains speed and never tries to slow herself down.

Later, when we're on the teeter-totter, she confronts me about my mother.

"Your mother told me about your talk at Hettie's, what you found out. She never meant to keep it from you, Nellie. It's a hard thing to talk about."

I nod, watching the sunbathers pack up their things. "I just wish I had known before, that I didn't have to find out like that."

"Some news comes hard, no matter how you tell it." She fixes her barrette with one hand. "I thought telling my kids they were adopted was going to be easy. I thought we'd just tell them real early, when they were practically babies, so they didn't ever remember not knowing. But it was still hard to make them understand. Caitlin kept forgetting, or maybe she just wanted to hear the story again, but every few months she'd walk over to me and tap my belly and say, 'Mommy, what did it feel like when I was growing inside you?' And I had to start all over again."

"Well, whatever you did worked on me. I can't remember ever being told that they were adopted. I just feel like I've always known."

"Well, good," she says. "At least it worked for somebody. I don't know, maybe it's the brain's way of protecting you. Maybe you remember what you want to, and you forget what you have to." She slips off the bench, holding it down with her arms so I can get off without falling. I stand up slowly, getting used to carrying my own weight.

"It must have been hard for you, all those years of not getting pregnant, and to know that my mother had just—"

"No, Nellie, don't say that." She shakes her head. "Don't even think that. One thing doesn't have a lick to do with the other. Yes, I wanted babies, and I was heartbroken when I couldn't have one, but I never once thought about your mother. She didn't take that baby from me, she took it from herself, and she's the one who's had to pay for that, not me."

She steps onto the sidewalk before shaking the sand from her sandals. Then she walks down the street without waiting for me to catch up.

I'm standing outside the pizza parlor when I notice a green Ford Galaxy drive by. I watch it come to a stop in the middle of the street, then reverse slowly, coming back to me. Dallas leans over to talk to me through the passenger window.

"You hitchhiking again?"

"No, my aunt's inside."

"Have you eaten?"

"Not yet."

"Then have dinner with me." He holds up a pizza box. "I just picked mine up."

"But we're on our way home."

"To do what, eat pizza?" He opens the car door from the inside. "Come on, you'll eat with me and then I'll bring you home."

When Aunt Maisie comes out I tell her to go ahead without me, that I'll get a ride home with Dallas. She looks suspicious until I tell her that he works for Palmer. Then she smiles and says, "You kids have fun." When she drives away I can see her looking in the rearview mirror.

We park by the water and sit on the hood of the car to eat. Dallas tells me that he likes the job with Palmer, that he likes work so exhausting he can fall right to sleep at night.

"I can't complain, it's good money. And it's keeping me busy, which is nice since I don't really know anyone around here."

"You know me."

"You know what I mean. I don't have anybody to go out with. Anybody my own age." Dallas eats two slices at a time, folded together like two hands praying. "How's it been for you, now that your mother's here?"

"It's the same; it's always the same with her." I bite into my slice slowly, making sure I don't get burned. "She's one of those people who asks a lot of questions but doesn't stick around to listen to the answers."

"Most people are like that."

"But she's my mother. She shouldn't be like most people." I throw my crust onto the ground and watch two birds fight over it. "She's just selfish, that's all. She says she's doing things for me, but they always end up helping her more. She lies, she keeps secrets, and then she pretends she did it for me."

He eats the ice from his soda. "Sometimes parents have to keep secrets to protect their children."

"Protect them from what? Finding out their mother's a liar?" I can't cover the anger in my voice.

He puts down the cup. "I'm lying to Serena. When she asks me where her mommy is, I tell her she's sleeping in a big cloud up in the sky, and when she asks why, I say because God needed more angels to watch over her."

"But that's different, that's because she's too young to understand death."

"Right, but when she's older, and she asks how she died, I'm still going to lie. I'm going to tell her it was cancer or an accident, that she got hit by a truck crossing the street, anything but the truth, anything but the fact that she walked into the woods in the middle of the day and hung herself from the tallest tree."

He picks the slices of pepperoni off the pizza still in the box, but doesn't eat them. Instead, he stacks them on top of one another like poker chips.

"I don't know, maybe I'm wrong. Maybe I should tell her the truth someday. I just don't want it to change how she feels about her." He closes the pizza box. "I don't want her to think that her mother was this crazy, depressed person that didn't love her enough to stick around. I don't want that one thing she did, the last thing, to somehow add up to be more important than all the other things, all the good things, so that in the end Serena won't have any other images of her. She will only be able to picture her hanging from that tree." He looks away from me for the first time. "I don't want her to think all the things I do."

I reach out and put my hand on his shoulder. At first he doesn't move, but then he leans over and puts his arm around me. We sit like this for a long time, staring out at the lake. The sun has set, and as the sky darkens I watch the cabins around the lake light up like lanterns.

It doesn't make any sense, but I feel like I know him better than anyone else on earth right now. Like I will never know anyone better.

He looks down at me and smiles. And then he squeezes my shoulder so lightly I almost think I've imagined it. I lean over to kiss him, to answer a question I've been asking since I first saw him in that park, but he pulls away.

"Nellie . . . we can't. I'm sorry."

I turn away, my face on fire.

"Look, it's not you, okay? I like you, you know that—"

"Forget it. Don't say anything." I jump off the car like he pushed me.

He stands up. "It's my fault, I shouldn't have started this. I'm not right for you."

"Whatever." I start to walk away.

"Nellie, come back. Where are you going?" I hear his boots on the path behind me. "At least let me give you a ride home."

I wave him off. "Don't do me any favors," I say, without looking back. Then I cut through the playground and disappear down a dimly lit path.

I take the side streets, just in case Dallas is following me, and in ten minutes I'm on the other side of town. I find a pay phone by the bank and call Aunt Maisie's house. The line is busy. I hang up and dial Uncle Flint's. I let it ring a dozen times before I hang up. It doesn't make any sense, there is always someone home in that house. I hang up and dial again, this time letting it ring more than thirty times. Jesus, even if they were swimming, or next door at our cabin, they should be able to hear the ring. I dial Aunt Maisie's again, and slam the phone down as soon as I hear the busy signal. I lean against the phone booth, watching a mosquito hover around the light, and wait for it to land.

I inhale deeply and pick up the phone again. I dial Uncle Flint's number slowly this time, pausing between each digit as if I didn't have it memorized. I listen to it ring, deciding not to count, but just to stay on as long as I can stand it. If I don't get through here I'm going to have to call Luke.

I'm just about to hang up when someone finally picks up. After a long second she speaks.

"Hello?"

"Who's this? Marley?"

"Who's this?" the voice spits back.

"Nellie."

"Oh. What's up?"

"Jess?"

"Yeah?" She sounds annoyed.

"What are you doing there?"

"I wasn't here, I was next door. But when the phone started ringing for five fucking minutes I came over to see what the emergency was."

"Where is everyone?"

"How should I know? I just got back."

"Oh." Her dinner with Renny. "How was that?"

"Fabulous. Just fucking fabulous."

"Listen, is anyone around? Uncle Flint, Dawn?"

"The lights were off when I got here. I think they're all up at Maisie's. Renny was talking about some card game or something."

Good, that should keep them busy for a while. "Listen, are you doing anything?" I try to sound relaxed. "Do you feel like coming into town?"

"On what, Jake's tricycle?"

"No, you can borrow Uncle Flint's car, the big red Crown Victoria next to the barn. He won't care, he let me drive it to the post office last summer and I didn't even have a license."

"Why? Did you break down or something?"

"No, it's a long story." I'm trying not to get frustrated. "I just need a ride home. Will you help or not?"

"You want me to go up to Maisie's and step over all the beer bottles to ask Flint for the keys to his car?"

"You don't even have to ask him, the keys are always in it."

"So you want me just to take it?"

"Either that or ask your father to borrow his car."

"Yeah, right."

She's quiet for a minute. I figure there's a fifty percent chance she'll do it, and a fifty percent chance she'll hang up on me.

"All right, where are you?"

"Just turn left out of the driveway and stay on the road till you're in St. Croix. I'll be in the Western Trust parking lot on your left."

"I'll be there in a few minutes."

Then she hangs up the phone.

I'm sitting on the curb when Jess pulls into the parking lot in Uncle Flint's car. All the windows are down and the radio blares some terrible rock song. She barely slows down to let me in, and we're back on the road before I can even buckle my seat belt.

Within three blocks it becomes clear that Jess is a terrible driver. She claims she passed the road test but I'm thinking she paid the guy off in the parking lot. She hasn't used the turn signal once, and consistently speeds up before stop signs and red lights. Walking home would have been a lot safer.

"So what happened? A date go bad?" she says, finally turning down the radio.

"Something like that." I roll up the window to stop my hair from whipping me in the face.

"Well, I didn't have any five-star night either," she says, lighting a cigarette. "'Dinner with Dad' had to be the longest meal I've ever sat through." She ashes her cigarette out the window and the whole car swerves. I'm starting to worry about her ability to smoke and drive at the same time.

"He took me to some barbecue joint named Regal Ribs, but it wasn't even good barbecue. The ribs were all dry and the cornbread tasted like birthday cake. Ugh, and those poor people think they're eating the real thing."

"Enough about the food, how'd it go with him?"

"Like you'd expect. He drank a few beers and talked about his other kids, how he wants me to get to know them finally. Then he started in on Shell and what a pain in the ass she was to live with and everything. How he didn't want to leave me but couldn't stay with her. I could tell he wanted me to say it was okay, that I forgive him or whatever."

"So what'd you say?"

"Nothing. I just sat there and ate that shitty barbecue and looked at the floor every time he said he was sorry. Then that Kenny Rogers 'Gambler' song came on and he asked me to dance."

"Now *that* I would have paid money to see."

"Are you crazy? I said I had to go to the bathroom and I stayed in there until the song was over. When I came out he was by the jukebox dancing with his beer. Christ, it was embarrassing." She takes a drag on her cigarette and starts speeding up.

"Slow down, the driveway's coming up."

She keeps her foot on the gas. "I was thinking, what if we just keep on driving? We could go to the Cities or Canada or some shit, whatever's in this direction."

I look over at her, not sure if she's serious. After a few seconds she smiles and takes her foot off the gas.

"I had you scared there for a minute, huh?" She pulls into the driveway and slows down when we get near Aunt Maisie's house.

"Cut the lights so they don't see the car."

"Then I won't be able to see anything."

"I know this road like my own face." I reach over and turn the lights off. "Just keep going straight, now veer to the right a little bit, watch out for the raspberry thicket."

"What the fuck is a thicket? Is that a real word?"

"Yeah, and it's a real bush so don't run over it. Uncle Flint would be more pissed off about you killing that bush than crashing this car."

I help her guide the car down the road without hitting anything. She parks next to the barn and turns off the engine, leaving the keys in the ignition. Then we roll all the windows back up. Jess tries to put her cigarette butt in the ashtray.

"Wait a minute." I grab her arm. "They don't smoke anymore, that'll give us away."

"Then what's this?" She pulls a half-smoked rolled cigarette out of the ashtray. She smells it. "Damn, they really smoke. This is the good stuff."

"No way." I grab it from her and sniff it myself.

"Maybe Uncle Flint used weed to get off cigarettes."

I hand it back to her.

"Or maybe Dawn needs to relax after all that studying." Jess starts to crack up. Then she lights it and inhales deeply.

"Are you nuts?"

"Come on, it's no different than drinking." She's trying to talk and hold her breath at the same time. "Aren't you even tempted to try it?" She holds it out to me.

BRASS ANKLE BLUES   187

It smells sweet and burnt at the same time. I shake my head. "We got away with the car. That's enough risk for one night."

She takes a final hit and then puts it out against the bottom of her sandal. "There, they won't even notice," she says, tucking it back into the ashtray.

I get out and quietly shut the door behind me. Jess meets me near the trunk.

"You're too good, Nellie." She puts her arm around me. "You've gotta work more adventure into your life."

"Why, so we end up like them?"

"No," she says, suddenly serious. "So we don't end up like them."

We walk back to the cabin in silence. She doesn't remove her arm until we get to the front door, which is too narrow for us to walk through side by side.

In the morning I feel hungover, like I spent the night drinking instead of having my heart stepped on. I walk down to the beach, hoping the water will wake me up, but the sun is covered up by clouds and it's too cold to swim. I tuck the towel around my waist and sit on one of the swings instead. Part of me is afraid to sit down, afraid of breaking the entire swing set, but a another part wants to be able to sit here comfortably, to pretend I'm still small, still a child. I let my feet out from under me and slowly start to swing; the chains squeak under my weight, but don't drop me. I keep swinging, wishing the wind would blow in one direction to keep the hair out of my face, wishing I could always go forward.

After a few minutes Jess shows up, without warning, as only Jess can do, and sits down on the swing next to me without saying a word. Now I'm certain the whole swing set is going to bust, but miraculously, it holds us both. The only sound I hear is the squeaking of the chains and the quiet whir of Jess's body each time she swings by me. She swings effortlessly, never even pumps her legs.

"My daddy doesn't love me," Jess says suddenly. Then she lights a cigarette and holds in the smoke like she's trying to get high again. I don't say anything, but I look back at the houses to make sure no one can see us.

"I don't even know why it bothers me. I mean, I don't love him either. Christ, I still don't even know him. And what I do know I don't like that much. But it seems like it should be different for parents, you know? I thought they all felt unconditional love for their kids, no matter what they do. Isn't that some sort of instinct or something?" She looks at me like she wants me to answer. I move my head, not quite committing to a nod or a shake. She looks away and starts talking again.

"You know those guys on death row, the real killers, the ones who gun down nursery schools or whatever, do you think their families still love them? I bet they do, I bet their mamas still go visit and bake them sweet potato pie, still try to hold their hands through the prison bars. That's what all parents should be like, no matter what their kids do; they should still be able to love them."

"But you're not like those guys in prison. You haven't done anything wrong." I pick some rust off the chain on my swing.

"Don't say that, Nellie. Please don't tell me there's no reason. Don't you see how that makes it worse?" She lowers her voice. "I want it to be because of something I did, something I had control over. Maybe I cried too loud when I was a baby or maybe it's because I'm a lousy student and I lie sometimes. Or because everything I have doesn't really belong to me. Maybe this is fate or karma or whatever, getting back at me for all the stuff I've ever done wrong."

"Don't do this to yourself, Jess. It's not worth it."

"Yes, it is. I have to be honest with myself. For once I want to tell the truth." She glances at me with a crooked smile. "Isn't that what you've always wanted?"

"I don't know what I want," I say, but now I am the one who's lying. I want my cousin to feel loved and to love herself. I want to be able to tell her that she's wrong about Renny, but I don't want to be another person who lies.

"Maybe it'll be different when it's just the two of you. Maybe you'll talk and get to know each other and you'll forgive him, and he'll say all the right things."

"Come on, you don't really believe that. You've seen him, you've heard the way he is; he isn't going to change for me."

"So you don't have to change for him either. You'll be even."

"And what if I want to change?" she says. "What if I'm already changing?" She says it like she's growing a third leg. I can't help but laugh.

"So what? You're allowed to change without getting permission. It's not like you owe him an explanation, right?"

"I guess not." She sounds disappointed, like she wanted the responsibility. She takes another drag off her cigarette and blows the smoke over her shoulder. "So what happened the other day at Hettie's, between you and your mother?"

I shrug. "Nothing."

"Come on, you rode back with Uncle Flint and she didn't say a word during our drive home. Plus her eyes were all red for the rest of the day."

"Was she crying?"

"Not then, but she looked upset, the way she's looked ever since she got here. I don't know, maybe that's just her look."

"No, usually she's all smiles. I guess it's this trip, being upset about her grandmother or whatever. . . ." I don't know why I don't just tell her the truth.

Jess suddenly stops swinging. She digs a small hole in the dirt with her big toe and drops her cigarette butt into it, then covers it back up.

"You know when we first met, not when we were kids, but just a few weeks ago, I thought we were total opposites. We didn't like the same music, the same food, the same clothes, the same boys—nothing, we really didn't have anything in common. And now this." Jess starts twisting her swing around, winding the chain around itself. "It's funny, I just never would have predicted it."

"Predicted what?" I stop swinging. "What do you think we have in common?"

"Anger." She looks at me. "We're both really fucking pissed at our parents. We're holding on to something from the past, something they did a long time ago that might not have even had anything to do with us, but we're still holding on tight, riding that anger like a wild horse we're scared to jump off of."

I picture these spotted gray horses galloping down a dusty path with Jess and me riding their strong backs without saddles, holding on to their matted manes, and it almost makes me smile.

"I can't," I say, my hands still tight around the chain. "I've tried, but I can't let it go."

"I know," she says. "Neither can I."

She finally stops twisting the swing and kicks her legs out, spinning around and around as the chain unwinds. Her eyes are closed and she throws her head back, letting out a long howl. It echoes a few times around the lake. Then a couple of dogs start barking as a loon cries out in the distance, other spirits returning the call.

Chapter 18

Like most farmers, Uncle Flint can predict the weather. He reads the sky, no matter what time it is, and can interpret the flight of the clouds. A few days later, we pass by him on the way down to the cabin from a night spent watching TV at Aunt Maisie's. He's standing on top of the picnic table in his backyard.

"Storm's coming. A real pisser, I think, could last the better part of the week."

"How soon?" I ask.

"Midnight, maybe sooner. I'd get those towels off the line tonight. And close the windows on the north side so your old lady's plants don't spill."

"Okay, thanks." I start walking away.

"Hey, you girls want to make a few bucks?"

I hesitate, afraid where this could lead. Jess turns around.

"Sure," she says.

Uncle Flint pulls a wad of bills out of his shirt pocket and peels off two fives. He gives one to each of us, then hands us each an empty ice cream bucket.

"Pick everything you can off the bushes by the lake, then get the ones behind the barn. Don't worry about the cherries, they're too young, but get all the raspberries you can. Derry and Ty are in the garden already, but holler if you need them."

Then he gets into his truck and drives off.

"This is a two-gallon bucket," Jess says. "How many bushes are there?"

"Enough to make jam for everyone on the lake."

"Damn." Jess shakes her head. "We should have asked for more money."

"At least we can eat on the job," I say, heading down to the lake. "Tyler and Derry are probably picking rhubarb."

We finish the lakeside bushes in about an hour and move up to the barn, our buckets half full. It's dark back here, but the bushes are partially lit by a bug zapper that hangs on the side of the barn. It sizzles every few seconds, another mosquito drawn into the bright fluorescent light. The berries are so ripe they come off the branches with the lightest touch, their plump bodies falling into my hands like raindrops. If I pick fast enough, each handful of berries is timed perfectly with the death of another insect. Planning this makes the time pass faster. I stop after a while, my hands tingling and covered with the dark juice.

Thunder cracks in the distance, so loud it almost makes no sound. Jess jumps and makes a noise that should only come from an animal. I feel my heart pounding in my chest. A lightning bolt divides the sky in the distance; the tail touches down on the top of a tree so gently that I think of an old man petting a cat. The thunder booms again and then the wind picks up, so I don't hear the truck when Uncle Flint pulls back in. I see the headlights, though, the high beams floating over the fields like searchlights. He drives up to the barn slowly, and I notice that the back end of his pickup is overflowing with stuffed garbage bags. Then I see Dallas in the passenger seat. The thunder continues to swell, creating a sound track that doesn't match the scene unfolding. It's like watching a Charlie Chaplin movie in the middle of a bombing raid.

Uncle Flint parks in front of the barn and they start unloading the bags. Dallas stands in the back and tosses them to Uncle Flint, who stacks them in the barn next to the squared bales of hay. They work at a steady pace, each man completely focused on his task. Dallas tosses the bags effortlessly, as if they were filled with popped corn. We are less than fifty yards away but they don't even notice us.

"What, they raked up all the hay?" Jess yells over the noise, motioning to the stuffed bags.

"I don't know," I say, even though I know exactly what's inside. He cut his crop early, before the storm had a chance to ravage the plants.

The first raindrops feel like tears hitting my cheeks. I look up at the sky, thick with clouds and not even the hint of a star. The darkest patch is directly above us, a wide front that must extend to the next county. It covers the sky like one massive blanket, but there are layers within it, and colors ranging from a smoky gray to the darkest indigo. It looks like something out of an oil painting, where the colors are so rich, so vibrant, you'd end up with paint on your fingertips if you touched the canvas.

Dallas speeds up as the rain starts to come down harder. He grabs the bags in twos and tosses them into the barn without worrying about Uncle Flint being ready to catch them. He stops only once, to push the hair out of his face. Now it's slicked straight back like he just came up from underwater. When the back end is empty Dallas hops down from the truck and joins Uncle Flint in the barn. He closes the door behind him.

Soon the rain is falling harder, heavy drops that feel like nickels when they land on my skin. The water collects in my eyelashes and even though I blink as fast as I can, I'm barely able see a few feet ahead of me. Within seconds my clothes are so wet I must look like I was just thrown into the lake. We grab our buckets from the muddy ground and run toward the cabin. I lean over the berries, trying to shield them from the downpour. It feels like someone is spraying my back with a fireman's hose. As we pass the barn I can't help but look back. I see Uncle Flint through a crack in the door, standing on a ladder with twine in one hand and a bouquet of marijuana in the other. If it were Christmastime I would think he was preparing to hang garland, proving to his children that he can be like any normal father: one who litters the yard with plastic decorations to re-create the manger; one who donates his scarf to the snowman on the front lawn and makes walnut shells look like eyes; one who sprinkles little white lights throughout the trees, making sure that Santa and his team of reindeer will find their house, their chimney, their stockings, on even the darkest winter's night.

But Christmas is not in July.

Three days later and it's still raining. It happens every summer, these thunderstorms in late July, but we act shocked each year, angry to be locked inside. We bake cookies, watch *Beverly Hills Cop* (the only videotape my cousins own), and play cards to make the time pass. We'll play almost any game: Bullshit, Spoons, Oh Hell, High-Low-Jack, poker, gin rummy, and Go Fish, but the vicious rounds of Hearts are the most time-consuming and the most important. One year a game lasted seventeen hours, split between two days. Today, Cody and I are partners and we're losing to Derry and Tyler, who hate to be on the same team yet manage to play well together, as if they are linked by some sibling bond. Caitlin had to go to her grandmother's so she dropped out after the first round, and Jake and Marley aren't allowed to play. Jess is playing solitaire at the end of the table. She's been watching us play, but is still trying to learn the rules.

"So the hearts are each a point?" she asks.

"Yeah."

"And points are good?"

"Yeah."

"So the more you take the better you are?"

"Right, but only if you're shooting the moon."

"And that's when you want them all?"

"Right."

"And if you're not?"

"Then you don't want any."

"But you have to take at least one," Derry adds.

"Right, 'cause otherwise the other team would have them all," Tyler says.

"And that's not good . . ."

"Right."

". . . because then they would have shot the moon."

"Right," we all say together.

"See how easy it is?" I say.

"I don't know, spades seems a lot easier."

"Spades is too easy," Cody says. "You don't even get penalized if you overbid—where's the challenge in that? Hearts is a game with balls. You either got it or you don't."

"Oh, we got it," I say, laying down the ace of hearts and taking the final trick.

"Yes." Cody puts his hands in the air. "The moon has been shot."

Jess stares at the cards. "But they had the queen of spades, that's thirteen points."

"But I had the ace," I say. "Hearts were lead so the ace takes the queen."

Jess still looks confused.

"You'll get it by the end of the summer," Derry tries to reassure her.

"You have to, hearts is like a family tradition," Tyler says.

"Some families play the lottery," Cody says, glaring at Jess while he shuffles the deck. "We play cards." He's been mad at her since he lost his Walkman and it showed up on Jess's bed.

It takes us a few more games to turn the tide and beat Derry and Tyler. We stop to make lunch: leftover potato salad and chicken pot pies. I'm slicing up the watermelon for dessert when Tyler walks out of the kitchen, heading for the front door. He opens it up and leans his face against the screen door like a sick dog.

"I can't stand being inside another minute."

"But it's still raining, where can we go where we won't get wet?"

He pauses. "Well, let's get wet then. Let's go swimming."

"In the lake? You know they won't let us, not with the lightning."

"Come on, it's just a drizzle now. The storm's passed."

"Still, you know they won't. Go ask."

"I'm fourteen. I shouldn't have to ask to go swimming."

"Don't then. And I'll set the timer to see how long it takes Uncle Flint to come down the hill and drag you out."

He's quiet for a while.

"Let's go to the pits then."

"The mud pits?"

"Why not? After all this rain they've got to be filled. It'll be just like the lake, maybe warmer. And no one around to see us."

"Except the guard."

"On a Sunday? Come on, he's asleep or watching the football game. Besides, he's never caught us yet."

"Does that mean we should push our luck?"

"Yes, it means we have luck, and we should use it." He pushes the screen open and walks out into the rain in just his T-shirt and shorts. I follow him, half knowing I want to go myself, and half pretending I'm just going to stop him. By the time I catch him the rest of the cousins have caught up with both of us. We let Derry, Cody, and Jess come, but send Marley and Jake back to the house with promises of candy if they keep their mouths shut.

The gravel pit is on a huge chunk of land across the road from Aunt Maisie's house, more than twenty acres filled with mountains of sand and gravel that look like pyramids, the mysteries of Egypt in our own front yard. In back, behind where they park the dump trucks, there is a dried-up mud pond that fills up in the rain to become a perfect swimming hole: half water, half mud. Every year we sneak over at least once and stage our annual mud fight on state property. When it ends, and we are covered in mud from head to toe, we sneak back down to the lake to show off, posing for photos like heroes come back from the battlefield. Our parents, never happy with our deception, are nevertheless impressed by our ingenuity, shrieking in horror as they take more pictures, and ask for more details. My mother, always feigning the most outrage, combs my hair later that night and tells me how soft the mud has made it, and how the skin on the back of my neck glows.

Instead of walking down the driveway, we cut through the field behind Uncle Flint's barn, so none of our parents will see us leave the property. We hide under the sumac trees by the edge of our land and sprint across the highway when it's clear, jumping into a ditch before the guard can see us. The ditch is filled with rainwater, but we're already wet and don't even notice that we're standing up to our knees in water. It smells like wet hay and horses. My heart is beating quickly and I wonder if repeating this act over and over again for the rest of my life will be the only law I ever break. Cody acts as lookout, climbing onto a lamppost to get a look at the guard's desk. He waves us on and we run across the parking lot in single file, a row of ducklings trying to make it to the pond. We pass the dump trucks without incident and gear up for the most dreaded leg: sprinting over the Mountain.

We call it the Mountain because it's the tallest hill in the gravel pit. Instead of fine sand it's filled with sharp gravel pieces, and in the past, if we went too early, before our feet had time to toughen up, we would all come out with cuts in between our toes. It's also the most dangerous part since there is nowhere to hide; you just have to keep running and pray that the guard isn't looking. Luckily, the area at the base is clear today, and we all try to pick up speed on the straightaway. Still, the first step into the Mountain always slows momentum, and soon I am using my hands to climb up through the avalanching gravel. The rain has softened it, and with every footstep another layer crumbles, threatening to wash me to the bottom. But I stay up, pulling my legs out of the cold pebbles only to thrust them back in, afraid to watch as they disappear below the knee. I climb faster with each step even though my legs feel like sandbags. When I make it to the top I have to resist the urge to stand and throw my arms up like I've just conquered Mount Everest. Instead, I tumble down the other side, letting my body fall in every direction, resting only when I know I'm out of sight.

Only now do I think about anyone else. Cody is in front of me, doing somersaults down the Mountain. When he gets to the bottom he stumbles around like a drunkard. I look behind me to find Tyler and Derry coming over the top together, as if they had helped each other over. Normally, I would never believe it, but it looks like they are still holding hands. Suddenly I realize I don't see Jess. I look around, hoping maybe she passed me during the climb, but she isn't on this side of the Mountain. If she got caught we'd hear the trespassing bell (Uncle Flint set it off picking up sand one year), so all I can think is that she's hurt. I stand up and run back to the top.

I find her on the other side, lying on her back as if she were sunbathing. Her arm is covering her face, bent at the elbow to shield her from the rain, or to hide her tears.

"What's wrong with you, are you hurt?"

She moves her arm away but doesn't look at me. "I'm done."

"What?"

"I'm done, I can't move," she says.

"So you're just going to sit here?"

"Just go ahead without me."

I think about walking away, about taking long strides down the side of the Mountain away from her, but I don't.

"It's a fifty-dollar fine if you get caught."

She shrugs and looks away. I notice a crane hovering over a sand pile in the distance. It reminds me of a child's outstretched arm sprinkling sand onto a castle at the beach. I take a few steps toward her.

"I'm not leaving you."

"Forget it, Nellie, it's not a big deal."

"We've never gotten caught before and we're not getting caught today."

I grab her by the armpits and start dragging her up the hill. She tries to help, pushing her feet into the crumbling earth. They are red and cut up, her skin not as strong as mine. When we get close to the top I sit down and go over backward on my butt, using gravity to pull us both over the top. The gravel burns my skin as we fall down the Mountain, but I hold on to Jess and try to remember to breathe. We come to a stop right before the bottom and I finally let go of her.

We both take a while to stand. I wipe the sand and grit off my legs and start walking to join the others at the mud pond, trying not to hobble. She catches up to me, wincing with each step, but not giving up.

"You'll feel better in the water," I say. "The mud helps."

She nods. "Thanks."

The water is warmer than I remember, but the mud seems a lot colder. I sink into the mud up to my knees, stuck like a plastic soldier. We stay all afternoon, throwing mud balls at each other like hand grenades. After, when the war is over and we are all dead, we bury ourselves in the mud, using the damp earth as a balm to cover our wounds, to heal the things we don't even realize are broken. Eventually the rain stops falling, but we don't even notice.

The guard is gone by the time we leave so we only have to sneak past the security camera and hop the fence. We walk side by side in front of the camera, arms linked like we're a group of protesters, knowing the mud is a disguise that no one can uncover. I can't help but imagine the guard's face when he sees the tape tomorrow, wondering, if only for a brief second, if we are human. We pass over the weight scale, a metal slab the size of a parking space, and I am amazed that anything can hold all of us in the same grip. Our collective weight is 767 pounds. Even together we are no match for a mountain of sand. Alone, we would not even register.

We stop at the edge of the highway, waiting to cross. The cars slow down as they drive past us, just like during the car fire. But this time we stare back, pointing and laughing, howling at them like they are the real freak show; Jess even moons a truck driver. We are all tougher under the shield of mud, the cloak of a brown mask. Since they can't see us, can't trace this behavior to our names or families, we act like we are totally separate from our bodies; like there are no repercussions to our actions. For just this moment, I have the freedom of invisibility, and I relish it. When we all stand next to one another, I finally feel like I belong, like I'm no different from my cousins. In this moment, we are the same color, with the same thick locks of tangled hair, the same clumped and crackled skin, the same grotesquely distorted features. We are all monsters.

When there's a break in the traffic, we run across the road together, leaving a fresh trail of lake water and mud, the footprints of our family swallowed up in the tall grass as we disappear one by one into the shadows of the sumac trees.

There are no photo sessions when we get home this year. We slip into the lake unnoticed and spend the evening washing off the layers of hardened clay. We each wash our hair at least three times and make sure to clean our fingernails and the curved canals of our ears so that we leave no trace of our afternoon adventure. From the beach I can see that the tree house got battered in the storm; it looks like the entire roof was torn off. Tomorrow, in the daylight, I will assess the damage. I look across the lake and wonder how Dallas and his tent survived the rains. He is probably asleep in the arms of an evergreen, laughing at the rest of us who are holed up inside, afraid of water.

When Jess and I sneak into the cabin after sunset my parents don't ask any questions. They don't even look up from their reading material: for my father, the local newspaper; my mother, a book of poems by Robert Frost.

"There's dinner in the oven and fruit salad in the fridge," my mother says. "Don't forget to turn the oven off."

We eat dinner in our bathing suits, wrapping the towels around our waists. This is the only skirt I've ever felt comfortable in. After eating, Jess rubs cocoa butter onto the skin between her toes and puts on a pair of athletic socks we find in the closet. I'm pretty sure they are Marcus's, from the one season he played football in high school, but when Jess imagines them to be my father's, surviving thirty years on the bottom shelf and carrying the legacy of undergraduate tackles, I don't correct her. She pulls them above her knees and exaggerates her stride, running in slow motion to cross the carpeted end zone, both hands raised above her head in victory.

When she goes to bed I make the mistake of retrieving my book from the living room.

"Because that's what we're supposed to do," I hear my father say. His tone isn't particularly harsh, but the sentence still makes me stop short. I try to back up without being seen but the old floors give me away.

"I was just getting my book," I say, reaching over the couch to the end table.

"It's all right, Nellie, you can come in."

"We were just talking, honey." My mother sounds like she's apologizing.

"I'm going to bed anyway." I pick up the book and turn to leave.

"Nellie," my mother says.

I stop. "Yeah?"

"Quite a storm, huh?" She points to the cover of the newspaper on my father's lap. The photo is of a telephone pole resting in the middle of a minivan. "We were lucky we didn't lose more trees."

"Yeah, I guess."

"How'd the tree house make out?"

'I couldn't really tell, it might need a new roof."

"I'm sure Cal or Palmer will give you some lumber."

"Sure, okay."

"Now that the storm has passed," my father starts, "and it's safe to travel again, your mother—"

"I'll be leaving next week," my mother finishes. "I'll stay for Caitlin's party, but then I have to go home."

I flip through the pages of my book and don't say anything. They stare at me like I am a photograph they just found in the bottom of an empty drawer. If I ever found a picture of this moment I'd tear it into a hundred pieces and sprinkle the ground with the colored shreds.

"Is there anything you want to talk about, since we're all to-gether?"

"No." I shrug and try to look nonchalant.

My father sits up in his chair and clears his throat. The sound of him clearing his throat, usually into a microphone at the beginning of a poetry reading, is one of my earliest memories of sound. Sometimes I like to imagine the first time I heard it, his tall frame folded into a rocking chair next to my crib as he prepared to recite a nursery rhyme from his childhood, while other fathers across the country struggled to get through *The Cat in the Hat.*

"Hettie's death was a surprise, something no one was expect-ing, but it doesn't change anything. It can't make us go back in time. We already decided what was best and we have to stick with that, okay?"

"Sure, whatever."

"Nellie . . ." My mother sighs.

"What?"

She turns away, shaking her head.

"Don't act so cavalier," my father says.

I stare at the lamp that separates them, sitting on an end table that might as well be two miles long. The filtered light divides the living room into two equal parts, where each of my parents can exist in their own space. It's easier to see them like this, apart, even in the same room, and easier still to not look at them directly.

"What do you expect me to say?"

"Whatever you want. Something."

"Did you know that this is the first time I've been alone with the two of you since Noah's graduation? He and Marcus went to that brunch at the Biltmore, remember, and we stayed home and had French toast with Aunt Maisie's plum jam and leftover pork chops." They're listening so attentively I decide to go on. "Then we did the dishes together. I washed and you guys both dried. You had matching towels, the green-and-white-checkered ones, and somebody smeared grease on the water glasses but you both denied it and walked away with your towels slung over your shoulders, keeping the evidence just like a little kid would." I mimic them with my own towel and they both smile. "Do you guys remember that day?"

"Sure, of course," my mother says.

"I didn't think it was a big deal then, I didn't try to remember it, I just did. Don't you think that's weird, that I can remember the details of something so insignificant?"

"No." My mother shakes her head. "You've always had the best memory in the family."

"The youngest one always does," my father says, finally sitting back in his chair. "My sister remembers things about my life that I didn't even know she was alive to see: my homeroom teacher in fifth grade; who I took to the junior prom; how many questions I missed on my driver's test. She kept track of my life like there was going to be a quiz later."

"That's just her personality," my mother says.

"No, that was her role. She was the record keeper, just like Nellie."

"I don't want that role," I say. "I don't want to remember all those details, all the things nobody else cares about. I'm sick of being the only one."

"You're not the only one," my father says. "You know that."

"We all remember different things, Nellie, that's what makes it interesting."

"Like what?" I question her. "What interesting things do you remember?"

"Come on, I remember lots of things, too many to count."

"I'm not asking for a list. I'm just asking for something. One thing."

"I remember when you were five, and you convinced Caitlin to cut off your braid. Then you taped it to your pants and walked around saying you were a raccoon and that was your tail." She smiles at the memory. "I remember the crush you had on your Spanish teacher in the eighth grade. And soccer, I remember being at every home game, even the ones you didn't tell me about, and I remember the semifinals, when you saved that goal by heading the ball out and how your coach yelled out that he loved you from the sidelines."

"My coach. Not you."

"But I was there. And I remember all those moments—"

"Do you remember Mrs. Thatcher, the sub I had in the second grade who weighed the entire class and then announced that I was the heaviest second grader she'd ever weighed? How I cried on the school bus when the kids called me Dumbo? Or how about that Halloween when I had to squeeze into my old clown costume from the year before?" I hold on to the back of the couch, leaning over her. "Do you remember my chicken pox, how they were in my throat and my ears and I couldn't sleep or look at myself in the mirror for almost two weeks, how I cried into my pillow and the tears burned my scabs? How I thought I would never look normal again, how I hated myself? Do you remember any of that?"

She speaks softly. "No, I'm sorry. I didn't know you went through all that."

"Because you weren't there. Because you left."

"It was only a few months, Nellie—"

"That's a lifetime to a seven-year-old."

"I just needed the time to think. I was always coming back." She looks at my father, as if still explaining it to him. He looks away, unwilling to help her.

"How could I know that? How could I trust anything you said or did?"

"That was years ago. Things are different now."

"How? Here we are, eight years later, and you're doing the same thing."

"I don't see it that way, Nellie. A lot has changed."

"You're right." I stand up. "This time I don't want you to come back."

She shakes her head. "Don't say that. Please, don't mean that."

"Look at you: You've left your parents, your brothers and sister, your high school boyfriend. You've left your husband and your children. You've left everything and everyone you've claimed to care about. Every place, every home, every hobby. You're so used to being the one who leaves that you don't even realize that you can also be left. That this time we're leaving you."

I walk out of the room, the weight of my footsteps making the floors creak, covering up her silence and the sound of my father clearing his throat.

Chapter 19

There is enough light coming from the movie screen to see that Luke and Paul Newman have the same color eyes. I used to think that Paul Newman's were fake, that the camera somehow made them more vibrant, but then I noticed Luke's. His blue eyes are so vivid it looks like they're wet, like the color is still setting.

"What, you don't like it?" He looks over at me.

"No, it's good." I turn back to the screen. "For an old movie."

We're at the Lake View drive-in outside St. Croix, watching Paul Newman and Joanne Woodward in *The Long Hot Summer*. Drive-in movies have always seemed like magic to me, the way the voices just come out of the speakers. It seems so intimate, like they're acting for our car alone.

"Come on, look how cool he is"—Luke gestures toward the screen—"outbidding everyone else to buy her lunch just so he can be alone with her." He puts his arm on the headrest behind me. "This is when she falls for him."

"Are you kidding? Look how angry she is, she's just going along to be polite."

"Girls don't do that. If she really didn't want to, she wouldn't go."

Onscreen they're walking along a river that looks like almost any part of Redwood County. When they stop at a picnic table, Paul Newman bites into her finger sandwiches as if he were tasting a part of her body, something she wrapped up just for him. She looks like she can't stand to see him enjoying anything that much. Then she picks a fight and leaves.

"See, there she goes," I say.

"That's just because her boyfriend showed up. She's playing them against each other."

I reach for the popcorn that's sitting between our hips. "Maybe she just doesn't know who she wants yet."

"Come on, how could she not want Newman? The other guy's a total loser."

"Well, maybe she wants them both."

Luke looks at me. "What's she going to do with two men? Marry them both?"

"She could keep one as a lover, on the side, like men have done for generations." I toss the popcorn into my mouth, one kernel at a time.

"And I suppose you consider that progress, women acting as foolishly as men? That's equal rights?"

I smile. "Just because it's equal doesn't mean it's progress."

"Exactly," Luke says. He reaches for the popcorn and flicks a few kernels toward my face. I open my mouth like I'm trying to catch them and he laughs.

I don't mean to think about it, but suddenly I remember that we almost shared a sibling. Is this the right moment to tell him that? Is it even my responsibility? It's weird, but I feel more connected to him now, almost like we're related, even though nothing has really changed. Even if the baby had been born it wouldn't have made Luke and me siblings, and yet somehow things seem different. I feel more attached to him, like people who go through a crisis together and all of a sudden feel this new bond. I saw something on television once where strangers who had survived a plane crash stayed in touch afterward, and told one another things they couldn't explain to their own families. They shared this one little moment, this disaster, but it became bigger than all the other, regular moments in their lives. They became obsessed with the tragedy, and how they were able to survive. I guess their real obsession was with survival.

My mother lost her virginity at this drive-in. It was the night before Palmer's graduation from high school; she was still a sopho-more. This is the part of their story that I've always known, the part she told me when we talked about waiting to have sex. She said she didn't really want to do it, she felt too young, but she didn't want to disappoint him. Of all the things she could have told me she shared that moment. It was two years later when she got pregnant, sometime before her graduation. I wonder if on that night, he was worried about disappointing her.

"I guess our parents used to come here a lot," I say, sipping my soda. I suddenly want to find out how much Luke knows.

"Really? Like on a double date?" His raises his eyebrows but doesn't take his eyes off the screen.

"No, I mean in high school. Your father and my mother."

"Oh. I guess that makes sense. This thing's been around for-ever."

"Don't you think it's weird?" I ask.

"That they came here or that they dated?" He stuffs a handful of popcorn into his mouth.

"Both, everything, this whole situation."

"It's kind of funny, I guess." He glances at me. "That here we are, more than twenty years later, doing the same thing."

"Is that what's happening, we're doing the same thing they did?" I try to sit up but my thighs are stuck to the leather seats. When did I start sweating?

Luke pauses. "Well, not exactly the same . . ." He turns toward me. "It's different because it's us, not them. We're not the same people."

I lean back and roll my eyes. "Thank god."

"Plus, we're already screwing up." He sips his soda and tries to hide his smile.

"How's that?"

"Because we're at the drive-in actually *watching* the movie. My dad would have never done that." He looks almost proud.

"I bet you're right." I make myself smile.

"Listen, Nellie, this is our thing, okay?" He moves over to me and grabs my hand out of my lap. "It's totally new and different. It's . . . whatever we want it to be." He kisses my hand, leaving a buttery imprint of his lips on my knuckles like I punched him in the mouth. I smile, but it turns into a laugh.

"What, that's funny?" He leans back.

"No, no, it's sweet." I pull him toward me. "You're sweet." I kiss him quickly on the lips. "And salty." I kiss him again. "And buttery." This time when I kiss him he doesn't let me pull away. Instead, he guides me backward until I'm lying down on the seat with most of his body on top of mine. I think of my mother, who lay in this same position with her own Jasperson boy two decades ago. I wonder what she thought about as she felt the weight of all his desire resting on her adolescent frame. Did she feel his heart galloping against her own? Did she love him?

The last image I see on the movie screen is of a barn going up in flames. The air in our car is so thick and hot it feels like the fire is in the engine. The sound of sirens pours out of the speakers like smoke, filling our car with an urgency, a desperation, that is almost suffocating. I hold my breath as long as I can, but when I have to, I breathe Luke in, take his spirit into my lungs and hide it in a fold that no one has ever seen. But I won't take his body to that same place; I'm not ready to show that landscape to anyone. I will keep something for myself, careful not to make the same mistake my mother made.

Of all the chaos wreaked on Redwood County during the thunderstorms, the damage to my tree house hurts me the most. The main room looks okay, having lost only a few side boards, but the roof is completely gone, as if it never existed. I spend the first few days after the storm fixing it up alone, enlisting the help of Jake and Marley to steal nails and two-by-fours from Uncle Flint's tool chest. Jess hangs around a lot, watching me work from below. She has a lot of ideas about the design even though she's afraid of heights and claims that she'll never set foot in the tree house. She sits for hours against the base of the trunk like it's a beach chair.

Without the roof, the view from the main room is amazing. I consider leaving it completely open, like a sundeck, but then think about the colder days, when shelter from the wind is more important than sunbathing. I look across the lake, my eyes subconsciously searching for Dallas's clearing. I know that I will never be able to see it from here, from any spot on the outside, but I wonder if I will ever stop looking. I think about going over to visit him, but decide against it. At this point, what is there to say?

I hear footsteps below and a soft whistle; my heart instantly starts beating faster. Did I conjure him? I hang my head over the edge and look down below, expecting to welcome Dallas as my first official visitor to the construction site. Instead, I'm looking at my mother.

"How's it going?" she asks. She's wearing her swimsuit and holds a tall plastic cup.

"Not bad," I say, straightening up and going back to work. The trunk blocks her from my view.

"Jess says you're almost done."

"Not really. I have the whole roof to rebuild."

She's silent for a minute and I hope that means she's left. She hasn't.

"I brought you some lemonade."

"Thanks."

"Here, I'll bring it up."

"No, just hand it to me." I lean over to grab the cup but she's already halfway up the ladder, the cup clenched between her teeth. She stands on the top rung and pokes her head through the front door, inches from my feet. She places the cup on the plywood floor and looks around.

"I never knew it was so big inside. From the ground it looks like it's only built for one person."

"What would be the point of that?" I ask. "It's for all of us. All the cousins." My eyes go to the spot on the trunk where we each carved our initials into the bark, using this tree as our family bible. We thought we remembered everyone, but now I realize that Jess was missing.

My mother pulls herself inside and stands up, looking out over the lake. "Nice view," she says, cupping her hands over her eyes. She spins around in a circle. "You can see everything here—from Maisie's house to Miller's Point. You'd never guess that this was such a good lookout."

"It'll be different when I finish the roof," I say. "This top part will be closed off." I start hammering nails into a two-by-four between my feet just to make some noise.

"That's too bad," she says. "It's nice to be in the open air, to be able to see everything without anyone seeing you."

"I'm not up here to spy on anyone."

"I know, that's not what I'm saying." She leans back against the center tree trunk. "Sometimes it's good to have a different perspective, that's all. Just a different way of looking at the same things."

Her double meanings aren't lost on me, but I decide to let it go. I look out at the still lake water, wishing I could dive right in from here.

"The lake is still the lake," I say, "no matter how you look at it. That will never change."

"You're right," she says, smiling. "Isn't that why we keep coming back?" She leans her head back, her hair spilling onto the bark. "My father always predicted that. He used to say that if you grew up on a lake you could never get that water out of your blood, and would never be happy living some place where you couldn't dip your ankles within three minutes of realizing they were hot. Every time I talked about leaving he'd say, 'You'll be back, maybe not for us, but you'll come back for the lake.' I guess he was right in the end."

"So that's why you came, the lake was calling?"

"No, not just the lake. I missed a lot of things." She runs her fingers along the bark. "I missed you," she says. "I still miss you."

212 RACHEL M. HARPER

When I turn to her she's looking at her feet. Her toes strum the
withered plywood board one at a time. It's weird how hours in the
sun washes the color out of wood, making it brittle and gray, but
those same hours on our skin makes it darker and more vibrant.
My mother needs those hours. The skin not covered by her swimsuit looks pale and vulnerable, like planks of freshly cut pine that
need a coat of shellac before they can face the elements.

"I've got a lot of work to do up here. If you don't mind . . ." I
gesture to the ladder with my hammer.

"Sure, yeah." She takes a step toward the door, her foot dangling
over the opening. Then she changes direction midair and steps
closer to me. "Nellie, listen, I came up here to tell you something, to
tell you a story that I should have told you years ago. Now, maybe
you don't want to hear it and maybe I don't even want to tell it, but
I have to, we both have to, and then hopefully we can get over this
thing and get back to being mother and daughter . . . friends, even."
She leans into the railing overlooking the lake.

"When I was your age I wasn't like you. I wasn't confident and
strong-willed, I wasn't smart or independent. I was scared and I was
immature, but I was a good actor, so I never let any of those feelings
show. I pretended I was everything you are so I could survive my
childhood, my family, and when I grew up and moved away I never
took the time to stop and realize that I was still acting. The real me
was so hidden under all these layers I'd been wrapping myself in
that I didn't even know where the fake person ended and my real
self began. And the sad part is that I still don't know, not really. I'm
forty years old and I'm just beginning to know myself." She stops
and fixes the barrette that's been slowly falling out of her hair. "I'm
not saying this as an apology or so you'll pity me, I just want you to
know where I'm coming from and what I've been dealing with, or
not dealing with, for most of my life." She adjusts her swimsuit,
pulling up the straps to give her more support. Then she grabs the
railing again.

"Palmer Jasperson was supposed to be my ticket out of here.

He was smart and handsome and ambitious and he was going to build a life for us: in the Twin Cities or California, overseas, wherever we wanted to go. But then he graduated and started to work and worry about the future and things started to change—"

"And you got pregnant," I add.

"Yes, I got pregnant, but things were already beginning to shift, we just refused to look at it. He was working in St. Croix, building docks for the parks department and living in his mother's basement and he was happy. That was always the difference between us: he was happy with a simple life, with familiar things, and I was restless. I was sick of Redwood County and the drive-in and Friday nights at the Dairy Queen and swimming in the same lakes and working in the same fields and eating with the same silverware. I wanted things I couldn't even ask for, and that want, hidden and unnamed, began to drive a wedge between us. And then I got pregnant." She exhales. "Palmer was thrilled, he wanted to get married that summer, right here on the front lawn. He even put a down payment on a little two-room cabin on Blackfoot Lake, right next to the Tower. He had everything planned. He had even named the baby: Ava, after his mother."

"It was a girl?" I ask. I had a sister?

"No," she says quickly. "Well, I don't know. But he wanted a girl. He wanted a life with me, and he thought that his desire was enough to make it happen, and to keep me happy. So I left. I left before I could disappoint him, before I knew where I was going."

"And you went to live with Hettie?"

She nods. "Just for the summer. It was exactly what I needed, hours alone in the cornfields, time to sit with myself, time to dream. And during that whole time we only talked about it once. She said that after seventy years on this planet, and forty of them with my grandfather, she only had one regret: that she didn't see more of the world. She never even left the state of Minnesota. There will always be time for a husband and babies, for making a home, she said, but the time for yourself runs out."

"So Hettie encouraged you to get the abortion?"

"I don't know if 'encouraged' is the right word . . . but she supported my decision. She let me know that it was an option, that's all, and it was all I needed her to do. That was all I needed from anyone, but no one else would do it."

She grabs the railing like a gymnast about to pull herself up on the bars. She looks strong in this moment, like she has the strength to pull the entire tree out of the ground. "So that's it, that's how it happened. I'm sorry I kept it from you all these years. I never knew it would make you so angry."

"I'm not angry." And as the words come out I realize that I'm finally telling the truth. "I just have one question." She looks at me with an openness that's frightening. "Do you love my father?"

"Oh, Nellie . . ." She drops her head like I slapped her.

"What, that one's too hard?"

She exhales. "I'm trying to love myself."

"But did you ever love him?"

"Yes, of course. And I looked up to him. I loved his work, his confidence in front of an audience, the way he changes a room with his voice. I loved all of that—"

I cut her off, my voice strained and barely recognizable. "And him, do you love any part of him?"

She lifts up her hands and stares at them. "I love his hands, the way his fingers taper like a pianist's. You know what I mean, you have the same ones. And his hair, the smell of his scalp, those are the things I would miss when he traveled. I used to stand in the closet and smell his collars or the inside of his wool cap. I don't think I'll ever get over that." She finally looks at me. "But that doesn't mean that we're good partners, that we were ever good friends, and that's the part that makes a marriage last."

"But you had a family . . ."

"Yes, and that's the only thing we ever really agreed on, having you kids. We both knew we wanted to be parents and we did that part together. I think we did it well."

"So now that it's over you can go your separate ways? We're finally old enough to be okay without a family?"

"You have a family, Nellie, a big one, in fact, filled with lots of people who care about you. None of that is going to change. We're just shifting around the details. Everything will be okay in the end, you'll see."

"Why? Because you say so?"

"Because you're stronger than most people, and stronger than you think you are."

"You think I'm always strong? You think I'm tough? Well, that's not how I feel on the inside. I feel weak and lonely and scared. I feel like a child—I am a child—and I just want to know when I get to act that way. When I get to be innocent again."

"I don't know," she says, rubbing her bare arms. The skin looks soft, but the muscles below are strong. Even her skin is deceiving. "When was the last time you felt innocent?"

"You don't want to know the answer to that."

"Yes, I do. I think maybe I have to."

I breathe in slowly. "Provincetown," I say. "That weekend we camped by the ocean."

She looks down at her hands, flawless against the weathered wood. I keep talking.

"I remember walking along the beach by myself, looking for crabs or starfish, anything that was alive. It was a perfect summer day, sunny and warm, with almost no breeze, and I had a pair of goggles on my head, the rubber strap real tight so they wouldn't fall off. I was carrying a snorkel in one hand and a red plastic bucket in the other."

She scratches at the railing with a fingernail, pulling up shavings of wood like it's dead skin.

"I was following a pack of seagulls for some reason, and they had me racing around in circles, so dizzy I could barely stand up. When they all flew away, I started running through the sand dunes, just running in my bare feet, not once thinking about what could be buried in the sand, not once thinking I would find you there. And you want to know the worst part? At first I didn't get it, I didn't know what you were doing with that man, what you could possibly be doing under a blanket in ninety-degree weather. I wanted to know if you were all right, if something had happened to you. I wanted to make sure you didn't need me. And then he looked up and saw me, gave me this look that made me think that I'd been caught doing something wrong. Like I was the one who was going to get into trouble. So I didn't say anything, I just turned around and walked back to the beach. I sat by the water and spent the rest of the day burying my feet."

"Nellie . . ." Her voice is barely audible.

"No," I say, "I don't want you to say anything." I can feel the sand on the bottoms of my feet, and the icy slap of the Atlantic on my toes. "That was the moment, though, that was the last time."

She nods, still looking straight ahead. There is a part of me that wants to toss her over the railing, and a part that wants to wrap my arms around her and never let go. Her lap is still the most comfortable chair I've ever sat in.

"I like it up here," she says suddenly. "It's like being above the clouds, like no one even knows you're here." She turns away from the lake and steps onto the top rung of the ladder. "Watch me when I swim out, okay? Yell if you see any speedboats."

I nod and watch her climb down the ladder with slow, cautious steps. When she gets to the lake, she walks onto the dock and dives in without hesitation, her form still as perfect as a lifeguard's. Then she swims out to the raft in one breath, leaving a trail of waves big enough for any boat to see. When she lifts her head out of the water she looks up at me, making sure I'm still watching. She waves as if to say, "I'm okay," then turns around and heads to the other side of the lake. I wave at her as she swims away from me.

I stare at the bandage on my arm, so familiar I hardly recognize it as being different from my own skin. I've worn one all summer, weeks after my burn still needed to be covered, but suddenly it feels unnecessary. I tear it off with one strong pull and slap the bandage onto the wall next to me, as if to protect the tree house. There is a lighter band of skin where the sun wasn't allowed to go, proving just how dark I have become. The scab has fallen off already, and only the new skin is left behind, as smooth and vulnerable as the inside of an eyelid. It will heal eventually, will fill in with color to match the rest of my arm, but there will always be a mark there. I am like Dallas now, or Sethe, graced with a permanent scar that makes me easily identifiable. Soon it will help define me, creating my individuality as much as the shape of my fingers or the flecks of color in my eyes. Is this where we find our identities, in the smooth, defiant flesh of our scars?

Chapter 20

If you've never seen an agate it's hard to explain what to look for. Some have a striped pattern, while others are solid; some are shaped like an egg, while some have almost no shape—they're just a bunch of jagged lines; some are copper or chestnut brown in color, while others are so light they're almost clear, with gray-blue lines tracing a path through their center. My favorite ones are the color of rainwater collected in the bottom of a rusty pail. When you hold an agate up to the light, no matter how big it is, the sun should shine straight through it and throw a rainbow across your face. In some ways, finding an agate is like finding a piece of a star.

For us, agating is a family tradition, right up there with farming and playing hearts. The best time to go is after an intense rain, when the gravel roads are packed down and the dust has settled. And the sun has to be shining, that's when they are easiest to spot. This year the perfect agating weather coincides with Caitlin's adoption day, so we end up taking the party out to the gravel roads behind our property. There are at least a dozen of us, scattered down a long stretch in the road. Jess and I are at the head of the line, pushing up the hill that leads to the other side of the lake, to Luke's house and the clearing in the woods that Dallas calls home.

I find a round amber stone and pop it into my mouth, sucking off the dirt as if it were chocolate. I am always surprised by how warm they are. Jess spits onto her agates to clean them and then shines them on the front of her cutoffs. She's picked up agating like she's spent her entire life on these gravel roads with us, and her pockets are already bulging with the stones.

"So I've been thinking about something lately." Jess is bent over a pile of rocks at the edge of the road.

"Oh yeah?" I hold my agate up to the sun, trying to count the stripes.

"I've got an idea of what I should do."

"About what?" I walk over to her.

"The future, who I want to be." Her hand floats over the ground like a metal detector looking for gold. "I think I'm going to be a lesbian."

"What?"

"You heard me."

"Going to be?"

"Yeah, in the future. Not now, not yet, but someday."

"Did you just come up with this today, right now?"

"No, I've been thinking about it for a while, for years, maybe."

"Maybe you're just sick of guys."

"It's not about the guys, it's about the girls. That's the whole point." She picks up a dust-covered stone and spits on it. "I think it'll be different. Softer."

"Some guys are soft," I say, imagining the inside of Luke's wrist and Dallas's top lip, his voice over the bonfire.

"Not the ones I've known. They don't make it if they're soft."

"There has to be some kind of compromise, something in the middle."

"That's a hard place to be," Jess says. "You know that."

I stand at the top of the hill, looking down in both directions. "Yeah. But sometimes it's the only place you can be."

I hear the rumbling of tires on gravel and a few voices yelling "car" in the distance. The clouds of dust come first, then the spit of an old engine, and finally the front grille of Uncle Flint's truck. All the windows are down, and the dust is swirling around in the cab like smoke. I can't even tell who's behind the wheel. It barrels up the hill, but slows down as it reaches the top, coming to a stop in the middle of the road in front of us. When the dust settles I can see Uncle Flint and Renny in the cab; Dallas squats on a tarp in the truck bed. He smiles at me as he stands up.

"Somebody lose their watch?" Renny says, leaning out the window.

"We're agating," Jess says, holding up her biggest rock. "You do know what an agate is, right?"

"Girl, are you kidding? I've been agating these back roads since before you were born. Bet we've already picked all the best ones."

Jess turns her back to them and starts scanning the ground again.

"Bullshit," Uncle Flint says. "They put fresh gravel down every year, don't worry about running out."

"Yeah, just like the Easter Bunny puts out more eggs each year, just for the little kids to hunt." Renny tips his head back to finish his beer, the can never touching his lips.

Dallas hops out of the truck and walks toward me. "Easter egg hunts," he says with a smile, "now that's another tradition I never understood." He takes an agate from my hand, the one that was just in my mouth. "So this is what an agate looks like?"

I nod, still shocked by his presence. I want to smile but I don't let myself. Let him work for it.

"It's beautiful." He looks up at me. "And you found it right here, just lying on the road?"

"Yeah. We've found hundreds over the years. Thousands, maybe."

"It's like having your own seashore, I guess."

"Is that what you're doing, Jess? Looking for seashells?" Renny calls after her but she doesn't turn around. She keeps walking down the hill, her gaze tipped to the ground.

"So this is how you've been filling your days?" Dallas says, gesturing to the road, or maybe the sky.

I shrug. "It beats work."

"Wish I could say the same. We just finished that motel outside Edison last week. It came out pretty nice, too. If you're ever driving by, check out the roof. I spent three days nailing in those shingles." He mimes hammering a nail into his palm.

I nod. "Well, I'm glad it worked out for you, the job and everything."

"I'm getting by." He nods toward the truck. "And your uncles are keeping me busy."

Uncle Flint leans across Renny's lap. "You coming?" he says to Dallas.

"Yeah." Dallas walks backward, still facing me. "You should come by some time, if you're ever in the neighborhood."

"I live across the lake. I'm always in the neighborhood."

"You know what I mean. If you ever want to hang out."

I cross my arms. "I thought you were wrong for me, that this wasn't right."

"That's not exactly what I said."

"Well, that's what I heard."

"I miss seeing you, Nellie. I just want to be friends again."

"Is that what we were?"

Uncle Flint revs the engine. Dallas is about to climb back into the truck when he spins around.

"Hey, I've been meaning to show you those pictures." He reaches into his back pocket and pulls out two four-by-six prints. "The ones you took in the park that first day, of Serena and me."

He hands me the photographs, which are bent from living in his pocket. The first, a picture of the two of them, is exactly how I remember that moment: the brilliance of Serena's yellow dress and Dallas kneeling behind her, brushing the hair from her face. It makes me want to be a child again.

"She's grown up so much lately, but I only notice it in the photographs. It's like I can't see it with my own eyes." He blocks the sun with his hand.

"All parents say that."

"It's still true," he says, looking down at me.

"Let's go," Renny calls out, slapping the top of the cab.

Dallas grabs the photo and climbs into the back of the pickup truck. He leaves me with the second one, a double print, I guess.

"Keep it," he yells as the truck pulls away. "Something to remember me by."

I smile and follow him with my eyes, watching the truck until it drops behind the next hill. Does he really think I need a picture?

Now that he's gone I look down at the photograph. I was wrong, it's not the one with Serena. It's the second shot I took, the one of him alone, falling back against the oak tree. The strange thing is that his expression is surprisingly calm, like he doesn't know that he's lost his balance. No, it's more confident than that: he's aware of falling, but doesn't seem to care. Like a bird that drops from his nest, knowing he can fly.

The best part of Caitlin's adoption day party is the slide show at Aunt Maisie's. After the cake and ice cream, after the limeade toasts and opening the presents Caitlin will never wear, we all cram into her living room for a pictorial walk down memory lane. Like most country people, Aunt Maisie measures the passage of time by the changing seasons, which she captures on film and catalogs in spiral-bound photo albums. Each year she starts the slide show with photos from the previous year, laid out in chronological order: the first day of school, Halloween pumpkins, Cody's birth and adoption days, the buck Maisie shot that's bigger than she is, the first snow, Christmas morning, Cal setting up his icehouse, a neighbor's goat being born, the crocuses blooming, a robin's nest, the first swim in May (only the kids are brave enough to try), and finally, our arrival at the lake. She shows us these photographs, snapshots of a year in their lives, and tells herself that we are caught up now, that we've lived it as much as they have, and are now equal. It's as if we never left, like we've lived down the hill the entire time. It's the way we know we're still family.

The last picture on the first carousel is of Uncle Flint putting the raft into the water, one of the official markings of the beginning of summer. Aunt Maisie clicks past it to an empty slot, projecting nothing but light onto the empty screen. She gets up to change the carousel as we all wait in the dark.

"That's it?" my mother says. "No arrival shots this year?"

"You all came separately, what could I do?" Aunt Maisie takes her seat again. This second round is my favorite, a random sampling of shots from the past thirty years. Sometimes it's obvious, but often we have to guess who's who.

"Now comes the fun," Aunt Maisie says. "I found a lot of old stuff in Hettie's hope chest; we'll have to see if the kids can tell us apart."

The first slide is a black-and-white shot of a really chubby baby sitting in a wheelbarrow.

"Renny!" the sisters yell out in unison.

"No way, I was never that fat," Renny says, tapping his flat belly.

"Yeah, right," Uncle Flint says. "Ate nothing but cheese for the first three years."

Aunt Maisie advances the projector with a remote-control switch. The next slide is a group shot of all the cousins sitting on the front lawn in an inflatable raft. It's easy to find Marcus, Noah, and me, three brown bodies in a sea of pink and white. I'm wearing a dress with blue flowers on it and look like I'm about to cry.

"Aww, look at how cute Nellie was, with all those curls."

"Who's that girl next to Marcus? Was that me?" Caitlin asks.

"That's Tyler," Aunt Maisie says. "Dawn refused to cut his hair till he went off to kindergarten."

"Where am I?" Marley asks.

"You weren't born yet," Derry tells her. "Neither was Jake or Cody."

Marley looks back toward the screen. I can see her fingers in the air, counting. "So where's Jess? Wasn't she born?"

Derry tries to whisper. "Yes, but she didn't live out here."

"Nellie didn't live out here either, but there she is." Marley points to the screen with one hand and to me with the other.

"But she came to visit."

"Why didn't Jess come to visit?"

Derry takes Marley into her lap and starts whispering into her ear. Aunt Maisie advances the projector to the next slide: two couples standing in front of an old convertible, the girls dressed in pastel gowns with long white gloves. Both guys are wearing white tuxedo jackets and black bow ties. Prom night.

"Oh god," my mother says. "What it took to get those gloves on."

"And that dress—Mom had to practically sew it on to you." Aunt Maisie leans back, laughing. "I remember Palmer complaining on the dance floor about getting pinpricks every time he tried to dip you."

"He couldn't dance, that was the problem," Cal says.

"And you could?" Aunt Maisie asks.

"Look at my hair." My mother reaches up to touch her head. "I think it fell out of that twist as soon as the picture was taken."

"Well, riding in that convertible didn't help."

"All right, all right, we should have put the top up." Cal opens another beer. "I've been apologizing for twenty years, what else do you want, woman?"

I try to make out my father's face, but I can't see his expression in the dark. He clears his throat as we move to the next shot. This one's of a blonde toddler eating an ice cream cone. The ice cream has dripped all the way down to the elbow, making a chocolate stream the child's tongue is meticulously following. The swing set and a corner of the lake are in the background.

"Derry?" someone calls out.

"Nope," Aunt Maisie says. "She was never that skinny."

"Cody?" someone guesses.

"I never wore pink," Cody says. "Did I, Mom?"

"Is this a second cousin we don't know?" Tyler asks.

"No, you know her."

"Marley likes ice cream," Jake says. "Especially chocolate."

"It's not Marley." Uncle Flint shakes his head.

"It's Jess," Renny finally says. "I took that picture myself, down by the lake." He looks over at Maisie. "How'd you get it?"

"You must have sent it to Hettie. I found it in her things."

Renny sips his beer. "I don't remember doing that."

"You don't remember what you did last week," Uncle Flint says to him.

"Maybe Shelley sent it," my father offers.

"Shelley wasn't around that summer."

"Why not?" Jess sits up. "Where was she?"

"She went down to Florida to visit her folks. So I brought you up here."

"I was here as a baby? I was here with you?" Jess sounds like she doesn't believe him.

"You stayed in the cabin with Grandma and Grandpa," Aunt Maisie says. "Before Malcolm and Ginny bought it. You stayed in the same room you're staying in now. Isn't that funny."

"I forgot about that trip," my mother says to Jess. "You were such a sweet baby, so quiet."

"I was?" Jess looks shocked. "Shell always said I was loud, that I talked to myself even when I didn't know how to."

"No, you were just singing. Your father used to do the same thing when he was a baby."

Jess looks across the room at Renny. His eyes are locked on the screen, on the life-size image of his baby girl.

"Did you ever tell her about the swing set?" My father looks at Renny, who shakes his head.

"What swing set?" Jess asks.

"The one right there," my father says, pointing at the screen. "The one at the beach. Your father put it up so he could swing you to sleep at night."

And I always thought that swing set was ours.

"That's mine?" Jess says, struggling to grasp the idea of ownership.

Renny nods. "You always liked movement," he says softly. "Had to be going somewhere."

No wonder she always swings so effortlessly.

The next shot is of my parents, standing in the shallow waters of our beach. They both look skinny and young, so it had to be taken before I was born. My mother is standing on my father's shoulders, and he's holding on to her ankles, trying to stabilize her. Her arms are stretched out in front of her like she's looking for something to grab on to. Or maybe she's about to dive in. Even though she's about to let go, it's the first photograph I've seen where they're touching. It's long overdue, but it still makes me smile.

"Didn't you have a dock to jump off?" Cody asks.

"Your uncle was better than any dock," Aunt Maisie says. "He used to stand there like a tower and let everyone jump off. Oh, I never flew so high."

"No, not that day," my mother says. "We were playing chicken, remember? We had just beaten you and Cal."

Aunt Maisie laughs. "How can you remember all that?"

"My bathing suit," my mother says. "I only wore it that one time. It was too small and the straps kept falling down. Then I got pregnant with Marcus and never wore it again."

"Too bad, it looks great on you."

"It wasn't practical. It wasn't something a mother should wear."

"How old were you there, Aunt Ginny?" Caitlin asks.

"Nineteen, I guess, almost twenty. Not that much older than you guys."

"But you were married, that makes you seem older."

"Yes, I guess it does."

I'm no longer watching the screen as the slide show continues. Instead, I look at the people in the room, try to make pictures in my own mind, filling in the shadows with my own imagination. I decide for myself who's smiling, and who's about to cry; who looks for her likeness in every shot, and who's incapable of looking at himself; who is open to the past, and who will never tell the truth, even when it's captured in a photograph.

It's dark outside since the moon is gone, and we walk along the gravel road by instinct. My mother and Jess stayed to help clean up, so my father and I walk home alone. It feels like we haven't been alone together since the beginning of the road trip, before we picked up Jess, but I can't really remember if that's true. The silence between us is comfortable, like sitting next to him in the car. After a while he begins to whistle. He keeps starting the same song, but doesn't finish it. Not a good sign.

I feel his eyes on me and hear him take in a deep breath. He exhales into the colorless air.

"We're getting a divorce, Nellie." He fixes his eyes on the blackness in front of us, as if he can see in the dark.

"I know."

"Oh." He looks down at his feet, the straps on his sandals unbuckled. "Did she tell you?"

"No, it's just the way things have been looking."

For the first time I feel how cold the pebbles are on my bare feet. I remember how he used to give me piggyback rides down this same path, my head resting on his broad back.

"It's what I want, just so you know." He looks at me. "It was my decision to finally end it, not your mother's. She wanted to give it more time, but—" He cuts himself off. I wait, but he never finishes.

"I understand," I finally say, wondering how to make that statement true.

"You do?" He makes himself laugh. "You might be the only one."

We keep walking, the crunch of our feet on the gravel almost deafening.

"You need closure in order to move on."

"Closure?" he says, sounding like I'd said the word "denture" instead. "Is that what I need?"

At first I think he's angry, but then I feel him smiling in the darkness, like seeing someone laugh with no sound. "How'd you get so smart?" he says, combing out my hair with his fingers.

"Good genes," I say, copying a line his father used to say.

He slows down before we get to the cabin, like he's not ready to go inside, to be confined to a space with walls. We finally stop under the crab apple tree and face each other. The porch light is on, and it lights up half my father's face.

"We're going to have to sell the house, the one on Tremont Street, not this one. We'll always keep this for you kids, so you'll have some place that's yours, no matter what. We agreed on that." He runs his sandal over the ground, crushing the fallen apples. "Your mother's going to stay in Boston so you'll be in the same school district. You can go back with her now, or you can fly back after Labor Day. It's your decision."

"Where are you going to be?"

"I'm going to stay here for a while and work on my manuscript. When my sabbatical's over, we'll see."

"Can't I stay with you?"

"Well, the schools out here, I mean, they aren't exactly college prep."

"But it's only one year."

"It's part of your foundation."

"You're my foundation," I say, realizing this is beginning to sound like a love scene in some terrible movie. He reaches out to hug me as I try to stop myself from crying.

"I'll talk to your mother about it, okay? Maybe we can work something out."

"I can't go back there. She doesn't really want me."

"Don't say that, Nellie. Don't make our problems about you."

"She told me herself." I pull back. "She said she had to focus on her right now, not us."

"She's always going to be your mother. No matter where you live, you have to accept that." He takes his glasses out of his pocket and starts cleaning them on his shirt. "And in some ways she'll always be my wife. No piece of paper can change the way you feel." He puts on his glasses and climbs onto the porch.

"Well, what about Jess?" I call after him. "What's she going to do?"

"I don't know." He turns around. "Go with Renny, I guess. Wasn't that the plan?"

"Come on, he's no good for her. He doesn't know what to do with himself, let alone a teenager."

He shrugs. "He's her father."

"No, he's not. He just got her mother pregnant."

"You're out of line, Nellie."

"Why, because I'm the only one willing to say it?"

He waits at the door. "Think about her for a second. Maybe she needs him."

"She needs a parent."

"So that's what he'll become." He opens the screen door for me. "You know what my mother used to say? 'We are what people need us to be.' Maybe she's right."

I walk into the cabin without responding, determined to be different, to be what I need to be.

Chapter 21

It's sunny on the morning of my mother's departure, and hotter than it's been all summer. Dawn and Uncle Flint send her off with their annual pancake and venison-sausage breakfast while Aunt Maisie walks around with her camera, capturing the moment for next summer's slide show. We pack her things into the rental car while she hugs everyone, wishing them well in the next year, promising to return before they have missed her.

"The bus leaves at ten," my father says, looking at his watch, "and it's already twenty of." It's only a seven-minute drive to the station but I guess he really doesn't want her to miss this bus. He starts the car and slides a tape into the cassette deck.

"Okay, okay." My mother looks around. "Is that everything?" She picks up her purse and brushes it off. I take a step toward her to hug her good-bye. "Aren't you coming to the station?" Her question is more of a plea.

"I didn't think there was any room." Actually, I had wanted to make the good-bye as quick as possible.

"We'll make room," Jess says, restacking the boxes in the backseat.

I squeeze in next to her suitcase, remembering how Jess rode more than five hundred miles in the same position. It's strange to be back in this crowded rental car, pulling out of the driveway with my parents as if the summer were over and we were leaving the lake today. As if we were leaving together.

When we get to the bus station (it's really just a gas station with a ticket window) my father unloads the boxes into the storage compartment under the bus. My mother and I go up to the window.

"One ticket to the airport, please." She takes out her checkbook.

"Round-trip?"

"No, just one-way." She sounds like she's apologizing.

"Nine-fifty."

When she writes out the check she signs her name slowly, like she's spelling out the letters. I wonder if she'll change it back to Christiansen after the divorce. Even if I get married I will never change my name. I am a Kincaid for life.

The cashier hands her the ticket through the half-moon opening at the bottom of the glass window. "You're the only one getting on here," she says, "so you have your pick of the seats. He'll take off in about ten minutes."

My father stands next to the bus, holding up my mother's jacket. "Everything else is underneath. Just check it at the curb, that way you don't have to try to carry it all."

She takes the jacket and folds it over her arm.

"Here." My father hands her a twenty-dollar bill.

"I don't need any money, Malcolm."

"You'll need some cash for tipping the skycap. They don't take checks."

"Thanks." She tucks the bill into her jacket pocket, still letting him take care of her.

"Have a safe trip," he says. Then he touches her shoulder as if to tell her he really means it.

There's no bathroom at the station so I end up using the one on the bus. When I look out through the window my parents are no longer touching. My mother says something that makes him nod, and he takes a step backward. Then, just before he reaches the car, he changes his mind and steps toward her. He hugs her with one arm and kisses her quickly on the cheek, as if he just realized it might be the last time he'd touch her. When he pulls away her jacket falls to the ground.

When I come out of the bathroom my mother is struggling to open the window next to her seat. She seems tired already, as if this were the end of a long trip instead of just the beginning. After several attempts she abandons the window and picks up her purse.

"Damn, I forgot my book at the cabin." She drops the purse. "Oh well, I'll just buy a magazine at the airport."

"I'll send it to you if you want."

"No, you keep it," she says. "Read it when you're lonely or bored."

I sit down on the armrest of the seat behind her. "I already read it."

She laughs, resting her head on the seat. "It's poetry." She says the word like she's talking about a rare and beautiful flower. "You never read it just once."

Outside, the bus driver stands at the ticket window, laughing with the cashier. They speak as if there is no glass between them.

"Okay, then . . ." I stand up and walk toward the front of the bus, passing my mother's seat.

"Nellie, wait. Don't go yet."

I turn around to find her sitting on the edge of her seat. She tucks her hair behind her ears even though it doesn't need it.

"I've been thinking about our talk the other day, what you said about losing your innocence. I was wrong to let that happen, but I didn't know any better, I couldn't be any better." She stands up. "I'm sorry for that."

I look out the window, watching my father play with the dials on the car radio. She follows my glance, focusing on the man she will never hold again.

"There were things that I needed—"

"And the rest of us, what about our needs?" I ask.

"If you're worried about your father, don't. He doesn't need me, he never did."

"I needed you." I'm still not looking at her.

"And I was there," she says. "Maybe not those few months in second grade, but every other year I was there."

"And now?" I turn to look at her. "Where are you going to be now?"

She pauses, as if really thinking about the answer. "Do you need me now?"

I open my mouth but nothing comes out. I don't know if I still need her.

"Let me know when you figure it out," she says, touching my sleeve with her fingertips. She takes in a deep breath and smiles. "I couldn't have been all bad," she says. "Look how you turned out."

I shrug. "I'm not that great."

"Don't say that," she says. "You're one of the best things we ever did. Don't take that away from us." She steps into the aisle, looking smaller than she has in years.

"When I left for California that summer after high school, my mother brought me here to this same station. I'll never forget what she said when she put me on the bus: 'You have everything you need, Virginia. Right now. Don't let anyone tell you different.' "

She wraps her arms around me in a squeeze so tight I can hardly breathe. Her hair tickles my eyelashes, and for a second I think I could cry.

"I want you to remember that, when you're thinking about the past and all our mistakes. You have everything you need, Nellie, and you belong anywhere you want to be. Don't let anyone tell you differently."

When she pulls away, our hair is still entwined. She tries to separate it with her fingers, but a long strand of my hair stays with her, hanging from just above her ear. The color blends perfectly, and it looks like it's growing from her own head, the lone curl from a leftover perm. I wonder how long it will stay there, hanging onto the foreign strands of her straight hair, until it's blown away or just surrenders, dropping softly to the floor.

Once my mother leaves, I finally finish reading *Beloved*. I don't think I'll be able to dream for at least a week. I haven't felt this way since finishing *Invisible Man*. I don't know if I understand all of it, but that's nothing new. I don't understand much of my own story.

Sometimes my father will begin a poem on the edge of a napkin. He says he likes the way the ink bleeds into the cotton. He can't write on a typewriter, he needs to feel the weight of a pen, to watch his hand move across the paper. He says sometimes a line just comes to him, or an image, or even a sound, and he has to stop what he's doing to write it down, even in the middle of the night or during a class. Even if he doesn't know what it means. He has a notebook filled with these pieces, napkins waiting to grow into poems.

If I had a journal, this is what I'd write down:

Notes on Interracial Relationships—

1. The black woman is running.
2. The white man is making amends.
3. The black man is proud, proving something to the community.
4. The white woman is independent, making her own choice.
5. Where the white partners are idealistic, the black partners are realistic. They know they are fighting in a war, and will battle known (and unknown) enemies every day.
6. The white partner has the freedom to pretend she's not fighting. It is her choice.
7. The children are revolutionaries. There is no choice.
8. I am not made of brass.
9. Love. (It has to be there somewhere.)
10. I am not a mule.
    I am not a.
    I am not.
    I am.

Part III
The Cabin

I have Dutch, nigger, and English in me,
and either I'm nobody, or I'm a nation.

—Derek Walcott,
"The Schooner *Flight*"

Chapter 22

———✦———

The first book I remember reading to myself was *The Adventures of Huckleberry Finn*. My father lent me his copy, the unabridged version, and asked me to write a book report on it. It was summertime and the report had to be typed. Using his typewriter, I took three days to pound out a four-page synopsis of the plot, with a detailed breakdown of every character. I was nine.

I chose the book because I already knew the story, and was drawn to the devilish Huck, who had just the right blend of adventure and compassion to keep me interested. He also had a sense of self-preservation that I admired. My mother had introduced me to the children's version, condensed into a fourteen-page picture book, which I held in my lap as she read to me, refusing to turn the page until I had memorized each image and could close my eyes and re-create the scene: Huck and Tom whitewashing the old picket fence; the frayed straw hat that never left his head; the dilapidated shack that Huck called home; the corncob pipe he sucked on but never lit; and of course Huck and Jim on the raft, floating down the wide banks of the Mississippi on water drawn as black as Jim's skin. It was the raft that stuck with me the most, a symbol of the freedom and opportunity I wanted to have in my own life.

My dream came true on a fall day just after I turned five. I was playing on the front porch while my mother brought in the clean laundry from the clothesline. She went inside when the phone rang and I wandered over to the basket of clean sheets and towels. Within minutes I was standing on six of the towels in the middle of the driveway. I had laid them out like pieces of a patchwork quilt and was jumping from one to the other, hoping they wouldn't blow away or sink into the murky waters of the river our driveway had become. When my father came home he drove right through the laundry, destroying my raft and damaging the linens beyond repair. I guess I was lucky he didn't run me over, too. He blamed my mother for not watching me; she blamed him for driving recklessly. Either way, I had to be punished, and as we walked up to my bedroom together I knew that I was about to get my first spanking. I remember being thankful that it was going to happen in private.

It was cold and dark inside my room, and it seemed emptier than when I'd left it that morning. My bed had become as hard as the ground, the comforter a rough tarp against my hands. Even the stuffed animals looked mean, or to my guilty eyes, disappointed. I leaned over the bed, my cotton underwear the only thing between my butt and my father's large hand. I tried to imagine that I was walking through a patch of ripe strawberries, looking for the ones as big as my fist. Then I heard a knock on the door. I looked up to find Marcus standing in the doorway, his socked feet barely making a sound on the wood floors. He had his head down, his eyes locked on his feet.

"Don't hit Nellie, Dad." He spoke slowly. "Hit me. Hit me instead."

My father didn't respond. Marcus took another step into the room, his small body shaking as he tried to stand still. His hands were balled into fists at his sides. I could live a hundred years and never again have someone make such a gesture. I lay there motionless, afraid to look either of them in the face. I didn't want to see anger or love so closely. I heard my father clear his throat, and then shift his weight behind me. When I turned around he was leaning against the wall, looking out the window into the front yard. A tear had fallen from his left eye but it was trapped behind his glasses. He didn't move, he just stood there staring out the window, tears collecting behind a wall of glass.

My first lesson in loyalty.

*   *   *

Labor Day brings out the black people, the first to ever come to the lake who weren't related to me. My father decides to have a barbecue, but instead of inviting our neighbors from around the lake, he invites a few friends from Minneapolis, who in turn bring their neighbors. By noon our front yard is filled with women in lawn chairs and men sweating over charcoal grills, looking like a family reunion in rural Alabama. My cousins love all the excitement, and have pulled out every toy they've ever unwrapped in an attempt to entertain all the children. The raft is so heavy with people that it appears to be sitting only a few inches above the water.

I survey the view from the top of the yard and wonder what my grandparents would think if they were still alive. Grandma Floss, who loved parties and poetry and thought my father was probably too good for her daughter, would have loved to see such a turnout, but I'm not so sure about Grandpa Brant. Would he wish for the raft to sink, carrying all the brown bodies to the lake's muddy bottom, or would he fry his fish on their grills and play five-card stud until the sun set? The sad part is, I don't even know.

"Hey, Mama," a soft voice calls from behind me, "where've you been all my life?"

I turn around to find Lonnie Potts, one of my father's childhood friends, standing on the porch with a pitcher of lemonade and a plate of hot wings. He has the solid figure of a man who used to lift a lot of weights, and unlike my father and Oliver Scott, he has managed to remain a bachelor. When I was younger I wanted to marry him myself, but now I just wish he could replace one of my uncles. My first memory of him is the time he ran his hand down my back, pretending it was a saw. He said he wanted to cut me down the middle and take half of me home with him, and if my father was nice he'd leave him with the other half. It was the first time I thought of myself as two halves of a whole, as something that could be divided in two.

"Lonnie!" I run to give him a hug.

"So how have you been, Miss Nellie? Breaking hearts out here in the country?" He smiles the carefree smile of someone who loves children but has none of his own.

"Better than having mine broken, right?"

"I can see you've remembered some of my lessons." He laughs a deep laugh that doesn't match his soft voice. It makes sense that he's a musician, that he uses instruments to speak, instead of his voice. "We have to have a little talk, though . . ." He puts his arm around me as we walk toward the picnic tables. "What's up with all the white boys?"

I look around. "We're in rural Minnesota, Lonnie, what did you expect?"

"And the ones in your bedroom?"

He's talking about the pictures from *Teen Beat* that Jess pinned to the walls. "My cousin put those up," I say defensively.

"Where are all the brothers?"

I shrug. "There aren't any in the magazines."

"Okay, I need to have a talk with your daddy." He looks around the yard for my father. "Malcolm!"

My father's head pops up from behind the grill. Lonnie walks over to him, still yelling like he's on the other side of the yard.

"Why don't you buy your daughter an *Ebony* magazine?"

"Oh, Christ." My father shakes his head.

"What, you can't afford it?" Lonnie leans on his shoulder.

"Aren't you supposed to be on my side, Nellie?" he yells to me.

"I thought you didn't want me to pick sides," I say from across the yard, laughing as they argue over the smoking grill.

"I've seen your subscriptions." Lonnie starts listing with his fingers. "*The New Yorker, Sports Illustrated, Newsweek, Playboy,* even, yet you can't cough up a few dollars so your daughter can see some brown faces in a magazine? That's a shame, brother." He rubs my father's back with pity.

"No," my father says, " 'the Top One Hundred Black Bachelors in America,' that's a shame."

"Why you got to be jealous, man?"

"Why are you pretending you're in the top hundred?"

"Top hundred? Shit, I'm in the top ten."

"Man, you're sick." My father elbows him out of the way but I can still see the smile on his face. He seems to have lost almost ten years since this morning.

Jess sits alone, leaning against the trunk of an oak tree. She has a full rack of pork ribs on her plate and a huge smile on her face.

"Finally some real barbecue," she says, taking a greasy bite.

I gesture toward the yard. "And how about the people? Are they real enough?"

She shoots me a confused look, bits of pork and burnt barbecue sauce in between her teeth.

"Are they dark enough? Does their hair have enough kink?" I squat down next to her. "Are they really 'black'?"

She cleans her teeth with a plastic fork. "Of course they are."

"But did you see their cars? Some of them are driving BMWs," I tease her, remembering our conversation back in Iowa. "I think a few of them even went to college."

"I was wrong before, okay?" She bends the fork in her hand, almost breaking it. When she tries to straighten it out it won't go back. I hand her a new one from an empty place setting.

"Thanks, Nellie," she says. It's the first time I've ever heard her use my name.

She looks around the yard, taking in the scene as if it were air. "You know, we could be in Virginia right now. The food, the smell of the grill, the people—it's just like being at home."

Interesting that being in rural Minnesota with a bunch of black people finally makes her feel at home.

"Don't you miss it, though, being in a familiar place?" I ask her.

"Sure, sometimes. The times like these. The good times."

"Well, maybe this will become a regular thing out here, now that my mother's gone. Maybe that was his plan all along, to get some black people out here and to finally integrate Redwood County." I laugh, imagining faceless black people in speedboats, fishing off docks, and falling in love.

"You've already done that," Jess says, looking straight at me. "You integrate every town you walk through."

I make myself laugh. "Are you kidding? I'm not even integrated myself. The only time I feel black is in a room full of white people, and the only time I feel white is in a room full of black people. And unfortunately, I'm never in both rooms at the same time."

"That's a shame," Jess says. "It should be the opposite, you know. You should be at home anywhere, everywhere."

I think about that for a moment, wondering if it could ever be true. If a child can integrate a family, does that family then integrate the town, that town the state, that state the country? If so, we are on our way to a blended world, where people like me not only exist, but are held in high regard, becoming the bridge that connects separate islands, a steel frame built to sway or expand with the changing weather, but never to crumble and fall.

Renny walks by, trying to light a cigarette with an empty lighter. Jess reaches into her pocket and tosses hers at him. He lights the cigarette, then walks over to return the lighter.

"Thanks, kid." He rubs his hand on her head. "Way to look out for your old man." He nods toward the tree. "What, are you guarding trees now?"

"What?" Jess says.

"The way you're sitting there, I figure maybe you don't want anyone else to climb it."

"Please, she won't even climb it herself," I say. "She hasn't even made it up to the tree house, and that has a ladder."

"Why not? You scared of heights, in this little tree?" Renny leans his head back to look at the top of the tree.

"I'm not scared. I just don't know what the big deal is. I can see the world just as well from down here."

He looks down at her. "I used to think that, too. Until I started climbing the redwoods in Northern California. Now I'm not talking about some regular old tree here, I'm talking about the tallest trees on earth. Skyscraper tall. They don't even have branches for the first one hundred feet so you gotta use pulleys and harnesses like you're rock climbing. That's something to be afraid of, when you know you're going against nature, against what's supposed to be humanly possible."

"Why do it then, if it goes against all that?"

" 'Cause it's so fucking amazing. To be up there looking down at the world, where everything's so small and insignificant. It gives you instant perspective." He leans against the tree. "We're not all that special, human beings, we're here seventy, eighty years, maybe. That's just a blip. That's like two feet on a redwood tree."

"It sounds crazy if you ask me."

He shrugs. "You'll have to decide for yourself. When you're standing beneath one." Then he touches her shoulder before he walks away.

He doesn't see it, but he actually makes her smile.

Playing croquet is one of the few lake activities that reminds me of my mother. She loves to play, and used to keep the field set up for days, making sure everyone played at least one round. She wouldn't quit until she'd knocked each of our balls into the lake, forcing us to walk through the lily pads in order to retrieve them. She even made us stand in the shallow water to hit them out, claiming that those were the official rules. One time every player except her was standing in the water looking for their ball, when she knocked hers against the final post and won. She took a picture of us and called it "Clamming." I wonder why Aunt Maisie has never shown that one during a slide show.

We're still playing croquet when Luke arrives in his speedboat. I walk down to the dock to greet him, forcing myself to be nice to his cousin Chad, who has always been somewhat of a bully, even though he's small for his sixteen years. He is also Melanie's younger brother, another reason I don't like him that much. Chad does a double-take when he sees that most of our guests are black. He stares at the kids in the water, seeming surprised that black people can swim.

"Would you rather go swimming?" I ask him, nodding toward the lake.

"No, no, croquet's fine." He picks up a mallet and swings it like a baseball bat. Why do men love to hit things?

We convince Jake and Marley to go swimming and have Luke and Chad replace them in the game. Things are calm until Chad knocks Derry's ball into the garden. She claims he cheated and never even went through the ring; he calls her a liar. Luke has to calm him down behind the chokecherry tree before we can resume play. Chad wins the first two games with a smug smile that I am determined to get rid of. My opportunity comes halfway through the next game, when our balls are vying for the same position. I have the chance to go through the ring and advance my ball or hit his ball and knock him wherever I want. I choose to knock him. He's immediately pissed and starts walking toward the garden, assuming I will hit his ball in that direction. Thinking of my mother, I step on my ball and knock his right off the field and into the lily pads next to the dock.

"What the hell was that?" he yells, storming over to me.

"That was a knock," I say calmly. "Don't worry, you can hit it out from the water."

"What are you, nuts? You think I'm standing in those lily pads to get your fucking ball? No way."

"Come on, Chad, it's just a game." Luke gestures with his stick, which Chad slaps out of the way.

"Yeah, well, fuck this game." He walks down to the water and tosses his mallet into the lily pads.

"Are you crazy? That's a fifty-dollar mallet." I follow him down to the water's edge. "You better jump in and get it."

"Sorry, I don't have my swimsuit on. Why don't you ask one of them to go get it. If those niggers can swim that far." His smile is a slap across my face.

"What?" I stare at him, feeling my face get hot. "What'd you say?"

Chad shrugs. "Relax, they didn't even hear me."

I take a step toward him. "Do you think this is a fucking tan?" I point to my face, my finger shaking.

Chad looks at me, seeming to see me for the first time.

"I was only joking. Luke, tell her I was only kidding around."

"Let's go." Luke nods his head toward their boat, refusing to make eye contact with me. When Chad steps onto the dock, he mumbles something under his breath. The only word I can make out is "nigger," shooting from his mouth like spit.

Before I can even think of what to do, I find myself tackling Chad into the lake. We land together in the shallow water, and he instantly begins to sink under my weight. I pull him up and turn him around, start slapping his face like he's a drowned victim I need to revive. I hit him so hard that it feels like I'm slapping a block of ice. He tries to swim away, but I grab his shirt with the other hand, scratching at his hairless chest. I see the blood come in and the water wash it away, trying to cleanse him. I know there must be noise around me, people yelling, at least, but I hear none of it. The only thing I can hear is my heartbeat.

I don't know who finally pulls me off. Maybe Luke or Tyler, maybe even my father. When I'm lifted out of the water, my hair is covering my face and I cannot see. I stand on the dock and feel the water pouring off my clothes, running down my legs in rivers. I push the hair from my eyes and look down at my feet, outlined in water that bleeds into the weathered wood. I'm about to take a step toward the shore when I change my mind. Instead, I walk to the end of the dock and dive back into the lake, trusting that the water will hold me when nothing else can. I swim with labored strokes, as if swimming upstream, but when I finally lift my head I am almost at the other side of the lake. I hear someone calling my name, but I don't look back. When I get to the shore I stumble out of the water as if I've never walked before. My legs sink into the loose sand, two anchors drawn to the bottom. I make it to the edge of the woods as quickly as I can, then disappear into the dense pine trees, making a path as I go.

He doesn't ask any questions. When I finish my first cup of tea, Dallas fills my mug again, then returns to the piece of wood he's been carving with a pearl-handled switchblade. He doesn't take his eyes off me.

"I have something for you." He reaches into his pocket and pulls out a small, round object the size of a peanut M&M. When he hands it to me I realize it's an agate.

"So you found one," I say, holding it up to the light.

"It found me, actually, when I was getting gas. I dropped my keys on the ground and there it was."

"Eggs like this are really rare; you should keep it." I hold it out to him.

"It reminded me of you," he says. "See the top there, the way the rings are darker around the edges like the trunk of an old oak tree. That's how your eyes look in the sunlight."

"My eyes look like an oak tree?" Obviously, he doesn't know how to compliment women.

"The rings," he says, drawing a circle in the air with the knife. "Just the rings."

I stare at the agate again, trying to see something of myself in the almond-colored rock. Could any part of me be so clean and beautiful?

Behind the bonfire, in the shadow of the flames, I notice the empty field where the marijuana plants used to grow.

"You've been busy." I nod toward the field.

"Nah, your uncles did all that. They've been picking that shit for weeks now, drying it out in the barn. Flint said the early spring really gave him a jump-start."

"So what happens to the field now?"

"They turn over the soil. Clean it up and get rid of all the evidence."

"I thought the real evidence was in the barn."

"Well, right, but once it dries he'll just wrap it up and take it out west."

"I guess that's Renny's job, huh?"

"I guess. I don't really ask a lot of questions. The less I know the better."

I wonder if Renny's going to take it when he leaves with Jess, her duffel bag jammed into the trunk along with the pot. When did children become less valuable than cargo?

"So how's the tea?"

"Fine." I stick my finger into the water but it's still too hot to drink. I suck the tea off my finger and pretend to be interested in the sky.

"How long are you going to sit there until you tell me what happened?"

I exhale into the mug and let the warmth from the steam cover my face; the pores in my skin open up like a fist relaxing. I lean back onto the log that doubles as a deck chair, wondering how wood has the strength to grow so tall, so hard.

"I just beat this kid up," I say nonchalantly, pulling a piece of bark off the log. I try to roll it into a ball but it crumbles into dust in my hand.

"He must have deserved it." Dallas shaves a piece of bark off his carving in one stroke. The inside is a pale yellow, like the fruit of a Golden Delicious apple.

"Yeah." I rub my hands together, sprinkle the log with its own dust. My palms sting, like they've been asleep for hours. "My hand still hurts."

Dallas nods. "It'll hurt for a while. You should ice it so it doesn't swell."

I blow on it, as if my breath were frozen. "So I guess you've hit a lot of people?"

"I've been in a lot of fights."

"How'd you feel after?"

"Sore." He puts his knife away and comes over to me, sitting next to me on the log. "Here, let me look at it." He takes my hand and squeezes it sideways. "Does this hurt?"

I nod, trying not to wince.

"Open it up now, move the fingers." I extend all the fingers, wriggle them around. "You'll be fine," he says, letting my hand drop onto his leg. I don't move it. Heat spreads through my hand, as if his leg were just taken out of the fire.

"Your hair is so straight when it's wet," he says. "Just like mine."

"When I was little my mother used to comb it out at night, after my bath. Then she'd braid it while it was still wet so I wouldn't cry as much. I was seven before I realized I had curly hair."

He reaches out to tuck a stray piece behind my ear. His hands smell strong and spicy, like homemade soap or a soup you can only get in Chinatown. What wood could be so fragrant?

"It's grown a lot this summer," he says. "I wish mine grew that fast."

"Yeah, I guess I should cut it."

"No, let it grow. It's too pretty to cut off." He tugs softly at the ends, as if to help it grow faster.

"Why do men always say that? It's the same hair, even if there's less of it."

"But you can't braid it when it's short. That's the difference." He turns me around so my back is facing him, then starts combing my hair out with his fingers. His touch is so delicate I can barely feel it. I wish my mother had had his hands.

"So this is what it takes for you to come visit, you hitting some kid?"

"I wanted to come before, you know that. I just didn't want to bother you."

"You don't bother me, Nellie. You confuse me. There's a difference."

"What's that supposed to mean?"

"I don't know. I thought I knew what I wanted, what you

wanted, but then . . . things just don't make sense anymore. One night you're with me, the next you're out with your boyfriend—"

"My boyfriend?" I turn around quickly, tugging my hair through his fingers.

"Come on, Nellie. I've seen you two together all summer."

"Where, at the pig roast? That was two months ago."

"Not just there. At the Tower at Blackfoot Lake, at the drive-in . . ."

Has he been spying on me? "Why didn't you ever say hi?"

"I tried to once, but you looked kind of busy." I can feel him smiling at the back of my head.

"And what about you," my voice gets louder, betraying me, "going out with Melanie that night, letting her hang all over you—"

"Are you kidding?" He laughs. "I'm not interested in Melanie. That girl is an open book, one I've read dozens of times." He separates my hair into three chunks and finally starts braiding them together. "Plus, she could drink a sailor under the table. I can't be with any woman who likes the bottle as much as she likes herself." He sweeps his hand across my forehead with every twist, trying to catch stray hairs. His fingertips feel hot and flawless, like the pads of a kitten's paw.

"Look, it's not what you think, between Luke and me. . . ."

"You don't owe me an explanation. You're just acting like a typical teenager."

"I'm not a typical teenager." I reach back to feel the beginnings of the braid, the smooth cords too perfect to grow from my head.

"You know what I mean. It was the same for me the first time, with Serena's mom."

"But it's not the same." I shake my head, feel the strength of his arms drawn through the braid. "He's not going to tattoo my name onto his arm. I'm not going to have his baby."

Dallas pulls at the braid, making sure it's tight enough. "I'm just trying to say that I understand, that's all."

"And I'm just trying to say that it's not what I wanted. It just sort of happened."

He shrugs. "That's life, that's how it always works."

"Then why didn't it work that way with us?" I turn around, the braid swinging behind me like a cat's tail. I can't believe how light my head feels. "Why did you push me away that night at the lake? Don't tell me it's because I'm too young."

He exhales slowly. "Well, you are young, Nellie. Or I'm old. But either way there's a gap between us—"

"My parents are nine years apart."

"And look how that turned out."

"You think that was about age difference?"

"Maybe. I don't know." He reaches for my arm, holding the elbow tight like he thinks I'm going to run away. "Look, what I'm talking about is an experience gap. We're just not in the same place."

"We're both here."

"But for how long? You're only here for the summer and I don't know where I'm going to be next week."

"The summer's already over and I'm still here. I'm not going anywhere."

He looks at me, not quite following.

"They're selling our house, back in Boston, and my father and I are staying here. My mother already left."

He releases his grip on my elbow but keeps his hand resting there like a paperweight, so I don't blow away. "You're staying?"

"At first they didn't want me to, but I wanted to stay with my dad. I wanted to stay here." I touch my head softly, like I'm wearing a wig that could fall off any second.

He nods toward the braid. "Don't worry, it looks good. Makes you look older." He smiles, knowing he walked into that. "But it still doesn't change anything."

"I know. Nothing ever changes anything. And then suddenly everything's just different."

He laughs. "You've got a pretty good handle on the world, Nellie. A hell of a lot better than I did when I was your age."

"That doesn't count—you were getting drunk and stealing cars when you were my age."

"Exactly, and now I'm drinking herbal tea and roofing houses." He takes a sip from his mug. "See how things can change, if you really want them to—"

I cut him off by putting my mouth on his, covering his lips with my own. He tastes like how the tea smells when it's brewing, fruity but not as sweet as the mango itself, more like how I'd imagine the leaves to taste: crisp, oily, somewhat bitter, alive. He kisses me back with an intensity that I wasn't expecting. It reminds me of drinking the red wine in Iowa, of tipping the glass to get the last drops, of wanting to chew on the cork just to get another taste. Passionate, like a good-bye kiss at a train station, like something out of a black-and-white movie, actors rehearsing for hours to make it look spontaneous. Like how you kiss someone when you think you're never going to kiss him again.

He holds my head in his hands, traces small circles on my neck with his fingertips. My heart starts to race, the beats tripping over themselves. He must feel my quickening pulse and imagine a newborn kitten lying in his hand, the body no more than a sheet draped over the pounding heart. I breathe him in, trying to take every piece of the night into my expanding lungs, memorize even the scent.

He was carving a piece of ginger.

Chapter 23

———◆———

The canoe rocks when I lift myself out of it, threatens to toss me into the shallow water of the outlet. I could have paddled right into our beach, but I'm not in the mood to run into anyone, to explain where I'm coming from at this time of night and whose canoe I've borrowed. Even Dallas doesn't know I took it, since he was asleep in front of the fire and I sneaked away without saying good-bye. I can believe that I stayed out past my curfew, that I ate sunfish grilled over an open fire, and that I held on to Dallas like he was a balloon I didn't want to float away, but I can't believe that I fell asleep. That I trusted him enough to fall asleep.

My feet are still in the sand when I hear the swing, it's rusty chains strained in flight. I see two silhouettes in the distance: one leaning against the swing set, arms braced along the top bar, the other sitting on the swing, not moving. My father is the one standing, his frame recognizable in any light, but the other person, sitting underneath him the way one might sit underneath a tree, is a mystery. Maybe it's Jess, although I can't imagine her staying still for so long. I sneak up to get a better view, hiding in a forest of intersecting shadows.

"I can't do it." The voice is low, apologetic. "I thought I could, I wanted to, but I can't." A bottle lifted to an opened mouth. Renny.

"You haven't even tried."

"You don't have to try walking on water to know you're going to sink. Some things you just know."

"You don't know her." My father lets go of the swing set. It shakes as if he'd dropped it.

"I know myself. That's enough." Renny kicks out his feet, starts swinging a bit. My father turns to walk away, but Renny stops him with his voice.

"Do me a favor, will you?"

"Don't you owe me enough?"

"Wait until I'm gone to tell her."

My father takes a step back. "Are you kidding me?"

"Just wait until I'm gone, then you can say whatever you want."

My father shakes his head. "I'm not telling her, Renny. I'm not cleaning this up for you."

"She looks up to you. She trusts you."

"But I'm not her father." He walks away, letting his sandals scrape along the sidewalk.

"Her loss." Renny finishes his beer, then tosses the bottle onto the grass. When it rolls into a plastic bucket I hear him whisper, "Two points."

He leans back in the swing, his legs together and pointed toward the stars, frozen in a half-pike, a diver with no pool. After a few seconds his legs drop. He catches them before they hit the ground and starts pumping with the enthusiasm of a child, determined to build speed from a standstill. He lowers his head and pushes into the wind, tries to knock down all resistance with the strength of his face, the fortitude of his small frame. He soars through the sky like a bird on a leash, the swing pulling him back when he threatens to fly too high, the chain clipping his wings in midflight.

Even though I try to catch it, the screen door slams behind me as I sneak into the cabin. I can feel my father's presence in the shadows, before I make out his frame on the couch.

"Hi." I greet the darkness with a bowed head.

"Where have you been?" His voice is as sharp as a blade of grass.

"I went for a walk around the lake."

"That's a pretty long walk."

"I needed to clear my head." I reach back to feel the braid and wonder if he will say anything. When he stands up the whole room creaks.

"Jess told me what happened, what the boy said." He walks across the room, stopping in front of me. "Do you think you can solve all your problems by punching someone in the face?"

I look down at my hands, the palms still sore. "No."

"If you try to hit every person who calls you a nigger or thinks you're a 'nigger' or writes 'nigger' across your locker, you're going to spend your whole life fighting people. I didn't raise you to use your fists, Nellie, I raised you to use your mind."

I look up at him, blinking quickly to stop the tears. "What should I have done, sat down and had a conversation with him?"

His face becomes a scowl. "I'm not concerned with him, or any other boy who comes in here and thinks his opinion is the god-damn law. My concern is with you. My responsibility is to you."

"I didn't know what else to do. It all happened so fast." I wipe a tear before it falls, pretending to remove an eyelash.

"How many times have you seen me hit somebody?"

I look away, hoping this is a rhetorical question.

"How many times?"

"None."

"What?" He cups his ear.

"Never. I've never seen you hit anybody."

"And why do you think that is? Do you think I never get angry?"

I sink into the wall, which feels as cold and pliable as clay. "I know you get angry."

"Right. And yet I never let that anger translate into violence. Do you want to know why? Because I don't want to give them an excuse. An opportunity to say I'm inferior or uncivilized, or to look at me as if I were a monster. I'm not one of them, you know that, but I'm playing by their rules—I have to if I want to succeed, that's the way this country was built." He leans in and lowers his voice like he's telling me a secret. "Listen, I'm not saying that he didn't deserve it. I'm certain that he did. But you shouldn't be the one to punish him, you shouldn't let his hatred become your own."

"How do you do that? How do you not hate people who hurt you?"

He hesitates. "I don't hate your mother."

"But you could. You have the right to."

"And who would that help? Not me, not her, not you or your brothers. So why bother? Hating someone who hurt you doesn't make your pain go away. Haven't you figured that out by now?"

"But it doesn't seem fair. It's like she got away with something."

"Your mother has suffered, too, Nellie, in ways you weren't around to see." He takes off his glasses and rubs the mark they've left on the bridge of his nose. The skin there is darker from decades of holding the weight. "When Marcus was born and we were living in San Francisco, three miles down the road from her aunt, the one she had lived with until she met me, the one whose children she took care of—did you know she wouldn't give your mother any of her children's old clothes or toys? And what we did get, the crib and the stroller, we had to pay for, like we were strangers?" He cleans his glasses with a napkin but doesn't put them back on. "So, yes, she made mistakes, she betrayed me, but she was also betrayed. She's flawed, like all of us. She's human."

I cross my arms and take a deep breath.

"I knew. I saw them." Tears well up in my eyes. My father reaches for me but I pull away. "I didn't tell you, I didn't tell anyone."

"It's okay, Nellie. It wasn't your job to tell." He holds my face in his hands. "Listen, you didn't do anything wrong."

"I was afraid." Tears are streaming down my face. "I'm still afraid."

My father hugs me, both arms tight around my back. "It's okay, Nellie. I don't blame you."

"But maybe if I had said something, if I had done something, you wouldn't have wasted all those years—"

"Stop, don't say that. I don't have any regrets about that decision, okay? I forgave your mother, I took her back, and we tried to move on. We have a lot of good memories, we shared all those years, and just because we're splitting up now doesn't mean that was all a waste. We all need to move forward now, not back. And that includes you." He lifts my face up to meet his. "You have to forgive her, okay? And you have to forgive yourself."

I nod, wiping my face with my sleeve.

"You're strong enough to do this. I know you are."

I tuck my hands into my pockets, the flesh still tender. "Why does everyone think I'm so strong?"

"You're a survivor, Nellie, and you've got tremendous will. How else could you have survived this family?"

I give into a smile. Then I reach behind my head and start pulling out my braid, one twist at a time.

"No, don't take it out yet." He shakes his head slightly. "It reminds me of when you were a little girl. How your mother used to fix it after your bath."

"I'm not a little girl."

"I know," he says, tucking the damp strands behind my ears. "I know."

Later that night I find Jess in the bedroom, standing on the top bunk in order to take down a poster of Duran Duran. She picks the tape off each corner with surprising delicacy and wraps the poster so tight it could be used as a weapon.

"Sick of them watching you undress?"

"Nah, I just figure I should get ready. Summer's officially over, you know."

I notice her duffel bag packed in the corner, the seams bursting.

"Besides, every time I see Renny he's got this stressed-out look on his face. I want to be ready whenever he says the word."

"So you're still planning on going with him?"

She shrugs. "Why not? There's nothing back in Roanoke calling my name. At least with him I get to see another part of the country."

"Maybe you should give it another chance back home. Don't you miss school and your friends, your mother, maybe?"

"In case you forgot, I got kicked out of school, and as far as my friends go, I promised them a postcard from Disneyland and I can't go back empty-handed." She climbs down the ladder, the poster held in her teeth. When she gets to the floor she spits it out. "I do miss Shell sometimes—when we play cards, or when I hear someone swearing in a movie. But then I think, You know what, she doesn't miss me. Shit, she probably hasn't even realized that I'm gone yet." She walks into the closet. "You really expect me to go back to that?"

I sit on the edge of her bed, twisting the sheets around my hands, and say nothing.

"So where'd you disappear to?"

"I just needed to get away from here. Uncle Flint has some land on the other side of the lake—"

"Yeah, I know, Renny told me all about it. He was bragging, like he wanted me to be proud of him."

"Well, Dallas is staying there. We got to talking and . . ."

"That's what I figured." She sits down next to me. "Don't you get confused, going back and forth between him and Luke? It seems like a lot of work."

"I don't know," I say, "it just kind of happened. I didn't plan it this way." I grab the edge of the bed. "They're so different, you know, and I'm different when I'm with them. It's hard to know which one makes more sense."

"Are you in love with either of them? With both of them?" She looks so concerned I realize I have to tell her the truth.

"I like Luke a lot, I care about him. We have fun together and I'm comfortable with him. But I don't think about him all the time when I'm not with him. And he doesn't make me feel all sick and scared inside. At first I thought that was a good thing, that I wasn't as vulnerable then. But that sick feeling, that terrified feeling, I get that all the time when I'm with Dallas, and it makes me feel like I'm alive."

"Well, there you go, there's your answer."

I lie back on the bed and cover my face. "But he's nineteen and he's got a little kid. I don't even have my driver's license. I'm not ready for all that." I look at the cracks in the wall and the peeling wallpaper, and wonder what it would take to fix them.

"Don't stay with Luke because he's easy, because he doesn't scare you. That's not fair to him. You might make him feel all sick and scared—shit, I know you do—and he deserves that back. Everybody does."

I stretch out on the bed and tuck my hands behind my head. "I've been pissed at my mother for almost half my life. I've been judging her and blaming her; I've been hating her. But what she did when I was a kid, how's that any different from what I'm doing now?"

"Come on, it's not the same. She was married. She had a family. She hurt a lot more people."

"So I'm better than her because I'm hurting fewer people? I don't want to hurt anyone."

"So stop. Figure out what you want and go after it. And don't compromise. I think that's why adults are all fucked up and depressed. They think that growing up is more like giving in. Don't do that, not if you know what you want."

I look up at the ceiling. "But that's all I've ever done. Christ, I am a compromise."

"No." Jess speaks as surely as I've ever heard her. "Maybe that used to be true, but that's not true anymore. Look around, look at where you are and who you're living with. You got what you wanted." Jess picks the rolled-up poster off the floor and taps it softly against her hand, a hollow beat.

Maybe she's right. Maybe I have stopped compromising. And now, like it or not, it's her turn.

Renny packs up his car before the sun rises, the dark the only friend he's ever trusted. He doesn't see us in the field, isn't expecting witnesses at such an early hour, but we are here nonetheless, choosing the silence of the cornfield instead of our restless beds. I didn't even have to wake Jess up; she was lying with her eyes open, reading the underside of the bunk bed. She left the cabin without an argument and followed me into the field automatically, as if we were migrant workers who spent every sunrise picking cold fruit off rigid stalks. She didn't even stop to put on shoes.

We hear him start the engine, watch him back out of the driveway with his lights off. He turns them on once he's away from Aunt Maisie's house, shining a spotlight onto our distant faces as if he were the one catching us. As he approaches, he slows down with slight hesitation, like someone lost in a bad neighborhood and afraid to ask for directions. The backseat of his car is filled with duffel bags, and his dog, Wolf, is strapped in the passenger side. He rolls to a stop beside us, and leans his head out the window.

"Hey." He taps on the side of the car with an open hand, not quite committing to a wave. His arm is dark against the faded yellow of his old VW, a picker's tan from hours in the fields with Uncle Flint.

"Hey," Jess says, taking in the site of the packed car. I look up but don't say anything, trying to make myself invisible.

"So I'm taking off," Renny says. "Gotta make it to Idaho tonight so I couldn't wait." He gestures to the back of the car. "Got a full load."

I wonder if he's talking about his clothes and fishing gear, or the pounds of marijuana hidden in the trunk where a spare tire should be.

"You're leaving right now?" Jess asks. "Alone?"

"Yeah. Cops are less likely to stop you in the morning. They don't think the criminals like to get up early."

Jess stares at him. "I'm up," she says, just above a whisper.

He drops his gaze. "Maybe next summer, okay?"

Wolf barks and tries to squirm out of his seat belt. Renny tightens it and pats him on the head, scratches behind his ears. Then he looks back at Jess.

"Come here, I got something for you." He digs into his shirt pocket and pulls out a hundred-dollar bill, holding it up between two fingers. It flaps in the wind like a miniature flag. Jess doesn't react.

"What, you don't need it?" he asks.

Jess shrugs. "It's not my birthday or anything."

"So it's a little early. Come on, take it."

"It's a little late," Jess says. "My birthday's in February."

"I know when your birthday is. I meant early for next year."

"Shucks," Jess says as she walks toward him. "And here I was hoping for a convertible." She runs her hand along the roof.

Renny looks up at her, squinting against the rising sun, or maybe the brightness of her face.

"So how long are you going to stay out here?"

"I don't know," Jess says. "Till they kick me out, I guess. That's usually when I decide to leave." She tucks the hundred-dollar bill into her bra.

"You must get that from your mother," he says, lighting a cigarette. "I always leave early—that way you know they're going to miss you."

"Really?" Jess says. "I hadn't noticed." Then she leans toward him, like she's going to kiss him good-bye, but ends up plucking the cigarette from his lips. She takes a drag from it and then offers it back to him.

"Keep it," he says. Then he pulls out his pack and lights another one. They each let their cigarettes dangle from the corners of their mouths, finally having something in common.

"Well, drive safe." Jess taps on the roof of the car. "Don't get arrested."

"You neither." He smiles at her like a friend or an old running mate, but not a father. "And say hi to your ma for me when you get back home. Be sure to give her my best." He reaches his hand out as if he's going to touch her, but at the last second swipes at a mosquito.

"Sure," Jess says. "I'll do that." She spits onto the ground, just missing his tire.

"See ya." He nods in my direction before putting his foot on the gas. He pulls away quickly, kicking up a cloud of dust in his wake. Jess watches until he turns onto the highway, his car disappearing with the road. She puts her cigarette out in the gravel and smooths over his tire tracks with her bare foot. I'm surprised by how dark her feet have gotten during the summer, during her time with me, as if I'm rubbing off on her and slowly making her black.

We finish picking the corn in silence, listening to the dragonflies as they fight for position on the stalks. It feels warmer as the sun begins to climb up the sky, and I can already tell that the weather will be perfect for the rest of the day.

Jess finally speaks. "He wasn't even going to say good-bye."

She snaps a piece of corn off the stalk. When I look up, she's holding it in her hand like a knife.

Chapter 24

It's mid-September and the trees are already turning, trading in their green leaves for a new color scheme: burnt oranges and honey browns, the violence of a cranberry red. My favorite is the occasional yellow leaf, a canary hanging from a thin branch.

Jess and I are sitting beneath the maple trees, staring up at their outstretched limbs. They are always the first trees to turn, their leaves so brilliant that from across the lake they might look like they're on fire.

"I love the colors out here," Jess says. "Nobody could paint that."

"Don't the leaves change in Virginia?"

"I don't know," she says. "I've never noticed."

I lie back and contemplate a nap right here in the middle of the lawn.

"It's too quiet," Jess says. "Where is everyone?"

"Uncle Flint took his whole family down to Hettie's place to clean up the house for the real estate agent. Everyone else is at Cody's football game. I think my father even went."

"It's kind of sad when nobody's here."

"We can go to the game if you want."

"No, I might as well get used to being alone." Jess sits up. "At least I can smoke in the open." She lights a cigarette, tossing the match on the ground. When the grass threatens to catch fire she stomps it out with her bare foot. Surprising what a few months can do.

A splash from the other side of the lake interrupts the silence.

"What was that, a loon?" I don't look up.

Jess glances at the water. "That's a big-ass loon. I'd say it looks more like a seal."

"This is fresh water. I bet it's just someone out doing laps."

"Yeah," Jess says, drawing on her cigarette. "That special someone."

I sit up to get a better view, watching Dallas as he powers through the water. There is something deliberate about his strokes, the timing as precise as a machine. In the last twenty yards I see him take only one breath.

"Jesus Christ, can he swim," Jess says, shaking her head.

He glides into the beach and climbs out of the water fully dressed.

"You always swim in your clothes?" I call out.

"I wasn't planning on swimming," he says, gesturing toward his canoe, which lies in the grass behind me.

"Sorry." I cover my mouth. "I forgot to bring it back."

"Where's your uncle?" he asks, trying to catch his breath.

"He's at the farm, in St. James."

"How far is that?"

"A few hours. Why, what happened?"

"Some guys just showed up at the clearing, undercover cops, I'm guessing. I heard them say they'd been watching him for weeks, seemed to be pretty angry that all the evidence was gone."

"And they let you go?"

"They never saw me. Not today, at least." He wrings the water from his shirt. "I'm taking off, I just wanted to give your uncle a heads up. I owe him that much."

"Wait a minute." I stand up. "If the evidence is gone, what's the problem?"

Dallas points to the barn.

"But I thought Renny took it."

"Not everything. Stuff's still drying in there, maybe half the crop. That's a hell of a lot to get busted with."

"Why don't we just call him at Hettie's?" Jess interjects.

"There's no phone in the house," I say. "They turned it off when she died."

"So there's no way to get in touch with him?" Dallas asks.

I shake my head.

"Well, there's nothing I can do then." He runs his fingers through his hair and for the first time, it stays out of his eyes. It has finally grown.

Jess looks worried. "And what about when the cops show up here?"

"Just tell the truth: you don't know anything." Dallas heads for his canoe. "I wish I could say the same."

"Dallas, wait." I run after him. "This is insane, you can't just leave."

He turns to me. "Listen, Nellie, this isn't a game, okay? Your uncle chose to take this risk; hell, maybe that's why he did it in the first place, but I didn't. I'm not getting locked up again, I can't."

"But you didn't do anything."

"I did enough."

He gives me a quick hug, then kisses me hard on the forehead. It feels like his lips could break the skin.

"I'm sorry to leave like this." He runs his finger down my cheek, tracing tears that haven't yet fallen.

"Where are you going, back to the reservation?"

"I don't know, for a few nights, maybe. That's not home for me anymore." Then he lowers his voice to a whisper. "This isn't it, okay, this isn't the end."

I nod, incapable of speech.

He drags the canoe into the water and gets in. "You're going to be fine, Nellie. Trust me." Then he looks at Jess. "Don't do anything stupid, just tell the truth. You don't know anything, okay?"

He steers the canoe into the outlet, quickly disappearing into the tall grass. His paddle, lifted in a wooden salute, is the last sign I see of him. And then he's gone.

I hate this moment, this scene I've watched in so many movies, where the person left behind just stands there, paralyzed by her own sadness. I wave at the water, his wake slowly dissolving, just to know that I am still able to move.

We only have one book so every match counts. The inside of the barn is dark, even with the door open, so I twist an old newspaper into a torch and light the tip on fire. One down.

Jess finds a gasoline can and begins watering the crop with a stream of unleaded. I follow behind her with the torch, lighting each bundle with a quick dip of the flame, as easy as lighting candles. The plants burn slowly at first, the outer leaves just dusted with ash, but when the fire reaches the gasoline-soaked centers, the bales ignite into balls of brilliant red. It looks like a scene right out of *The Long Hot Summer*. Call me Ben Quick.

Now the inside of the barn is lit up like noontime, a piece of the sun burning on the dirt floor. I've never seen the barn this bright, without any places to hide. I try not to look around, to see all the things that are about to be destroyed, but I can't help it. The walls call out to me, displaying the past in a hazy hue: the wooden sleds we took down Smithson's Hill during the blizzard of '78; the stuffed head of a buck my grandmother shot, figure skates hanging from the antlers; Aunt Maisie's first sewing machine, which she used to make her own wedding dress; a lantern my father bought but never used; the Raleigh bicycle I learned to ride on; a baby carriage with a canopy top and only three wheels; my grandfather's fishing poles, the ones we weren't allowed to touch; a teddy bear I remember seeing in photographs but don't ever remember holding. There is still time to save something, one thing, but what should I choose? Which memory, packed in a box and placed on a shelf that I can't reach, holds the most value?

I finally look away, deciding to let it all go.

The fire grows quickly, it's graceful flames climbing along the walls and into the hayloft, where the bales of old hay ignite in unison. Soon smoke fills up the barn, turning the air into a dense, sweet-smelling fog. After a while I can no longer see the flames, just the red glow of the fire hidden deep in the cloudy darkness. The surroundings are different, but the heat is familiar; it reminds me of sinking into the melted tar of the Ohio Turnpike. A cord of firewood, stacked against the back wall, starts to crackle and pop as the fire consumes it, and I wonder if, in the distance, it sounds like gunfire.

"We should get out of here."

"Wait," Jess says, inhaling, "I at least want the contact high."

I drag her out of the barn by a broken belt loop, knowing we will sample these fumes for hours. We close the barn doors and turn the latch, locking in the fire. I'm amazed that such fury can be hidden so easily.

"Shouldn't we call the fire department?"

"Not yet. If it was an accident we wouldn't know until we saw the smoke."

We stand in the yard, sweaty and out of breath, waiting for the first signs of fire. It takes a few more minutes, but slowly the evidence leaks through: a stream of gray smoke, no thicker than the tail of a kite, escapes from the roof and quickly becomes a thick mass, hovering over the barn like a thundercloud. The first flames appear small and harmless, but as they spread across the rooftop they look like bright orange waves, swelled in a storm. The roof, already a blackened raft, floats in those turbulent waves, until it sinks into the fiery surf and drowns in the embers below. Without the roof, the flames fly out of the barn in long liquid streaks, like hair streaming from a convertible. The fire looks surprisingly fake and incredibly beautiful at the same time, and because of that, because I know how and why it started, it doesn't scare me. There is comfort in the ownership of fire.

"I can't believe it," Jess says. "I can't believe we did this."

"We had no choice," is all I can say.

There is a split second of warning before the first wall collapses. A terrible scream, so piercing it sounds almost human, tears through the air as the wood breaks from its frame and falls slowly into our backyard. It floats like a sheet on fire. The flames spread across the dry grass quickly, licking their way up the side of a maple tree until even the leaves are burning, the entire tree lit up like a Christmas pine.

"Jesus Christ."

"Call the fire department."

While Jess runs to Uncle Flint's, I race toward our cabin and turn on the outside faucet. I follow the hose to the end, picking up the sprinkler to fan the grass around me with water. I wet down the whole yard and the sides of our cabin, even though the windows are open and I know that later I'll get yelled at for ruining books. I walk closer and wave the sprinkler at the flames, trying to calm them. The fire spits the water back at me, warmed now, like it was coming from an out-door showerhead, something my brothers always wanted to have. I unscrew the sprinkler and use the hose alone, spraying water at all the trees that aren't yet burning. The force of the water strips some of the branches, littering the ground with wet orange leaves.

The wind begins to pick up, blowing off the lake with a strength usually reserved for storms, and the flames of the fire continue to grow. I feel the heat on my back and turn to face the maple that's burning right next to my bedroom window. I keep the hose on the tree for what seems like hours, but the stream of water isn't strong enough to put out the blaze. The fire continues to burn through the tree, moving gracefully from one leaf to the next. When it reaches the top branches, it's passed to the leaves of another tree, a fluid baton in a relay race. The maple tree slows down now, catches its breath, as the old, reliable oak takes off. The fire spreads through the huge limbs of the oak as smoke builds in the canopy, blocking out the sun like a storm cloud. I look up, half expecting raindrops to fall onto my face. Half praying.

Jess returns with a large plastic bucket full of freshly picked car-rots. We dump the carrots onto the ground and fill the bucket with water, then drag it to the maple tree. We lose half the water on the way, yet we can barely lift the bucket high enough to douse the flames around the base of the tree. The ground sizzles as the fire is extinguished, a small patch saved. I bet we could do as much by just spitting onto the flames. Still, we head back to the faucet to do it again, trying to save something.

By now there is so much smoke that I can no longer make out the structure of the barn; the fire looks like it's holding itself in the air. Finally, with a noise so loud it sounds like applause, the entire barn collapses onto the ground. The remains continue to burn in a splintered heap, a bonfire taking up most of our yard. Jess looks at me with her mouth open but no words come out. I drop the bucket, pick up the hose again, and spray down the grass around the rubble. Jess picks up pieces of the fallen barn—half-lit two-by-fours that would make perfect torches—and tosses them back onto the heap. There is no way to slow down this fire, but we don't give up, desperate to keep it from reaching the cabin.

The hose has flooded the yard, making shallow pools in the short grass. The water is so warm it's indistinguishable from the air, and we don't even realize we're walking on it. Something squashes under my foot and I almost slip. Even the carrots are cooked.

I don't hear the fire trucks, but soon the firemen are next to us, spraying down the area with lake water filtered through their mammoth hose. They ignore the barn—already a pile of ash—and head straight for the maple tree, which burns like a cross on our lawn. It takes two men to hold the hose as they blast the tree with water, knocking burnt limbs to the ground. In a few minutes they have doused the entire tree, drowning all the flames. The sight of the naked tree, a charcoal sketch of its former self, makes my eyes well up. It looks like a child's version of a tree in winter, a violently drawn symbol of loneliness and death.

"You girls need to get out of the way," yells one of the firemen as he brushes past me. The buckle from his jacket slaps into my arm like a branding iron and leaves an L-shaped welt. Life. Laughter. Loyalty. Loss. (Later I will think of Love.)

We back away slowly, watching them work on the fire in the oak tree. They stand directly under it with their hose aimed up at the limbs, but the water seems to bounce off as if there is a force field protecting the flames. It rains back down on them in thick drops, but they don't avert their eyes. One of the firemen puts a ladder against the side of the cabin and scrambles onto our roof to get closer to the tree. He holds the hose like an automatic rifle and shoots into the blaze, waiting for casualties to fall. Blackened leaves drop from the tree like sparrows, fluttering wingless until they hit the ground. Above, in the dark, crooked limbs of the magnificent oak, the fire continues to blaze.

By now Jess and I have backed our way down to the tree house. I climb up to the top and stand in the lookout tower, watching the treetops burn. Of all the things I thought I'd see from this view, the oak tree ablaze over our cabin wasn't one of them. When I turn around, Jess isn't behind me. I look over the side to find her standing below, her hands on the bottom rung of the ladder but her feet still planted on the ground.

"Come on," I yell, waving for her to climb up. "What are you afraid of?"

She looks up at me and then over to the fire. Finally, she pulls herself up, climbing each rung carefully. When she gets to the top I hold out my hand and pull her onto the platform. She stands up, holding the railing with both hands.

"We made this thing ourselves, you know it'll hold."

She nods toward the fire. "We made that, too."

It's slightly cooler down here by the water, but when the wind blows it covers us with a warm blanket of soot. My eyes are so dry that blinking offers no comfort. Even closed, they still feel the heat, and replay the image of a dazzling inferno onto my eyelids. I hear the flames roaring in the distance and the sound of water rushing like the force of a flood. A broken dam spilling. Later, I recognize it as the sound of blood flowing through my veins.

A mosquito lands on my hand but I don't move to kill it. I

watch it prick my skin with its stinger but feel nothing. When it flies away, its body full of my blood, I follow it with my eyes, wondering where it's taking me. I lose it in the darkness a few seconds later, somewhere over the lake. When, I wonder, did the sun set?

"What happened?" Jess whispers, as if anyone could hear us. "What went wrong?"

I don't have an answer, so I decide to say nothing instead of making one up. I put my arm around her, hoping that will tell her something. She turns into me, hugging me with a force I didn't think she was capable of. For the longest time, neither one of us lets go.

I look back to the cabin, the trees, the firemen, just to make sure everything's still intact. There is a strange stillness to the scene, like all movement has been slowed down to make it easier to consume. Then a burning limb suddenly breaks from the oak and plunges into the roof of our cabin, slicing through the frame like a knife. It falls swiftly, without apology, and disappears into a cloud of smoke. The fire continues to burn in the trees, its flames floating softly in the air, bending like a field of poppies in the breeze, to show off its beauty to the sky.

The hardest part is going inside. They make us wait until the next day, but then they let us in, to see the damage and decide how much we want to save. The fireman in charge escorts us around our cabin like a tour guide—no, a security guard—who follows our every move. He tells us not to touch the walls, to walk only on the plastic rugs, to be careful of the furniture we've spent years breaking in, to put down photographs we posed for and framed. He talks of smoke and water damage, of structural compromises, of how much it will cost to rent a crane, of the best way to lift a tree limb out of a house, like it was his specialty, something he's done every week for the last twenty years of his life. Who knows, maybe this is a common occurrence in this county.

"Here, I'll take you to the impact site," he says, leading the way to my bedroom. He says "impact site" like he's talking about the place where an asteroid hit.

The door to my bedroom is gone. We crowd around the open doorway, no one brave enough to step inside. I'm surprised by how dark the room is; the windows, normally full of afternoon sun at this time of day, are completely covered by the tower of splintered pine that used to be our bunk beds. The only light in the room comes from the hole in the roof—hazy diagonal rays that remind me of a cartoon image of heaven. The limb from the oak tree looks like a trunk from up close. It lies in the middle of the room like a beached whale, water still dripping from the bark. Underneath its body, smaller branches are smashed against the floor, arms broken in the fall. Chunks of the wallpaper are missing, peeled off in wide scratches. It looks like this room housed a wild animal who took its escape through the roof and left a fallen tree in its wake.

The fireman tells us that my bedroom and the attic are the only rooms with significant damage. I guess I deserve that.

"The arson guy will be coming by to check out the barn, but that shouldn't hold things up over here. My guys saw the tree fall with their own eyes so there's no mystery about what's to blame. It should only take a few days for them to label it an accident."

Jess and I look at each other.

"Well, it was an old barn," my father says, "I'm actually surprised it never happened before."

"Oh yeah, those old barns are just a fire waiting to happen. Especially this time of year, when everything's so dry. You guys are just lucky that nobody was hurt." Then he hands my father a list of qualified contractors; Palmer Jasperson's name is first, with an asterisk next to it.

"What's the star for?" my father asks.

"Free estimates."

My father tucks the list into his pocket and walks away, heading to his study. He finds the room perfectly intact, except for his smoke-dusted books whose swollen pages are filled with the lake water that was meant to save them.

"Don't you worry, girls." The fireman puts a hand on my shoulder. "As soon as the insurance money comes in they'll rebuild this thing as good as new. Hell, probably even better." When he takes his hand away I still feel its weight.

Jess leans into the bedroom to pick up her duffel bag, which was protected by its hiding place under the desk.

"I wouldn't bother," the fireman says. "You'll never get the smell out."

Jess shrugs and puts the waterlogged bag over her shoulder. She looks around the room, looking for something of mine to salvage.

"I lost everything the first time, remember?"

"But your suit's outside on the line," she says. "And your books are in the living room—that's something." She puts a consoling hand on my arm.

"I'm not worried about what I lost," I say, stepping inside to look at my old room for the last time. I glance up at the sky, which I have never seen from this angle, and can't help but picture another limb coming down, falling out of the tree like a child.

"Wait," Jess says, unzipping her bag. She rummages through the wet clothing until she pulls out a sweatshirt from the bottom of the bag. "Here." She hands me the sweatshirt that Dallas gave me more than two months ago. I take it, even though I know it has lost all traces of his smell.

Outside, Uncle Flint is walking through the pile of ash that used to be the barn. He sifts through the charred remains like a gardener looking for the last potatoes of the season. He glances up at the trees and then over to the cabin, tracing the path of the fire with his eyes. He looks puzzled, relieved, and furious at the same time, the same expression he's worn since he pulled up to the house late last night, surprised by the presence of firetrucks and the men in matching brown suits who knew his name. He was calm while they searched his house, and even wore the hint of a smile as he walked them to their car, slapping the roof as they drove away, his hands not cuffed.

He picks up a short piece of crooked metal, what used to be the handlebars to a ten-speed bike, and starts to clean if off with his T-shirt. He will spend all day in that debris, trying to salvage something, trying to figure out who or what to thank, who to curse.

Suddenly he looks in my direction, as if sensing that he's being watched. I duck behind the clothesline, hide in a fortress of billowing sheets.

This is the biggest secret I will ever have to keep.

Chapter 25

We spend the first few nights after the fire in Aunt Maisie's house, my father in the guest room and Jess and me on the floor in Caitlin's room. I wake up on the third day with a note from my father next to my pillow, telling me to meet him at the cabin when I get up, telling me to come alone.

He's on the phone when I get inside, a strange sight since we've never had one in this cabin before. It's a wall-style, just like the one in our kitchen in Boston, the pale yellow matching perfectly with the appliances. I think it's the first new thing to be added to this room since my mother walked in fifteen years ago holding me.

"He said he was going to call you. . . . Yes, I know that's not your fault, that's not the point. . . ." He looks at me, points for me to sit down. "Nellie and I are staying on here, but I'll put Jess on a plane when you say the word. . . . No, there's no rush, but school starts next week and I thought—Okay, well, when do you think would be a better time?" He nods his head, opens his mouth but doesn't speak. "Uh-huh . . . I know, Shelley, I know . . . I'm not judging you. . . . No, that's not what I think. . . . I was there in the beginning, remember? I know you did. . . ." He turns away from me, still nodding. "Listen, Shelley, I can't talk right now. . . . No, I'm not just saying that. . . . Yes, I'll tell her. She's fine, really . . . I know you do, I know . . . Okay, take care. . . . Good-bye." He hangs up the phone, holds it in place to make sure it won't fall.

"When was that put in?"

"The guy came this morning." He pulls out a chair to lean on.

"Listen, that was Shelley on the phone." The chair creaks under his weight. "She says she's not ready . . . I mean, she thinks it would be better—"

"She doesn't want her back," I say, cutting him off.

He pauses, then nods, a look of embarrassment on his face. "She needs a break, I guess, to focus on herself."

"How original." I can't cover the bitterness in my tone.

He taps his fingers on the back of the chair, long and tapered just like mine. His mother wanted him to play the piano, but he traded the keyboard for a typewriter. We all disappoint our parents, I guess. And they disappoint us.

"So . . ." He leans forward, eyes locked on mine. "What do you want to do?"

My eyes scan the kitchen, stopping everywhere but on his face. Nothing has changed in my lifetime in this cabin, not the table-cloth, the butter dish, or the flower vase. Not even the wallpaper, a country scene drawn in faded brushstrokes, repeated over and over along the wall. When I look closer I realize that what I thought was a barrel rolling down the hill is really a little boy wrapped in a potato sack. He is falling down all around me.

"She should stay with us," I finally say.

"Are you sure?"

I look him in the eyes. "Yes."

"It's a big deal, to take someone into your home—"

"She's been in our home for months."

"I know, but it will be different now, more permanent." His fingers are still tapping, searching for notes. I notice that he finally took off his wedding ring and now wears a band of flesh lighter than me. How long until the sun erases it, until it becomes a memory?

"She's family," I say. "What's more permanent than that?"

There is a bowl of ripe peaches on the table, the smell strong even in the wake of the fire. No matter what happens, this room will always smell like peaches, like summertime, like everything familiar.

"I've got some decisions to make about the cabin, how we want them to fix it, what changes we want."

"What do you mean, 'changes'?"

"Well, they can build on another room if you want. For Jess. Or we can make your room bigger, take it out toward the driveway so you two can have more space."

"What about the attic?"

"Haven't you noticed the hole in the roof?"

"But after they fix it, couldn't they put up a wall and make it into bedrooms? Marcus and Noah used to sleep up there."

"I don't know, Nellie, it's not even winterized." He tries to cover his skepticism. "Is that what you want?"

"I just think it might be better to start fresh, you know? Plus, there's a view of the lake from up there."

"Pretty soon you're going to tell me you want to sleep in the tree house." He shakes his head, smiling. "Okay. I'll talk to Palmer when he gets here."

"Thanks." I move to stand.

"Hold on a minute." He stops me with his hand. "Listen, we haven't really had a chance to talk since the fire." He leans forward, his arms still resting on the back of the chair. "How are you doing with all of this?"

"I'm fine, Dad."

"I know you're fine, that's not what I meant. Is there anything you want to talk about?" He turns the chair around and finally sits down. "Anything you want to say?"

I shake my head slowly, eyes on the table. Does he know something?

"The report on the barn came back. They said it was inconclusive, too many variables to tell for certain. They're looking hard at your uncle Flint, of course, but since he's not filing for the insurance money there's nothing they can do."

"What about us?"

"We're okay. Thanks to all the witnesses, they know it wasn't our fault."

I look down at my hands and realize that they're clasped together on my lap as if I were praying. I close my eyes and promise that if I get away with this lie, it will be my last.

My father clears his throat before speaking again. "We're entering a new phase, Nellie, and things are going to be different from here on out. Don't be afraid to ask for help, okay, to tell me if something's bothering you." He reaches out to rub my head, smoothing out the loose ends of my hair. "You're allowed to be upset sometimes, to get frustrated, to feel . . ." He runs out of words but his mouth stays open, a bird clipped of his song. "To feel," he says again, his eyes softening.

I sit back in the chair, my hands hidden in the pocket of my sweatshirt, balled into fists. I take a deep breath and let them relax, feeling my fingers open like flowers.

"It's so quiet here, especially at night. Now that all the windows are closed, and everyone's inside . . ." I lower my voice. "Sometimes I miss the sound of cars driving by, of strangers talking outside the window, all the things I used to hate about the city. It's just weird to still be here. In the fall, I mean." I rub my hands together. "It's so cold already."

"Maisie swears it's not that bad," he says. "Once the snow comes it's so pretty you won't even notice the cold. At least that's what she keeps telling me."

"I bet the lake freezes by Christmas. If I buy you a pair of skates, will you go ice-skating with me?"

"Are you crazy? Black people don't ice-skate. I barely trust the sidewalk."

"How about cross-country skiing?"

"Too much work."

"There's a sled in the basement. . . ."

"Too small."

"A snowmobile?"

"Too dangerous."

I laugh. "So what are you going to do all winter?"

"Read. Write." He smiles. "And raise you girls."

"Maybe I'll cause some trouble, just to keep you busy."

"Don't get any ideas. Better yet, don't give Jess any ideas."

I look out the window toward Uncle Flint's house. The sun is shining on it, making the wood look much brighter than it actually is.

"Will it bother you to be in the country all year, to live with these guys, but without . . . everyone else?"

" 'Bother' isn't the right word." He spins the bowl of peaches with the tips of his fingers. As it moves faster the fruit begins to blur.

I decide to push him. "But it's not where you want to be, is it?"

"It's not the same for me as it is for you. I didn't grow up here like your mother did, like you did. It was never meant to be that for me." He clears his throat, and I feel a lecture coming on.

"When we moved into this cabin your grandparents lived next door. That's why we bought it. We wanted you kids to spend your summers here, to grow up next to them, so you knew that part of where you came from. Now, I wasn't expecting Flint to move up from the farm or your grandmother to get sick, but that's what happened, and I didn't want to change my plan just because things got hard. It wasn't ideal, but I thought it was necessary—I still think it's necessary—and that's why I'm still here." The sound of the spinning bowl, a whir that sounds almost mechanical, takes over the room like a fragrance. He stops it with one finger.

"Maybe I made a mistake. Maybe I should have bought a place on the Cape or Martha's Vineyard—Oak Bluffs has a huge black community—and then the drive would have been hours not days. But that's not your legacy. This is."

"I get it, Dad, I understand. It was just easier—"

"It was never easy, Nellie. Driving across the country, sticking out like I had a bull's-eye painted on my back, but I wasn't about to let anybody tell me where I should and shouldn't go, where my children did and didn't belong. I wanted to give you kids a place that was your own, a spot that you could have all to yourselves, where nothing from the outside world could touch you. Maybe that's changed now, or maybe it never existed, but I spent the last fifteen years trying to make it possible, trying to show you that there's more than one way to live, more than one place where you belong." He picks a peach out of the bowl and checks it for bruises. "This cabin is the first thing I ever owned, the only thing I've paid off, and I'm not going to let all those sacrifices mean nothing." He offers me the peach. "This is for you, Nellie; for better or worse, it's yours."

I take the ripe fruit, the one he has chosen for me. "It sounds like a marriage."

"Maybe." He pushes the chair in. "Hopefully it will last longer."

It's strange to have so many Jaspersons in the cabin. Palmer, who's never even sat at our kitchen table, now walks freely through the house, his toolbelt hanging low on his waist, hammer slapping against his jeans. Most of his crew, including his own sons, are scattered throughout the cabin like a litter of kittens, popping up in unexpected places. Most days Palmer eats his lunch in my father's study, leaning against a shelf of Harlem Renaissance poetry; Troy works in the attic with the cleanup crew, boxing up my toys and baby clothes; Luke spends all day in my bedroom, throwing out pieces of the bed I used to sleep in. Palmer, who left a job renovating the bowling alley to work on our cabin himself, promises to have everything fixed in three weeks, including the attic insulation and a wall to give Jess and me our own rooms. Now we will fight over who gets the window facing the lake.

We aren't supposed to be at the construction site without the workmen, but sometimes I sneak in after hours to grab a forgotten book or deck of cards, using any excuse to visit. I come often because I want to see the transformation; I don't want to walk in one day and feel like it's no longer my home.

Tonight, I go straight up to the attic to see the new floor. The whole room smells of sawdust and varnish, and the gloss on the wood is so flawless it still looks wet. I test it with my toe, then walk out under the hole in the roof and stare out at the night sky. The view has opened up since they cut down the remains of the oak. I imagine that I'm standing on the deck of a huge ocean liner, the star-filled sky close enough to touch. I hear footsteps on the stairs, soft, patient ones. My first thought is to duck, but there is nothing left to hide behind. I'm standing in the middle of the room when Luke walks in with a flashlight, holding it out like a sword.

"I thought you'd be up here one of these nights."

"I came to check on your work." I grab the new frame like I'm testing it.

"And?"

"Not bad." I slap the wood. "You guys work pretty fast. I hope you don't compromise quality for speed."

"Don't worry, my dad's running this one himself. He's not going to let anything happen to your mother's house." He takes a few steps toward me. I back away.

"Here, I saved this for you." He holds out a small doll covered in soot. "I thought it might be from your childhood."

When he hands it to me I'm surprised by how light the doll feels, like a bird perched in my hand. I try to wipe off the soot but it only gets smeared around, gray swirls on her once rosy cheeks. When I stand the doll up her eyes flutter open, big blue marbles still perfectly intact. When I lay her flat they close quickly, her straight eyelashes clamped together, a forced sleep.

"It was my mother's," I finally say.

"Wow, I guess it's older than I thought."

"My grandmother gave it to her when she was pregnant with my aunt Maisie. She wanted her to practice being a big sister, to learn how to support the doll's head and burp her."

"Did it work?"

I shake my head. "My mother kept putting her down to nap, just to make her eyes disappear. When Maisie didn't do that my mother lost interest." I walk over to the window and sit the doll up on the windowsill. Her eyes are wide open, peering out at the lake.

"The view's nice from up here," Luke says, a slight hesitation in his voice.

I nod, keeping my back toward him. "This is going to be my new room."

"I heard."

The beam from the flashlight bobs against the sloped walls of the ceiling as he walks up behind me.

"Nellie . . ." He throws my name out like a flag, hoping for a truce. "I'm sorry about the other night, the barbecue, everything that's happened. I wasn't prepared for any of it." He reaches for me but stops his hand short of my arm. I see the shadow on the wall, grasping the air. "You have every right to be mad at me."

"I'm not mad, Luke." I sit down on the sawhorse in front of the small window, still looking away from him.

"Come on, you've been avoiding me for days. You didn't come over for my birthday, you don't return my calls, you won't even look at me."

I turn and look him straight in the eyes. "I'm disappointed. There's a difference."

"Look, let's just start over, okay?" He starts talking faster. "Just wipe out the summer and start again."

"You know we can't do that, we can't go back. I don't even know if I'd want to."

"What does that mean?"

"It means I don't have any regrets. We had fun this summer, Luke, but it's over now. Let's just move on."

"And if I don't want to?" His face is half lit by the flashlight, giving him a look of not quite being formed.

"You don't really have a choice. Things change, they end, and we don't always have control over them."

"Wait a minute—" His face is full of surprise. "You're admitting you don't have control? That's gotta be a first."

"I don't have control over lots of things." I turn back toward

282 RACHEL M. HARPER

the window. The doll still sits in the windowsill, keeping tireless
watch over the lake. I reach over and I lay her down, relieving her
of her duties. Her eyes snap shut as she falls asleep.

Luke finally sits down next to me. "Just tell me that things are
okay between us. That you don't hate me or anything."

He looks so sincere that I can't help but smile.

"You worry too much, Luke."

"And you could hold a grudge forever."

I turn back to the window and smile at my own reflection. "It's
one of my only flaws."

"Yeah, right," he says, matching my smile. Then he puts his arm
around me, at first gently, but then tighter as he gets more comfortable, as he remembers. "That, and you can't do the breaststroke
to save your life."

I elbow him softly in the ribs. "Who cares, it's a lame stroke."

I look out at the lake, its still, black waters the most comforting
I've ever known. "At least I can do the butterfly. Do you know any
other girls who can do that?"

He shakes his head slowly. "You're the only one. I've been
telling you that all summer." His arm feels heavy across my shoulders, and I know that soon I won't be able to carry it.

I am my mother's daughter.

Our car is back. Almost two weeks into the construction it shows up
in the driveway: a 1978 Volvo station wagon parked quietly under
the crab apple tree. It looks exactly like the one that burned in the
car fire, right down to the cream-colored leather seats and silver
hubcaps. The only difference is the color of the paint: this one is a
dusty green that blends right into the landscape; a country car, a get-
away car. It would be so easy to go back in time, to erase the memory of the car fire and convince myself that everything this summer
had never occurred, to just wipe out the past with a new paint job.

Up close I can see that it is, in fact, a different car, unburdened
by my family for the last decade. There is no oil stain on the ceiling

from my father's pomade; no box of mixed tapes on the passenger floor; no bottle of sparkling cider tucked into the seat pocket; no frayed seams along the backseat's bench. I wonder how many used car lots my father had to search to find such a perfect replacement—the same make and model, even the same year. Now we'll never have to think of this as a different car; instead, we can pretend that the old car was renovated, just like the cabin. All part of the plan to redesign our family, to refurbish our lives.

When I step back from the car, I realize that something's missing, that it still needs one thing to be complete. I go down to the basement, searching through the old boxes we pulled from the car during the fire. Finally, I find the right box, the one with the AAA sticker on the outside. The old license plate is tucked inside, resting against a stack of magazines. It still smells like hot tar and burnt rubber, like no time has passed since I salvaged it from the front of our burning car. I clean off most of the soot with an old towel, but the smell refuses to wash away. I grab a screwdriver from the toolbox and bring the license plate out to the car, where I attach it to the holder on the back end, tightening each screw until it's secure. Then I slap the AAA sticker onto the bumper and smile at the new old car, as if I had saved it from the ashes and resurrected it myself. Now there is no doubt: it is ours.

I take the screwdriver and head inside to find Jess, ready to do something we should have done a long time ago. I drag her off the couch and down to the tree house, where she reluctantly follows me inside.

"Here," I say, handing her the screwdriver.

"What's that for?"

I point toward the spot on the trunk where every other Christiansen grandchild has carved their name. "It's your turn."

"Are you serious?"

"Come on," I say. "Everyone else did it."

She holds the screwdriver like a pick and jabs into the thick bark, scratching her initials next to mine.

"Well, look at that," she says with a sly grin. "I guess I'm one of you now."

And finally, she's right.

The sun is low in the sky as I head out to the mailboxes. The driveway is already covered with fallen leaves that crunch below my feet and drown out the sound of the wind. This will be a long, cold walk in the winter. The trees along the road look thin without their leaves, and weak, like they could barely hold the weight of a snowfall. I look through their branches to the highway, then across the gravel pit to a cluster of homes on a hilltop I never knew was there. The electric lines hang loose from their poles like an old web I could pluck from the sky with two fingers. Everything seems more open now, more vulnerable; even the sun doesn't have a cloud to hide behind.

The only piece of mail is a postcard from my mother. It's a picture of a map of Minnesota with a sign above it saying LAND OF 10,000 LAKES. She circled a tiny blue dot in the middle of the state, drew an arrow out from it, and wrote in *Silver Lake—we made it!* I guess that means we finally exist, since we can find our home on a map. Part of me doesn't even want to read the card, but I'm halfway through before I realize it. She doesn't say much, just that she's moved into the new house and hopes I'll come back to see it before Christmas. The last line says, *I'm here if you need me,* and then she wrote down a new telephone number. I knew it was coming, but it still seems too quick. Everything from our old life is gone now, even the phone number, the first ten-digit pattern I ever memorized. I tuck the card into my pocket, knowing I will eventually call, but not wanting to commit this one to memory.

I'm about to walk away when I notice something else inside the mailbox: a short curved stick that has been stripped of its bark. When I pick it up I see that it's a miniature canoe, the inside hollowed out so that it could actually float. I think back to the day I watched Dallas carving it with his switchblade, remembering the gentleness of his touch. There's a hole at the tip, so I can hang it around my neck on a string. I bring it to my nose and breathe in the smell of ginger. The scent is still strong even though it must have dried out weeks ago. I touch it quickly with my tongue and taste the sweet spice of the ginger root, the only wood I've ever longed to eat.

I look around but of course there is nobody there, no one to witness what I will always consider a miracle: the first time I've ever enjoyed being surprised. I tuck the tiny canoe into my pocket and continue to rub it, as if it were a rabbit's foot or a lucky feather. I walk out onto the highway, looking up and down the paved road for a sign, for something familiar. A few cars pass by me, nothing unusual, but suddenly someone slows down and pulls over to the shoulder. I don't recognize the truck, a tan Dodge with busted tail-lights, but I still walk to the passenger side hoping to recognize something. A little girl with dark, wind-blown hair rolls down the window.

"Need a ride, lady?" the little girl says. An older woman is be-hind the wheel, fixing her lipstick in the rearview mirror. She blows a kiss at her reflection and smiles.

I look at the back of the pickup, imagine myself crammed in next to a week's worth of firewood and enough cement to pave a road to the Cities.

I smile at the girl. "No, thanks. I'm just out walking."

"On the side of a highway?"

"It's all right, I'm almost home."

She shrugs and rolls the window back up, careful not to catch her hair in the jamb.

I stand there as the truck pulls away, thankful that I'm no longer on the road, that I'm no longer paralyzed by the need to move. I watch them until they reach the railroad crossing, then look away before I see which way they turn.

I walk with my head down, watching the asphalt turn into loose gravel and become softer with each step as I leave the highway behind and turn into our driveway. Ahead I can still make out my footsteps through the fallen leaves, but I take a different route this time, turn over new leaves, kick pebbles I don't recognize. Yes, this is a path I know, with the same trees and gravel, the same corn-stalks at the edge of the grass. But I am not always the same, so I make the road new. The road, the lake, the cabin: they are all old and new at the same time, just like I am.

Foreign and familiar.

Urban and rural.

Black and white.

Here and there.

Everywhere—even in you.

Epilogue

There is a color between black and white; sometimes it's a shade of gray but other times it's almost brown, and when the moon is out and the stars are lighting up the sky, it may look silver or even brass. It is a rare tone, a color you won't find on its own, but it can be blended from other colors, from any color that occurs in nature, and sometimes even if there is no color, but just an idea. Created and re-created.

That is my color.

And if that color were a road, that would be where I walk, somewhere between the tar and gravel. There are no signs, but I know my way on this road, and even if it doesn't show up on any map it still exists. It is my road. I know it like I know my own color. Like I know my own home. It is not a constant thing—it changes—but I change with it. Still, my road always knows me. Even in the dark it doesn't ask any questions—it already knows where I am and where I'm going, where I've been. Like how a tree knows to drop its leaves in autumn, and a lake knows to freeze in the winter, and a flame knows to grow so hot it can't be held, and a girl knows to make herself whole.

Acknowledgments

I would like to thank all the family and friends whose encouragement helped me during the dark hours of writing (and rewriting) this book. I am particularly grateful to my early readers—Graeme Fordyce, Daniel Alexander Jones, Lori Pope, Brett Schneider, and Shay Youngblood—for their enthusiasm and grace.

Special thanks to my father, Michael S. Harper, for his immeasurable faith, and to Stephanie Blank, for all that she said and did not say.

I am forever indebted to the Corporation of Yaddo; the Rhode Island State Council on the Arts; my wonderful agent, Ira Silverberg; and the hardworking staff at Touchstone, beginning with my editor, Brett Valley.

My final thanks is to Neda Ulaby, for believing in a short story called "Barefoot on the Ohio Turnpike."

Discussion Points

1. Consider how the elements of Nellie's journey have been divided in the novel into three parts. Discuss why the author chose to arrange the events of her story in this way.

2. Why does Nellie feel closer to her father after her parents decide to separate? Why does she ask her mother not to come with them to St. Croix, when it is her mother's family they are visiting? Once you learn the whole truth, do you sympathize with Virginia, or do you agree with Nellie's opinion that she is selfish?

3. What does Aunt Frances mean when she tells Malcolm that now his kids "really won't know who they are"?

4. After their car catches fire, what prompts Jess to suddenly defend her uncle and cousin? What makes her open up to Nellie at the motel?

5. While hitchhiking to Silver Lake, Jess argues with Nellie over whether or not her family is "really black." Nellie says that she "chooses" black. What prompts her to say this? Contrast this moment with the end of the novel, when Jess points out that Nellie shouldn't have to choose white or black, but that being both should make her feel at home anywhere. Do you agree with Jess? Does this statement reflect a change in the way Nellie sees herself and her place in her family?

6. What is it about Dallas that draws Nellie to him? What parallels can you draw between Dallas's relationship to his hair and Nellie's relationship to her skin?

7. Nellie finds herself torn between Luke and Dallas, the small-town white boy and the exotic Indian man. What are the various elements of the two worlds that they represent to Nellie? What is the significance of Luke's behavior (or lack thereof) when his friend calls Nellie a nigger?

8. What changes for Jess and Renny in the moment she learns that he brought her as a baby to stay at Silver Lake? What does the swing set he built for her—and her current love of swings—reveal about Jess?

9. Nellie gets injured repeatedly throughout the novel: when she steps on Jess's cigarette, when her would-be kidnapper burns her arm, when the wasp bites her shoulder at the funeral, etc. Do you think the author creates this pattern deliberately? Why or why not? What does Nellie mean when she wonders, "Is this where we find out identities, in the smooth, defiant flesh of our scars?"

10. *Brass Ankle Blues* encompasses three major destructions: the car fire, the barn fire, and the collapse of the cabin. Discuss what each of these events means in the grand scheme of the novel and what is lost (both physically and metaphorically) with each.

11. The last line of the novel reads " . . . a girl knows to make herself whole." How do Nellie and Jess make themselves whole? What about Virginia?

Author Q&A

1. **This is your first novel. What inspired you to write this story?**

   Like many writers, I was an early observer, and the first group of people that I watched intently was my family. They were an interesting collection—every member quite unique—and I was aware of that from an early age. I knew I was living a life that few people get to see, with the blending of quite disparate worlds (both racially and economically), and I thought my perspective would be fresh. This novel is fiction, as none of the events actually happened, but the framework is fairly autobiographical. For me, writing a novel was already a huge challenge, and I knew I needed to write about familiar themes and dynamics if I wanted to survive it; that's why I chose this story for my first outing.

2. **There are many race, class, and age collisions in *Brass Ankle Blues*. Is your own family as multifaceted?**

   It's a terrible cliché now, but I do tend to "write what I know," and Nellie and I have several things in common: being biracial, spending summers in rural Minnesota, coming from a farming family, and having a large extended family. Many of the feelings Nellie expresses are ones I've dealt with personally. I think that give me an authenticity of voice that's invaluable in a story as complex as this one, and why I chose to include so many of those elements.

3. **What made you choose a Native American man as the object of Nellie's first forays into romance?**

   After a lifetime of feeling like she doesn't fit in, I thought it would be interesting for Nellie to connect with someone who also doesn't fit in. Dallas grew up in that area, and has ancestors that could claim original ties to the land, yet he now lives as an outsider in the community, and is somewhat disconnected from his own family. Having him be racially different from Nellie, yet look and feel similar to her, was a way for me to get her to start examining her own definitions of what it means to belong—to a tribe, a race, or a family. I also wanted her to be able to see herself in another person—one she wasn't related to—to examine whether that made her feel any differently about the idea of kinship. I wanted her to begin to understand that feeling connected to someone doesn't have to be tied to looking alike, or sharing the same culture.

4. Have you ever suffered from an identity crisis similar to the ones Nellie and Jess struggle with throughout the novel?
Most teenagers go through periods of feeling at odds with the world, their parents, or their community, for a myriad of reasons. I can absolutely relate to feeling like an outsider at that age, even in my own home. I remember struggling to assert my individuality in all the wrong moments, times when my family thought I should focus on the good of the whole, and there was quite a bit of conflict. But just like a good story needs conflict, every family needs some conflict, too, so I don't think it's a bad thing. If it's productive, conflict can be a very healthy thing.

5. There is a kind of war, and also an uneasy alliance, happening between the children and adults in this novel. Do you relate more to your young or your adult characters?
I relate to all of my characters. They all come from me, of course, and I think they all have pieces of my own personality—both strengths and weaknesses—as I've tried to make them as realistic as possible. They are all failing and succeeding in different ways, and that is what makes them interesting to me. I am a bit harder on the adults, perhaps because they've had more time to figure things out, and should therefore have a better understanding of the world. But this isn't always the case, of course, and the older I get, the more I begin to forgive them. Experience isn't only measured in days on earth, and I think we can all do better just remembering that.

6. **The three-part structure of the novel—and Nellie's journey—is very interesting. What made you choose to arrange the story in this way?**

I like to read books that are broken into sections. It's like serving a large meal in courses—it's just easier to digest if you take it in phases. I plotted the story and then stepped back from it, trying to see where the natural breaks occurred. Part One is "The Road" and it obviously ends when they arrive, but it was more difficult to figure out when to end Part Two, "The Lake." I eventually decided it should be with her mother's departure, because that is what leads Nellie to create a new family, which is rebuilt (literally and figuratively) in Part Three, "The Cabin."

7. **Do you see *Brass Ankle Blues* as a coming-of-age story, or as something broader?**

I like to think of it as something broader, although I am not offended if someone refers to it that way. Nellie is the protagonist, and she is on a quest that is typical of the form. But what makes the novel more than that is the fact that several of the characters are also on that quest—that search for autonomy and self-definition—regardless of their age. In my opinion, the issues dealt with in a "coming-of-age" story can surface at any time, and I decided to burden several of my older characters with that dilemma. I think the novel tells the whole family's story—not just Nellie's—and its struggle to define itself and survive during tumultuous times. What I want to acknowledge is that a family is a living, breathing thing that doesn't have one constant definition. It can change or evolve as time goes on, and we often have to restructure it if we want it to survive.

8. **The last line of the novel reads ". . . a girl knows to make herself whole." How does this statement reflect your own life's challenges? Do you think you know how to make yourself whole yet?**

Nellie's realization by the end is that she, and only she, can make herself whole. It is her job to unify the paradox of her own identity. And I came to that realization myself, probably when I was in college. But knowing you have to do it doesn't mean that you know *how* to do it. That is a lifelong battle, I think, one that I'm sure will be the theme of several books I'll write in the future.

9. **What do you hope readers come away with after reading this graceful novel?**

First and foremost, I hope to have engaged and entertained the reader. That is my first job. If they have learned a thing or two—about an experience they weren't familiar with or people they didn't recognize—that's even better. Writing is a way for me to connect—to the reader and to myself—and that is why I do it. I'm trying to connect with people in a small way—one reader at a time, one book at a time—and my hope it that those connections can become part of a larger framework that can unify, rather than divide, this huge world we live in. We have so many labels now, so many disparate identities, but I don't think that has to be divisive; in fact, it can't be if we're all going to survive together.

10. **Are you working on a second novel? If so, what is the premise?**

Yes, I just finished my second novel. It's also a family story, but the family makeup is quite different, as is the setting, so it feels like a very different book. It takes place in Providence, my hometown, and is about a family trying to survive the unique challenges of an urban landscape. It is not *Brass Ankle Blues, Part II;* it's a completely new story, and I'm grateful that it came to me when it did. As sad as I was to leave my old characters behind, it was a relief to know that I could create another world that would challenge me and hold my interest throughout the lengthy writing process. I feel very lucky to be able to tell these stories, and I hope to continue to find an audience who appreciates them.